Sirens Cove

Allie Belle

eBook ISBN: 979-8-9936371-1-2

Paperback ISBN: 979-8-9936371-0-5

Book One of The Sirenborne Chronicles

Edited by Alyse Bailey

Proofread by Alexandra Leonhardt

Book Cover and Map by Mary Dublin

Formatting and Interior Illustrations by English Proper Editing Services

First Edition 2025

To the ones whose minds are always lost at sea... This one's for you.

TRIGGER WARNINGS

Sirens Cove is an adult fantasy that dives deep into dark waters. Within these pages, you'll find violence, blood, gore, torture, drowning, and death. There's harsh language, explicit sexual content, and moments of grief and trauma. Manipulation, power, and pain all have their place here. This story isn't gentle. It isn't meant to be. This world is not for the faint of heart.

But beneath the brutality, you'll find resilience, healing, and the kind of love that claws its way out of ruin.

Once you hear a Sirens song, there's no going back.

PLAYLIST

Power Over Me ~ Dermot Kennedy

Eyes Don't Lie ~ Isabel LaRose

Middle of the Night ~ Elley Duhe

Figure You Out ~ VOILA

Sailor Song ~ Gigi Perez

War Of Hearts ~ Ruelle

Skyfall ~ Adele

LET THE WORLD BURN ~ Chris Grey

Dark Paradise ~ Lana Del Rey

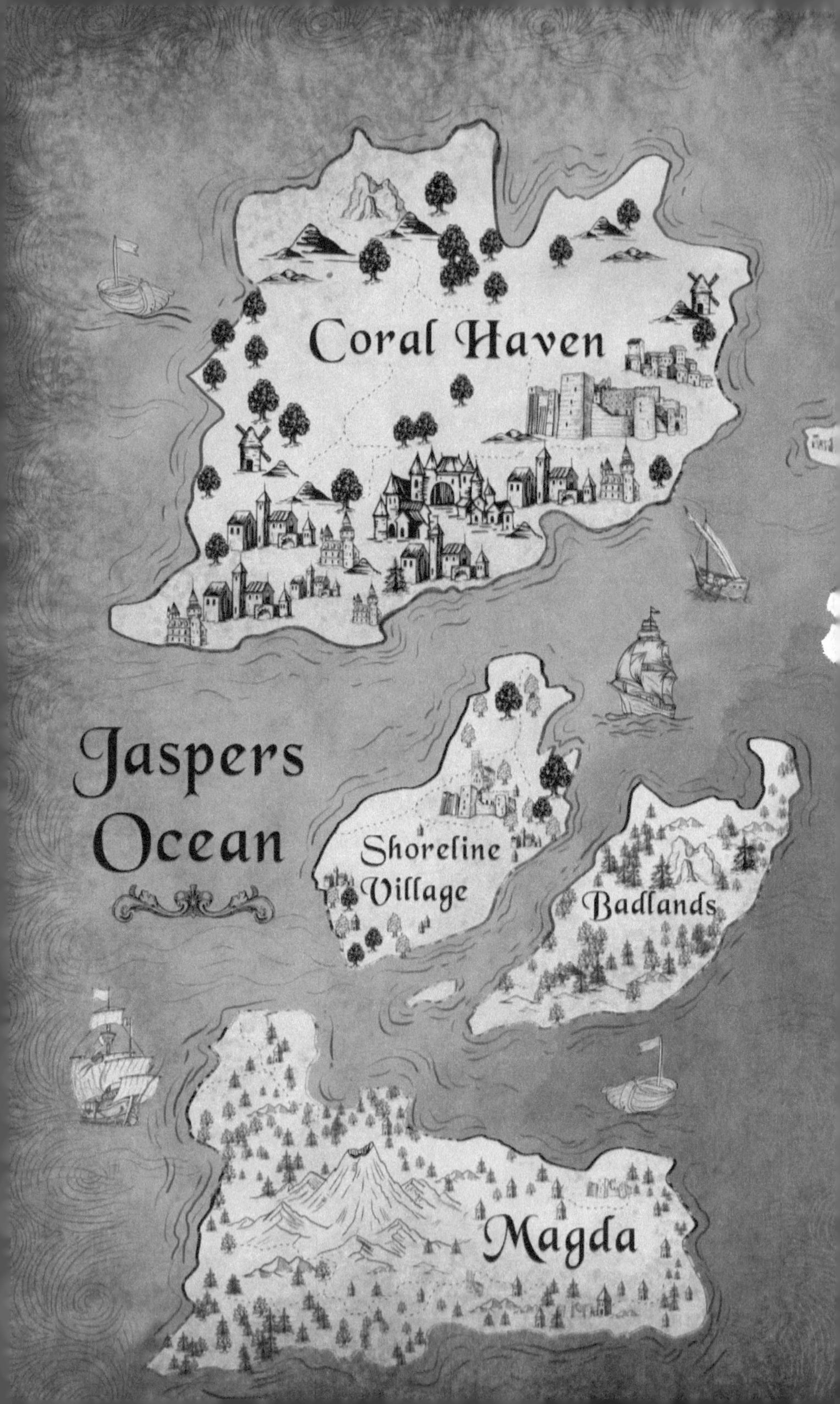

Coral Haven

Jaspers
Ocean

Shoreline
Village

Badlands

Magda

CHAPTER ONE

MIRA

BRUISED

When I was a little girl, my father used to whisper stories of the Fountain of Wishes like a prayer. It was his greatest dream to bring my mother back from the dead, then wish for eternal youth so we could remain together, forever unchanged. Every moment he spent chasing the cursed fountain was stolen from me. Life aboard a pirate ship carved loss into my bones at an early age. I knew he wanted a son, an heir, not a daughter. But I still tried to become the legacy he longed for. And now that the sea has claimed him too, I have only one purpose left: bring them both back. And gods help anyone who stands in my way.

I took command of my father's ship, *The Siren*, a vessel born of old magic, feared across the seas, with a will of its own and a name spoken in equal parts awe and envy. They said the sea wasn't meant for women, that no woman should ever captain a crew of pirates, let alone a ship like this. But I became captain at nineteen, the youngest in our history, and one of the only women to ever claim the title. I didn't inherit the role. I bled for it. After my father, Captain Bleu, was ripped from me during an expedition just a year ago, there was no one else worthy enough to take the helm.

The irony? It was the ship's namesake that killed him. We were fighting for a fragment of the map when the sirens rose from the water, not women, not monsters, but something in between. Shadows spun from ocean song, cloaked in beauty, sharpened by death. Their voices weren't just a lure, they were a curse. Haunting. Fatal. Designed to seduce men into the depths and silence them forever.

My father had always been immune to their charms, too clever to fall under their spell. But that day was different. The sirens weren't alone. Sea wraiths poured from the trenches, soulless creatures with hollow eyes and claws that dripped venom. I watched from the quarterdeck as crewman after crewman fell, torn apart in a single slash of those claws. The first sound was always a scream, raw, animal, ripped from the soul. The rest... too gruesome to stomach. Whatever god birthed such creatures was no god of mercy, only one of cruelty. It was chaos. I didn't know who was fighting who. Maybe we were never their enemy. Maybe we just arrived at the wrong time. But in the confusion, my father stepped too close to the shore. His biggest mistake.

That's when she reached for him. A siren, rising from the waves, her arm slick with seawater, her blue-black scales shimmering in the moonlight. Her fingers were long, claw-tipped, webbed at the base, and inhumanly strong. She coiled her hand around his ankle like a serpent and yanked him into the sea. He didn't fight. Not from what I saw. I watched him vanish beneath the black surface, the ocean swallowing him whole. A scream ripped from my throat, echoing across the shore and out into the endless sea. The sound of a girl who loved her father, but hated him just the same. And in the end, I could do nothing, only watch as he died before me, helpless. Leaving me to carry on the Bleu name.

The water turned red with blood as the battle raged on. We lost so many that night. I gathered what was left of my crew and fled, half alive, wholly heartbroken.

When we finally returned to port, after licking our wounds and counting the dead, the crew made their choice. With no son to inherit the title, I became the next best thing. Or so they thought. I was nineteen, just a girl in their eyes, but I took the helm anyway.

I know I'm small for a captain. I've heard the whispers. But I was trained from the cradle to fight, to survive, to command. I've taken down men twice my size without blinking and slain creatures that crawl from the deepest parts of the sea. Strength doesn't just come with size; it comes with guts and training.

As the sun warmed my olive-toned skin and the salty breeze stung my face, I watched the crew hand me my father's hat and his title. I wasn't nervous. I'd known this day would come. My father had always been reckless, too consumed by his own madness to care about much, especially after my mother was taken from us. He fought recklessly against his greatest rival, Captain Eldoris. The two of them were always chasing the same treasures, their clashes leaving one or both bleeding before the day was done. Their feud burned for years, a fire neither man could put out, until the day Captain Eldoris committed the unthinkable. From that moment on, my father lived for only one purpose: to slaughter Eldoris's son, as payment for what had been stolen from him.

Kai Eldoris. Infamous Pirate Lord. Feared across every sea. The youngest, most powerful captain to ever sail and the only pirate known to wield real magic. Not borrowed from a witch. Not stolen or cursed. Magic that pulses in his veins. It belongs to him. A mortal man who should've never been given that kind of power.

They say he was born for war. That he held a blade before he could speak, fired a pistol before he could ride the tide. That he's been fighting alongside his father since he could walk. Now he commands *The Leviathan*, a ship said to vanish into fog and reappear miles away, faster than wind, cursed by the sea itself. While Captain Eldoris rots from illness, too weak to even stand, he remains shut away on Kai's ship. Guarded by Kai and the few crewmen he trusts, no one ever lays eyes on him. If I could, I'd make him bleed myself, but he's too well guarded. And unlike my father, I don't have an itch for a death sentence. Good. Let the bastard wither where he lies.

But I haven't forgotten. And I'll never forgive. No matter what power Kai holds, no matter what title sits on his shoulders, he is still my enemy. And one day, I'll make him pay for what his father did.

"Captain, we've hit port. The men are heading out for supplies before we set sail again," Smith says.

I've known Smith since I was a baby. He taught me everything that made me who I am: how to fight and when to hold back, how to splice a rope and tie a knot that won't give, how to load a pistol cleanly, and how to grip a cutlass so it lands true. He showed me where to strike a man so he never rises again and how to live with the cost. He turned a headstrong little girl into a captain. I owe most of what I know to him.

He was my father's first mate, and now, he's mine. He's a middle-aged man with shaggy brown hair streaked with gray, chestnut eyes sharp as broken glass, and a scar slicing down the right side of his face. He's a force in battle, can face down three enemies at once and walk away with nothing more than a scratch. My father trusted him with his life. And so do I.

However, ever since I took the role of captain, I've felt his resentment simmering beneath the surface, though he hides it well. But there was never a world where he could claim my ship. *The Siren* answers only to blood, my bloodline. Without that bond, I fear the crew would have chosen him long ago. My father would never have passed her to someone who doesn't carry that legacy in their veins. *The Siren* chose me. Smith never had a chance. I couldn't imagine life aboard *The Siren* without him here to help run it.

"Aye, I'll be down in a minute," I call back, perched in the crow's nest, the ship and sea laid out below me. It's where I go when I need a breath. When the weight of everything, this journey, this war, this map, settles heavy in my bones. I keep waiting for answers to surface. For fate to speak. Especially with Kai Eldoris out there, chasing the same legend as I am. We're all chasing the Fountain of Wishes for one reason or another, but if his father's legacy is any indication, Kai's reason is bound to be dark, hungry, ruthless, maybe even diabolical.

He still has his father. Still has Eldoris guiding him, even if the man is a shell of what he once was. But Eldoris is sick, not silent. He's still speaking, still scheming. And I can't afford to fall behind.

I make my way down to the dock, where I meet our dealers. Finally, the sweet scent of Magda hits me, the rich, smoky aroma of bonfires laced with laughter, mingling with the salt spray on my skin. The sun warms my face, and for the first time in what feels like forever, I feel at home again.

I hand the silver to Corvin, a well-known trader on Magda's docks. He's young but always has just what everyone needs. He is quite wealthy and very trustworthy. Would never tell another soul what you bought, as long as you don't ask where he got it.

"Thank you, Corvin. I always appreciate doing business with you," I say with a slight smile. His sea-blue eyes catch the sunlight beneath the brim of his worn straw hat, freckles scattered across his sun-browned skin like grains of sand. A gold chain glints at his throat, hinting at wealth he doesn't flaunt but can't quite hide.

"Anything for you, Mira," he answers, his voice slick with charm. He's always had a little thing for me, one I have no interest in. I nod, turning back toward the ship to steal a moment's rest before the night unravels.

Word's already spread that I'm recruiting, so we'll be docked here until morning. One night. Just enough time. It's important to let the crew stretch their legs, do what they please and who they please. I'm not that soulless of a captain.

Tonight, we'll head to Pebble's Pub, the kind of place where the most wanted criminals, future pirates, dealers, and crime lords gather to drink, gamble, make deals, and start fights they rarely finish. It's where my father always stopped to visit old friends during his excursions. And if I'm lucky, it's where I'll find the next additions to my crew.

Pebble's Pub is run by my oldest friend, Neressa, though sister might be the better word. A stunning woman, fiercely sought after, but don't let her beauty fool you. Between running her underground gambling ring and dealing half the island's drug supply, she's the deadliest slayer I've ever known. A hunter. A killer. And her reputation reaches farther than mine ever will.

My father trained her, more than he ever trained me. Though, I'm happy someone gave her time. I had my father day in and day out on *The Siren*. When he was off at sea, he hired the fiercest, most lethal killers to shape her. She had many mentors, most of whom she eventually killed. She's wealthy, powerful, and more than capable of handling herself in any situation.

The only thing she struggles with is being out at sea. She's bound to land—the ocean hunts her. Something waits in its depths, old and cruel enough to twist the tides themselves. She is safest ashore, for if she were ever taken, gods know what would happen. We would never see her again. So she made the shoreline her throne, turning curse into crown. Queen of pirates, yet she cannot sail beside them and still, they answer to her all the same.

Magda is the one island the guards won't touch. Too many pirates call it home, and even the royals know better than to test Neressa's rule. If word ever spread that Magda was under attack, every pirate across the sea would return to defend it.

Coral Haven, though, is different. North of Magda, it's the royals' stronghold, where common folk live under their rule and pirates are nothing more than enemies to be hunted. The guards there would sooner string us from the gallows than let us set foot on their shores, though that doesn't stop them from trading with the wealthiest pirates when it suits their pockets.

Magda is a safe place. It always has been. My home away from the ship. We spend most of our time here whenever we're on land. The town is full of color, small, crooked buildings with no two alike, every corner painted in different shades and stories. Musicians line the streets, chasing silver and gold with battered instruments and hopeful eyes. Nearby, prostitutes lean against doorways, laughing and calling out, each hustling for their next quick coin.

There are no street addresses in Magda, only names for the buildings: The Crooked Tooth, Blackbone Alley, Wren's End, Tarlock's Teeth.

And no one ever sleeps. There's always something happening, parties, deals, fights, love, betrayal. Magda breathes. It lives and burns and sings louder than any place I've ever known. Like a raging fire.

It's also home to one of the largest volcanoes in the sea. The last time it erupted, it scorched half the island into ash. But the locals didn't flinch. They rebuilt in the lava's shadow like it was nothing. That's the magic of Magda, wild, dangerous, and definitely alive. Just the way us pirates like it.

The sun dips low over the ocean, casting fire across the waves. It's time to pay our old friends a visit. I gather my crew and head down to the pub. Smith walks beside me, his hand resting near the hilt of his blade. I can feel it too, that sensation crawling up the back of my neck. We're being watched. Someone's lurking in the shadows.

A small smile tugs at the corner of my lips. "Hello, sister," I say, voice laced with mischief. Neressa steps out of the alley like a cat, smooth and slow, leaning casually against the wall. She's a sight to behold, obsidian curls framing her face, crimson lips that promise danger, and skin kissed bronze by the sun. Freckles scatter beneath her eyes, delicate and deceptive, and her gaze? The impossible color of a cool fog, unreadable, unshakable and rare.

She smiles slowly, then opens her arms for a warm embrace. "Mira, love. You've been docked all morning and didn't come say hello?" Her voice is low and raspy, the kind that makes men and women swoon. Neressa has eyes all over this island. If you so much as breathe the wrong way in Magda, she'll know.

She pulls me into a tight hug, holding me like it's been years. "I was resting," I say as I breathe her in. "It's good to see you."

Neressa looks at me with those dangerously gray eyes. "Always good to have you home." She slings an arm around my shoulders, steering me toward the pub like she owns the whole damn island, which, in a way, she does. "Come grab a drink. You know you never have to pay." She's only a few inches taller than me, but somehow she still manages to look down with that same amused, wicked gleam in her eyes.

"Aye." I smirk. "I could definitely use one."

The moment we step inside, the live music playing from the drunken pirate band dies. So does the laughter. The air turns thick, and for a second, it's like the pub itself is holding its breath. Usually, Neressa's the one who stills a room; her presence alone is enough to make even the boldest men go quiet, not just from her piercing beauty but from her lethal reputation. But this silence feels different. Heavier. Wrong. They're not looking at her like they usually do. No teasing smirks. No drunken attempts at flirtation. Just wide eyes darting between faces, as if they've all just seen a ghost.

A chill prickles at the back of my neck. Something's off. Magic runs through our world like water, twisting everything it touches, bleeding into cracks it was never meant to fill. And right now, it feels like it's soaked into the walls. Then I see it. A woman, barely clothed and barely worth noting, glances to her right, then quickly back at me. Her gaze lingers just a second too long. I follow it. And there he is.

Kai.

He sits casually at the center of the room like he owns it, two women draped across him, laughing, whispering into his ear. His presence is a gravitational pull, and somehow, without saying a word, he has the entire pub in the palm of his hand.

I hate to admit it, but even now, after all these years of hating him, I can't look away. His sharp jawline. That dark brown hair falling just to his chin. And those glowing hazel eyes, cutting through the dim light like they can see every part of you. Even the parts you'd rather bury. The ones you've nearly convinced yourself don't exist.

The scar down his right arm. A brutal, jagged thing. The kind that whispers of death and survival. A remnant from the siren battle that nearly ended him. I've heard stories about it, each more outrageous than the last. Some say he killed three sirens alone. Others say he never even bled. Hard to know which pirate tale is true. He was just a boy, after all.

He hasn't looked at me. Not yet. Or maybe he has. His eyes haven't moved, but his men have. They're on alert. Tense. Watching the room like they feel it too. The shift as thick as morning fog.

Kai's body is a map of violence. Muscles carved from years of battle, inked skin like scripture, with waves, storms, sea creatures, the Kraken he slayed to earn the title of Pirate Lord. Every inch of him screams survival. A legend in flesh. But not a single mark, not one, tells the story of a siren, from what I can see. He commands a room and expects to be listened to.

Kai rises from his chair like it's nothing. The two women draped across him slide off with the wave of his hand, dismissed, discarded. He adjusts the weapon at his hip, casual and calculated. A predator playing dress-up as a king. He starts to slowly walk straight to where I stand.

My crew steps forward instinctively, closing rank. "Move," I command. My voice slices through the pub like a blade. They flinch, then part. I step into the space between us, unflinching. Unafraid. The air stretches tight around us, taut as a drawn bowstring. "I want to see the bastard whose father killed my mother."

His brows arch, slow, amused. That wicked gleam dances behind his hazel eyes. A slow, almost lazy smile spreads across his lips, like he's savoring the challenge I've just laid at his feet. "Big words from such a tiny girl," he purrs. His voice has been sharpened by years of danger and dark deals, laced with something older. Something crueler. He's in front of me now, towering over me by a full foot. His presence wraps around the room, heavy, arrogant. Those eyes dare me to flinch. I don't.

The scent hits me next, sea salt, tobacco, and something sweeter. Rum, maybe. Pirates aren't supposed to smell like that. Not like power wrapped in sin. I refuse to back down. I meet his gaze head-on, heart pounding like war drums in my chest.

I don't speak. I let the silence stretch. Let him feel the weight of me, the fury, the history, the name I carry like a weapon. He tilts his head, studying me like I'm a puzzle he's halfway to solving. "So you're the one who's been following me..." A pause. "*Captain Mira.*" He drags out the title like it's a joke and a compliment all at once.

"Don't see many female captains these days," he drawls. "Heard this dump is your usual haunt. Kind of dirty... but raw." His grin is wolfish. "Just the way I like it." I let my eyes drag over him, slow, deliberate, then flick to the two women he dismissed like afterthoughts. Then back to him.

"It seems you've made yourself quite at home," I say, voice low but sharp enough to slice. I don't blink.

He chuckles, deep, smooth, entirely unbothered. Like the whole room isn't being crushed by just his presence alone. "Jealous?"

I roll my eyes so hard it almost hurts, disgust curling in my throat like smoke. "Please." My lips twist into a sneer. "I wouldn't touch you if you were the last man alive on a raft in siren waters." That only makes his grin grow wider.

He stares straight through me. Those hazel eyes, flickering between green-gold and stormy brown, like the ocean deciding whether to drown or spare. My body stiffens. But my soul refuses to strike.

Not yet. My fingers curl around the hilt of my cutlass. His eyes cut that intense eye contact with me to see where my hand moved to. "I wouldn't do that, *treasure,*" Kai says. The word drips from his lips like honey laced with venom. "I've got men at every corner of this pub. Let's play nice, aye?"

He's infuriatingly calm, and it makes my blood boil. My grip tightens. "There's nothing to play nice about. I want you gone from my town before we have to force you out." But his gaze doesn't waver. It sinks into mine, deep, endless, and suddenly, I'm not in a pub anymore. I'm in a memory that doesn't belong to me. Warm arms. Lullabies wrapped in seafoam. A glowing map tucked around me like a blanket. A siren circling a crib, her body pulsing with light beneath the waves. Guarding me.

I blink. Hard. My heart slams against my ribs. I know what this is.

Magic.

"You control thoughts," I determine, voice turning to ice. "Stay the hell out of my mind." Then I spit at his feet. He laughs. No one knows exactly what kind of magic Kai Eldoris holds. But for someone of his rank, with his bloodline... any kind is lethal. Especially if he can read minds.

"I didn't show you anything that wasn't yours already," Kai says, voice calm. Almost amused. "Those were your memories. Buried. Forgotten. Wished away. I only unlatched the door." The entire pub is suffocating in silence now. Every eye is on us. Even the filthiest criminals don't dare breathe too loud. You could hear a coin hit the floor and it'd echo like thunder. Rare, in a place where pirates never shut the hell up.

I glare at him, every nerve in my body on edge. He tilts his head, smirking like this is a game he's already won. "Seems like we're after the same thing, *treasure*... Do stop chasing me. It's getting a bit embarrassing."

Then he turns and waves me off like I'm some tavern girl begging for a coin. Dismissed. But then, he stops. Slowly, he looks back over his shoulder, locking eyes with me once more. His voice drops. "I'll let you live this time." He takes a small step closer, "But come near me, my ship, or my treasures again, and I won't be so kind. Would be a shame if history repeated itself. Like the last time your family was on *my* ship."

The words hit harder than steel. And for the briefest second... I swear I hear my mother's scream echo through the salt-heavy, muggy air of the pirate pub.

Anger surges through my veins like molten lava. I don't think, I move. One quick stride. My hand cracks across his face, the sound sharp and explosive, echoing like thunder in the tight, suffocating air. Pain blooms instantly in my palm. But the sting is almost satisfying. Before I can blink, he catches my wrist, twisting it behind my back with iron strength. Too fast. Too smooth. His grip burns against my skin. Heat shoots through me, like gold struck alive.

Then, chaos. My crew lunges forward. His men surge to match. The pub explodes into a violent symphony of clashing steel, snarled curses, and overturned tables. But Kai doesn't flinch. His eyes fixate on me. He leans in, close enough that I can feel the warmth of his breath graze the shell of my ear.

"I could crush you as easily as I scrape barnacles from my ship," he murmurs, voice low, sinfully smooth, dark as a storm rolling in. "Never touch me like that again... unless I ask for it." His words sink into my bones like poison, no, like fire. I want nothing more than to smack him again, this time harder. He's absolutely infuriating.

Kai shoves me into the heart of the brawl, where chaos and fury churn thick in the air. I unsheathe my cutlass, slashing, blocking, taking down anyone foolish enough to cross my path. But something's off. I'm not fighting to kill. I'm just moving. Reacting. Like instinct has taken the helm of my body, steering me with nothing but rage.

Across the room, Kai strolls in the opposite direction, completely unfazed. A glass of rum glides through the air from the bar like it was summoned, floating straight into his open hand. He takes a sip, never once looking back at the chaos erupting behind him.

His presence slices through the brawl. No one dares to go near him. No one even tries. It's like the air around him hums with something unseen, something waiting to strike. Magic clings to him like a second skin, quiet but coiled. He doesn't need to lift a finger to command fear. Maybe it's a spell. Or maybe it's just him. Either way, Kai Eldoris isn't someone you cross, because to cross him is to lose *everything*.

Neressa's back presses against mine, steady and familiar, as we fend off a group of drunken bastards, men easily a foot taller than either of us. But size doesn't matter when you're fighting like we do, furious and precise, shaped by a life balanced on the blade of violence. She lands a swift kick to a man's gut, sending him crashing down with a satisfying thud. This is nothing more than a warm-up for her.

"You couldn't have told me he was here?" I grunt, deflecting a wild swing from a thick-armed brute.

"He wasn't here when I left to find you," she says, calm as ever, knocking another man out cold. "But I heard rumors he was in town. Follow me." Without hesitation, Neressa grabs my wrist and pulls me toward a narrow hallway, cutting through the fight with practiced ease. The chaos fades behind us, swallowed by distance and shadows, as we move deeper into the dark hallway.

"What the fuck, Neressa?" My voice is low. Dangerous. "Hiding something like that could've gotten me killed. Do you even understand that?" She smirks like she has no remorse. She never has. Neressa kills for a living. Buries her guilt six feet under and pours herself a drink over it. And I know that, I always have. Even though everyone tries to keep information hidden from me. Still, the fire in my chest is spreading fast. I narrow my eyes. "What's going on with your face?" She bursts out laughing. That laugh, like we're in the middle of some joke I haven't been let in on, only makes my face flush more.

"Do you really think he'd kill you?" she teases, grinning like the devil herself. "Did you not see the yearning in his eyes?" She leans in, voice sing-song and deadly. "My sweet Mira, men aren't just for a crew."

I shove her. Hard. She hits the wall with a thud, not because I'm strong enough to throw her like that, but because she allows me to. I put distance between us, just in case she tries to grab me again. Her laughter echoes down the hallway, unapologetic and wild. And I can't tell if I'm angrier at her or at myself for not knowing which part of her is right.

I try to walk away, anger bubbling inside me like a storm waiting to break. But before I can take more than a few steps, Neressa steps in front of me in a feline-like manner. "There's more than meets the eye, little sister. Play your cards right. That man is the biggest Pirate Lord on the seas, the most cunning and lethal. If you really think I was going to kick him out of my pub and get marked..." She pauses, her eyes flicking toward the pub, where the brawl still rages on. It'll continue until either I leave or Kai does.

Her fog-colored eyes narrow, locking with mine. "Then you're surely mistaken." I don't look away.

My gaze stays sharp. Unforgiving. I know she cares for her business and her title. But choosing Kai's title over blood? Or is there something else she's keeping to herself? "His father killed my mother when I was a child. You knew that. She was like a mother to you, too." I step closer. "There was no *yearning* in his eyes. He wanted to kill me. Wanted my blood on his blade." My voice turns razor-sharp. "For someone who kills for a living, I'd expect you to be able to recognize bloodlust."

I hold her stare, letting the venom in my words settle like poison. For just a moment, something flickers behind her eyes. "I don't kill without intent," she slickly says, then whispers under her breath the number *thirteen*. I know her past with killing hasn't been easy. Being trained as a slayer is some of the most brutal training you can endure. And starting at such a young age? It's inhumane. In a selfish way, I'm glad my father didn't train me like he did her.

The lantern light catches her irises, igniting her usual icy calm with a flickering flame of something else. It unsettles me that death is her trade. Rich beyond measure, still she commands the deadliest slayers in the world. She's unmatched, unstoppable, yet she never seems to rest her blade, only bury it in another body. I think she's scared to put her blade down. Maybe it's the quiet that terrifies her the most. The way she does it without a flicker of hesitation, without even a blink. She'll slit a throat while holding their gaze, steady as steel. I resent her for it, even knowing it's all she's ever known. She's stopped slaughtering the innocent, but the truth is, Neressa is as hard as diamond. Beautiful, yes, but it's the flaws that cut, the imperfections that make her dangerous and stunning. I could never hate her for what she is. Neressa is the dark to my light, the shadow I will always need. She doesn't unmake me; she balances me.

I don't say another word. I walk past her. She leans back against the wall, cutlass still in hand, relaxed, but watchful. If she had more to say, she would've stopped me.

Even as I leave her behind, it isn't Neressa I can't shake, it's Kai. And if he finds the fountain before I do, gods help us all.

CHAPTER TWO

MIRA

WITCHWATER

I wake to sunlight spilling through the windows, its golden warmth spreading across my face like a gentle embrace. For a fleeting moment, I bask in it. Letting it chase away the chill of the night before. But then my gaze drops to my wrist. The pain is sharp. A bruise already blooms there, dark, angry, and unforgiving. A perfect imprint of Kai Eldoris's grip. He hadn't even grabbed me hard. Not really. But the mark says otherwise, like it was his magic imprinting itself inside me. If that was him holding back, I can't imagine the full strength he's capable of.

Last night, we left the pub with a few new recruits in tow, fresh blood, eager eyes, and the kind of desperation that turns men into pirates. No one died in the chaos, though I'm sure we earned a few new enemies along the way. My father's name was whispered through the streets long after we left.

His legacy. His madness. His map. Everyone still talks about it like it's gospel. Like it's worth dying for. And maybe it is. But the obsession... It burns in them the same way it once burned in him. It makes my blood boil. And at the same time it leaves me hollow.

I'm sure Neressa had a hand in persuading some of the new recruits. She always does. People bend around her like smoke, charmed, convinced, or cornered. But still, the irritation lingers. I love her. I do. But last night? Her actions of not telling me who could be walking through Magda. Knowing there were rumors, it was a selfish move on her part. Even for her. She's always been about the business. About survival. About stacking gold over sentiment. And I get it. But putting me last? Choosing power over blood? That's not how sisters are supposed to act. Blood or not.

I push the thought aside. We have leads, faint, shifting trails pointing toward places most don't return from. The journey ahead won't be easy. The truth we're chasing lives in the hands of the hidden and the haunted.

I step onto the main deck and announce our next heading. Alek. A cursed town where witches are bred and born. There's one witch in particular who may hold the answers I seek. But every answer she gives comes with a price, and she's never been known to play a fair game. Alek lies far to the northeast of Magda, hidden deep within the heart of Jasper's Ocean. We sail for three sunrises and two moon-soaked nights. The winds slow. The sea turns silent.

Then the huts begin to appear. First just shadows at the edges of the fog, crooked silhouettes that vanish if you look too hard. Then suddenly, they're just... there. Weather-worn, bone-stitched, covered in symbols that seem to shift when you blink. None of it makes sense. But Alek never does.

The fog thickens until it breathes, stealing air right from our lungs. It wraps around the ship like a serpent, curling over the deck, slithering between my boots. It presses against my lungs, not choking, just claiming. The air is wet with whispers I can't quite hear. The water is no longer water, it's black glass rippling with things that never breach the surface. The type of water you never want to fall into.

Alek feels alive. Hungry. Watching. It should because this is Taika's domain, the most powerful witch born of salt and blood, her very name a curse. Her magic is never given, only endured. And whatever price she demands will haunt you for the rest of your life.

If you're lucky enough to leave, or live with your soul intact.

The last time we came to Alek, Taika asked my father for a baby hippocampus. Alive. She needed one for a ritual, to harvest pieces of its soul and sell them to those who'd lost theirs. Hippocampi are pure. Too pure. And purity, in this world, is a dangerous thing. It rots in the wrong hands. Harming a hippocampus is a sin, one that could place bad omens upon your soul.

I was too young to understand the full horror of it then, but I remember the screams. Blood-curdling. Unnatural. The sound of something so sacred being torn apart, body and soul, deep below deck. It still haunts me. It was the moment I realized my father didn't have a heart anymore.

I steer *The Siren* toward Alek, one hand gripping the wheel, the other gripping my thoughts before they spiral. But it's no use. My mind is a storm. All I can think about is Kai. A gust of wind blows my curls violently, like a warning. Looking forward, I start to see a small storm forming over the horizon. That could only mean one thing: we're close.

The way he touched me, not tender, not kind. With power. The kind that reaches past skin and muscle and sinks into your bones like poison or desire. I don't know which is worse. He moved through my mind like he owned it. Rearranged things I didn't give him permission to touch. And what's worse, my body let him. I'm supposed to hate him. I do hate him. So why does the memory of his hand still burn? Why do I ache in places that I have never known want?

It infuriates me. The thought of him, out there, chasing the same wish I am. Wanting the same truth. Holding all that power and knowing how to use it. Sometimes I wonder if we even stand a chance, but that's a fleeting weakness. Because while he may have magic in his blood, I have it in the wood of my ship.

From what I know, the Fountain of Wishes has a few unbreakable rules. You can't ask for a wish that's already been made. You can't wish death upon anyone. And you can't wish for the tides to turn in anyone's favor. That last one I still don't fully understand. Maybe it's a metaphor. Or maybe it's a warning.

But one thing is certain: break any of these rules, and you'll turn to dust where you stand. Not metaphorical dust. Bones to ash. Gone. The fountain was once just an old sailor's tale. Whispered in taverns. Traded in drunken slurs around bonfires. A bedtime story for children too afraid of the sea. Until it wasn't. Until it resurfaced, real. And far more dangerous than any legend should ever be. It's sparked the dreams of many pirates and claimed even more lives. The path to it is cruel. Not just perilous, but cursed.

No one's laid eyes on the fountain in over a hundred years and lived to tell the tale. The map that leads to it was shattered, split into pieces and scattered to the corners of the sea. Each fragment cursed, hidden, nearly impossible to find... or so the legends say.

But pirates, we love a tale as old as time. Especially if it ends in blood, gold, and power.

We drift into a black fog thick as tar, heavy as grief. It clings to our ship like claws, choking the air from our lungs. *The Siren* groans beneath me, the sound sharp and strained in the unnatural quiet.

"I know, girl," I whisper, tightening my grip on the helm. My fingers dig into the rich, enchanted teak, as if I can anchor us both through touch. The fog unsettles her. It unsettles me, too.

Around me, the crew coughs, harsh, rasping gasps. Some collapse where they stand, their legs folding like broken sails. I yank the brown bandana from around my neck and tie it across my nose and mouth, forcing myself to breathe only when absolutely necessary.

The darkness swallows us whole. It's suffocating. Hallucinatory. My vision swims, my balance teeters. "Light the lanterns!" I shout, voice ragged with urgency. The thought of steering blind into the unknown, of running aground or worse, twists something deep in my gut. I won't lose her, my ship. Not to this. Not to fog born of curses and things with teeth.

She's more than a ship. She's family. The only piece of it that I have left.

The ship jolts, then stops. Not with anchors, but just a sudden, silent halt, as if gripped by unseen hands. The black fog begins to peel away, slow and steady, like smoke retreating from fire. And then it appears, a narrow bridge stretched out across the water, conjured from nothing. No splash, just magic leading the way. "Smith!" I call, voice slicing through the thinning haze.

He rushes up the deck, breath sharp in the cold air. "Yes, Cap'n?"

I look down from the helm. "You're coming with me." He nods, crisp and wordless.

"Cap'n, want me to come with you?" Nate's voice cuts through the mist. I turn toward him—my third in command, steady as stone even when the sea's against us.

"No, Nate," I say. "Keep your eye on *The Siren* while we're gone."

He nods once, no argument, just loyalty. The red bandana tied around his head is damp with fog, his jaw set as he breathes through the sickening air. "Aye, Cap'n," he mutters, voice rough.

I step down from the helm, the wood cool beneath my boots, and begin strapping on more weapons to my belt: blade, dagger, pistol, another blade. Each click of metal grounds me.

Smith does the same. Shadows my movements like the soldier he is. We descend the rope ladder, each rung slick with sea mist. The moment our boots hit the bridge, it groans beneath us. Not like it was made from wood but from cursed bones. I step cautiously. One foot. Then the other. Smith mirrors me, silent and ready.

The farther we walk, the more the fog thins, revealing a crooked hut at the end of the bridge. As though the hut had drowned once, then clawed its way back to the surface, resurrected. Vines snake across the rotting wood, tangled with twitching insects and patches of pulsing moss. Something skitters in the shadows, a rat, or worse. How anything can live here, I'll never understand. The air reeks, like rotting fish and old boots left to bake in the sun. It hits the back of my throat, sour and unshakable.

The hut is barely lit. A faint, flickering glow leaks through the warped wooden slats like a dying heartbeat. Still, I know where we are.

With magic guiding us, we've made it to Taika's.

CHAPTER THREE

KAI

MARKED

The morning fog had thinned by the time I stepped out here, leaving the horizon stretched wide and endless over the sea. A cup of hot coffee warms my hand, a pipe resting easy in the other.

I set my coffee on the ship's weathered rail and let the ocean breathe beneath us, then run my fingers along the scar on my forearm. Once it was only a pale crescent beneath the skin; now it throbs with small, electric stabs that jumped down my arm, short-lived but painful. I don't like that. I never liked anything it reminded me of. But this pain... It's new and unexpected.

The memory of her claws tearing into my right arm, the world collapsing into the black ring of water she carved around us. In that circle there was no up and no down, just pressure and the sound of my own breath turning thin. I blew bubbles, traced their path with my fingers, hoping they'd lead me to the surface. They did.

I crawled onto shore under moonlight, the flames of the nearby battle flickering in the distance. My arm was mangled, bloodied, dangling by sheer will. I was certain I'd lose it that night. But it healed. Looking back, I think my magic had something to do with that. I was just a child.

My best friend, Jack, had been a victim of the sirens that night. He never fell for their songs and was always the first to mock the poor bastards who did. But one of them called him by name. Her voice wasn't like the others, wasn't haunting or seductive, it was soft. And her eyes... They were piercing blue. Curious but sparked with sadness. Not dead like the others. Her long black hair moved through the water like oil, and when she smiled... it didn't look like a threat. She didn't have razor-sharp, unsettling teeth like a siren typically does.

Even I hesitated. Sirens aren't beautiful. Not like that. Not in ways that make you forget what they are... but she was different. And there was something else in her gaze, something almost human. Jack stepped toward her like he'd been waiting his whole life. She took his hand, then his arm, and dragged him beneath the waves. Kissed him as he drowned, and he let her.

The sea stilled where he vanished, moonlight spilling over the surface like silver. I screamed his name. But he didn't hear me. Or maybe he didn't want to. I never saw him again.

He was a few years older, more like a brother than a friend. And the ache hasn't dulled. But the way he looked at her... I can't stop thinking about it. Like maybe he chose her, or she chose him, or they had known each other. Maybe it wasn't her voice that lured him in, but something entirely different.

And if that's possible, if it's even remotely possible to fall in love with a siren, then everything we've been taught about them is wrong. Worse... It means they're not just killers. They're something far more dangerous.

After I watched my closest friend, my brother in every way but blood, vanish beneath that silver-streaked, black water, I sat there. Sat there while the sirens sang their death songs. While men screamed. While fire consumed everything around us. I sat there, blood pouring from my mangled arm, every heartbeat pulsing with the sound of his name. He was the first and only person I ever cared about losing. I swore to myself to never get attached to anyone after that night.

Sirens don't just drown you. They unravel you, piece by piece. They toy with your memories, make you believe you're home, that you're safe. And then they drag you under, and you beg for death to come faster. They don't kill you outright. They make you fall apart, one memory at a time, drowning at the same time.

Last night's encounter lingers in my mind, unwanted, unexpected, and something I would've preferred to keep buried. I take a slow sip, the bitter heat chasing its way down my chest, steadying me from the inside out. Then comes the pull of smoke, soft and familiar. I exhale into the rising light, watching the cloud curl and scatter, wrapping itself around the thin shafts of sun as if the day itself were reluctant to wake.

I know she's been following me for months. Her trail is messy, erratic at best, but I can't tell if that was her doing or the result of her incompetent crew. She first caught my scent back at Shoreline Village. Small island. Strategically wedged between Coral Haven and Magda. Too tiny to matter, but just big enough for pirates and common folk to barely coexist. The guards have their districts. The locals know which taverns to avoid, the ones we've claimed as ours, where pirates drink, deal, and disappear.

I'd heard whispers that someone there knew the location of a map fragment. Just one. But it only takes one piece to start a war. And when I want something? I get it by persuasion or by force.

I spotted her ship a few ports down from mine, carelessly docked, sloppy as ever. Mira's rise to captain after her father's death was the worst thing that could've happened to that crew. And that ship, *The Siren*, it's a waste in her hands. A vessel carved from enchanted teak, steeped in old magic, whispered about in every port from Coral Haven to the Barrens. I can feel it when *The Siren* is close. The magic radiates off her hull, thick and cloying, tainting the sea like perfume on a corpse.

That ship is the only reason Captain Bleu ever made it out of battle alive. The only reason anyone remembers his name. As someone who commands magic myself, I can't help but want it. A ship like that? It's priceless.

My ship, however, *The Leviathan*, is the fastest vessel on the sea, an unholy beast carved from nightmares and legends. She doesn't just slice through water, she hunts, silent and ruthless. But it's my quarters that are the heart of her. A place no one has stepped foot in since I was a child. As I grew, so did the walls I built around it, thick with secrets, soaked in blood and memory. Every item inside is sacred. Untouchable. I've grown... territorial. Obsessive, even. I don't let people near the things I care about. Not my weapons, maps, or space. It's not about privacy. It's about control. I can't afford to let anything, or *anyone*, get too close. Because once something's mine, I don't let it go.

As for Mira, she's not ready. She doesn't know how to lead. She lacks the steel, the instinct, the kind of edge it takes to make the hard choices and walk away while the rest are left bleeding inside. She's no Neressa.

Now, she's a killer. Mira can hold her own in a fight, sure, she's been trained. But you can see it in her eyes. There's too much soul left in her.

With my father growing sicker by the day, command of the ship and crew has fallen to me. Rightfully so. It was always my birthright. This vessel runs like a well-oiled machine beneath my hands, powered not just by discipline, but by magic. My magic. And my crew, they're stronger than most, because they follow someone worth bleeding for. The title of Pirate Lord wasn't handed to me, it was earned. In blood, bone, and fire. And I intend to keep it that way.

Using magic on Mira, her mind was easy to invade. All I had to do was make simple eye contact. Manipulating a mind to unlock what once was hidden, dark secrets, untold truths... Except when I tried to use magic on creatures born from magic, sirens, mermaids, witches, their minds were too strong to alter. Humans, however, I could twist their minds into something dark, easily.

They say the power came from my mother's bloodline. She was a witch, strong, feared, and long gone. She vanished after I was born, leaving me behind with my father and a legacy wrapped in secrets. I've tried to slip inside his mind, to claw out whatever scraps of truth he's hiding about her. Just one image is all I need, but his thoughts are sealed and the key thrown away. And if he ever knew I'd tried? He'd skin me alive. Her name was never spoken to me. It has been something that has haunted me my entire life. But I know this: what I've uncovered so far about my magic? It's barely the surface. I can feel it just under my skin, waiting to wake.

The magic hums in my veins, steady and relentless, like a storm waiting to break. It sharpens in battle, in every encounter where a choice could mean blood or breath. It feeds on my emotions. Anger makes it flare, despair makes it burn. Sadness is rare, but when it strikes, the magic swells with a ferocity I can't control, as if it refuses to let me die.

But it's wild. Untamed. A weapon I don't yet know how to wield. I've been hunting for a mentor, someone who can sail beside me and show me its true reach. How to bend it, shape it, unleash it. Until then, it remains unknown, raw and dangerous.

And that makes it mine.

I was there when Mira's mother was slaughtered in front of her. Back then, I still had a heart, if only barely. I was young. I remember feeling something. Maybe pity, maybe guilt. Her father didn't fight—he was taken down, bloody, beaten, completely broken. My father didn't care. Mercy wasn't in his blood. Killing them would've been kind. Instead, he left them to rot in their grief, soaked in blood beside the woman they loved. He shattered that crew without lifting more than his blade and walked away as if it meant nothing.

That was the day I realized my father wasn't a man anymore. He was something else. Something carved from cruelty. He created his greatest enemy that day.

Mira's father spent years trying to kill me. To avenge the woman my father butchered. But I was never worried. My crew is stronger. My magic, darker. I've taken down sea beasts older than time, creatures whispered about in the same breath as Charybdis, the Kraken, tarlocks, and the Leviathan. And now that the merciless siren has dragged the old man into the black water and drowned him, I know I was right not to fear him. He fell for a siren's song, one voice a pirate should never let into their minds. That, to me, screamed he was weak minded.

The thought of sirens pulls my eyes to the horizon, searching for the sea's telltale shift to black, their omen, their feast, their graveyard. I listen hard to the crash of waves against the hull, bracing for the kind of song that could unravel a man's mind and drag him willingly into the depths.

They say the first sirens weren't born of the sea. In ancient myth, they were once muses, cursed by the gods, their beauty twisted, their voices turned into weapons. But ours? Ours are worse. Forged in salt, souls, and vengeance.

Touching Mira that night in the pub was unlike anything I've ever felt. It was as if my hand had been set ablaze, fire igniting beneath my skin, a heat only her touch could quench. I've never known a connection so raw, so visceral. With just a single contact, I could see straight through her. And she didn't resist. Didn't flinch. It was as if I could feel the warmth of her mother's arms, the way she must've felt as a child, safe, loved, protected.

But then came the vision. A siren circling her bed, not with malice, but with grace. Gliding through glowing water like a guardian, not a predator. It sent a chill through me. Why did she see that siren? Why wasn't it attacking her, especially while she was defenseless? And why was the water glowing, when it should've been black?

So many questions. Too many. The Bleu family, it seemed, was built on secrets.

I hadn't seen her since the day her mother died, and she'd changed. Grown. A tiny thing with a sharp tongue and fire in her deep emerald green eyes. She spoke with the confidence of someone twice her size and hit just as hard. Those emerald eyes, feral, alive, could bring a lesser man to his knees. Her frame, all soft curves and wildfire, was a contradiction I can't ignore. I'm not supposed to want her. I'm supposed to kill her.

But back at the pub, no matter how hard she pushed, I couldn't do it. My blade stayed sheathed. Something inside me whispered *don't*. I thought it was my magic leading me, so I listened.

Only now, that whisper hasn't stopped. It echoes in my bones, hums beneath my skin when I think of her. Magic doesn't lie and mine is restless. Like it's trying to lead me somewhere. To her. I keep telling myself I only hurt her a little. That maybe my grip was too tight. That maybe I crossed a line. But I had to send a message that I don't tolerate being followed. Anyone else would've died for less.

Jay, my second, hasn't let it go. He's always been that way, ever since I was a reckless boy running headfirst into fights I couldn't win and he was the one dragging me back out again. He's always pulled me in the right direction when I veered too far, kept me sane, or as sane as a man can be on a ship like this. Yesterday he said I've gone soft. But there's *nothing* soft about me. Not even when it comes to her. Especially not then.

Searching for the map fragments has been nothing short of hell. No one truly knows how many there are or what forms they take; they shift and hide as trinkets, stones, even pieces of living things. The only lead worth following is this: the oldest creatures of the sea might remember where they lay, and coaxing answers from beings older than time is never simple.

My pursuit of the fountain isn't about some selfish wish, it's about closing a wound. My father failed; he left a trail of shame and weakness I refuse to inherit. I hate him for what he was, and I live to prove I am better in every way. If the fountain can finally finish what he started, no matter what I would wish for, it will stand as proof that I am the man he never was. That kind of hunger does not stop for mercy.

This hunt has buried more legends than it has crowned. I will not be another footnote. I will find the fountain, and I will kill anyone who stands in my way.

Before his mind turned to rot, my father knew nearly everything, where the pieces were hidden, the curses tied to them, the monsters guarding them. Now he rages at shadows, forgets my name, talks to ghosts that never answer back.

Pirates don't mourn. We survive, and survival means never getting attached, to crew, to blood, to anyone.

We set sail for a place called Pike, a strange, reclusive town buried deep in the jungle, where vines grow thicker than rope and the air tastes like earth and secrets. It rests right on the borderline between Jasper's Ocean and Sapphire's, an eerie place where the sea changes color and depth without warning. It was put there by the gods to separate magical beings and mortals. Our goal is to find Veyra, a woman said to live in the jungle's heart, and one who only appears if she chooses to. Veyra is rumored to be in direct communion with Mother Earth herself. She doesn't just hear the land and sea, she feels them, breathes them, becomes them.

Many have ventured into Pike seeking her wisdom. Most are turned away. Some leave cursed, marked by omens that follow them to their graves. Veyra doesn't entertain fools or those with darkness in their hearts. She's a brutal judge of character, and if she senses something off, she won't just reject you, she'll ruin you. Quietly. You won't even realize you've been judged until it's far too late.

Visiting Veyra is a dangerous move, but she may be the only one who can get me closer to what I need. I won't pretend to be a saint, but I'm not wicked either. Somewhere in between, maybe. I'm counting on the magic I carry to draw her in. Maybe even earn her trust. What I can do is rare, feared in most parts of the world and outlawed in the rest. I've spent my life keeping it buried, hidden beneath sharp smiles and sharper blades.

But power like mine doesn't go unnoticed. There are things that feed on it. *Nyx.*

Few speak of them anymore, and those who do whisper like they're afraid the shadows are listening. They're old, older than sirens, older than sea magic. Born from the dark when the gods stopped watching. They walk like men, but they're not. Their eyes are dark and their smiles like shards of broken glass, hidden behind whatever skin they wear. Draining magic from the living, slowly, methodically, until nothing's left but an empty shell for them to inhabit. No screams or blood. Just... gone.

Most believe they're extinct. A myth to scare children, to scare witches. But magic like mine calls to them. And I've felt eyes on me when no one else was around. They say there's no way to kill them. I don't know if that's true. I just know if I ever come face-to-face with one... I'll have to try or I'll end up dead.

"Cap'n! Ship off the starboard side, full sail and heading straight for us!" one of my men shouts, yanking me from my thoughts. I pivot toward the west end of the deck.

A vessel I've never seen before carves through the fog, its inky black sails rippling like shadows torn from the underworld. A chill scrapes down my spine. Something ancient clings to that ship, something foul. Wrong. "Ready the cannons! Battle stations, we're under attack!" I bellow. Before the words leave my mouth, their cannons ignite. Wood splinters. Shrapnel sings. *The Leviathan* groans as the blasts hit, precise and brutal. Anger boils inside me from the hit.

Figures swing aboard, thick ropes hissing through the air. Half-man, half-creature. Their snarls sound like metal grating bones. Clawed feet slap the deck. I've never crossed paths with these creatures. But I know what they are: kappas. My crew meets them head-on, blades drawn, the clash of steel ringing across the chaos. "Hold the line!" I command. "No one crosses over. We fight here. That ship looks like a place no pirate ever returns from." Or worse. A place that keeps you. *Changes* you into one of them.

Dark, twisted magic rolls off them in waves. One of them barrels toward me, a grotesque thing, half-hammerhead, half-human, dragging a saw-toothed sword behind it. I duck the first swing, sidestep the second. Fast, but clumsy. I counter. Slice clean through its arm in one motion. It stumbles. Then straightens. And the limb grows back.

My heart hammers once, hard. Sea beasts can do that. But they don't breathe above water. This one does. They're not just monsters. They're something from the depths of hell, twisted in dark magic.

My mind sharpens like a blade. I already know the solution. You want to kill something like this? You take its head. I stay light on my feet, dodging each vicious swing, every move calculated, clean, survival honed into instinct. His strikes are wild, fueled by rage, but I'm faster. I duck, pivot, drive a brutal kick into his gut. He stumbles back with a guttural snarl, hitting the deck hard.

I don't give him time to recover. One clean stroke. My blade severs his head from his shoulders. Blue blood gushes out, thick and oily, staining my deck with the stench of something that should've stayed buried in the deep. His body spasms once. Then goes still.

I scan the chaos. My crew is struggling, blades glancing off flesh instead of tearing through. Panic flickers behind their eyes. "Behead them!" I roar. "It's the only way!"

"I wouldn't do that to your new allies, son. We've only just met, and you've already spilled one of my men's blood." A deep, rasping voice cuts through the chaos behind me, like barnacles scraping across a ship's hull. I turn fast, blade ready. And freeze.

He stands at the edge of the deck like he's always belonged there, like the sea birthed him for this moment alone. Towering. Composed. Rotting with elegance. Purple-black urchin spines fan out from his skull like a twisted crown. His skin is a grotesque collage, scaled, barnacled, water-swollen. One eye is milky and bulbous, the other a piercing silver, too focused, too knowing. His left arm is a massive crab claw, dripping saltwater, while his right remains human, sort of, tattooed, muscular, blue as drowned flesh. Where his nose should be, there's a gaping blowhole, glistening and pulsing as he breathes.

What unsettles me most is his calmness. The way he tilts his head, studies me like I'm a puzzle he's already solved.

"Allies?" I growl, my voice sharp as steel. "You storm my deck, spill my crew's blood, and expect an alliance?"

He doesn't flinch. "I fear you have no choice, Kai," he says, voice smooth, anchored with eerie calm. "We're chasing the same storm. You lead me to what I seek... and I'll make sure you live long enough to reach it."

I don't trust him. Not the way he speaks my name like it's already his. Not the hunger in that glinting eye. "I don't work with others," I snap. "My crew makes no alliances. You've wasted your breath." His smile widens, not with amusement, but certainty.

Then the sky breaks. The storm hits all at once, like it's been waiting for my refusal. Rain slams down in sheets, sharp and icy, needling into my skin. Winds howl from the deep, ropes snap against the masts, and the ocean surges, rising in violent, unnatural swells. It was clear just moments ago. Now, it feels like the ocean is punishing me. Or worse, like he called the storm.

"Unfortunately for you, boy, this isn't an offering," the creature sneers, his crab-like arm sweeping toward the chaos unfolding around us. "You'll either work with me... or for me. Choose wisely."

I glance around. My crew is losing ground. Too many are falling, bloodied bodies strewn across the deck. I'm not used to losing. Not like this. My gaze drops briefly toward the lower deck, where my father lies, safely. His mind is fractured, rotting, but when it clears, he's a vault of priceless knowledge.

I tighten my grip on my sword, knuckles bone-white, and take a step forward. "What do you want?" I growl, my voice colder than the wind tearing across the deck. "What could I possibly give you that you don't already have?"

"You, son, are the key," he says, voice cold and calculated. "The sirens are terrible gossips, and that scar of yours is a crucial part of the map." His one eye flicks to my arm. I follow his gaze, staring down at the jagged scar, rain and seawater dripping off it, twisted, brutal, a relic I've spent years trying to forget.

My jaw tightens. My mind races. "My scar... is part of the map?" I ask, forcing the words past the weight in my chest. "The map to the Fountain of Wishes?"

He nods, slow and sure. "A siren gave you that, didn't she?" he says, each word a blade digging deeper.

Behind me, the clash of steel and the screams of pain continue, my crew still locked in combat. "Call off your men," I demand, stepping forward, sword still in hand. "I'll bargain. But no more bloodshed."

He watches me for a beat, his single eye unreadable. Then he taps his sword on the deck.

Once.

Twice.

Three times.

Instantly, his crew stills, frozen mid-strike, their bodies rigid, spellbound. Without a sound, they withdraw, slinking back to their ship like a tide reversing. Vanishing into the thick mist and storm.

He turns to me again, voice smooth as silk. "Come aboard," he says. And without hesitation, I follow. Knowing if anyone should cross over into the ship that looks like it was wrenched from the deepest depths of the sea, it would be me.

The fog parts just enough for me to see the name carved into the blackened hull. Letters etched deep, glowing faintly in the stormlight:

Urashima's Curse.

The ship pulses like a heartbeat. And still, I follow.

CHAPTER FOUR

MIRA

THE WITCH'S HUT

"Taika," I say, my voice smooth. "Nice to see you."

She turns slowly, her long, dark brown locs swaying, strung with bones, beads, moss, and gods know what else. Her smile is wicked, eerie. It never reaches her eyes, eyes the color of dirt after rain, rimmed in shadows as deep as the trench. Her lips are slicked in something thick and black, tar-like and wet.

"Captain Bleu's daughter," she says, her voice soft and slithering, curling through the air like smoke. "I wondered when you'd come. So many questions, I imagine. Questions I could answer..."

I glance around the hut, my eyes adjusting to the dim, flickering light. Cages line the walls, some made of bone, others of rusted iron, housing creatures in varying stages of decay. One twitches violently, skin hanging in strips, its eyes gone but somehow still watching. Another is nothing but a ribcage and claws, rattling softly as though whispering secrets to the dark. A third lies motionless, lifeless eyes staring up, yet its limbs jerk like a puppet. My eyes flick to Smith, leaning in the doorway. Waiting for any move she might make to hurt me.

My stomach churns, bile rising in my throat. But I don't flinch. I meet her gaze and speak calmly. "Aye. I believe you're the one who can help me." I let the words land, solid and unafraid. "But what do you want in return?"

She glides across the room, her steps near soundless. With a graceful flick of her fingers, she plucks a vial from the chaos of her shelf. Inside, the liquid glows faintly, like starlight trapped in glass. It shifts, shimmers, catching the low lantern light and throwing ghostly shapes on the walls.

"Mermaid tears," she says, holding it between two fingers, her smile never quite touching her eyes. "They heal even the most grievous wounds. Might just save a life." I narrow my eyes, studying her face, trying to unravel the game beneath her words. There's something she's not saying. Something more.

Her voice softens suddenly, almost maternal, but it's the kind of softness that makes my skin crawl at the same time. "My dear girl," she says, tilting her head just slightly, "I don't need you to help me. I simply want a wish. One little wish, made in my name."

Shock pulses through me like a lightning strike. A wish? She wants me to make a wish for her? I try to hide the way my chest tightens. Taika is the most powerful witch in all the seas. If she wants something, can't she just take it? Bend the tides, speak to the dead, twist the world to her will? Unless there's something stronger than her. Something even she can't touch. Or that she's afraid of...

"How do you know what I'm after?" I ask carefully, each word measured. I keep my voice low, guarded. Her laugh coils around me, like a snake wrapping its prey tight.

"I know everything that happens in the sea," she says. Her eyes flash. "What pirate isn't chasing the cursed fountain by now?"

I lift my chin, letting the weight of her words settle without sinking me. I straighten my shoulders, spine tall, tone steady. "I see," I say. "And what is it you want to wish for?"

"Girl," Taika says, voice heavy as storm clouds, "I will not tell you my wish yet. It is dark and it must remain a secret. Spoken only to your ears." I blink, the weight of her words pressing against my ribs. But she doesn't wait for my reply.

Her gaze cuts to Smith, lingering. Then back to me, sharp, unreadable, almost hungry. "Do you wish for him to leave us?" I ask evenly, keeping my tone firm, calm. Reassuring. "He's harmless. Let him be." Taika moves slowly toward Smith.

"Hurt him," I warn, my fingers resting against the hilt of my cutlass, "and I'll kill you where you stand." She pauses mid-step. Her eyes narrow, her expression shifts, mocking, cruel.

"You wish to protect those with bad blood running through their veins?" she whispers, the words thick with meaning. A chill runs down my spine. My instincts bristle. She said it low enough only my ears could hear it. A secret.

"What are you talking about?" I press, but she only shrugs, like I'm not worth the effort of an answer. Like the future has already unfolded behind her eyes. She turns without another word, vanishing into the shadows of her hut. Smith stays rooted to the doorway. Watching. And though nothing moves, the air feels colder now.

Taika's figure is swallowed by the flickering gloom, but her voice lingers, low, echoing, as if the very walls breathe with her magic. "I want to help you," she says. "You are the only one meant to find the fountain. I have foreseen it. You are the key."

As she speaks, the lantern hanging above flickers unnaturally, once, twice, and then steadies, casting long, twitching shadows across the floor. Bones in a nearby cage rattle softly, as if stirred by her words. She reappears, gliding back into the dim light. Her smile is gone.

"I do not know how," she continues, "but something about you is different. Special." Her gaze sharpens with concern as she slowly shakes her head. "If I can see it, others will too. You will be hunted. A heavy bounty will be placed on your head." A gust of cold air rushes through the hut despite no open window. The flames dance violently, casting shadows on the walls.

There's something in Taika's voice, something that clings. Maybe she needs me alive for that wish she refuses to speak aloud. I square my shoulders and meet her gaze. "You don't know how I'm the key," I say, each word measured, "but you're certain I am?"

She hands me the vial, her beady brown eyes locking onto mine with unsettling force. "I foresee things, child," she murmurs, her voice dry and brittle. Her fair skin is caked in layers of grime, and the bitter sting of potions clings to her like perfume gone foul.

"Things you do not wish to see. Things that weigh." She pauses, the air around us pulsing faintly, as if the hut itself is listening. "I see you finding the fountain. Fighting for your life in glowing water. I see you falling. I see you wishing. I see your heart breaking..." Her voice dips. "... and I see your soul being saved. I see you saving another soul."

She tilts her head, as if catching a whisper carried by something I can't hear. When her gaze returns to mine, there's a shadow in it—something that wasn't there before. My thoughts scatter, no matter how hard I try to focus. Questions claw at me. Whose soul am I meant to save? Why would I not want to see what my future holds? That one thought alone chills me to the bone. The riddle she's speaking of, the one she refuses to explain, feels like the deadliest truth of all.

"I see your father, smiling at you. I see you running to him. And I see your mother... but that vision is unclear. Clouded. As if she does not wish to be seen." A chill bleeds into my spine. Her words wrap around my thoughts, pulling them tight. Does she see my father alive? Or is this the afterlife? The images twist in my gut, gnawing at my calm.

Taika tilts her head, watching me like a predator reading the last twitch of its prey. "You're confused. Good." A thin smile curls her lips. "Confusion makes you think. You'll need that, for the road ahead is long. And it will not be kind." She steps back, the shadows folding around her. "But I will help you." She lowers her voice. "Now tell me... What is it you came here for?"

I honestly didn't know what I came here to take. I came for information. A path. A sliver of direction in all this madness. "Then I will give you a path," Taika says, her gaze slicing through me like a blade of glass. She sees everything. Every buried thought, every flicker of doubt. My heart sinks.

"Get out of my head," I snap, voice low and sharp. Taika only chuckles. She turns her back to me and begins rummaging through the chaos of her hut. Vials clink. Bones rattle. She retrieves a tattered scrap of parchment and uncorks a twisted vial shaped like a mutilated skull. Thick black tar drips from the mouth of it like poison. With one long, grime-coated finger, she begins to swirl it across the page.

"Young one," she croons, amusement dripping from every word, "I am a witch. I have been inside your mind since that enchanted ship of yours first touched my shore." She pauses, glancing over her shoulder with a feral grin. "Never tell a witch what to do." Then her grin stretches wider, feral and strange. "Unless, of course, you wish to be turned into an eel."

She lets out a raspy, unhinged laugh and for a moment, I wonder if she's truly mad. Maybe if I lived here, surrounded by rot and ruin, stirring the dead with every breath, I'd be mad too.

She presses the worn, rolled-up piece of parchment into my hands. Her dirt-caked fingers brush against mine, and the chill of her touch shoots goosebumps up my arms. "Follow this map," she murmurs. "It will lead you to what you are yearning for. I am connected to it and through it, to you. I will be your eyes. You will follow what I say. You *will* trust me."

Oddly enough, a part of me does trust her. Even as every other part of me screams not to. I nod slowly and unroll the map. It's blank. I frown, scanning the page, searching for any trace of the black tar she swirled. But it's gone, vanished, like it was never there at all.

"What is this? Why must you play these mind games with me?" I snap, frustration slipping through my guard.

Taika's expression darkens. A flicker of annoyance and danger sparks in her eyes. "The map will reveal itself when you draw nearer to what it is you truly yearn for," she says, voice laced with ire. "It listens to your heart, not your eyes." She leans in, her breath colder than before, a low hiss curling from her lips.

"Don't be fooled, some pieces don't show where to go, but whom to find." Her long nails graze the skin on my arm, sending goosebumps down my body. Smith moves forward with his hand on the hilt of his sword. I motion for him to back down. If she really wanted to hurt me, she would have done it already.

She crosses to the far side of her cluttered hut and plucks a small shell from a crooked shelf. Blue, laced with black and white shards like splintered glass. Holding it to her lips, she whispers something, a secret meant only for the sea, before pressing it into my palm. "If you need me," she says, "speak into this shell. I will hear you." Then her tone sharpens like the crack of a whip. "But heed my warning: lose it, and you lose me. Question me again... and you lose me forever."

Her dark, beady eyes lock onto mine like a curse. "Your soul is tied to something strong. Something that will change who you are to your very core." She pauses. The air stills. "Find out who you are. Find your destiny." A beat.

"Now go. And stay alive. You are a key, child. And we all need you to live."

My hands curl into fists before I know it. The words sink into me. First comes anger, hot and sharp, because she's just handed me a debt I never asked for. "A key," I breathe, tasting bile. "You're making me into something I didn't choose." My voice cracks on the last word, equal parts fury and a small, ugly fear. For a second I want to curl up and hide. So many impulses fight in my ribs until the breath from my lungs comes out cold and steady. I hold her stare, not backing down.

"I did not fashion you, child. This was born with you, your destiny from the first breath. I answer to it no more than you do. Leave now." Her words fall like a chill, her dirt-covered hand waving me off as she turns around.

The hut begins to darken, shadows stretching like hungry fingers until Taika vanishes completely into the gloom.

Smith and I don't hesitate. We turn and cross the crooked wooden bridge that docked itself to *The Siren*, treasures clutched tight in my hands. The moment our boots hit the deck, the cursed fog begins to burn away, hissing, evaporating in curls of black smoke as if it never existed.

Light pours in, golden and sudden. The skies above shift from slate to sapphire, and the sea sparkles like polished glass. A scene so breathtaking, so impossibly peaceful, it could have been painted by the gods themselves. And yet every detail felt wrong. Like this was some facade made by Taika.

As if Taika and the horrors we saw in that hut had all been a dream. A terrible, whispered dream the ocean is trying very hard to forget.

Taika believes I'm some kind of key to finding the fountain. I always wondered why so many fought to protect me growing up. And now, with both of my parents gone, that protection is gone too. Maybe they were the only ones who truly knew the truth.

I lean against a rum barrel, casual but unyielding, watching Smith strike his pipe alight. "Did you know?" My voice cuts sharp, eyes locking on his. He shakes his head. "Words, Smith. Use them."

His jaw tightens, eyes narrowing. "I knew you weren't just the captain's daughter," he says slowly. "But I didn't know you're the key to finding the fountain."

I tilt my head, just enough to show I've heard, and look to the horizon. Then down at Taika's little treasures in my hand. "Interesting. Here's the thing, I'm done being kept in the dark. If you're holding anything back, now is the time to speak."

"You know as much as I do," he answers, earnest. I study him, eyes trailing up and down, searching for the crack. I have never had any reason to doubt him, but it seems there are many secrets being hidden from me. For now, I believe him. But Taika's warning still etches itself into my brain. She doesn't trust him. She said he has bad blood in his veins.

"Okay," I say. "Thank you for being there."

He gives me that small, loyal smile. "I'll always be right there." The words warm some buried part of me. Smith has been my father figure growing up, the one who taught me all I know. I walk away with many emotions stirring inside me.

Anger curls in my chest, low and hot, building with every breath. Why didn't they tell me who I am? Did they really think they'd live forever? My parents weren't even close to finding the fountain. My father was always chasing something else, another map, another myth, another thrill. He should've focused on the one thing that mattered.

But he didn't. They both failed me in that. I was nineteen when my father died. I was old enough to know the burdens I carry. But they left me in the dark. And now I have to light my own way. I can handle that. I just wish I didn't have to do it blindly.

The only thing my father was ever truly loyal to was my mother. In its own way, that was beautiful, but what about everything else? I never really understood love. I've never taken a lover, never even come close to trusting a man that way. The men in my life, the role models I grew up with, didn't exactly inspire faith. I don't see the point in chasing someone who'll only end up letting me down, bedding another woman, or finding new ways to break me.

Unlike Neressa, who can have any man she wants. She holds power over them, courted by nobles and commoners alike. She thrives in that world. I guess I never had that kind of interest. Or maybe I never had the chance to want it.

I move toward the helm and meet the gaze of one of our newer crew members, relieving him of the wheel with a nod. My hand glides across the enchanted teak wood, its magic seeping into my skin, steadying me.

One hand grips the helm, the other holds the so-called map Taika gave me, its pull guiding our course.

The map Taika gave me is fragile, barely holding together at the edges, and despite her cryptic promise that it would guide me to what I yearned for most, I've spent days staring at the parchment with nothing to show for it. Out of desperation, we sailed to the farthest reaches of the sea, hoping that answers might rise from the unexpected. When that failed, I gave the order to head toward civilization. Restlessness gnawed at me with each passing day, my patience wearing thin as the ocean stretched on endlessly and our supplies dwindled faster than I liked. Gold is running low, especially when it has to feed an entire crew. There's always my hidden stash buried beneath Pebble's Pub, a vault Neressa and I quietly maintain, adding to it over time. It's our shared insurance, for moments just like this.

The map begins to darken, inky black spots bleeding across the bottom right corner. My heart skips. "Turn the ship southwest!" I shout, snapping the wheel as the crew rushes into motion. As we shift course, more spots bloom across the parchment, scattering faster now, until the map is drenched in black. A full signal. We're heading the right way.

"What do you think it means, Captain?" Smith asks, hovering beside me, eyes narrowed on the page. I glance at him, then out to the endless stretch of sea.

"I don't know," I admit. "But it's showing us where we need to go. And I trust it. So we follow the map." Smith doesn't respond right away, but I feel his doubt. He always questions my decisions, quietly, but it's there. He forgets I'm the captain now.

We continue moving southwest, following the map's direction day after day, watching the sun rise and set. The anticipation grows with each passing moment, and I begin to grow frustrated, wondering if what Taika gave me was even a real map or just some kind of distraction. Then, I hear laughter coming from below deck. A woman's laugh.

I'm the only woman on board. A sudden wave of unease sweeps over me. My first thought? A stowaway. Someone who'd slipped past my crew.

I head down to the main deck and catch sight of them—mermaids. They swim alongside my ship, laughing and leaping from the water like dolphins. They're beautiful. Far more so than sirens. Sirens are all teeth and claws, pale skin stretched over sharp bones, alien eyes and scaled flesh. Weapons born of the sea. Mermaids, though? They can be sweet, when they choose to be. Creatures of charm and color, their satin hair flowing like ribbons in the tide, skin glowing under the sun, eyes glittering in every hue. Their tails shimmer in pastel tones, like seashells made flesh.

My men lean over the edge of the ship, slack-jawed, catcalling, practically falling overboard to get a better look. I roll my eyes. Idiots. Risking their lives for a chance to flirt with something that would never let them close. Men really aren't the smartest creatures in the sea.

I glance down at the map and the black spots are gone. "Shit. We've gone off course," I mutter under my breath. My boots slam against the deck as I charge up to the helm. The wheel is abandoned. No one at post.

I snap my gaze across the deck and there he is. Sully. Leaning over the edge of the ship, making doe eyes at the mermaids like a damn fool.

I storm toward him, grab the back of his collar, and shove him aside. "Back to your post," I growl. He stumbles, muttering an apology, like he's drunk. Useless.

I quickly make my way back to the wheel, trying to get us back on track. Nothing. No black spots. I shift the course again. Still nothing. The mermaids laugh behind me, taunting, high-pitched giggles that pierce straight through my skull. Fury burns hot beneath my skin. We lost the path. Because of him.

I storm over to Sully, fury coursing through me, and slap him hard across the face. "You idiot! You lost our heading so you could flirt with mermaids you'll never touch," I hiss. The crew falls silent at my outburst.

I've always had a temper. While my father taught me to fight, my mother taught me how to deliver a slap that stings both pride and skin.

"Sorry, Captain. Won't happen again," Sully mutters, a sour sneer twisting his face. I step closer, the power in my voice making up for my small frame. I might be short, but I carry more command in the tip of my pinky than most men hold in their entire spine. "No," I say coolly. "It won't. Scrub the decks."

"You can't be serious," Sully has the nerve to say, letting out a cocky little laugh.

"I've never been more serious," I snap. "You don't understand what you've cost us. You'll pay for it with labor. Now get to it. And don't test me."

I spin on my heel before he can open that arrogant mouth again, fury still simmering beneath my skin. My eyes drop to the map just in time to see the parchment shift, darkening into a deep, solid black. My gaze flicks to the horizon. *The Leviathan*, Kai's ship, is there looming in the distance, unmoving, like it has been waiting. Waiting for me. The map doesn't fade. It stays black as I turn the wheel toward him. What in the hells does he have to do with this?

Smith steps up beside me, his voice low, dry, and far too amused. "Looks like you found what you truly desire."

CHAPTER FIVE

KAI

HOLLOW DECKS

Stepping aboard the kappas' ship, dark magic seeps through every crack. These creatures are half-man, half-monstrosity, once drowned, dragged back to the surface by the ocean, their flesh twisted into something inhuman. Resurrection is agony, bones cracking, skin splitting, lungs collapsing only to regrow with gills, claws sprouting where fingers once were. No man survives that kind of death unless he's already gone. The kappas aren't alive, not truly. They breathe air they shouldn't, living contradictions of death and life, bound to the ocean's will. For them to walk the surface at all means something is broken, an imbalance deep within the ocean.

What makes them dangerous isn't only their claws or their unnatural bodies, but their bond to the deep. They've mated with sirens, forged connections that left them less man, more monster, and far too attuned to the sea. The ocean doesn't forgive, and neither do they. With their secrets, their ancient knowledge, they are an army born of dark magic and bone. An army that cannot die. Behead them, and they'll only grow anew.

Maybe I should consider an alliance after all. They hear things. They know things. The only question is, can they be trusted? Or are they just another piece in the ocean's endless, merciless game? Something vile churns beneath the surface.

"Son, take a seat. Make yourself at home," the captain says, gesturing to a chair fashioned from whale bone and algae. I sit, keeping my eyes on the ship around me. It's skin and bone, literally. An eerie carcass of a vessel that somehow stays afloat, despite the water that trickles through the walls and the gaping holes in its hull. It looks like it was wrecked long ago and dragged back from the bottom by something that refused to let it die. Just like its crew.

I glance back at the captain. "What's your name?" I ask. "We never exchanged, but you know mine. Seems only fair I know yours."

A smirk pulls at the somewhat good half of his face. The other side is missing, eaten away or never returned to him. "Varn," he says. "Name's Varn. I've captained this ship for the last seven hundred and fifty years."

Shock punches through me, hard. Seven hundred and fifty years? That's ancient, even sea beasts don't last that long. I steady myself. "Alright then, Varn," I say, leaning forward, elbows on my knees. "What kind of deal did you have in mind?"

"Your scar," Varn says, his tone steady, touched with something cold. "The one running down your right arm, it's not just a wound. It's a key." I freeze. "It will start to grow things," he continued, gazing unblinkingly. "Claws. Teeth. Pieces of her. The siren who gave you that scar has passed, and now, parts of her will begin to emerge through you. Rare fragments, laced with her power. When you reach the fountain, you'll need them. They must be cast into the water to unlock its magic, proof that the siren trusted you with herself. Only then will the fountain trust you in return." He leans in, his single eye gleaming with something unreadable.

"When they start to show," he murmurs, "pull them out. Keep them safe. Do not lose them. Do not share them. They're yours. And now, they're mine too. Because I've shared this truth with you, you will help me make a wish." He shifts in his seat, and only then do I notice the table between us. It's covered in strange objects, sea-worn trinkets, glass vials glowing faintly, flickering in the low light. Each one shimmers with droplets of rain, like the ocean had cried into them herself.

My brow lifts, suspicion threading through my voice. "And what would you wish for?"

Varn's eye hardens. For a moment, something flickers there, regret, maybe. Or exhaustion so deep it feels older than the sea itself. "I wish to be free of this cursed existence," he says quietly. "I've lived longer than any man should, trapped in an endless loop, bound to the ocean, unable to die. I am the longest-living creature in the sea, but that's no gift. It's a sentence."

He pauses, letting the weight of his words settle. "I want it to end. I want freedom. True death. Peace. That is my wish. You will grant it, no matter the cost. That is our deal: I give you the truth, and in return, you help me break the bond." His voice is steady, but I can hear it, the centuries of torment buried beneath every word, echoing in the silence that follows.

A strange wave of pity rolls through me. I can't fathom the torment of being trapped in a body that isn't your own for seven hundred and fifty years, bound to a life you never chose, never wanted. To crave death and be denied rest... It's a fate more brutal than any I've known. I wonder if, in all that time, Varn had loved ones. A family long gone. A love lost to the waves. Maybe he still dreams of them. Maybe that's the worst part. The weight of it settles on me, heavy and quiet. Agreeing to share the fountain wasn't part of my plan. But I can't ignore the truth that having these creatures on our side, creatures bound to the sea in ways I'll never understand, might be the twist we need. The one thing that tips the odds. However, allying with them is risky; they're unpredictable and violent creatures.

If I help them, they'll help us. I steel myself, locking down the flicker of hesitation in my chest. "I'll make a deal with you," I say, my voice firm. Steady. Decided.

"I will free you. You have my word." I extend my hand, ready to seal the pact. Varn's cold, blue fingers reach for mine, but then he hesitates. His eyes narrow, and the air around us thickens.

"One more thing," he says, voice low and laced with weight.

My brow furrows. One more thing? Of course there is. "The girl," Varn murmurs, a rare softness in his tone. "She is important." Confusion knots in my chest, but I already know who he means.

"Yes, boy. Mira," he confirms, as if plucking the name straight from my mind. "She is the key. If you truly want to find the fountain, she's who you'll need. She doesn't know how important she is yet, but she will. And soon, the entire ocean will know too."

I rake a hand through my rain-soaked hair, trying to make sense of it. Why Mira? Why is she tied to something as ancient and closely guarded as the fountain? "What is it about her that makes her so valuable?" I ask.

Varn leans forward, his voice certain. "Her blood," he says. "She's part siren and they trust her. And trust goes farther than magic with those wicked little creatures." Disgust curls in my gut. A siren, the one creature I hate the most. I would rather come face to face with a nyx before a siren. Varn continues, "Her birthmark, it's the final key to the map. Without it, nothing unlocks. Not the path. Not the power. Nothing. She must be protected at all costs."

"Protecting someone I loathe will be... challenging," I breathe slowly, measuring the angle of this new plan. "Fine. I'll keep her alive, if it gets me to the fountain."

My mouth is careful, but my aim is not. Finishing what my father started, what he broke himself on, becomes my calculus. I will be steadier, smarter, and colder. I will become everything he wasn't and complete everything he failed to do. If Mira is the key, then I'll treat her exactly like one: useful, expendable, and precise. I'll hold her close, pull what I need, and walk away when the lock clicks open.

Varn stares at me for a moment, then speaks. "She's the female ruler of the ocean," he goes on, reverence softening his voice. "A force more powerful than even she understands. When she unlocks what she is, she won't just belong to the ocean. She will be the ocean." He looks out toward the waves, as if something ancient stirs just beyond sight. "The sea cannot carry her soul forever," he says. "Even it must rest. Mira was chosen before she even took her first breath. The ocean marked her in her mother's womb." Varn's voice lowers, barely more than a whisper. "Her family knew. But they passed before they could tell her. She was left unaware and yet, she's the only one who can carry the ocean forward."

Mira is the new Soul of the Ocean? The one living force that keeps the balance between dark and light in a sea crawling with wretched creatures. The power in her veins is ancient, and once she inherits the Soul, nothing, not blade, not beast, not god, will be able to touch her.

"Seems she's found you," Varn says, his eyes narrowing like he can sense her through the waves. His gaze drifts past me, sharp, knowing, and settles on something in the distance. I turn slightly, following his line of sight. *The Siren* is approaching, gliding through the water like a ghost returning home.

"I must go," he says, still watching her. "We'll need to take her eventually since she holds the most power. No one can know about our bargain. Not your crew. Not the girl. Keep her safe until the time comes. Let her find who she is. Do not tell her, or the prophecy will need to be rewritten. She is meant to find who she is on her own. Collect all the pieces of the map. They will arise when they are meant to." A pause. Then, calmly, "I'll be seeing you soon."

I never agreed to handing her over. It seems she will be more valuable when she's with me. He can think what he wants for now.

He extends his hand, blue, bloated, slick with death and sea rot. I take it. The cold seeps into my skin like a curse. We have a deal. Without another word, I return to my ship. I watch as his vessel cuts through the water with impossible speed... then dives beneath the surface like a predator. Gone. No trace. It's easy to see how no one escapes them. How their enemies vanish into ocean myths, never to be heard from again.

I take my place at the helm, one hand resting on the worn wood. The sea stretches quiet and endless ahead. Her ship is approaching fast, like fate barreling toward me. I watch as the sails cut through the mist and the crew scrambles to dock, but all I see is her.

She's here. A destined collision I would've given anything to avoid. My burden. My responsibility. The key to the fountain and the unraveling I never saw coming. And still, somehow, my newfound treasure.

CHAPTER SIX

KAI

UNDONE

The wind tangles through her long, curly brown hair, the strands dancing like wildfire, catching the last remaining beams from the sunlight as her ship draws closer. She really is a sight to behold, though I hate that my chest tightens when I look at her. My mind wages war against itself. One side urges me to end this, to seize the enchanted ship, to sever her bloodline and claim the power for myself, like my father before me longed to do. But the other hesitates. I know she's a vital part of this journey, one I can't afford to lose. So she'll live.

I still can't help but have a certain pull towards her. When she's out of sight it's easy for my hatred to boil. But when she's in front of me, the world turns on its axis. I felt it the moment I saw her at the pub on Magda. One glance and the world narrowed to just her. Touching her was like brushing flame, her skin burning mine, branding something ancient into my bones. I fought to keep my face unreadable, to wear a mask never taking it off. Not in front of anyone, anyway. But I slipped. Just for a second. And Neressa saw it. I caught the shift in her expression, the flicker of realization. She saw what I didn't want anyone to see. Mira didn't. She was too consumed by her fury. But her friend saw the truth. The part of me that doesn't want to destroy Mira. The one split second of vulnerability.

I order my crew to stand down. They hesitate, trained to strike the moment *The Siren* appears. Mira's bloodline has always been our greatest enemy. Generations of bad blood don't die easily. But things are different now. I know who she really is.

What does inheriting the Soul of the Ocean mean for her? Will the sea one day swallow her whole, strip away her mortal shell piece by piece? Or will she live a full life on land until the tide calls her home? The answers are buried deep, but I need them. First, I need to find out how much she knows, by breaking down her walls one brick at a time.

Mira and her crew pull up alongside mine. No raised weapons. No battle stance. Just eerie stillness. Too calm. It sets something off in me and in my crew. Instinct screams trap, but logic presses pause. She must've ordered them to stand down. That means she knows. She knows we need each other if we're going to get what we both want.

Our ships groan as they meet, wood creaking beneath the weight of silent expectations. Then, like a vision conjured by myth, she swings across on a rope, hair wild in the wind, sea-green eyes locked on mine. Her landing is fluid, too fluid, graceful in a way that shouldn't belong on the deck of a warship.

I blink once, grounding myself. She doesn't smile, nor does she speak. Just observes. Her eyes narrowing, looking at each member of my crew, watching their hands for any sudden movements. Smart, I'll give her that. She's tiny compared to anyone on board. I move toward her slowly, every step measured. Our crews fall in line behind us, like two halves of a brewing storm. Only a handful of her crew step onto my deck, handpicked, hardened, the kind who don't flinch without orders and never move without purpose. She's playing this smart. Calculated. And I don't know if I should be impressed... or very, very worried.

"Captain Mira," I say with a smirk, "what did I tell you about following me?"

She rolls her eyes instantly, sharp, unapologetic. "Kai, we need to talk. It seems we may need each other after all." She stands tall, unshaken, meeting me head-on. There's steel in her spine, but I can see the storm in her eyes. She doesn't want to be here. That alone tells me she's desperate.

I step closer, my shadow stretching over her, and watch as her gaze trails my movement, slowly, before rising to meet mine with sharp, measured defiance. I meet her challenge. "Captain Kai," I correct, letting the title bite. "You're on my ship. Address me as such." She narrows her emerald eyes. So small, yet full of heat and fight. I half expect her to spit in my face or at my feet again. Part of me wishes she would.

"*Okay*, Captain Kai," she snaps back, voice slick with sarcasm. "Anything else?" The fact that she gave in, just a little, sets something inside me burning.

"No," I murmur, voice low. "That'll do. For now." I find myself gesturing toward my quarters, an instinct I can't explain. No one's been allowed past that threshold in decades, and yet my hand moves like it's forgotten how fiercely I've guarded that space, how dangerous it is to invite anyone in. Yet I still open my mouth. "Why don't you join me for a chat? Something tells me we have a lot to discuss."

She hesitates for half a beat, just long enough for me to catch it, then walks ahead, not behind. Her back is straight, shoulders squared, daring me to underestimate her. And all I can think is, *This is the first time she walks into my quarters.* But the voice inside tells me it won't be the last.

"What can I do for *the* Captain Mira?" I ask, leaning casually against the door as it clicks shut behind us. But she doesn't answer. She's already moving like she owns the place. Her fingers skim across the shelves, ghosting over the artifacts of my life like she's studying me. She picks up a rusted compass, then a dagger with a jeweled hilt, items no one touches. And yet, for some damn reason, I let her. I let her touch my treasures. I don't even try to stop her. I only watch her every fluid movement, so intoxicated by everything she does. What the hell is wrong with me?

She moves with careful curiosity, taking it all in, not like she's admiring it, but like she's evaluating, deciding if any of it matters. If I matter. When she reaches the bed, she pauses. Her eyes sweep over the tangled maroon silk sheets, the black comforter draped carelessly across. Fancy bedding for a pirate, but I am a lord after all. Then her gaze shifts to the large window, where the last light of the sun spills into the room like blood in water. Igniting her, drenching her in a golden hue.

She looks like she belongs in it. But she's still quiet, so I let the silence stretch. Finally, she turns to me. "Your room," she says softly with a slight pause. "It's not what I would've expected." There's something in her voice, measured, curious. A flicker of surprise, maybe even a sliver of respect. But it's layered beneath something gentler, something harder to name. Something that lodges in my chest and refuses to let go.

"What were you expecting?" I ask, arms crossed as I watch her finally turn to face me. Her dark wavy hair bounces with the motion, catching the last streaks of sunlight.

"I don't know," she says, her gaze flicking across the room again. "Something colder. Less sentimental. I thought you were a man who burned through everything he touched, not one who kept pieces." Her words land sharper than she knows.

"So, you think I don't have a soul?" I ask, my voice cool, unreadable. She lifts a brow. "Do you?"

A beat of silence. I almost laugh. Almost. "Would I have let you walk away at the pub if I didn't?" I counter. Her eyes widen, just for a breath. But she masks it well. She doesn't back down. I admire that, even when it grates.

"Captain Mira," I say, tone hardening like drawn steel, "You boarded my ship. You've ordered your men not to attack. What is it you want?"

Her emerald eyes lock with mine, steady as a blade. "You let me board," she snaps back, voice low and pointed, not playful this time. "Don't act like you're in control when we both know I came because I chose to." That one hits. A slow grin curls across my face. I admire her fire.

I step closer, slow and purposeful. My voice drops. "Oh, Captain Mira," I murmur. "Don't play power games unless you're ready to lose." Her breath catches. Just enough. Her cheeks bloom with heat and this time, I see the truth. She liked that. This facade of protection might be easier to maintain than I thought. She wears her armor well, sharp tongue, steady hands, but there's something soft and vulnerable beneath it. And if I can see it, I can use it.

She pulls a folded piece of worn parchment from inside her jacket. Black as ink, its edges fraying like something timeworn. My eyes sharpen. "This map," she says, voice lower now, more guarded, "was given to me by a witch. A family friend. She told me it would lead me to what I yearn for most... what my heart truly desires."

She looks at me then. Really looks. Her eyes flicker with something raw. "It led me to you." For a heartbeat, silence reigns between us. Her words hang in the air, too heavy and too true. It can't be that easy, her just showing up on my ship, ready for me to take her.

"I think you know something about the fountain," she adds, her gaze steady, "something I don't." I step in, just enough to feel the heat rolling off her. My voice drops to a low hum. "There are a lot of things I know that you don't, treasure." Her breath hitches at the nickname. "But I do know one thing: we may need each other if we want to find the Fountain of Wishes."

She shifts, eyes flicking away as her shoulders square, barely, tension rippling through her like she's been caught. Fighting herself the way I fight myself. "I know," she says softly. The words barely make it out. "We do." But she still won't look at me.

I reach out for the map, palm open. She places it in my hand without hesitation. The second it touches my skin, the parchment shudders, black bleeding into a deep, violent red. Like spilled blood soaking through fabric. I glance at her, frozen, jaw slack, caught somewhere between shock and silence. Eyes locked on the map like it's just betrayed her. I half expect it to be wet, but it's dry and warm.

"It... it turns black when I'm near, or when I'm on the right path to what I yearn for most," she says, voice uneven. "I don't know what red means." I stare at the crimson-stained parchment. Then at her. My chest tightens.

"Not a thing," I say quietly. "But a person you desire."

She recoils. "No," she breathes, almost to herself. "It has to be a thing. Like information, power, a key. For some reason I trust the map. It led me to your ship, because you know something." But then her expression cracks, just slightly. Her eyes flick to mine and stay there. She *finally* looked up at me. Again, why do I even give a shit if she looks at me? The truth hits her like a crashing wave.

"No," she whispers again, shaking her head. "Not you." Her voice sharpens into steel. "It can't be you. Everything about you is *repulsive.*" Her jaw sets. Her spine straightens. She meets my gaze with fire now. "Your father slaughtered my mother. In cold blood. In front of me. In front of my father." She pauses. "While you *watched.*" Her eyes narrowed to a lethal glare.

Her words are sharp and precise. But I don't flinch. Tears brim in her eyes, and the sight scorches something deep inside me, something I thought long dead. "I saw you," she breathes. "You were old enough to stop him. But you didn't. You let that monster take her from me." Each word lands like a blow, pointed and merciless. She takes a slow breath and then fires the final shot. "It will *never* be *you.*" It feels like she spit venom at me.

The hatred in her voice cuts straight through me, sharp and unrelenting. It bleeds from her eyes, pure, raw disgust. I reach for her face, my fingers curling gently beneath her chin. Not rough. Just enough to make sure she sees me. A single tear slips from the corner of her eye, trailing down my fingers like a silent accusation. Something inside me wants to comfort her. No matter how tightly I cling to the hatred I've harbored, she keeps unraveling it, simply by being who she is.

"I'm sorry he took your mother from you," I say, low and steady. "But I am not him." She shakes her head, tries to pull away, but I follow, step for step. I don't let go.

"No, you're not him," she snaps. "You're worse." The words land like a blow to the ribs. My jaw tightens. Heat rises in my chest.

"I am nothing like my father," I growl. "Was he a great pirate? Sure. Ruthless. Cunning. Feared. But his heart?" I pause, teeth gritted. "Cold.

Black. He didn't care about anyone. Not even me. And if he didn't give a damn about his own son, he sure as hell didn't care about a little girl and her mother." I released her, not because she wanted to be freed from my touch, but because every single second my skin touches her a flame ignites, one I can't put out.

"But me?" My voice roughens. "I wouldn't do that. I couldn't. Not even to my worst enemy. I don't hurt children. Not even by accident."

She turns away without a word, her gaze fixed on the sea. Her back is straight, shoulders drawn tight. The silence stings. I stare at her, stunned by how effortlessly she turns her back to me, like she's not afraid, like she *knows* I won't strike, even if I could... even if I should.

"It doesn't matter," she mutters, eyes fixed on the horizon. She pushes down the emotions so effortlessly. The sun is nearly gone now, bleeding into the sea. "I need you. And you need me. We both know it." She pauses, then adds, voice sharp, final, "We can make a deal now, or I leave. And you'll never see me again." Her threat is sharp. Final.

The idea of her walking off my ship shouldn't bother me. But it lands in my chest like something heavy. She's the key. The only one who can get me where I need to go. That's all this is. That's all it *has* to be. Whatever else stirs beneath that, I'll bury it.

She won't survive on her own. Not when word gets out about what she is, what runs in her veins. But that's not the only reason I don't want her to go. I want to know more. Every scar, every secret she harbors, every storm she's hiding behind that sharp tongue.

I drag in a breath, stuffing the chaos down. I school my face into something easy, unreadable. "We can make a deal, Captain Mira," I say at last, a slow, bitter smile pulling at my mouth. "Where should we start?"

She turns, eyes guarded, and extends her hand. It's not surrender. It's a challenge. A warning. I take it anyway. Her hand is soft. Small against mine. But there's roughness too, calluses from a blade, maybe a cutlass. She's been training. She's not just a pretty face with a sharp tongue.

The second we touch, something shifts. A spark, instant, unwelcome. My body betrays me, igniting with something I have no right to feel. I'm supposed to hate her. I'm supposed to want her dead. Take her enchanted ship. Watch her crew fall. End that cursed bloodline. Bring honor to my name. That was the plan. Always the plan. But that plan is crumbling, fast. Now I need her.

"I think it would be best if you and your crew boarded my ship," I say, voice steady. "Yours is too well-known, too traceable. Mine is feared in every port. No one follows *The Leviathan* without a death wish."

Mira raises a brow. Not in surprise, just mild annoyance. "So you want me to just drop my family heirloom off and go roaming the seas with you? What are you hiding, Pirate Lord?"

I let out a small laugh. She's intelligent enough to question me. "Like I said, treasure, I know a lot you don't. What I can tell you is you're of value, I know you know it, and you will be hunted. My crew, ship, and most importantly myself, can offer you the protection we both need to get to the fountain. We'll be better if we travel with higher numbers."

"And where would I sleep?" She completely dismisses what I say.

I glance around the room. My quarters. The only space I've never let anyone enter. Not even my crew. Not even once. I hesitate, then gesture toward the bed, massive, cold, untouched on one side. "Here."

Her arms fold slowly across her chest, eyes narrowing. "You want me to sleep in the same room. Same bed."

"There's room enough not to touch," I say flatly. "I've survived worse arrangements."

She tilts her head, like she's trying to decipher what game I'm playing. "There has to be another room."

"There's not." A beat passes. "Not one that locks from the inside. Not one without eyes or ears." I shift my weight. I hate explaining myself. But she needs to understand, I'm not offering comfort. I'm offering control. "My father's still alive. He's on board. He gets loose sometimes. And if he sees you…" My jaw tightens. "He'll tear you apart before anyone can stop him."

Her lips part, just barely. But she doesn't flinch or cower. She calculates. I can see it in the way her gaze sweeps the room, not in fear, but in assessment. Measuring threats and *me*. "You think I can't handle him?" she asks.

"I think I've watched him slaughter men bigger than you without blinking. Creatures that haunt your nightmares." I pause. "He won't care who you are. Only that you bleed. But in your case, your blood is what he has been wanting to spill for far too long."

Another long silence. She doesn't yield. Just stands there, spine straight, daring me to treat her like less than what she is. And maybe I would if I didn't already know how dangerous she is.

"Hmm," she hums, brow arching. "You keep him locked away like some dog?"

The corner of my mouth twitches, almost a laugh. "His sickness is a liability. I won't let anyone near. Especially you." She nods, just barely. But it's not agreement, it's acknowledgment. Her eyes stay on me, like she's trying to read between the cracks. Like she knows I'm not telling her everything. And she's right.

"And my crew?" she asks finally. "Where will they stay?"

"In the sleeping quarters," I reply. "There's more than enough space. Plenty of beds." She just studies me like she's cataloging every detail of this deal, weighing its worth. I keep my posture loose, unaffected.

What I don't say is that my crew has thinned over the years. Not from death, but from purging. I don't let just anyone aboard *The Leviathan*. Everyone here has earned their place. Some I've known since I was a boy. Others I've fought beside, bled beside. Loyalty matters, but silence matters more.

Trust isn't handed out like rations. It's rare. And these days, with the sea turning restless and monsters wearing the skin of men, finding someone who won't slit your throat in your sleep is worth more than gold. I can't afford softness. Especially not now with *her* on board.

"And who will be the captain of the ship?" she says, standing straight and confident.

"Oh, Captain Mira, you sure have a lot of questions, but treasure, don't get confused. This is my vessel."

Her emerald eyes darken, "I won't leave *The Siren* if I'm not a captain of my own men... so how badly do you want this alliance, Captain Kai?" Her words are slick and full of taunting.

I can't help but smile. She's clever. Sharp. Bites back like she has no reason to fear me, a refreshing shift from the usual silence and flinching I've grown used to. Everyone else walks on eggshells around me. She strides through them barefoot. "We can both captain our crews," I say, tone even, decisive. "Together."

Another nod seals it, and she turns toward the door without waiting for a response. But just before she reaches it, she pauses. She's still glowing like a flame bottled in a lantern. She pivots, eyes lit with something wild and steady.

"By the way." Her voice is soft, but commanding. "I want the side that overlooks the ocean." A demand, not a request. She's already claiming space.

"I'll allow it," I reply, masking the amusement behind a casual shrug.

"And we make for Magda," she adds, already halfway gone. "I only trust one person to look over my ship."

"Neressa," I say before she can.

She glances back, a flicker of approval in her eyes. "Yes." Her eyes wander for a split second, "Also, Captain Kai," she says, pausing in the doorway with her back still half-turned to me, "let's get one thing straight." Her voice doesn't rise, but it sharpens. "No one controls me. I do what I want, when I want, and I'll make whatever decisions I damn well please. You don't hold power over me. Not now. Not ever."

She meets my eyes then, like she's daring me to argue. "As long as that's understood, maybe this alliance has a shot."

Then she turns fully, her hair catching the soft light from the pink and orange painted skies as it swings behind her, hips swaying with that same deliberate grace. I watch, helpless against it, as she glides out of my quarters like the sea itself just parted for her. My lips twitch again. A smile threatens. I catch it too late.

She's gone. And I hate that I let any trace of that feeling show, even in private.

She heads back to *The Siren* to speak with her crew, to explain the shift in command. I don't envy her. Pirates hate change. Mine won't take it well either. They'll bark, bite, maybe even draw blood. Let them. I'm not here to entertain their opinions. There's more than enough room in the crew quarters, and if anyone has a problem with Mira or her crew, they're welcome to try their luck with me, or whatever nightmare waits beneath a pirate ship. Let them grumble. Let them fight. This alliance changes everything, and I'll drown every last objection before I let it fall apart.

"We've got changes ahead," I announce, stepping onto the quarter-deck where the crew's already gathered. "Big ones. And you're all going to need to be on board."

A ripple moves through them, confusion, tension. Arms cross, brows furrow. They know something's coming, but not what. "Why hasn't their ship pulled off?" someone yells. "Aye! Why'd you stop us from gutting them when we had the chance?" Another, "They've got some damn nerve thinking they're welcome aboard this vessel!"

The crew erupts. Grumbles become shouts. Frustration spills into fury. I let them go, let them bark, let them growl. Let them show their teeth. Then Jay's voice cuts through the noise. "Enough!" he roars. "Let Captain Kai speak. Whatever he decides, it's what's best for us. Don't let your pride cloud the truth. And if you can't trust your captain, your Pirate Lord, then go ahead and jump. Swim to shore and pray the sharks show mercy." Silence drops like a guillotine. Jay's loyalty hits me square in the chest. I nod once, sharp, thankful.

I look down at the crew gathered on the lower deck from the helm, weathered faces, narrowed eyes, every one of them itching for a fight. "Captain Mira and I have formed an alliance," I begin, voice steady, slicing through the murmurs of wind and sail. "She holds information we don't. Knowledge about the Fountain of Wishes. She's essential to our mission. And she needs protection." That word hangs. Protection.

"We've lost too many mates in recent battles," I go on, my gaze drifting to the empty spaces where familiar faces once stood. "Her crew will help fill the gaps." Silence falls. Among pirates, quiet never means peace. It means they're weighing their odds, obedience or mutiny.

Finally, someone grunts from the crowd, voice low and wary. "So... they're comin' aboard here?"

"Yes." Voice stern. "They'll live among us until we reach the fountain. That's the deal. That's the command." A storm brews behind their eyes. Murmurs rise like crashing waves, disbelief, resentment, anger. I don't need to hear every word. Their glares are loud enough. Let them rage now, while she's not aboard. Let them spit their venom into the wind.

"They'll board soon," I declare, my voice cutting through the tension. "And hear me clearly, if anyone lays a finger on them, speaks out of turn, or breathes wrong in their direction, you'll walk the damn plank." I pause, just long enough for the silence to shiver down spines. "And if anyone touches Mira or so much as looks at her sideways" —my voice lowers, ice cold now— "I will *personally* make sure you regret it." The threat hangs heavy in the air, thick as fog. They've seen what I'm capable of, what inhumane things I'm willing to do. "Understood?"

"Aye, Captain!" the crew answers in unison, tension clinging to every syllable.

"Then get back to work," I snap, voice sharp, final. I lean against the rail overlooking the main deck, watching as the crew scatters back to their posts, boots thudding against wet wood.

"And what of yer father?" Jay says. I don't answer right away. The thought of that man still breathing makes my stomach twist.

"No one is to tell him about Mira being on board," I say finally, each word deliberate. "He'll stop at nothing until her blood is spilled."

Jay's expression hardens, but he nods. I rake a hand through my hair, the sea's dampness clinging to my fingers. "See to it no one speaks to him and no one new tends to him except the ones I've already approved." I turn fully toward him, meeting his gaze. "Can I count on you to do that?"

"Aye, Cap'n. No one will tell him."

I narrow my eyes. "And?"

"No one new will care for him," Jay adds, more firmly this time.

I nod once. "Good. Then we're in agreement." My voice softens, barely. "She'll be safe here." Jay groans but obeys, trudging back toward his favorite post, the helm, where he's spent more nights than his own bunk.

My gaze drifts over to *The Siren* where Mira stands on a pair of overturned rum barrels, commanding her crew with nothing but fire in her voice. She's ridiculously small, and yet she's the first thing I see. The only thing I see. By all accounts, no pirate should take her seriously. But they do, every single one of them listens. I realize, with a sharp twist in my gut, that I may have underestimated her far more than I should have.

I turn away, heading for my quarters, heart pounding like war drums in my chest. I'm always calm. Always in control. But with her it spikes. I need to prepare. She'll be aboard soon. And nothing on this ship will ever be the same.

CHAPTER SEVEN

MIRA

SALT & LEATHER

I step out of Kai's quarters—or are they mine now? The alliance feels uneasy, yet inevitable, like this was always the path waiting for me. His crew watches as I pass, wide-eyed, bracing for me to strike. They don't fear me yet, but they will.

I seize the rope dangling from the mast, sprint, and swing. The sea wind whips through my hair as I arc across the deck, landing on my own ship with practiced ease. The moment my boots hit the wood, my thoughts surge. I pause, steadying myself, then climb atop the stacked wine barrels near the helm, rising above my crew, ready to claim the space that's mine.

I know I'll have many coming after me, Taika warned as much. Kai knows something I don't, and I need to start digging. Why am I suddenly so priceless when it comes to the fountain? My father never said anything about it while he was alive, but he always called me his ocean-born miracle. I thought it was just a father's love, a nickname wrapped in pride. But, he never loved me the way a father should. He loved blood. Gold. Power. Sea beasts and slaughter. He was obsessed with what he wanted, and I was just another thing to protect, not to love. Still, he kept me safe, but now I wonder if I'd been something else to him. If I meant something more. Not just his daughter, but part of a prophecy, a curse, a piece of the fountain's legend.

During battles, he'd lock me in his quarters, post his fiercest men at every entrance. I'd hear him bark the same words, over and over: "She's special. You protect her. If someone tries to take her, you kill them. And if they best you in battle, you lose your life with a blade in your hand, fighting for hers."

Locked away, I used to sit and listen, steel clashing, men screaming, the chaos of battle kept just out of reach. Every time he barred me in like that, fury burned through me. He knew I could protect myself, but still he sequestered me, like something fragile, tucked away on a shelf. I could have broken out if I wanted, but it was never worth the fight with him. Instead, I waited for the door. Never knowing if my father would be the one to open it, never sure if I'd see him again. Every night, I prayed it would be his face that met me in the morning. Was it love that he felt for me? Or was it possession?

Despite everything, I loved him. I cared for him. He had a soft spot for me, but I wish he'd been more of a father than a captain. I'm grateful for the skills he taught me, how to fight, how to survive, but eventually, he lost interest and handed me off to Smith to finish my training. He did the same with Neressa. Found her on Magda when she was young. I don't know the whole story, but she's always just been there. It still frustrates me, how he'd invest in us just long enough before pawning us off to whoever was available. Though Neressa's story is much darker than mine, I still don't know her full truths. I don't think I ever will. Neressa didn't take kindly to being pawned off. She grew powerful, so powerful that she killed most of her mentors. In fact, I don't think a single one is alive.

Kai's words were intense, but his touch was molten. That damn stare, those hazel eyes, melted me. I hate that my body urges me to be near him and feel the warmth of his body when I want nothing more but to end him where he stands, for everything his bloodline has done to mine.

The hate I feel for him has roots, deep, tangled ones. It goes back to my father's rage. It goes back to the little girl who watched her mother die. It goes back to all the blood and all the pain and tears. But the other half, the part that could never quite deny the pull toward him, thrilled at the thought of sharing a bed with the most feared pirate on the seas. The Pirate Lord. The one women would sell their souls to lie with. Now, I'll have all the time in the world to figure out what I really want from him and what he knows.

It wasn't a choice I ever expected to make. And then there was my ship. She's family. She's blood. I've always been there to guide her, to speak for her. Leaving her behind feels wrong. But what choice do I have? Sailing the seas in *The Leviathan* is smarter. More strategic. It's the most feared ship in all the seas. *The Siren* is a known ship and easy to track down. *The Leviathan*, on the other hand, is the fastest ship there is.

Staying away from Kai wasn't working. Not when he holds the truths I need, truths that could get me closer to the fountain, to the answers buried beneath the sea. And yet, the idea of him holding that kind of power over me burns like saltwater in a wound. But I trust the map that led me to him and for some odd reason, I trust Taika.

Once I board *The Siren*, I gather everyone on deck. Smith stands beside me, his silent presence steadying the buzz of unease rippling through the crew. One nod from him tells them all they needed to know, this is the moment we've been chasing. We've trailed Kai's ship for months, keeping to the shadows, tracking every breadcrumb he unknowingly left behind on the path to the fountain.

Pirates like us, raised under ruthless captains, hardened by betrayal, trained never to trust another soul, don't merge with other crews. It's rare. Reckless. Dangerous. But this time, it's the smartest move we can make. Kai is right, we're safer in numbers.

"Everyone, gather what you need. Pack light," I call out, my voice rising over the creaking of the ship and the thunder of the tide. "We board Captain Kai's vessel shortly. *The Siren* will be docked in a safe location, just until we find the fountain." I scan their faces, most unreadable, some uncertain. "I expect you to show respect. Get along with the new crew. No exceptions."

I step down from the stacked wine barrels I use for height, brushing off the uncertain looks thrown my way. My voice hasn't shaken, that's what matters. I make my way back to my captain's quarters, bracing myself.

Once I cross the threshold into the room that smells like him, salt, leather, and secrets, everything will change. His captain's quarters. This isn't just a shift in living arrangements. This is the start of something bigger, something irreversible.

I need to pack. But more than that, I need to search. For anything my father might've left behind. A letter. A journal. A sign. Something, anything, that could explain why he always calls me his ocean-born miracle. Something that might tell me why the fountain has chosen me... and what that means for everyone else.

When I was a child, my father's quarters were forbidden. He guarded them like a tarlock guards its breeding grounds, every journal, every trinket, every secret kept locked away behind that door. I learned early that his treasures were not mine to touch.

I was seven the day I forgot that rule. I slipped inside while he was on deck, curious, restless, drawn to the glint of a necklace resting on his desk. It was beautiful, the kind of thing a girl dreams of wearing. But before I could even lift it fully into my hands, I heard the footsteps. His voice followed, sharp and furious, and then... pain. So much pain. What kind of father strikes his daughter in the ways he did? My memory fractures there, splintered by the way he looked at me, not as his daughter, but as someone who had trespassed too far.

After that, I never went back. I never touched his things again. Even after his death, I couldn't bring myself to step across that threshold. His quarters have remained sealed in my mind like a wound that never closed. And yet, now I can't shake the feeling that the answers I've been searching for are buried beneath the dust he left behind.

I slide the key into the salt-rusted lock, and the door gives way with a reluctant groan. For a heartbeat, I almost expect him to appear behind me, boots heavy on the planks, voice sharp and scolding. But the only sound is the faint moan of the ship settling, the sigh of the sea against the hull.

The air inside is thick, stale with dust and the faint tang of salt. Moonlight pours through the wide windows, silvering everything it touches. I step across the threshold, and it feels like trespass, like stepping into a tomb, yet one still warm with his presence.

His bed lies unmade, the covers tangled as though he had only just risen. The pillow is flat, bearing the hollow trace of where his head once rested. For a moment, I swear I can hear him shifting there, muttering under his breath, alive again in the shadows. The sight makes my chest twist tight.

Across the desk, the moon ignites the treasures he once guarded so fiercely, scattered now like offerings left behind. I drift closer, pulled by their gleam, until my eyes land on the necklace. That necklace. Aquamarine, glowing like a piece of the sea itself, my birthstone caught in silver. I don't touch it. I can't. Pain lingers in my bones from the last time I dared, a memory carved too deep. It's beautiful, yes, but cursed by the moment he stopped being a father and became something colder.

The room hums with contradiction, empty, yet full. Innocent, yet haunted. For so long I convinced myself he was nothing but cruelty, but here, surrounded by the fragile remnants of his life, I feel the echo of something more. A soul, maybe. Or the ghost of one.

My gaze snags on a shape at the foot of the desk, hidden beneath a cloth. I sink to my knees, the teak floor cool against my skin, my hands trembling as I pull the fabric back. Dust billows upward like ash, and beneath it lies something he never meant me to find.

Journals. Dozens of them. I didn't even know he owned journals, let alone kept them. Honestly, I wasn't sure he could even write. Each one is worn, leather-bound, stuffed with notes, half-formed thoughts, and maybe secrets I was never meant to see. My heart thuds as I flip through the pages, then stops when I find another pile. Smaller. Softer. More delicate. My mother's diaries. I pause, fingers tracing the worn edges, the faded ink of her handwriting peeking out like a whisper from the past. Carefully, I begin stashing everything, his journals, her diaries, old maps, and anything he ever seemed oddly protective of, into my largest bag. I don't have time to process what any of it means. But I will.

Then I find them, tucked inside a small velvet pouch, as if they've been waiting for me all along. My mother's jewelry. Rings. Bracelets. Necklaces. Her wedding ring. The aquamarines and diamond catch the moonlight streaming through the window, scattering light across the floor like waves dancing in the tide. The diamond shimmers so fiercely it looks like it holds captured starlight.

I slide the ring onto the ring finger of my right hand. It fits perfectly. Aquamarine stones hug a round blue diamond, the colors mirroring the sea. If I remember right, the ring was designed to reflect the ocean and its beauty. And on my hand, it gleams like it was always meant to be there.

When I look into it, I see her. My mother. The most stunning woman I've ever seen. No wonder my father fell in love with her. Long, curly black hair. Bright blue eyes, like staring straight into the sea. Freckles scattered across her face and shoulders. Petite and graceful. Everything about her radiated warmth. She had a voice that made people feel seen. Heard. Understood. It was nurturing and wise. I wish I'd inherited that part of her. But I didn't. Still, I hope... someday, I can become her in my own way.

Smith agrees *The Siren* would be safest left on Magda, our home away from the sea. With Neressa. The ship creaks every time Neressa steps foot on her, like she recognizes her, trusts her. This ship means everything to me. I grew up sprinting across her decks, sneaking into the crow's nest, memorizing every creak and groan in her bones. She's the last piece I have of my parents, my home. Leaving her behind feels like carving out a piece of my heart. My last known family member.

But this alliance, this merging of crews, it's the right move. I need every ounce of help I can get. My crew's been off since my father died. The fight is still in them, but the spark has dimmed. He was an incredible captain, better than I'll ever be. Still, some part of me knows I'm meant for more than a captain's title. But the blood in my veins keeps me bound to both my crew and my ship. That bond doesn't break. Not even now.

Kai followed directly behind us the entire two-day trip back to Magda. He's making this transition easier than I expected, too easy maybe. Still, I can't help wondering what comes next, what it'll really be like sharing quarters with him.

Every time he touches me, something sparks. It's maddening how attractive he is. But it's more than that. He doesn't treat me like I'm fragile, like I'll crack under pressure. Even when his words are rough, they feel honest. Unfiltered. He also doesn't take any shit from me. That part is irritating.

Kai watches me from his deck. Always. I feel his eyes on the back of my head like a second shadow. I can't tell if it's because he feels what I feel, or if he just doesn't trust me yet. Maybe it's both. But one thing's clear, when we arrived, his crew showed me respect within seconds. Because he made them.

When I returned to *The Leviathan* to speak with Kai about docking *The Siren* in more detail, his entire crew nodded in unison, saluting me, calling me "Captain." I never thought I'd hear that from his crew. From Captain Eldoris's crew. Given our parents' history, it felt impossible. The chill that crawled up my spine wasn't from the wind. It was the weight of that name. The history behind it.

Captain Eldoris once ruled the sea, but not like some hero in a song. He was the pirate mothers warned their children about. The nightmare beneath every bedtime tale. His name alone could silence a tavern, not out of reverence, but fear. He was brutal, cunning, and relentless. I remember the stories. I remember the screams. I remember the blood.

When Kai took over as captain, he made it his mission to succeed where his father failed, to find the fountain and finish what Eldoris never could. But what the old man doesn't know is that I'm the key. *Me.* If he'd killed me like he wanted all those years ago, every twisted dream he ever had would've died with me. Funny, isn't it? The one thing he hated the most is the only thing that could have led him to what he wanted.

Chapter Eight

Mira

Anchorless

When we arrive in Magda, we dock *The Siren* at the edge of the island, as far from the main port as possible. A quiet inlet cloaked in stillness, where the sea whispers secrets only old ships could hear. The perfect hiding place. The perfect goodbye. Kai and I stand on the magic teak deck in silence a few feet apart, the moon spilling silver light across the wood, casting glittering trails on the water like scattered stars.

It feels like my chest is splintering, every beat of my heart cracking under the thought of leaving her behind. I know I'll see her again; she's bound to me. The magic in her bones is the same that runs through mine, a current that ties us together. She groans low, timbers shifting as if in protest, and I feel it echo inside me. She knows.

I press my palm against the rail, my fingers trembling over the salt-slick wood. "I'm so sorry, love," I whisper, voice breaking as the waves slap gently against her hull. "I'll be back for you soon." The ocean answers with a hush, carrying my promise across the dark water. Behind me, I hear Kai's footsteps approach, quiet, respectful, as if even he understands I am not just leaving a ship, I am leaving a piece of myself.

"She'll be well taken care of," he says quietly, not asking, just knowing. He can read it in my posture, the tightness in my jaw, the way my hand lingers on the railing.

"I know," I whisper, but it tastes like a lie. "It just feels wrong... leaving her here."

Kai steps beside me, his hand finding the small of my back, steady, warm, not possessive or commanding, and though every part of me screams to shrug him off, to keep him at arm's length, my body betrays me by leaning into the touch I swore I didn't want.

"Staying longer will only make it worse," he murmurs, his voice unusually gentle, almost human. I looked up at him, surprised. There's no smirk, no sarcasm, only something soft in his eyes, something I've never seen before. I nod once. He's right. And that quiet understanding between us? It's sweeter than anything I ever imagined from him.

"This isn't a normal ship," I start, my voice soft as I gaze out at the shimmering surface of the ocean. "She has magic. She won't be happy I'm just leaving her here for gods know how long."

As if on cue, The Siren creaks beneath my feet, a low, aching groan that ripples through the deck like a sigh. My chest tightens. She's speaking to me in her own way, letting me know she feels it too. The parting. The hollow ache of being left behind.

I place a hand on the railing, fingers brushing over the weathered wood like a farewell touch to a lover's cheek. "I'll come back," I promise. "You have my word. This isn't goodbye. Just a pause." Another creak answers me, softer this time, almost reluctant. She understands. But it doesn't make it easier.

Kai steps in front of me then, his broad shoulders blotting out the moonlight, casting a shadow over my skin. I don't look at him, not right away. I'm still with her. A chill slips down my cheek, a tear. I hadn't realized one had fallen. The sting of it infuriates me; I hate that I've let the crack show, that *he* can see what this is doing to me. And yet another part of me doesn't care, because the truth is heavier than pride: this bond between us, ship and captain, is splintering, if only for a moment, and I feel every fracture like glass breaking inside my chest.

But then his hand finds my chin, fingers gentle, coaxing, not demanding. His thumb glides along the curve of my jaw, urging me to look up. My eyes burn. I try to fight the tears. I have to stay strong in front of him. I don't want him to see any weakness. Not yet.

But I do. I look up. And those damn hazel eyes are glowing, lit from within, like the moon poured fire into them. No arrogance. Just quiet strength and something dangerously close to tenderness.

"I know what she is. I can feel her. Every time she's near, the magic bleeds off of her. Almost like it heightens my magic by just being near her," he says, voice low but sure. "She will be safe. I'll make sure of it."

I hate how easily I believe him. I hate that I want to. But there's something between us now, something that hums beneath my skin like an uncast spell. A pull I don't understand and can't fight. So I nod. I don't speak. I just trust, and hope I'm not a fool for it.

His gaze lingers a moment longer before it slips past me, scanning the horizon. Then his hand moves, slowly sliding from my jaw to my lower back, grounding me with the smallest touch. "Let's go, treasure," he murmurs. "We have business to handle."

When we step into Pebble's Pub, the scent of sweat, sea salt, and spilled rum hits me like a wave. And so do the hookers. They swarm Kai like moths to a flame, laughing too loudly, trailing fingers along his arms, whispering things I don't want to hear. I keep my gaze locked straight ahead, pretending it doesn't bother me. Pretending I don't see the way his smirk curves just for them. Of course they want him. Look at him. Maybe they already have him, and they just want more.

Jealousy twists low in my gut, hot, sour, and unfamiliar. It feels wrong, like I've swallowed something rotten. I know what jealousy can do to people—turn them cruel, make them betray even themselves. I've seen the nasty emotion within mermaids; it isn't pretty. I'm not going to be that girl. I shove it down and walk. One foot, then the next.

I beeline for the bar. I need rum. If I don't get it soon, I'm going to lose my temper and set this whole damn place ablaze.

Then she steps in front of me. *Neressa.* Dressed in black, eyes dark with a storm, which means only one thing. She's just come back from a job. She's taken a life tonight. It always makes me sick to my stomach how nonchalant she is about it. Lean, smug, and impossible to miss, she blocks my path like a gate I have to earn the right to pass.

"Back so soon, lil' sis?" she drawls, voice sticky with mock-sweetness. Her smirk says she hasn't forgotten our last fight.

Neither have I. I meet her gaze with a smile cold enough to freeze the sea. "It seems so," I say coolly, brushing past her like she's nothing more than smoke from a rotten pipe. The drink is calling, and I need it like air.

Neressa trails behind me, her boots clicking with purpose. "So," she purrs, voice laced with amusement, "I see you and the Pirate Lord docked at the same time... and walked in together? Interesting." She slides onto the barstool beside me like she owns the place, well, because she does.

The bartender doesn't need a word. Two glasses of rum hit the counter. She takes hers without looking, downs a generous sip, then taps her long, crimson nails against the wood of the bar. They're glossy and wickedly sharp. I wouldn't be surprised if she's slit a man's throat with them. Probably more than once.

"I did," I say at last, taking a slow sip to buy time. I feel her eyes on me, smirk tugging at her lips like a cat waiting for the mouse to admit it's already caught. "I guess you may have been right." There. The words are out, what she's been waiting to hear. A balm to soften the edge of the favor I am about to lay on her, to dull the sting of what I need to ask.

She lets out a short, musical laugh. "Funny how I always am, aye?" Her tone snaps like a whip, sharp and smug. Then her gaze narrows, curiosity slicing through her amusement like a blade. "But what I'm wondering is, why are you both back so soon? And together? It's barely been a month."

I finally tear my eyes away from the swirling amber in my glass and meet her fog-gray gaze, eyes that always seem to see too much. "I need a favor, Neressa. A big one. And I don't want a lecture."

Her brows rise, then her eyes lower into slits, her expression shifting from amused to intrigued. "What kind of favor?" she asks, voice curling with interest. Then a slow, wicked grin spreads across her lips. "Do you finally want me to kill someone for you?"

The way she says it, casual, almost hopeful, makes my skin crawl. "No," I say quickly. "You know I wouldn't ask you for that." I pause, the words bitter as brine on my tongue. "I need you to look after *The Siren* while I'm gone."

Her jaw slackens for a beat, just long enough to make my chest clench, then she snaps upright, her voice cracking like a whip. "You what?"

"I need you—"

Her palm slams against the bar, rattling both glasses, her nails leaving scratches in the wood. "I heard you, Mira. What the hell is wrong with you? Have you completely lost your mind?" Her voice rises with each word, sharp enough to draw blood. The sting of it lingers, but I don't flinch.

"I told you not to lecture me," I bite back. "I need what I need."

Neressa shoves off the barstool, eyes wild, motioning toward the room like she wants witnesses. Like she wants the entire island of Magda to know I've gone mad. "You're leaving your greatest heirloom, your entire family's legacy, to go after some old pirate tale?" She leans in closer. "And do you even trust him?" Her voice curls with venom, and the way she says *him* feels like a curse, and maybe he is. She jerks her chin to the other side of the room.

I follow the direction of Neressa's gesture. There he is, with his mouth on some hooker and his hands roaming like I was nothing more than seafoam lapping at his boots. Rage coils hot in my chest, rising fast, unforgiving. I shift in my seat, knuckles white around my glass. The urge to tear her away by that knotted mess of hair or slap the arrogance off his smug face blazes behind my eyes.

He's not mine. He's not mine, I keep repeating in my head. I know that, I really do. But damn it, why does it feel like he is? "This isn't about him," I say, forcing calm into my voice even as it splinters at the edges. My grip on the glass tightens. It's the only thing keeping me anchored.

Neressa eyes me sidelong, lips curling with the smallest, most infuriating smirk. "You don't have to play stone-hearted with me, love. I can see it, you're pissed."

She takes a slow sip from her glass, the amber shimmer of rum catching on her nails, turning them into little blades of light. "But it's not just your pride, is it?" She taps the rim of her glass on the bar. "A ship needs a captain. Especially that ship. And she doesn't follow just anyone. She answers to blood. *Your* blood." The truth of it hits like a blade touching flesh. I try not to flinch. Try not to think of *The Siren* waiting, sensing my absence like a wound that won't heal.

"You're the closest thing I have to a sister," I say quietly. "You are blood to me. The only one I trust with this. She'll sense that, she knows you." My voice barely rises above the hum of the tavern, but I know she hears me. "I'm not asking you to captain her. Just check in. Keep her safe. Live there, if you want. Just make sure no scallywags think they can take her." Neressa raises a brow, the sharp angles of her face softening, just slightly. And for once, she doesn't hide the flicker of something real in her eyes.

I let out a dry laugh. "Not that she'd let them. She'd drown the bastards before they even got close." *The Siren* doesn't suffer intruders. Her ropes slither and tighten, catching ankles, wrists—sometimes throats—before casting the unlucky bastards overboard. The sea always takes what she rejects.

Neressa places her hand over mine. It's a rare gesture from someone like her. "I'll take care of her," she says. "Just promise me you'll come back. Alive... and still yourself."

I look up, locking eyes with those rare grays. How many have stared into them right before they died? I wonder if they saw this softness, even for a second. "I'll do my best," I murmur.

"This isn't about him," I add, my tone edged with warning. "You know that, right? Something is calling for me to get to that fountain. I need to answer that call." She nods, but she doesn't meet my gaze. And that, more than anything, is my answer. I clear my throat and shift the weight of the moment. "I'm heading down to the safe. I need to grab whatever gold I can. Supplies. Weapons. Don't think I'll be back in Magda anytime soon."

"Take whatever you need," she says. Her voice is even, but her eyes soften just a shade. "Magda will be waiting for you, Mira."

I drain the last of my rum, the burn grounding me. I set the glass down on the golden wood of the bar and rise to my feet. "Thank you, Neressa. I know this isn't a normal favor."

She cuts me off with a wave of her hand. "This is destiny, love. I'll never stand in the way of that. Especially yours." Her voice, for once, is delicate. A word I never thought I'd use to describe her.

But then her eyes darken, like storm clouds curling at the edges of a calm sea. "However, if he hurts you, I'll hunt him down myself. And he won't want me coming. He would have much rather had the Kraken kill him than die at my blade." A chill scurries down my spine, but oddly, it comforts me. Because I know she means it.

"I have a feeling," I murmur, "he'll do *anything* but hurt me." And then I turn, walking toward the tunnels that lead to the underground vault, leaving behind the only person who's ever felt like family, entrusting her with everything I can't carry.

CHAPTER NINE

KAI

CINNAMON & STEEL

Silver is stunning, no doubt. I know that better than most—I've had her in my bed and know firsthand every curve of her body. But for some reason I can't pay her any attention, not when Mira stands in the room. Mira is a weapon, a rival I should cut down and be done with. Instead, I let the pull of her sink its claws in, hating myself for it. She's my enemy, yet every part of me strains toward her all the same.

"Silver," I say evenly, keeping my tone neutral. She giggles, flashing perfect white teeth, ice-blue eyes sparkling like frost under flame. Her long blonde hair swings with every calculated move.

"I love when you say my name," she purrs. "Couldn't stay away?" Another laugh, dripping with smug satisfaction. "Don't be embarrassed, most can't." She isn't wrong. Men line up for a chance with her.

"I'm afraid, I'm here on business, not pleasure," I say, lowering my voice as I lean closer. "Don't waste your time on me. Go find your next target, aye?" She smiles, then suddenly doubles back and presses her lips to mine. Uninvited. Fast. I shove her off without hesitation. And that's when I see her. Mira. Her eyes are locked on us, her face twisted in something between fury and betrayal.

Fuck.

I grab Silver by both wrists, my grip firm but controlled. My voice drops, low and lethal. "Whatever game you're playing, stop. I'd hate to ruin that pretty face of yours." I lean in just enough for her to feel the warning in my breath. "Now, like I said, move on. While you still can." The look in her eyes shifts instantly. The confidence drains out of her, replaced by dread. Like she's just heard a siren's call echo from the deep and knows, without question, it means death.

She swallows hard, throat bobbing. Still, she manages to gather the shards of her pride. "I'll be here when you change your mind," she says with a menacing little smile, brittle and forced. It only pisses me off more. I let go of her wrists, surprised she could still speak. She vanishes into the crowd of drunken pirates, slipping between bodies like smoke.

And I'm left standing here, with Mira's glare burning a hole in my back and a knot forming in my chest. Getting her to trust me has been hard enough. I have a deal I've made and I intend on keeping it. But now I've gone and made it worse.

I know Mira is safe with Neressa. I can read it in their body language. The two of them move like sisters, close and connected. So, I step outside for a smoke. I light my pipe and lean against the wall, letting the shadows swallow me. The moonlight stretches across the ocean's surface, each wave catching the light and scattering it in soft, shimmering ripples. The sea looks alive, whispering secrets into the night. If those whispers could speak, the stories they'd tell would be worth more than gold.

I lean against the wall, tucked in the shadows, trying to understand what Mira sees in this place. The night air is quiet, but I don't miss the sudden shift, the cold kiss of steel pressed to my throat in one swift, silent move. I don't need to look to know who it is.

"Neressa... you really are as sly as they say," I mutter, my voice low. She steps forward, the moonlight peeling across her features like a blade leaving its sheath. That foggy gaze swirls with something wild and unreadable, like a storm churning just beneath the surface. Her presence is sharp and dangerous. She smells of cinnamon. From what I've heard, she's like an orca, predatory and cunning, known for toying with her prey before delivering the final blow.

She presses the blade closer, slicing just enough to draw a thin line of blood. "Mmm, as sly as a fox, I've been told," she says. Warm blood trails down my neck, but I stay still. I could break her hold, pin her in seconds. But I don't. I want to know what she's after. Her eyes, swirling like sea fog before a storm, watch me without blinking. "If you harm her, I will gut you first, then I will kill you. I like to play with my prey before I end them. Do I make myself clear?" The blade doesn't waver. I lean into it, deepening the cut.

"Is that a promise?" I ask, smirking, not out of arrogance, but defiance. She narrows her eyes, trying to read if I'm bluffing. "If I hurt her," I add, "I'll end myself. But if you'd prefer to be the one to do it, you're welcome to try."

She lowers the blade and steps down from the old wooden chest she'd somehow climbed without making a single creak. Every movement she makes is catlike, silent, fluid, calculated. She and Mira are nearly the same height, both small in stature but dangerous in ways most don't realize until it's too late. Neressa reattaches her cutlass to her belt with a practiced motion, and I watch as the storm-dark shade in her eyes fades to a calmer gray, like clouds thinning after a squall. Still, her gaze stays sharp. "She's special. Very special... not just because she's like a sister to me." Her words settle like iron in the air. So, she knows. She knows everything about what Mira is meant to become. And she's kept it from her.

Does Neressa have some ulterior motive in keeping this from Mira? Sometimes blood isn't thicker than water when gold, wishes, and power are in play.

"I know," I reply, my voice low. Cold.

"I will tear this world apart for her, piece by piece. And you'll do the same. I hope." Neressa crosses her arms, her gaze sweeping over me like a predator sizing up a threat. "If her life's ever in danger, yours ends first. Is that clear?" She holds my stare, unflinching.

"Understood," I say, humoring her, though deep down, I know I mean it. Let her believe she's in charge.

Hell, maybe she is. With the stories I've heard, I wouldn't doubt it. Captain Bleu didn't just train her to survive, he forged her into a weapon, a living breathing weapon, then found others to sharpen the blade. Most of them didn't live long enough to tell the tale. Some of the mentors she had were close friends of mine. But now I see why. It was all for Mira. Even though Mira's more than capable of handling herself, what's coming for her is beyond any one person. She'll need every ounce of strength, every shadow-walker and sword-wielder on her side. She might even need an army. If Captain Bleu left one legacy worth remembering, it's this: The women in his life don't need saving. But gods help the fools who think they do.

"Great. You can start now." She pivots toward the front doors of the pub without another glance. A spike of worry stabs through me.

"Where is she?" I ask, voice low, edged with anger.

Neressa turns, meeting my glare without so much as a blink. "She goes down to the underground to grab some gold. They know better than to touch her, she'll kill them if they try." Her tone holds something dangerously close to pride. "She's just as clever as I am, just a little rusty. That's why they also know I'll finish off whoever she doesn't. And I'm not nearly as nice." Her words don't settle the fire in my chest. Letting her go down there alone? Into a place she'd call unsafe?

My jaw clenches. "Show me where the underground is."

I follow Neressa down a twisting descent of creaking stairs, the lanterns on the walls casting jagged shadows that dance like ghosts. With each step, the air grows heavier, damp with secrets and smoke. At the bottom, we stop at a splintered door, its surface worn and scarred from the memory of a thousand fists. Neressa knocks once, sharp and sure.

A grimy window slides open. Bloodshot eyes peer through. One glance at her. One blink at me, and then the door unlatches with a groan. Inside, the world shifts.

The underground buzzes with danger, a hidden den for gamblers, smugglers, and desperate kings in tattered coats. Gold clinks like wind chimes. Laughter slithers through the air, low and mean. Pirates, merchant lords, royals even, and criminals hunch over tables, gripping their coin and their pride with equal desperation.

The moment I step through the doorway, silence ripples like a dropped stone. Eyes turn. They know me. No one speaks my name, but the weight of it presses into the room like a drawn blade. I don't need to announce myself. I *am* the storm they whisper about in taverns. And every soul in the room feels it.

I scan the room, my gaze sharp, cutting through the haze of smoke and shadows. Then I see her. Mira sits at a table near the back, her posture relaxed, one hand casually dealing cards while the other cradles a dwindling pile of gold. Calm. Unbothered. Like this is just another game to her, and maybe it is. But I know better. She's always playing for something.

A tightness coils in my chest. "Did I give you a scare?" Neressa's voice slithers in beside me, all mockery and mischief. I turn toward her, jaw tight. She looks up at me with a grin sharp enough to cut, eyes full of wicked delight. "Oops," she says, tone dripping with sarcasm, a small giggle slipping from her. Then she strolls toward Mira without a care.

She leans in close, whispering something in Mira's ear that makes both of them laugh. That sound, her laugh, has a way of melting fury into something far more dangerous. Something tender. And I hate it. Because it's too easy to lose control when it comes to her.

Mira stands, her eyes locking onto mine from across the room. She walks toward me like the storm she is, graceful, steady, inevitable.

Every man in that bar gives me space, stepping back without needing to be told. They know better. And if any one of them even looks at her the wrong way, I'll happily remind them why the legends about me are all true.

"Neressa playing tricks on you?" Mira asks, her voice soft, threaded with amusement. There's a warmth in her tone that wraps around me like something familiar, something I don't realize I've missed until I hear it again. I meet her gaze. Those dark emerald eyes pull me. Beautiful.

"Seems like it," I mutter, my voice low, edged with steel. "If I hear you're in even a grain of sand's worth of danger, I'll be there."

A teasing smile ghosts across her lips, eyes flickering with mischief. Then, without a word, she brushes past me, the faintest touch of her shoulder sending a spark straight through me as she heads toward the door. Her scent trails after her, vanilla and sea salt.

I turn to Neressa. Her eyes meet mine, hard as cut glass. No words. Just a silent promise: *Hurt her, and I'll end you.* I give a single nod. Nothing more. A gesture of respect... and acknowledgment that I heard her loud and clear.

We step outside the pub. The night air snaps against my skin, cold and sharp, but it is nothing compared to the storm rolling off Mira as she charges ahead of me. She doesn't speak. Her silence has weight, heavier than a cannonball. I know exactly what she's angry about. The kiss. That damn kiss she saw.

"Mira," I call, cutting in front of her path. She doesn't stop. Just keeps walking like I don't exist. I grab her arm, not hard, but enough to make her turn. She resists, but I hold firm. "Listen to me." Her gaze stays on the ground, locked and distant. Frustration claws up my throat. "I didn't kiss her. She kissed me."

Mira lets out a sharp breath, a sigh laced with fury. Her eyes roll, slow and intentional, before they finally meet mine, dark, burning, disbelieving.

"You comfort me all night," she says, her voice low and shaking, "about leaving my ship, my beautiful, magical ship, behind. And then you go and shove your tongue down some whore's filthy mouth?" Her voice cracks on the last word, more rage than heartbreak. Her shoulders tremble slightly, the only crack in her steel armor. Then, with a slow shake of her head, she exhales, like she's trying to shake the image from her mind. She tugs at her arm again, trying to break free. I don't let her.

Her eyes drop to my chest, her voice flat but heavy. "You're not mine. I don't have the right to be upset, I don't even understand why these feelings are so strong. Maybe I'm just upset about leaving her." *The Siren.* She's more heartbroken than I know, and me doing what she thinks I did doesn't help. I tighten my grip, not to trap her, but to anchor her. To keep her from running when we both knew this needs to be said. I felt the tension in her muscles, the quiet tremor riding just beneath her skin. She can pretend all she wants, but this got to her.

"My tongue wasn't down her throat," I say, voice low, dragging out each word. "You can trust me. I'm sorry about you having to leave *The Siren.* I can see how much she means to you. But trust me when I say, I'm not looking at any other woman except the fiery one standing in front of me."

Even in the moonlight, I see the blush that climbs her neck, warming her cheeks despite the anger still simmering between us. And gods, it does something to me. But I don't let it show. "I don't like my integrity being questioned," I add, letting the edge slip back into my voice. "She came to me. Not the other way around."

I take a step closer, my eyes locking on hers. "I stood in the shadows all night, watching every move you made. Making sure no one laid a hand on you, I will continue to do that." Her gaze lifts, emerald eyes catching the moonlight like sea glass glinting at the bottom of the sea. I can't look away.

"We'll see," she murmurs, the words soft but threaded with steel.

We walk back to the ship in silence. The kind that wraps around your ribs and squeezes. Only the crash of waves against the rocks and the distant roar of drunken laughter breaks the quiet. But even that feels far away. Between us, the silence says more than we're ready to. And it weighs more than either of us is willing to admit.

CHAPTER TEN

MIRA

MOONLIT PROMISES

When we return to the ship, the crew is scattered across the deck and cabins, some finishing supper, others already asleep, and the rest lost in the rhythm of their usual tasks. Before we left, Kai made himself clear: no bloodshed, and no one dead by the time we returned. Shockingly, they listened. Not a single brawl or scratch. Most have already turned in for the night, resting for whatever storms tomorrow might bring. The ones still awake pass around bottles of rum, their laughter rolling across the deck like low thunder. They swap stories like old friends, their walls lowered for once. Some of them even seem to get along better than I expected, a rare and welcome change. With the road ahead long and uncertain, that thin thread of camaraderie might be the only thing that keeps us from unraveling.

I head straight for the captain's quarters. Kai cleared space for some of my things, not that I had much. Life at sea teaches you to travel light. A few shirts, worn-in pants, a couple of corsets, a skirt or two. Nothing fancy. I own more weapons than I do clothing. What will take up space are my parents' belongings, the ones I salvaged from *The Siren*. Their journals, especially, need to be hidden somewhere safe. I want to be the first to read them. Deep in my bones, I know the answers are there. Pirates always have secrets. My parents had more than most.

After unpacking what little I brought, I let myself take in the room for the second time. The large bed sits beneath tall windows that stretch from floor to ceiling, framing the sea in glass. The sheets catch my eye. He's changed them since I was last here. The black comforter remains, like a shadow draped over sheets that gleam like midnight waves under moonlight.

You'd never expect a pirate's bed to be this neat, but captains always live a bit more lavishly than the rest of the crew. He even added extra pillows. The bed is massive, more than enough space between us, if we wanted it. Secretly, I don't, even with how livid he made me earlier.

The rest of the room is cluttered in a way that feels intentional, like chaos with a system only he understands. Maps are pinned to the walls with knives. A carved pirate ship figure sits on a shelf, and small treasures lay scattered throughout the space. His clothes hang here and there, not many, but enough. I sit at the edge of the bed, letting the silk brush against my fingertips, and stare out at the sea through the tall windows. Just looking at her calms me, like she's whispering that I'm home.

There's always been a pull, an unspoken tether between me and the water, one that runs deeper than blood or bone. When I'm near the ocean, I feel understood and protected.

I hear the door creak open and turn to see a *very* exposed Kai Eldoris. He's soaking wet. Shirtless. Only a towel slung low around his hips. Water trickles down the sharp V lines of his torso, every muscle sculpted and sun-warmed. Tattoos cover him, ink swirling up his arms, across his chest, and all the way to his neck. His stomach is dominated by the image of the monstrous Kraken, its tentacles entwined with swords. Every inch of him tells a story through ink—none of them featuring sirens. Just a single mermaid, inked along the curve of his arm. I've heard whispers about how he became the Pirate Lord, how he's survived battles with sea beasts most wouldn't live to speak of. Especially the Kraken.

His shoulder-length dark brown hair drips from his bath, glistening in the low light. The scent of sea salt and tobacco curls in the air, subtle, unmistakable, and far too distracting. He glances at me, a slow smirk tugging at his lips. "Enjoying the view, Mira?"

I snap out of it and turn quickly back toward the windows. "Don't get too cocky, Kai," I say, keeping my voice flat despite the flush creeping up my neck. Still, I can't help stealing one more glance. He says nothing, just turns away and pulls a shirt over his head. I hate how disappointed I feel.

"So," he says after a beat, tone casual, "what do you think of where you'll be living for the foreseeable future?"

I turn fully toward him, still seated on the bed. "It's... cozy. The windows are my favorite part."

Kai steps closer, his eyes drifting toward the horizon. "Best part of the room," he murmurs. "The sunrises here are worth waking up early for."

I fall quiet. For a moment, it almost feels easy, talking to him like this, like we're something close to normal. But then his eyes find mine. Hazel and steady, too knowing. The kind of look that pulls the air right out of your lungs. My pulse stumbles. He doesn't look away, and I hate that I don't either. Whatever this is between us, it's coiled tight, waiting. And now, living under the same roof, I'll have to face it, whether I'm ready or not.

"I'm sorry about tonight," he says, his voice threaded with a sincerity I'm not expecting. I keep my stare. His eyes have softened.

"It doesn't matter," I reply, more defensively than I mean to. "I shouldn't have any feelings about you bedding others."

"It does matter, Mira." His voice is steady. "I wanted to give you space with Neressa, but I see now, I should've been sitting right next to you." I hold his gaze, narrowing my eyes, trying to get a read on him. A man like Kai has surely mastered every expression, every calculated tilt of the mouth, every well-timed flicker of softness in his stare. Pirate tricks. But this doesn't feel rehearsed.

"You should have been," I say quietly.

He steps closer. Reaches out. A strand of hair has fallen loose, and he tucks it carefully behind my ear. The touch is light, almost hesitant. Worry surges through me at how easily I allow it, how gentle it feels. "And for that," he murmurs, voice low, "I'm sorry."

His hazel eyes burn with flickers of green, gold, and brown, catching in the lantern glow. As furious as I am, his stare is its own kind of temptation, familiar, magnetic, impossible to ignore.

"I promise I'll always be right there for you," he says. His words send goosebumps rising down my arms.

"I'll hold you to it," I murmur, letting the ghost of a smile tug at my lips. "I have a question."

His eyes flick up, curiosity sparking like flame. "Yes, treasure?" He moves closer, sitting on the edge of the bed, not too near, not too far.

Just close enough that if he wanted to reach out, he could. And gods, I know he's aware of that.

"Your tattoos," I say, my voice barely above a whisper, "they're symbols of what you've defeated, right?" I know this because humans who possess magic don't choose their markings, they're chosen *for* them. A blessing and a curse, really. The magic decides what stays etched into your skin forever.

"Yes." His tone is steady, proud, carrying the weight of every victory.

"You've slaughtered a mermaid?" My hand drifts toward the inked figure of a mermaid curled along his arm, her tail coiling in soft, dark waves. My fingers hover, not daring to touch.

His eyes widen. "I would never hurt a mermaid," he says, voice low but certain. "This one, she saved my life." The words hit harder than I expect. I pull back, curling into myself before I can stop it. If he means what I think he does, then they're bound, connected by something deeper. A bond not easily broken. Sometimes, not knowing is better.

"Not all tattoos appear on their own," Kai continues, eyes shifting to the ink across his chest. "Some I chose. Some chose me."

"Interesting." My eyes break from his stare, drawn to the moonlit sea beyond the windows. Silver light ripples across the waves, catching like glass. "And what of a siren? Didn't you get attacked by one when you were young? Where's the tattoo for that?"

"I've never killed a siren," he says. His voice is steady. "If I did, I wouldn't want those dark creatures inked onto my skin."

I turn back to face him, shifting until I'm sitting cross-legged on the bed. The boards creak beneath me. "I don't know why, but I've never felt fear or anger toward sirens," I say.

"How could you not hate them? They took your father from you." His words aren't meant to wound, but they land deep all the same.

"Yes, they did." My voice softens. "They've never personally attacked me." His eyes search mine, quiet but unrelenting, as if he's trying to peel back every layer I keep hidden. I draw a slow breath, steadying myself before I continue. "When I was younger, maybe five years old, I was sitting on a dock in Magda, my feet dangling just above the water while my parents made deals with the merchants. The water was crystal clear that day... until I saw a razor-sharp fin slice through the surface."

I stop for a moment, realizing I'm saying too much. The air feels heavier for it. "Continue," he says, his voice gentle. Heat crawls up my neck at the softness in his tone.

"I quickly pulled my legs onto the dock and watched the water. A siren rose. But what was odd was the water wasn't black. She reached up and touched my face with webbed fingers. Her eyes—shaped like almonds and filled with stars, stared straight into my soul, like she was trying to read me. She was terrifyingly beautiful. I knew, even at that young age, she wasn't trying to hurt me."

"She didn't hurt you? At all?"

"No." My voice lowers to a whisper. "It felt like she just wanted to see if I was okay. Once she felt comfortable, she disappeared back into the ocean. Ever since then, during every battle, whenever sirens showed up, I've never been lured by them."

"That's because you're a woman. Only men answer to their songs," he says, so sure of himself it almost makes me laugh. I do anyway, a small, sharp sound.

"Do you really believe that myth?"

"It's not a myth." His face is perfectly innocent, which only makes it worse.

"It is," I counter, tilting my head. "They can lure anyone they want. It doesn't matter if you're a woman or not."

He shrugs, smug as ever. "I don't know. I haven't seen it with my own eyes."

I shove him lightly, grinning. "So, I know something about the sea that the great Pirate Lord doesn't? Maybe I should be crowned lord, then."

He lets out the smallest laugh, a low, rough sound I wish I could trap in a bottle just to hear again when the world goes quiet. I hate that I love it so much. "It'd take a hell of a lot more than knowing one little fact to earn that title, treasure," he says, smirking.

I smile, meeting his gaze. For a heartbeat, it feels like we've met before, like some old part of me recognizes him. "Anyway," I say softly, "I don't feel fear around sirens. Maybe they're just misunderstood creatures."

"I've seen firsthand what they're capable of," he says. "I'm lucky to still be alive. They're vile things, creatures that crave blood and souls. Men's and women's, I assume."

I know he adds that last part to soften the blow. "Well," I murmur, a hint of a smile curving my lips, "we can agree to disagree." My eyelids grow heavy, but I can still feel his gaze on me, steady, unyielding, warm enough to make me forget what we're talking about.

I turn away, slipping beneath the covers. The satin sheets are cool and comforting against my skin. I wear only my undergarments and the oversized, sun-bleached, long-sleeved shirt I always use during long days at sea. Tonight, it feels like armor of a different kind.

I choose the side of the bed closest to the window, drawn to the lull of the waves and the way the moonlight dances across the surface of the water. Resting my head against the cool satin pillow, I let the ocean soothe me. Kai doesn't say another word, but I feel him near, still and watchful. As the waves whisper against the hull, I let the ocean pull me under and pray he isn't the storm that follows.

CHAPTER ELEVEN

KAI

TWO BULLETS, TWO HEARTS

I wake before the sun does. I make my way down to the gunroom and light a lantern, the flame shivering before settling into a low, steady glow. Shadows stretch long across the walls, dancing over rows of polished steel. My fingers work a whetstone over a blade until it sings, a sharp, metallic hum that echoes through the cramped room thick with oil, salt, and old gunpowder.

I strike a match and light my pipe. The flame hisses, smoke curling into the dim. The air tastes of salt and smoke. The cold settles deep in my bones, heavy as ballast. Outside, the ship groans against the tide, and a new season rides the wind, cold enough to raise ghosts from the water.

Morning light slips through the slats, turning the steel of the weapons to molten gold. I've been down here long enough to lose track of hour and hunger when the crack of a pistol splits the silence. A breath later, the sound of screams follows, raw and eager, and something in me snaps taut. The whetstone clatters to the floor as I shove off the bench and take the ladder two rungs at a time. And if Mira's hurt, gods help whoever pulled that trigger.

As I shove open the door, a bullet screams past me, burying itself dead center in the head of a wooden target. I freeze. For a breath, all I can hear is the echo. Then I see her.

Mira stands amid the smoke, pistol steady, sunlight spilling through her dark curls like fire caught in motion. Her emerald eyes are narrow, shining like sea-glass in water. She holds the gun with lazy precision, like it's part of her. The shot wasn't luck. It was art. And gods help me, I can't look away.

For a moment, I just stare. The men cheer her name, voices rising, and I feel something twist low in my chest. Admiration. Bitter, unwelcome, and sharp as salt on a wound. She's my rival, my ruin waiting to happen. Still, I can't drag my eyes from her. The way she reloads, calm and unhurried, the sunlight glinting off her pistol. The crew feels her power, too. The air thrums with it.

"You're lucky I don't miss," she says, amusement tipping her voice. "I would've killed you." The corner of her mouth curves like a crescent moon.

Jay pads up behind her, steady as ever, his grin all teeth and pride. "Aye, fine shot, that one," he says to me, cocking his head as he takes the pistol from her. He raises it with casual precision and fires. The bullet lands clean through where a heart would be. "But I prefer to hit 'em in the chest," he adds, smoke drifting between his words. "Hurts longer that way." He taught me that when I was a boy—aim for the heart, not the head. Maybe that's why I never learned how to protect mine.

Mira laughs under her breath, and it's so unguarded, so easy, it knocks something loose in me. Smith stands at the stairs, pipe clamped in his teeth, watching with that knowing stillness of a man who's seen too much. He gives Mira a nod, brief, but not surprised. He knows what she's made of. He forged half of it.

Mira stands unshaken. And me? I'm just standing here watching them both, realizing I might be underestimating what kind of fire I've let aboard my ship.

I step forward, keeping my voice flat. I draw a pistol from my belt, let the metal catch the light for a heartbeat. "Let's make this interesting." I pace to the center, all eyes on me. "Hang those targets around the ship. Mira and I will swing from rope. Whoever lands the most in the heart wins."

"And what do I get if I win?" Mira steps closer, the challenge in her eyes.

I want to answer cockily, recklessly, but the words come easy. "Next round's on me when we dock. For both crews."

Her laugh is low, pleased. Jay claps once, Smith chuckles, pipe smoke curling like a benediction. Mira's crew erupts. Free rum is a promise no pirate ignores. The deck thrums beneath us, alive with shouts and salt and laughter. For a breath, I feel it too, the pulse of the ship, the heat of the moment, the pull between us. It's competitive, combustible, and threaded with something I can't name, something that will burn through more than any wager ever could.

"Okay, I'm in. Set up the targets, boys." She waves a hand in the air, pistol gleaming. Then she turns toward a hanging rope and reloads, movements smooth, practiced. Her confidence is a weapon all its own.

"You're not afraid—"

"Afraid of what?" she cuts me off, quick as a blade. "Losing to you? No." Her grin flashes, teeth white against sunburned lips, and for a moment I forget to breathe. I've never seen her smile like that before. It's reckless. Addictive.

"Well," she says, cocking her pistol, "pick your rope and get ready to lose your title, Pirate Lord."

"Oh, treasure," I drawl, matching her step for step, "I won't be losing anything. But I do love your confidence." A hint of pink creeps up her cheeks, and it's the first thing all morning that makes me lose my composure.

I cinch my hand around a ratline and begin climbing, boots finding the knots as the deck falls away beneath me. Mira follows, moving fluid as tidewater, through the rigging. We pull ourselves up onto the yardarm of the mainmast and crouch there, high above the foredeck, the world narrowing to rope and sea and the slope of canvas beneath our knees.

Smith stands on the quarterdeck, pistol raised. I scan the targets pinned along the rail from bow to stern, mark the angles, the swing I'll need to cut through them all in one long arc. I steal a quick look at Mira; she's already measuring the same geometry, green eyes bright as a flare. There's a heat in that look, more than competition. This is a battle of crews and captains now, and neither of us is stepping down.

The crew erupts in cheers. Smith fires his pistol, the signal. I push off the yardarm and swing down, body cutting through the air. The rope burns my palms, the rush of wind sharp as cutlass steel. My first three shots land true, each target splintering clean.

Mira follows close behind, her shot cracking through the air, two clean hits in rhythm with the swing. She moves like wind, fluid and fierce, her laughter carried off by the sea spray.

Then she's ahead of me, drops to the deck, runs full speed across the planks, and catches another rope. The move is reckless, brilliant. She launches back up, swinging opposite me, skirts of her coat flaring like fire. I keep my path steady, though my eyes keep wanting to find her. I land four more shots. Then five.

She hits six. I take seven. And then, she's flying in again, fast as a hawk diving for its kill, three perfect shots in a row. The crew roars. She's winning. I grit my teeth, twist midair, and mirror her movement exactly.

I glance to where the last target should be, but those sneaky bastards have moved it. Mira and I stand on opposite sides of the deck now, ropes in hand, boots balanced on the railing. The sea churns below, salt wind snapping at our coats. For a moment, all sound drops away.

We spot it at the same time, the final target, hanging high above the helm. A near-impossible shot. We move without a word, climbing the rigging higher and higher until the ship shrinks beneath us. The higher, the better.

I brace against the mast, plant my boots, and push off the wood for balance. I fire. Another gunshot answers mine in the same breath.

Two bullets. Two hearts. Perfect shots.

The crew erupts below, voices rising like a storm, but all I can hear is my own heartbeat and the echo of hers beside it. I'm not sure whether I've found an enemy or my equal. Because we hit the same spot, at the same exact time. We tie.

We land side by side at the helm, the boards shuddering beneath us. For a long breath, neither of us moves. Just the creak of rope, the crash of the tide, and her eyes on mine. The crew is silent, every man waiting to see which of us will break first.

Jay clears his throat, breaking the tension. He made his way up the stairs, standing between us. "Well," he says, half-grinning, "looks like we've got ourselves a tie, aye?"

I drag my gaze from her and look at him. "Seems so," I say, voice low. "But I'll still take the next round when we make port." She smirks, all pride and challenge, and it does something sharp to my chest. I turn away before she can see it.

Because what I felt for her at that moment wasn't part of the plan. And I don't like when my plans start to unravel.

CHAPTER TWELVE

KAI

UNRAVELED

The sea's balance has been off for over a century, but Mira doesn't know just how deep the roots of that imbalance reach. Whispers ripple through every dark cove and tidepool about the Soul of the Ocean, twisted and corrupted by something ancient and cruel. It's been birthing horrors, creatures of kelp, shadow, bone, and rage. An army of drowned things, growing slowly beneath the waves.

The corrupted Soul was once a mermaid, long ago. That's what the old stories say. But its original form is long gone, warped into something unrecognizable. Now, it can wear any face it wants, man, woman, monster, but it can never go back to what it once was. It chooses its victims carefully, pulling them under one by one until the sea has taken its due. Once it marks you, there's no escaping what comes next. You drown, but your soul doesn't rest, it festers, trapped beneath the waves for eternity, forgotten by the living and unwanted by the dead. And the worst part, they whisper, isn't the dying. It's the begging that comes after, the pleading for release the ocean never grants.

Being the new Soul of the Ocean is already enough to paint a massive target on Mira's back, but add her siren blood to the mix, and she's walking straight into a storm with no way out. Pirates have always despised sirens, me being one of them. They blame them for lost ships, dead men, sunken treasure. Most would kill one on sight, some out of revenge, others for profit. Siren blood is a powerful bargaining chip, passed between witches and pirates like dark currency. It's rare. Nearly impossible to come by. Few survive a siren encounter, let alone spill their blood.

But Mira, she carries it in her veins. If the corrupted Soul's army discovers what she truly is, the danger multiplies tenfold. They don't just hunt, they consume. Anything that threatens their queen's reign becomes theirs, body and soul. What keeps me up at night isn't just the threat, it's the question of how. How does she have siren blood? Was it a blessing from the ocean while she grew in her mother's womb? Or was she marked as an infant, touched by a siren, or something worse? Maybe her father's past holds more shadows than even Mira knows. Or her mother's past...

What terrifies me most is that the sirens know. They always know. And sirens protect their blood with a vengeance. Like she said, they've never attacked her. She feels safe with them, but that safety is an illusion.

Her story plays in my head again: a small girl on a dock, feet skimming the water, a siren rising from the deep to meet her. Any other child would've been dragged under, torn apart. But not her. She walked away untouched, even content. That kind of mercy doesn't happen by chance. If they've decided she belongs to them, they'll come for her. And I don't know if I could even stop them.

It's the morning after our little game. I tell myself it's for the best, that whatever's trying to claw its way to the surface needs to stay buried. Feelings complicate things. They make men weak, and I can't afford weakness right now. I've made deals with dark creatures, and I intend to keep them.

Still, when I catch the echo of her laugh somewhere on deck, it sticks like salt in an open wound. She slept before I did, sleeps longer still. Maybe she's trying to forget what happened between us. Maybe she already has. I wish I could say the same.

On deck, I check how close we are to Pike, the coastal town swallowed by thick jungle where Veyra lives. We were en route when the kappas made their unexpected appearance. Seeing Veyra will help. She sees, hears, and feels everything. A tether between us and the heartbeat of the earth itself. She keeps the land whole, while the Soul should govern the ocean's wrath. I'm not sure which burden is heavier.

Veyra faces the chaos of humans, politics, greed, war. The Soul answers to monsters, sirens, mermaids, pirates, witches, and the ancient things that drift in the dark. But Veyra has a way of getting along with all of them. Even the sirens.

I climb the stairs to the quarterdeck where Jay stands at the helm, his favorite place, hands steady on the wheel. The sun has just broken over the horizon, casting a golden glow across the sea. Everything shimmers: the sails, the waves, even the sky itself looks like it's been kissed by firelight.

"Are we close?" I ask, stepping up beside him.

Jay doesn't look at me right away. "Aye," he says after a pause. "Few hours out, give or take." *The Leviathan* is the fastest ship on the sea.

We can reach places days—sometimes weeks—faster than any other, depending on the winds and tides.

His tone is off. Too tight. Jay is always steady, always unshaken. But now, something in his voice makes my spine go rigid. "What is it?" I ask.

He turns his back to me, eyes fixed on the horizon like he's searching for something hiding just beyond the edge of the world. "Seeing Veyra might not be the best idea," he says, voice low. "She's not someone you can lie to. Or control." He hesitates, then adds, "She's close to a goddess, Kai. Closer than most men are comfortable with."

He isn't wrong. I've been dreading this visit since the moment we set course for Pike, long before Mira came aboard. Veyra's power runs deeper than most can comprehend. She doesn't just hear the whispers of the world; she commands them. But I also know she sees the truth in people. And if Mira is beside me, Veyra will sense it. She'll see who I truly stand for. That has to count for something.

"I wouldn't worry," I say, sounding more confident than I feel.

"That's what my father thought too... that he shouldn't worry."

My brow lifts. Jay never talks about his parents. That conversation has always been off-limits. "What?" I ask, still caught off guard that he even brought him up.

"My father, he was cursed by Veyra herself. Even sayin' her name feels like breakin' a law." He finally turns to me, eyes meeting mine. "I just hope you're confident enough to face someone of her rank. She's a goddess, a powerful one." His voice stays level, but there's something there, something sad.

"I'm never not confident in what I do," I say, meeting his gaze. "How did your father die? What omen did she place on him?"

He looks away from me, back out to the endless stretch of ocean. "He took her from him."

I have an inkling of who he means, but I ask anyway. "Who?"

He takes a long pause, and I wait. "My mother," he murmurs.

Shock ripples through me. Veyra is powerful, yes, but taking an innocent life to pay for another is ruthless. I can see the unease flicker across Jay's face, how dragging this memory out has cost him.

"I'm sorry," I say quietly. "I didn't know. You never speak of them." He grunts, lighting his pipe, a coping mechanism if I've ever seen one. He takes his time answering, drawing in the smoke, then releasing it slow. The smoke curls through the air, catching the morning light in ghostly ribbons.

He exhales through his nose, pipe smoke drifting between us. "My father thought he could bargain with a goddess and walk away whole. Thought he could cheat her outta what she was owed." He shakes his head, a low, bitter laugh slipping out. "But no one cheats Veyra. She takes what she's promised, one way or another."

He looks out toward the horizon, eyes dark. "He went to her thinkin' he could save my mother. That's the kind of fool he was, always tryin' to fix what was already broken. She warned him there'd be a price, but he didn't listen. When the sea came to collect, she took her first."

Jay draws in another long breath of smoke. "So if you're plannin' to face her, Cap', remember this. Veyra don't forget, and she don't forgive. If she sets her eyes on Mira... pray the sea takes you first."

I study him for a moment. His expression is serious, but he recoils into himself, his knuckles going white as he grips the helm tighter than usual. "I have it under control. When don't I?" I add with a smirk, trying to lighten the tension. Jay doesn't answer, just grunts, that low sound he makes when he knows better but can't say.

I turn toward the quarters, hoping Mira's awake. Just then, a sharp, electric pain crawls up my arm. I shove back my sleeve and freeze. My scar is pulsing, dark veins spidering out from it like ink spreading through water. Black. Not red. The ache settles into a steady rhythm, a heartbeat beneath my skin that isn't mine. I cover the scar. Some things are better left unseen and better ignored. There are more pressing matters.

My thoughts race back to Jay as I descend the stairs, his words echoing in my head.

He's sharp, steady, sees right through people. He was fiercely loyal to my father until the day he saw me covered in bruises. I was barely tall enough to grip a sword. Most would have looked the other way, but he stepped up. Took me in. Raised me like I was his own. Had the crew do the same. He was never afraid of my father's wrath when it came to protecting me.

He joined our crew young, maybe fifteen, and somehow still knew more about loyalty and piracy than most men twice his age. When I asked him once why he cared, why he stayed, he said, "He may have raised you with brawns, but I raised you with purpose." I don't know where I'd be without him.

Mira is just waking as I step back into the room. She stretches, arms rising above her head, and her shirt lifts with the motion, just enough to reveal a sliver of skin. A faded birthmark curves along her right side, sweeping across her ribs like it's been painted there by the ocean itself. I haven't noticed it before. Subtle, but striking. Like a secret only the sea has known until now.

She catches me staring. Her eyes meet mine, sharp green, aglow with the golden morning light streaming through the windows. She looks ethereal.

"Morning, treasure," I say softly, the words leaving me warmer than I mean them to. I want to break the tension we've had since yesterday. I need her to be on board with the plan to go pay a visit to Veyra.

She tries to suppress a smile but it slips through, soft and unguarded. "When did you get up?" she asks, no edge to her voice, just quiet curiosity. That alone stuns me.

"A while ago," I say, moving closer.

She throws the blankets off, revealing smooth, bare legs, her skin kissed by sunlight and sea air. It's the first time I've seen her like this. Unshielded. Bare. But still every inch in control. My pulse thuds. Every instinct screams to crawl back into that bed and devour her whole.

She catches the look in my eye, one brow lifting with amusement. "You're staring."

I don't deny it. "And?" I murmur, letting a small smile slip. Her cheeks flush instantly, that soft smile tugging at her lips, radiant in a way that knocks the air from my lungs. She looks like she belongs here, like the sun has always been meant to rise on her in my bed, in my life.

Without a word, she slips into her pants, keeping the white long-sleeved shirt she wears to sleep. It slides off one shoulder, just enough to tempt. My restraint is wearing thin.

"We're headed to Pike," I say, pulling myself together.

She pauses mid-movement, brows lifting slightly. "Pike?" Her voice tightens. "That's where Veyra lives." A beat. "Is that who you wish to see?"

If anyone else questioned me like that, they wouldn't have a tongue left to do it again. But her voice? Her words hit like honey and steel. Sweet, sharp, and utterly disarming. "Yes." I nod. "She's our best shot at information. Veyra knows and sees everything that moves across land

and sea. Risky, sure. But I have a feeling she'll speak to us. Might even help us find our way."

She falls quiet. Too quiet, for Mira. The silence stretches between us. I watch her closely. "Thoughts?" I ask. I can practically hear her thinking, feel the weight of her hesitation pushing against the air. Whatever she says next, it's going to matter. However, I refuse to ever invade her mind again.

"She's dangerous," she says, voice steady. "Kills more than she helps." Her eyes meet mine, unflinching.

"I have a feeling she won't kill us," I say.

"Why?"

"Because someone as pure as you," I murmur, stepping closer, "she wouldn't dare touch."

A faint smile tugs at her lips. "And you? You're not very pure." Her voice drags over the last word like ruffled silk. My gaze darkens at the accusation.

"That you know of." The space between us tightens. Veyra doesn't kill without reason, she never has. If she wants something from us, she'll take it.

Mira is quiet, calculating. I watch her pace across the room, sunlight slicing through the window and catching on her every step. It spills between her legs, tracing the motion like it can't help but follow her. "I think it's worth the risk. We need information. She's the best source." She stops pacing and looks up at me. "How close are we?" Mira's voice cuts through the quiet, her calm acceptance catching me off guard. I expected more hesitation.

"A few hours out," I answer, though my thoughts are tangled elsewhere. All I can think about is her voice, how it softened, how she didn't question the danger, how she's choosing to walk into the storm with me.

She reaches for her corset, looping it around her waist with practiced ease. The strings fall behind her in loose, winding ribbons. Her fingers brush them once, twice. She doesn't even flinch when I step closer, close enough to feel the heat of her skin.

"May I?" My voice is low, almost a murmur, as I reach out. My fingers graze the back of her shoulder, then drift down the length of her spine, slow and deliberate, tracing the soft curve until they find the cords of her corset. Her skin answers before she does, goosebumps rising like the tide returning to shore.

"Yes," she breathes. Just one word. Barely audible, but laced with certainty. Need. Surrender. It betrays more than she meant it to.

Then her scent hits me, sweet vanilla. It's so familiar it unsteadies me, like I've stood in this exact moment before in another lifetime. The air feels thinner now. Her presence pulls me under like a riptide, dizzying and unstoppable. And I know I'm already lost.

As I take the strings into my hands, she lifts her hair, a slow, graceful motion, like an offering. The top of her back and shoulders come into view, freckled skin kissed by the sun, each mark scattered like constellations across a night sky only I get to see. I ache to trace them, to memorize her in the quiet places no one else knows. To make constellations I'd gladly sail toward, again and again. Gently, I pull the corset snug around her frame, careful, slow, unwilling to break the spell between us. "Too tight?" I whisper, my breath brushing the curve of her neck.

She shivers but doesn't move away. Instead, she turns her head just enough for our eyes to meet over her shoulder. Emerald green. "That... works," she says softly. And just like that, I'm drowning in her. Not in her beauty, though gods, that would be enough, but in the way she looks at me. Like I might be worth unraveling.

Oh, this is bad. The slightest brush of her skin is enough to drown me. I'm sinking into her emerald sea, deeper with every breath. I want her. Gods, I want to close the distance between us, to cross the line that's been fraying since the moment I saw her. My chest tightens. The air grows thick. I tie the strings with a steady hand, but it's not enough to anchor the chaos rising in me. When I finally step back, I give her space, space to finish getting ready, space I need before I lose control. I should've stayed composed. But something in me is coming undone, unraveling in her presence like a tether slipping loose.

"Thank you, Captain Kai," she says, her voice laced with something I can't quite place. A challenge? Or just playful teasing? Either way, she's testing me, measuring how far she can push. My heart stumbles, but I cover it with a grin and raise a hand in mock surrender.

"Just Kai will do, treasure," I reply, voice low, controlled. The heat running through me is impossible to hide.

Her lips curve into a faint smile, the kind that hides more than it reveals. "Kai it is, then," she says, softer now.

I watch her move, slow and unhurried, fastening only her cutlass. A part of me relaxes. She must feel safe enough to let her guard down, at least a little. No full arsenal strapped to her thighs or her belt glinting at her hip. Just calm, collected Mira. The storm inside me is a jarring contrast. She passes me, and our hands brush, just for a breath, a second. But the air crackles. She doesn't speak. Just walks out to the waiting crew, and I'm left staring after her, pulse pounding, lungs burning, still trying to catch my breath while breathing in her sweet vanilla scent.

I stay where I am, pulse pounding, lungs burning, trying to steady the ache that follows her out the door. Because Pike waits on the horizon—and with it, Veyra. And if my instincts are right, one of us won't leave that island the same.

I've faced monsters, curses, and the wrath of the sea itself, but none of it feels as dangerous as Mira. If I lose control now, of her, of myself, I won't just lose this fight. I'll lose everything.

CHAPTER THIRTEEN

KAI

BREATH & VINE

"We've arrived, Cap'," Jay calls from the starboard side of the ship. I'm down on the lower deck, watching the waves slap against the hull and keeping an eye on Mira. She's been talking to Smith for far too long.

"Aye," I call back, turning to let her know we're close and to prepare for docking.

Mira and I are the only ones going ashore to find Veyra. She's not the type you simply stumble across. She hides deep in the jungle, somewhere the map doesn't reach. We're the only ones meant to walk this path to see Veyra. If we bring anyone else, she'll try to balance their souls too, and this journey is ours alone to take.

We board the small rowboat, the wood creaking under our weight as it drifts from *The Leviathan's* shadow. The only sound is the rhythm of the oars cutting through the water. The sea is calm and glassy, reflecting the bruised colors of dawn. Overhead, gulls cry and circle, their calls sharp against the stillness. Salt clings to the air, heavy on my skin, and every pull of the oars brings us closer to the shore waiting ahead.

I hold out a hand to steady Mira as she climbs out of the boat. She takes it without hesitation, and I help her down. "Thanks," she says. We move toward the tree line, where the jungle begins to swallow the beach. Mira walks close behind me, quiet, breath steady. Most would be on edge heading into Pike, with all the stories told about its cursed jungle and vanishing travelers, but not her. She's unshaken.

As we reach the tree line, Mira pulls out the map Taika gave her. "I think this should help us find Veyra," she says, unraveling it carefully. Small black specks stain the top left corner like ink spilled in warning. "We follow where it turns black. North. When it's completely black... we've found her." I glance at the map, then at her. If that map brought her to me, I trust it'll get us wherever we need to go.

The jungle engulfs us fast. Some parts are quiet and unsettling, shadows thick as tar between twisted trees, branches draped in moss that sway even without wind. Other parts feel almost peaceful, with birds calling overhead and the sound of water threading through narrow streams. It's the kind of place someone deeply tied to the earth might call home. Someone who doesn't want to be found.

Mira moves steadily beside me, alert but never tense. The deeper we go, the stranger it feels, like we've stepped into a place that sees us, weighs us up, waits for something. It feels like every sin I've ever committed is being judged here. Like the jungle decides whether I deserve to walk through it at all.

Animals slip between the trees, silent and watchful. A fox darts across our path. A line of unusually large ants crawls in perfect order over a vine-covered root. A snake slithers nearby, long and dark, its scales catching the faintest trace of light as it winds through the underbrush. I instinctively step in front of Mira. She doesn't flinch, doesn't slow, just glances at the creature with mild curiosity, like she's seen far worse. None of them come close, but none of them flee, either. It feels like we've been invited into their home, and they've opened the door.

What is it this cursed place shelters? The sea has its sirens, its kappas, its drowned horrors. What does the land have? The vines whisper, the air trembles. Whatever watches us now feels older than myths.

It's strange, feeling more unsettled on land than I ever have at sea. The ship is chaos, sure, but it's my chaos, one I can be in control over. This? This, something written by the gods, is a different realm.

Still, I tread carefully. I don't want to harm a single living thing before seeing Veyra. Even something as small as an ant under my boot. Her soul probably runs through every leaf, every stone, every bead of dew left behind by morning rain. This place feels sacred and I want to be respectful on her land, but if anything even tries to touch Mira, I'll burn the whole damn jungle to the ground.

Mira pulls the map out again. The black ink stains more of the top left corner now, the spreading shadow shifting our path. We veer slightly until we stumble upon a waterfall, its silver ribbons crashing into a crystal plunge pool below. The water smashes against the rocks, catching the light like scattered diamonds. Rain begins to fall. Soft. Warm. The droplets make the surface of the pool shimmer even more. It's mesmerizing, like this place was meant to be found.

The jungle heat wraps around us, heavy and wet. Our clothes cling to our skin, every breath thick with the scent of moss and rain. Mira glances at me, a sly, knowing smirk tugging at her lips, more playful than usual. "Should we go for a swim?" That smile of hers could undo kingdoms. Fighting my feelings of hatred towards her is getting harder, day by day.

"I would love to," I say, already pulling at my shirt. Mira's fingers are quicker, unlacing her boots, peeling off layers until we're down to nothing but our undergarments. She wears only a thin strip of fabric across her chest, completely see through. Her skin gleams in the golden haze of humidity.

She dips a toe into the water. The chill snaps at her skin, and she recoils with a small gasp. "It's freezing," she says, her teeth clenching through the shiver. "But we can get used to it." I let out a low laugh and dive in without warning. The cold bites hard, but it's sharp and refreshing. When I surface, she's still easing in, inch by inch. The water climbs her body, and she trembles against it.

There's no fat on her. No warmth to hold onto. She's all sinew, grace, and stubborn pride. A siren in her own right, but she has no clue yet. I look at her, her eyes wide with worry. "Your arm... It looks infected." I glance down. The veins have darkened, spreading up my bicep and down my forearm like ink spilled beneath the skin. It's getting worse. The pain comes in waves, sharp, burning, alive. When it hits, it feels like the siren herself is clawing to get out.

I move toward her, reaching to pull her in close. She tenses at the offer at first, but she gives into the warmth coming from my body. My arms wrap around her, pulling her in close. Her body fits perfectly against mine, like we were molded to belong to one another. Her arms slowly circle my waist, as though she's fighting herself to embrace me. She sinks into my warmth like she's been needing it, craving it, not fighting the pull. Her head rests right over my heart. For the first time in what feels like forever, I can breathe. Like I've been drowning my entire life and only now surfaced for air.

"Don't worry about it," I tell her, voice steady even as the burn crawls higher. "It'll fade." A lie, sharp and easy. The truth is uglier. Varn warned me it would reopen, but he never said it would spread like poison.

Her lashes flutter against my chest, soft, delicate, until they still. Her eyes close. Her body surrenders to the comfort between us. She stops shivering. She's so small in my arms. Fragile in a way I don't think she even realizes. But she feels safe. And that matters more to me than anything.

Mira looks up. Her emerald eyes, rich and dark like the forest around us, lock with mine. "If you say so," she says softly. I glance down at her, rain still dripping from my soaked hair. A droplet lands on her cheek and she scrunches her nose in protest. I chuckle.

The spark between us is impossible to ignore. She doesn't look away. Neither do I. Rain clings to her lashes like tiny diamonds. I've never liked this kind of eye contact. I can stare down an enemy across a battlefield, meet the gaze of a man I'm about to kill without blinking. But someone who makes me feel something real? That kind of gaze is harder to hold. Right now, I don't want to look away. I don't want *her* to look away.

She looks at the waterfall, jaw tight, eyes flashing with something sharper than the sunlight cutting through the jungle storm, gleaming off the water. "Don't use your magic on me," she says, voice clipped. "I don't like my mind being invaded." The accusation hits like a cold wave. I blink, confused, narrowing my gaze. "I haven't touched your mind since the night we were in the pub," I say slowly, brows furrowed. "Why would you assume that?"

She looks up at me, guarded. But behind the armor, I catch it, a flicker of vulnerability. Something raw. "I had some... feelings," she admits, the words thick, heavy, like they cost her something to say. "I thought maybe you were controlling them." A silence blooms between us. I want to touch her cheek, her jaw, anything to anchor her.

But I don't. Instead, I let my lips pull into a slow smile. "Feelings of what?" I know. Of course I know.

But I want her to say it. I want it spoken into the air, something real. Something undeniable. She looks away. Her jaw twitches. "It doesn't matter," she mutters. "We should get going."

She pulls from my arms and climbs out of the water, droplets trailing down her skin like silver threads. Her walls, which had started to chip away, rebuild themselves with every step. I let her go, respecting her boundaries. As much as I silently want her, I will never force anything on her.

Her warmth vanishes instantly. Like it was never there at all. After everything I've done. After the way I was in Magda. After a life where people only ever took from her. Especially with the weight of both our families' pasts, I don't blame her for putting up walls. I'd help her build them, if she needed me to.

She's shivering as she pulls her clothes back on, fingers trembling slightly as she laces her already soaked boots. I shrug off my shirt and offer it to her. "Here. Use this." She takes it without a word. Her fingers graze mine for a heartbeat too long. She presses the fabric to her skin, and finally, I speak.

"You have to know," I say gently. "I won't enter your mind again. Not unless you want me to."

She doesn't look up from what she's doing. "Okay" is all she says. It hits harder than I expected. So quiet. So unsure. But not a no.

A breeze stirs the trees above us. Leaves flutter like they're whispering. Something in the forest shifts, a rustle too purposeful, a shadow that moves without sound. She doesn't notice. But I do. Veyra is close. And she's listening.

I dress quickly, still watching Mira as she adjusts her corset, eyes downcast. We start walking again, side by side this time, not speaking. There's too much left unsaid. But we'll get there. One step at a time.

We keep a close eye on the map. It's been hours of trudging through the thick, humid forest, and finally, the black ink starts spreading again, slowly at first, then all at once. Nearly the entire map is consumed. We're close. As we near a quiet pond, the last patch turns black.

"We're here," Mira says, her voice barely above a whisper. She points ahead to a small house made of moss, vines, leaves, and mud, tucked beneath a curtain of vines and moss. It glows softly from within, the kind of light that feels alive.

"Stay behind me," I murmur. "One rule with Veyra, only speak when spoken to. She will ask her questions. Never speak out of turn." Mira nods, face solemn, and we step forward.

I hesitate before crossing the threshold of her land. It doesn't feel right to just enter. She'd know we were here. Someone like Veyra always knows. So we wait. And then she appears, not from the house, but from behind us, silent as a shadow.

Her skin glows golden, warm and otherworldly. Her eyes shimmer a bright, unnatural green, brimming with ancient knowing. Her hair is twisted into thick locs woven with twigs, moss, vines, exotic flowers, and bits of bark. She wears no fabric, only carefully placed moss, her form wild and sacred. She floats like a fairy, her presence wrapping around us like thick morning fog.

"Welcome to my home," she says, her voice like honey over stone.

"Thank you," I reply, keeping it short and respectful. My hand stays on Mira's wrist, gentle, but firm. A quiet promise that nothing will harm her. Veyra shifts her gaze to Mira.

"Mira," she says softly, tasting the name on her tongue. "I've been waiting for you." Her voice is calm, almost sweet, but it pulls a shiver straight down my spine.

CHAPTER FOURTEEN

MIRA

SEALED & TIED

All the blood drains from my face, my body frozen in pure shock. How does she know me? How do I respond without misspeaking, without offending someone so clearly not of this world? "You are just like me, child," Veyra says, her voice soft and melodic, each word falling like dew. "Can you not feel it?" Kai's grip tightens gently around my wrist. I anchor myself to that touch, steady, protective, familiar.

"I'm sorry, Veyra... I don't know what you mean," I say carefully, layering my voice with all the sincerity I can gather.

She tilts her head slightly. Her eyes glow. But her expression remains unreadable, still, serene, timeless. "You do not know? You truly do not know who you are?"

I shake my head, just slightly. A sting rises behind my eyes. "I don't," I whisper. "That's what I've been trying to figure out."

Veyra turns without a sound, gliding toward a nearby pond. A small turtle flails helplessly on its back. She kneels beside it, and with a single touch, graceful, instinctive, she rights it. The gesture ripples through the earth itself, subtle but undeniable. Then she turns back to me.

"Is that why you came to find me?" she asks, her voice like wind through the trees. "To remember what the world has made you forget?"

"I've been searching for guidance," I admit, my voice barely above a whisper. "To understand who I am and why I've always been told I'm different. Special. But no one has ever told me why." Veyra moves with a grace that doesn't seem human, her bare feet touching silently on the moss-covered earth.

She kneels by the edge of the pond again, where the small turtle drifts away in calm water. With a gentle touch, she trails her fingers through the surface. The ripples shimmer around her, like the water itself acknowledges her presence. She rises, turning back to me with a gaze that cuts through skin and bone. Like she sees everything. Everything I've hidden, even from myself.

"Child," she says. "You are a soul. A rare soul. A balance between what is and what was." Her eyes flick to Kai, her tone soft and steady. "And this young man"—she gestures—"is a part of that soul."

I glance up at him, my heart thrumming in my chest, eyes narrowing at Kai, at what I'm hearing. If she's saying what I think she is, then maybe, just maybe, these overwhelming feelings I've had all along weren't just mine alone. Kai's eyes meet mine, steady, warm. That familiar pull between us intensifies. The silence hums with meaning. The very blood in my veins starts to burn at his glance. His hazel eyes glow softly.

Anger surges through me. If Kai knew and said nothing, then he's been playing me from the start, using me like a pawn in whatever twisted game he's winning. "Did you know?"

He meets my stare. "No," he says, the word rough, honest—or close enough to make me want to believe it. "I just found out at the same time as you," Kai defends himself.

My eyes narrow. I don't fully believe him. Veyra continues, her words falling like sacred truth. "You feel it, don't you? The current between you both, it's ancient. It's powerful. The strongest energy I've felt in a pair in centuries." We're *not* a pair. But now is hardly the time to say that.

Kai steps forward. "There is an undeniable pull toward Mira," Kai says, his voice steady, reverent. "The connection I feel to her... it's unlike anything I've ever known."

Veyra tilts her head, gaze otherworldly, knowing. "She is the breath in your lungs? The hush of moonlight and the gleam of stars? She is the weight of gold and the warmth of flame?"

Her hand floats through the air in a graceful arc, as if painting the shape of my soul into existence. Kai's fingers slip from my wrist and interlace with mine. The moment his skin touches mine, something ignites, a spark that rushes through my blood like fire and salt and sunlight. And the anger I felt is just gone.

"She's everything I didn't know I was missing and everything I don't think I could survive losing," he says without hesitation, his hazel eyes shining with something fierce. Like a vow. Like truth. He looks at me like I'm something rare and irreplaceable. All the feelings inside me make sense now. We're bound by blood and prophecy. Something so much bigger than both of us.

The flutter in my chest is impossible to ignore. I've never wanted to kiss him more than in this moment. Veyra shifts her gaze to me. "And you?"

I pause, swallowing the storm inside me. "I feel the bond, the pull towards him." I admit. "But my walls are still up." Veyra's expression softens into something even more divine.

"There is no need for walls here. He is your shield, your storm. He was made to find you. To see you. You are safest with him. And he" —she flicks her eyes to Kai— "is safest with you." Her words melt something inside me I didn't realize was still frozen.

"I will trust you," I say quietly, lifting my eyes to Kai's. His gaze never wavers. He leans forward and presses his lips to my forehead. The touch is gentle but burns at the same time. And something in me shifts. For the first time, I'm not repulsed by the intensity between us. I don't flinch away from it. I welcome it. He makes me feel safe, like no one in this world could ever take me from him.

"Then you have my blessing," Veyra says, her voice like wind over water, soft, slow, eternal. "And my blessing is sacred. Do not break it. Do not bend it. You are tied together for eternity. Do not sever it. Not even death will unbind what I now seal." She extends her glowing hands, one toward Kai, one toward me. We place ours into hers. Her hands make both mine and Kai's hands glow brighter. Instantly, warmth floods through me. I feel it all.

His breath. His heartbeat, crashing in my ears like waves. His thoughts. His fear. His love. And his pain. She's connected us, body and soul. For a moment, it feels like I've absorbed a piece of him. Even his magic hums beneath my skin. The tether is complete. Eternal.

"You are now bound," Veyra says, her voice low and final. "Nothing can break this bond. Not even death."

Kai pulls his hand from hers but holds tightly to mine. "And what of death?" he asks, his voice shadowed with something heavy. "What if one of us dies?" Veyra's eyes, bright as starlight, turn to him.

"Then the other will die of heartbreak," she replies without hesitation. "There is no life without the other. And as for life after death, that is for you both to discover. You must find your way back to each other. In every lifetime. It is written." A hush falls around us. Thick with the weight of her words.

A strange peace seeps into my bones, though along with it comes fear. This life we lead is a dangerous one. Death isn't a distant threat, it's a constant shadow. And now, with our souls tied, if one of us falls, we both fall. We've become a target. Me, for whatever I am. And Kai, the Pirate Lord, now bound to me.

Kai nods slowly, steady as ever. "Understood," he says, voice quiet but resolute.

"Mira," Veyra says, her voice as soft as rain, yet each word lands with weight, "with the blood that flows through your veins, you are in danger. The witches whisper. The pirates plot. Even the mermaids stir beneath the tides. They are beginning to sense what you are. And a dark threat, the nyx, can smell your blood." My breath catches. I meet her gaze, heart pounding.

"My blood?" I ask. "What's in my blood?"

She shakes her head slowly. A serene sadness shines in her glowing eyes. "It is not what's in your blood, child. It is what your blood is. Who you are. What you were blessed with before your first breath. You are a very rare gem." She steps closer, her presence calm, but charged with something ethereal. Electric.

"Your blood carries a rare gift. One unseen in centuries. And because of that, your soul, your very essence, is the most important soul in existence. You're the balance between light and dark." The air around me grows heavier. The weight of her words settles into my bones like stone. My pulse stutters, uneven. I swallow hard, but the lump in my throat doesn't move.

I was told I was special my whole life. But no one ever told me why. Not like this. "You must find the fountain," Veyra continues, her voice wrapping around me like silk. "It holds the answers. And if it falls into the wrong hands..." She doesn't need to finish the sentence.

"What I was blessed with?" My voice cracks under the weight of confusion and frustration. My blood feels like it's on fire, boiling with unanswered questions. Rage builds in my chest. Not at Veyra, but at the unknown. At the way every answer always seems just out of reach. Like each question I ask is always answered with more riddles for me to figure out. Kai moves behind me, his hand gently pressing against the small of my back. His touch alters me. He must feel the anger pulsing off me, but his presence softens it, just enough.

Veyra doesn't flinch. Her glowing gaze remains calm. Celestial. "You will find your answers soon," she says, her tone airy but firm. "I cannot give them to you. I can only offer guidance, to lead you to the right waters." She turns and begins walking back toward her moss-covered home. But then she pauses and faces us fully.

"Seek out a mermaid named Anya. You will know her when you see her. She resides in the southern lagoon. Half the year, she calls it home. She can point you to those who know where to find the fountain." A flicker of something unreadable crosses her face. "But do not fully trust her," she adds. "Take what you need and leave. Immediately."

I glance at Kai, seeking stability in the storm. His expression shifts, serious and protective. I expect him to ask about the fountain. But instead, his voice is low and steady.

"How do I keep Mira safe? What can I do to protect her?" His question hits me like a tidal wave. He could've asked literally anything. Could've demanded a shortcut to the power he's been chasing. But instead, he chose me.

Veyra's face softens with something close to sorrow. Something sacred. "You protect her heart," she says, her voice like a vow. She locks eyes with Kai, deep, knowing, ensuring the weight of her words roots itself in his soul. Kai dips his head respectfully.

"Thank you for your time, Veyra," he says. "I know it's valuable. We'll be on our way." She offers a soft nod and turns, her glowing figure retreating toward the moss-covered doorway of her home. But a storm brews in my chest. We came for answers. Real answers. And now it feels like we're leaving with more riddles.

I step forward, unable to hold back. "Wait," I call out. "Veyra, is there anything else you can give us? Anything that might help us find the fountain?" She pauses mid-step. Slowly, she turns back, her eyes luminous beneath the dappled canopy light. Kai steps in front of me, slow and sure, like he isn't afraid to face a god-like being like her.

"Child," she says, her voice airy and ageless, "I have given you all that I can. Follow what I've said. Anya is your next step. And find out who you are. The sooner, the better."

Then, without another word, her form shimmers, flickering like a flame caught in the wind, and vanishes. Gone. I stare at the space where she stood, the hush of the jungle pressing in. Just like that, she was finished speaking.

"That went as well as it could have," I mutter to Kai, though the words taste bitter on my tongue. He looks at me with a sincerity that disarms me, jaw sharp, hazel eyes catching the faint glow of the jungle light.

"How do you feel?" Kai asks.

I snap my gaze to him, the humid air clinging to my skin like a second layer. "How do I feel?" My voice cuts sharp. "That I was just blindsided into having my soul tied to someone who's been my enemy since I could walk on a damn deck?" I let out a short, humorless laugh that tastes like anger. "Great. Just great. Now, let's go find that mermaid."

He opens his mouth, but I lift my hand before he can speak—a silent warning. The jungle hums around us, thick and alive, every sound too loud in the silence between us. I need a moment before my temper turns in a bunch of words that I'll regret.

We keep walking through the jungle, the air heavy with rain and the scent of earth. Leaves drip around us in a slow rhythm.

"I know you don't want to talk, and that's fine," Kai says, his voice low, careful. "But, Mira, you had to have felt it too—the reason we're so drawn to each other." His words carry softly through the mist. "I know I'm not the only one who felt the pull."

I stop and turn toward him. "I felt it." My fingers brush a rain-soaked leaf, gathering the small beads of water until they merge into one trembling drop. "I just... I don't know. I wasn't expecting that."

"That's fine," he says gently. "It'll take time."

I meet his gaze, unflinching. "Why are you so okay with this?" I ask. He smiles faintly, eyes glinting with something I can't quite name. "I don't get to pick and choose who I'm bound to. But if I have to be tied to someone, I'm glad it's someone as fearless as you."

Heat creeps up my neck and cheeks. I turn away before he can see it and keep moving through the dripping green. "How do you suppose we're going to find Anya?" I ask, pushing a branch out of our path.

"Well luckily, I know a few mermaids who can help guide us." Now I wish I let that branch hit him.

Of course he does. Mermaids, bewitching, elusive creatures. It's effortless to fall in love with one, yet nearly impossible to truly hold them. They choose who is worthy of their touch, and only the rarest hearts earn that trust. And that tattoo on his arm is burned into my brain, mocking me.

"I can feel your anger, Mira," Kai says, his voice dipping into a low laugh. "No need to be jealous, I know a few mermaids. I am a pirate, after all." His laugh is infuriatingly warm and as much as I hate to admit it, part of me likes it. But this isn't the time.

I forget he can feel everything now. Veyra's bond didn't just connect our souls, it bound our emotions. He knows my irritation, my walls, my flare of jealousy before I can even hide it. "It doesn't bother me," I snap, too quickly.

"If you say so," he replies with that maddening smirk. Then his hand finds the small of my back, steady, sure, guiding me gently through the underbrush. My traitorous body leans into him without resistance, betraying the storm still raging in my chest.

CHAPTER FIFTEEN

MIRA

BOUND

We didn't speak much as we made our way back through the jungle after leaving Veyra. The air was thick with unspoken words, but all I could hear was the steady, controlled beat of Kai's heart echoing in my ears. I felt every pulse of his emotions, his presence a constant hum beneath my skin. It was overwhelming, to feel so deeply what he was feeling, and yet it all still felt foreign. What was he thinking? What did he truly feel about me? I wish I could know. In a matter of seconds, Kai had become the most important person in my life.

When Veyra blesses you, it's said to be the most sacred thing in the world, an unbreakable bond. How can I possibly live up to that? How I can protect him as fiercely as I know he would protect me? The words he spoke to Veyra about me stir up a feeling I can't ignore. It's not just what he said, it's how he said it. The certainty in his voice. The way he looks at me like I'm something rare and precious, the most remarkable treasure he's ever found. And despite all my walls, despite how much I want to deny it, I wonder if I might be.

I can't deny the pull. Everything in the universe is screaming that he's the one. But gods, he's infuriating. The most stubborn, smart-mouthed man I've ever met. But when I stepped onto his ship, when the map led me straight to him... he was different. I was met with a kind of gentleness I didn't expect. Someone I could trust. I just didn't expect him to become this important.

Veyra's words keep echoing through my mind, the way she said he must protect me by protecting my heart. I can't stop wondering if he's truly capable of that. I want to believe he wouldn't break it. Not after everything. But the thought still lingers. He's a master of strategy, a man who bends fate until it breaks in his favor. Every word, every glance, feels like it's been placed with purpose, like I'm already caught in a web I never saw being spun. Why would I be any different? Just another pawn dressed up as destiny, another girl fooled into believing she was more than a means to an end.

It's too easy to imagine. And with the power I'm apparently carrying, whatever it is, underestimating me would be a deadly mistake. But would Kai underestimate me? Would he risk me for the map? For the answers? I don't want to believe that. I can't. But the truth is, there's so much I don't know about him and maybe even more that I don't know about myself. But for some reason, I feel like I know all of him at the same time.

We're heading to find the mermaid Kai supposedly knows, the one who can help us locate the lagoon Veyra mentioned. A mermaid. Just the word makes my stomach twist. Every time one is mentioned I think about that damn tattoo on his arm. I hate that he's close with them, that they seem to belong to his world in a way I never could. The thought of it makes my blood boil, jealousy simmering just beneath the surface. They're everything I'm not.

Dripping in allure, with their voluminous hair that moves through the air like it's still underwater, eyes that glimmer like the sea, fluttering lashes, and curves sculpted to tempt even the most faithful men into surrendering everything. Their beauty isn't just seen, it's felt. Everything about them is otherworldly, how they move, how they speak, how they own every room, every gaze, every silence. Their existence alone drips with bittersweet venom.

I've never struggled with self-confidence, not really. But whenever I'm near a mermaid, it's like the ground beneath me shifts. The world tilts, my senses blur, and something inside me begins to unravel. I know they can sense it. They smell weakness, unease, doubt, cracks. Mermaids lure. Sirens kill. They seduce you into death.

As beautiful as mermaids are, they aren't after your soul or your life, they're after your power, and they always seem to get what they want. That's what makes them dangerous. Kai knows them too well. What do they see in him? What has he given them? And worse, what has he shared?

"Mira?" Kai's voice comes from behind me. I'm sitting on the edge of the ship, feet dangling over the side, watching the sunset melt into the sea. But it's not the ocean that has me off balance. It's everything I don't know.

"I'm fine. I won't fall," I snap, not even bothering to turn around.

"I know you won't," he says calmly. "You just look deep in thought. I can feel your stress." I wonder, for a second, if he's only saying that because he doesn't want to feel the full weight of what I'm going through or if he actually gives a damn.

"Yeah, well, get used to it," I mutter. "I'm an angry, stressed-out, obsessive girl."

Kai moves closer, settling beside me. He wraps an arm around my lower back, gently, anchoring me like I might drift away if he doesn't. When his eyes find mine, there's no pity—just something fierce and unflinching, like he'd fight whatever breaks me if I'd only let him. Maybe I've been too hard on him. Maybe he really is trying. After all, he isn't the one who killed my mother.

"Mira," he says softly, "you are the center of my universe. I want to feel everything you do. I'll sit with you in silence for as long as it takes. I'll be there when you're red with rage, blue with sorrow, yellow with joy. I'll be there through it all." His voice doesn't shake. His eyes don't flinch.

"I've lost enough in my life to know when something's worth holding onto. And I'm holding onto *you*. So stop acting like I'm against you. I told you before, I don't like my integrity being questioned." The words hit like a wave to the chest. I blink, lips parted, trying to say something, anything, but nothing comes out. He hops down from the rail and walks away, confidence radiating off him.

His words pull me under, and I don't fight the drowning.

I hop down from the ledge of the ship and make my way toward our quarters. The wind howls, but my thoughts are louder. Everything's changing so quickly, and there's still so much I don't know. Maybe it's time I finally open my mother's journals.

CHAPTER SIXTEEN

KAI

CRIMSON TIDES

Finding Adella proves more difficult than I expected. She used to surface often, clinging to the edge of my ship with a smile full of secrets and seafoam, eager to spill whatever gossip the tides had whispered in her ears. Mermaids are eavesdroppers by nature, sly, curious, and dangerously perceptive. If anyone knows what the sirens are planning, it's them. And I need answers. About the sirens. About the kappas. About who or what is after Mira.

I haven't seen the kappas since Mira came aboard, and I hope it stays that way. There's something deeply wrong about the way they move, the way they look at you like you're already half-dead. They're selfish, erratic, and impossibly strong. If the corrupted Soul is building an army, I'd bet a bottle of blood rum that the kappas are already in it. What I'm afraid of is betrayal, sudden and clean. I know betrayal's language. I've taught men how to speak it. Trust is a currency they'll spend the moment blood tastes better than honor.

As the sun sinks below the horizon, staining the sky with fire, I give the order to head west, toward the last place I saw Adella. I haven't told Mira we're only looking for one mermaid. Not a group. I was worried she would start to ask questions, questions she didn't want the answers to. She has already pried more than enough into the story of my tattoos. But now, due to recent events, she has every right to know about every single one.

After talking to Mira, offering her the only kind of reassurance I know how, I can only hope it's enough.

We have the rest of our lives to unravel what this bond really means, but right now, getting to the fountain matters more than anything. I have to see this through, to become the pirate my father never was. The one who finishes what he couldn't. Every mile we sail is another step toward proving I'm more than his shadow. I can't ignore the black veins spreading from my scar anymore. The fountain might be the only thing that can save me.

It might be the key to unlocking what Mira is. The fountain is the most sacred power in all the sea, born of blood, legend, and prophecy. The ocean's changing—its obsidian waters churning, swallowing ships and creatures whole. It's building an army. Maybe Mira is the only one who can stop what's coming.

Pirates are closing in, and with a bounty that high on Mira's head, she's as good as dead if we don't move fast. Veyra warned us about the nyx—creatures even those with magic fear to name. But worse than them is the previous Soul herself. The Soul knows who Mira is, and she could strike at any moment. Ending the only thing standing between her and total dominion over the sea would shift the balance of the world itself.

Why hasn't she done it already? Maybe Mira isn't prey. Maybe she's the threat. Maybe the power inside her is stronger than the corrupted Soul's own. And if that's true—then she's not my salvation. She's my undoing.

The sun has gone to bed, and the moon has taken its place, casting silver light across the ship's deck. The stars burn brighter than usual, like even they know something is coming. I catch myself staring up at them, until a splash breaks the quiet. I glance down.

Adella.

She swims with effortless grace, circling the ship like a cat around prey, her presence unmistakable even before she speaks. I lift a hand, signaling to one of my crew to quietly slow the ship. "I heard you've been looking for me?" Her voice rolls over the air like silk, smooth, knowing, playful.

She emerges in the moonlight, perched atop a cannon, the closest thing on this ship to the sea. I make my way down to the gun deck, hoping she hasn't vanished already. But when I check each cannon, one by one, she's gone.

I hear her soft giggles echo through the gun deck. She's always loved the chase. The games that never truly end. The way she's teasing me now, hovering just out of reach, tugging at the air between us, tells me she's punishing me. Which can only mean one thing. She knows about Mira.

Adella is stunning, one of the most breathtaking mermaids I've ever seen. Her tail, a rare blend of violet and indigo, shimmers like oil on water, catching the moonlight with every graceful flick. She moves beneath the surface like liquid magic, more myth than creature.

We've shared a connection for years, forged in salt, silence, tears, and blood. She's healed my wounds with her tears, a sacred act, binding mermaid to man. A bond I'll never fully understand. Mermaids hold power that defies logic, beauty that bends the will, and magic that doesn't ask for permission. Adella's magic saved my life. She'll never let me forget that.

"Hello? Did you forget about me?" Her giggle rings out through the gun deck, light, teasing, infuriating. "Captain Kai? I know you hear me. Why aren't you looking for me?" She's baiting me. Dragging me into her favorite kind of game, taunting, elusive, always just out of reach.

"Adella," I call out, my voice edged in warning. "Come out. Stop this." A splash. Then silence.

I move cautiously toward the far cannon, senses sharp. And there she is, perched atop it like a siren on her throne, grinning down at me. Her bright blue eyes glitter with mischief. Crimson hair spills around her shoulders, catching the moonlight like fire woven with rubies. She is every bit the danger she pretends not to be.

"Hello, Kai," she purrs. "Did you miss me?" She leans forward, lips curved in a poisonous smile. "I heard you've got a new pet. How long until this one gets tossed back into the sea?" Jealousy doesn't suit her, but for a mermaid, it's the emotion they wear best. I step closer, locking eyes with her. "Call her that again, and I'll remind you why no one dares cross me."

"Oh," she spits, voice suddenly sharp, "you care for the thing?" I grit my teeth. I understand her pain, I do. But there was never a future for us. There couldn't be. She's a mermaid. And I'm not the boy she once healed.

"Adella," I say, my voice low, steady, "I get that you're hurt—"

"Hurt?" she cuts in, her voice dropping, low, cold, dangerous. Her features twist, the softness gone, replaced by something raw and furious. "No. I'm not hurt, Kai. I'm angry. And you don't want to see an angry mermaid." Her eyes blaze, twin storms locked on mine. "You lied to me," she hisses. "You said you'd find a cure. That you'd turn me human or become a merman yourself. I *believed* you. And now your soul is tied to her, an unbreakable bond, especially with Veyra involved."

I swallow hard. She's not wrong. I did promise her those things, once. I was barely eighteen, all raw edges and reckless dreams. We were drunk on possibility, on power, on the idea of forever. I never said those words to anyone else. Just her. And for a while, she was the only woman I let stay by my side. The only one who saw every piece of me, the rage, the ruin, the rare softness I never showed anyone else.

She meant something to me. She did. Just not enough to change everything about who I am. We both loved each other but we never chose. And love without choice, without sacrifice, was never going to survive.

She slips off the cannon with practiced grace, her tail slicing back into the sea, sharp and gleaming like a blade kissed by moonlight. "Of course I know about the bond," she spits, venom laced beneath every word. "I'm a mermaid, Kai. A force of nature. Whatever Veyra does, we feel. Instantly. So imagine how I felt, *truly* felt, when it happened. When my chest cracked open and I realized someone else had taken your heart." Her voice trembles, but her eyes, once as bright as sunlit water, have darkened with anger and betrayal.

"I'm sorry, Adella." My voice drops, steady but quiet. "I didn't mean for you to find out like that. I was going to tell you. But you and I... it was never meant to last. What we would've had to sacrifice, for either of us to switch, was too high a price."

She looks up at me sharply, the flicker of pain replaced by ice. Her eyes gleam like frozen sapphires, slicing through me. "I suppose you need me, then?" she says, too calm. "That's the only reason you'd come searching. Not for me. Not with your little toy on board..." My thoughts flick to Mira, hoping she's still in our quarters, out of earshot. Jealousy spews from Adella's every word.

"I do," I admit, meeting her gaze. "I need your help. I trust you. And I know you have the answers I'm looking for."

She flips backward into the water with a splash, vanishing beneath the surface. A moment passes. Then she emerges again, only her shoulders and head breaking the tide. The moonlight catches the strands of her hair, setting them ablaze. "Now why would I help you?" she purrs, voice slick with bitterness. "My heart was only ever soft for you, Kai. Now?" Her smile is a shard of glass. "Now it's stone."

"Because I know you care," I say, refusing to look away. "No matter how much venom you spit, I know you. You know who Mira is, what she means to the sea, and what she'll mean to you. If you don't help me, it hurts her. And if she's hurt..." I pause, letting the weight hang. "You know damn well that'll hurt you too."

She rolls her eyes, slowly, a hiss slipping through her teeth. "Mira." Her voice is edged with disgust. "She's the Soul of the Ocean. There hasn't been a new Soul in centuries." Her gaze sharpens. "She's valuable."

I watch her, still and quiet, as her mind begins to churn dangerous thoughts. This isn't just about love lost. This is about power. Adella was born to wield it but was never given the chance. She's a powerful mermaid from an even more powerful heritage. But she's the youngest in her family, so the throne doesn't belong to her.

"Adella," I warn, voice low. "Don't do anything reckless. Don't make me kill you." Her head snaps up, icy blue eyes wide, then narrowing, sparkling with dark amusement and wounded pride. "Oh? You'd kill me? For her?" she purrs, mocking me, but there's a raw edge beneath her words. "She must be quite the treasure for Kai Eldoris, the *Pirate Lord*, to unsheathe his sword so quickly. Especially towards the one he used to *love*." She laughs bitterly. "So what is it you need, Kai? Why must you seek me out?"

"I need you to tell me where I can find Anya."

Her expression shatters as fear flashes like lightning in her eyes. "Anya?" she echoes, voice tight.

"Yes." I narrow my gaze. "Is that a problem?"

She doesn't answer. She turns from me, the silence swelling, then slowly swims back, stopping just beneath the cannon. "She's... a very dark creature."

My brow creases. "What the hell does that mean?"

She props herself back onto the cannon, saltwater trailing down her hair and glistening tail. "She's dangerous, Kai. I wouldn't recommend going after her." Her tone turns sly, too casual to trust. "The sirens and her hunt mermaids for sport. That's what I've heard, anyway. But what do I know?" She shrugs, lips curling into a bitter smile. "I'm just a stupid, jealous mermaid."

I grab her face, fingers digging into her cheek. "Stop playing games, Adella. Tell me where to find her." She tries to jerk away, but I don't let go. Her eyes flash with something in between rage and need. "Don't kiss me, Kai." Her voice is a hiss. "Wouldn't want your little pet getting jealous."

My blood simmers. *Enough.* I shove her back, releasing her. "Anya is at the Wonder Lagoon," she snaps, eyes bright with venom. "You'll find it easily enough. Just don't say I didn't warn you." She sinks lower into the water, but pauses for one last dig. "Good luck training your new pet, sweets. See you soon. Or maybe not." With a flick of her shimmering tail, she vanishes into the onyx waves, leaving behind nothing but salt and silence.

CHAPTER SEVENTEEN

MIRA

FLAME & ASHES

It's time to finally go through my mother's and father's things. Part of me doesn't want to know the truth. Another part is terrified of what I might find. My parents had their fair share of secrets and enemies. I pray they hadn't crossed paths with the sirens.

I start with my mother's belongings. I reach for one of her journals, the cover worn and soft, the pages delicate, so fragile they feel like they might dissolve at my touch. Her handwriting is beautiful, flowing, like waves etched in ink. The date at the top reads over twenty-one years ago. Around the time I was born.

I settle onto the bed, the moonlight pouring through the window and over the pages. I slip into the past.

Mira. That's the name we've chosen for our daughter. It means female ruler, ocean, and admirable. Fitting, isn't it? She's not even born yet, and already we can feel how special she is. It's rare, nearly impossible, for a child to exist between someone like Bleu and someone like me. This is a blessing, a true miracle. I can't wait to meet her. To see who she takes after. If she's anything like Bleu, gods help us. We've agreed not to tell her everything. Not yet. If she's like him, she'll need time to grow into the truth. We'll wait until she's older, and when the time comes, we'll tell her together. For now, all we can do is protect her.

Taika granted me eighteen years in human form. Eighteen years to be her mother. When that time is up, I'll return to the ocean. If I die before then, my body will be cast back into the sea, and I'll return to what I truly am. She gave Mira the same blessing, or perhaps it's a curse. My only hope is that she survives. That she becomes strong, strong enough to face what's coming. Bleu and I will train her to be a weapon. That much we can do.

My heart stops. I stare at the page, rereading the words over and over, but they don't change. *"Return to what I truly am."* What the hell does she mean by that? She can't be what I think she is. She can't be. And if she is... Is she still out there? Is she alive? After all this time, the heartbreak, the tears, the suffering.

My pulse hammers in my ears, too loud, too fast. I can't tell if it's fear or rage crawling beneath my skin. My chest tightens, every breath shallow, like the world itself is closing in. The words blur, my vision swimming as I fight to steady myself, but the weight of what they might mean presses harder. If she's alive, everything I thought I understood—everything I've mourned—shatters.

I remember my father's face the day she died, haunted and hollow. I remember how carefully and gently he placed her in the ocean like it was some sacred ritual.

But I never asked why. I was so young. And now Taika's name is here. My blood runs cold. Why was she involved with my mother? And why didn't either of them ever tell me?

My mother looked so at peace as the ocean carried her away. But now that I think back, the water wasn't just red. It was black. I thought it was just the depth, the blood darkening against the salt. But no. Not anymore. Sirens bleed black. Mermaids bleed blue. Mortals bleed red. And my mother... My mother bled black.

The truth hits like a cannonball, tearing through everything I thought I knew. If my mother was a siren, what does that make me? All this talk about my blood being blessed. This isn't a blessing, this is a curse.

A violent chill snakes down my spine. I feel sick. Like the blood inside me isn't mine. Everything I've believed about myself has been a lie. And worse, Kai. Gods, Kai hates sirens with a fire I've felt in his every word, every warning. If he finds out what I am, what happens then?

I swallow hard and turn the page, my fingers trembling. The next entry is written in a different colored ink.

Mira is stunning. She takes after her father in almost every way, his eyes, his fire, his stubbornness. But there's something ancient in her too, something I can't quite explain. Human life will be difficult for her. The more people who discover who she truly is, the blood that flows through her veins, the more danger she'll face. There are those who would hunt her and kill her just for existing. She is the key to unlocking the fountain.

Bleu will make an excellent protector. A fierce teacher. He'll show her how to wield her strength, how to fight, and how to survive. But gods, I hope she gets to live first. To laugh. To be soft. To be a child.

I wish she could stay that way forever.

Not long after her birth, the sea came for her. Mermaids and sirens alike appeared, uninvited yet strangely welcome. I'd never seen them in harmony before, sirens, who usually hunt mermaids for sport, swimming side by side with them. It was unsettling. Beautiful. Almost like a dream. But it made my blood boil at the sight of it. It wasn't right.

Bleu went out to investigate. I remember the way he looked when he came back, ashen, urgent.

"We need to bring Mira," he said. "Now." I bundled her close and followed him outside. The ocean wasn't reflecting the moonlight, it was glowing from beneath. A thousand shades of blue and silver shimmered as mermaids and sirens sang in unison, their melody so achingly beautiful it stole the breath from my lungs. It felt like the entire sea was singing to her. For her.

Sea creatures circled the ship, dolphins, rays, even a whale in the distance, all swaying to the rhythm. And then, through the water's glow, my sister rose from the sea.

Anya.

"Dear Sirena," Anya said, "your baby has been chosen. Mira is the Soul of the Ocean, the one the sea has been waiting for, for thousands of years. It glows for her now. Her heart is pure gold, as beautiful as the sea itself. We must perform the ritual. Please... let me take her."

I looked at Bleu. He nodded. That was all I needed. With shaking hands, I gave Mira to Anya and followed them into the water. The ocean began to swirl the moment Mira touched it, like it knew her. Anya carried her to where the glow was brightest and placed her there. Then, a beam of light rose straight from the ocean, shooting up into the sky, connecting with the moon.

All of us stood, silent and still, watching in awe as my baby became something more, something the world would treasure, fear, and never understand. *Mira, the Soul of the Ocean. The most powerful gift the sea had ever given.*

The light slowly faded. Anya swam forward and lifted her gently from the glow, then handed her back to me. Her voice was soft, but there was weight behind every word. "She must be protected, Sirena. Her soul is rare. The ocean gave her to restore balance, but it will take her back if she's left unguarded. Never let her out of your sight."

I looked down at her. Mira was fast asleep in my arms. My precious, beautiful girl. My treasure. My soul.

I slam my mother's journal shut, completely and utterly stunned. Bile creeps up my throat, burning it, making me feel like I might throw up. "I'm the Soul of the Ocean?" I whisper. And Anya... she's my aunt? The weight of it all crashes over me like a tidal wave, my mother's secrets, the glowing ocean, the ritual, Anya. My mind spins, trying to piece it together.

That was the memory Kai unlocked in the pub.

"You are." Startled, I spin around so fast I nearly fall off the bed. Kai stands in the doorway, arms crossed, tattoos glowing faintly in the lantern's flame and the moonlight pouring through the windows.

"You knew?" I snap.

He steps toward the bed, calm as ever. "Of course I did, Mira. I've known since the day you stepped onto my ship. I vowed to protect you."

Anger surges through me like a rip current. "And you didn't think to tell me?! Don't you think that would've been helpful? What else are you hiding?" Kai shakes his head and sinks down beside me. Gently, he reaches out, brushing his fingers along the side of my face.

"Your story isn't mine to tell, treasure," he says softly, his hazel eyes catching the flicker of lantern light. "It's yours to uncover. But I'll be here, every step of the way." He glances past me toward the window, a slow, crooked smile rising to his lips. "And it looks like someone else is happy you're finally discovering who you are."

I turn, drawn to the glass. The ocean below burns like liquid starlight, glowing so brightly it stings my eyes. The water pulses with a rhythm that feels impossibly familiar, like a second heartbeat inside my chest. I look down and see my mother's wedding ring resting against my skin, shining just as fiercely as the sea. Something inside me shatters.

I bolt from the room, bare feet flying across the ship's wooden boards. Only the night crew is out, frozen at the strange glow rising from the depths. With a single sweep of his hand, Kai dismisses them.

I race to the railing, heart pounding like thunder. Below, sea creatures spiral through the illuminated water, carving patterns I can't begin to understand. My breath catches, too shallow, too tight. The pull is undeniable. The ocean is calling me home. I tear at my clothes, desperate to break free, to answer it. Then, his hand. Gentle, reassuring. Kai.

"I'll go with you," he says, his voice steady, low. He's already pulling off his shirt, moonlight tracing the lines of his skin like a blessing, igniting every single stroke of ink that stains his skin.

I hate to admit it, but gods help me. I love when his clothes are off. He's the most breathtaking man I've ever seen. All golden skin, sharp edges, and that storm in his eyes. We climb onto the edge of the ship, barefoot and balanced, hands clasped like we're anchoring each other to the world. We lock eyes. And we jump.

The second we hit the water, everything stops. Time. Sound. Thought. The glow swallows us whole. Moonlight flickers in his eyes and sparks through me, like the stars themselves fell from the sky and lit my blood on fire. All from one impossible look. Kai wraps his arms around my waist, steady and sure, holding me like I'm the very thing keeping him alive. He tries to hold on, but the ocean has other plans. And who are we to argue with her?

The current rips me from his grasp, dragging me under as if summoned by something ancient, sacred. Then, light. A radiant beam bursts through the deep, just like in my mother's journal. It wraps around me, warm and blinding, lifting me from the sea's floor like I'm nothing but breath and starlight.

I rise, suspended between sea and sky, hovering above the waves and under the stars. And then, I feel everything. I feel the waves battering distant cliffs, their fury echoing inside my chest. I feel whirlpools spinning like storms unchained, wild and endless. I feel sea creatures gliding far below, silent and sure, wrapped in the hush of the deep. I feel the ocean's pulse. Her rhythm. Her rage. Her reverence.

For the first time in my life, I feel whole. I've found myself. I've found home. It's as if the very heart of the ocean replaced mine with hers.

I glance down and see Kai in the water, staring up at me. There's something in his eyes, something rare. He looks proud. At peace. Like he's known this all along, and now I finally do too. Like he's my biggest fan, quietly cheering me on.

The ocean cradles me back to the ship's deck. My feet touch wood once more, soaked but steady. Kai swims toward the hull, ready to climb aboard, just about to reach for the ladder on the side of the ship, until the beam returns. This time, for him. The sea claims him gently, lifting him the way it did me. A blessing. A bond. The ocean chose him too, as the other half of my soul.

The water lowers him beside me, placing us back together where we belong. Below us, sea creatures scatter like falling stars. The glow fades into a soft shimmer, retreating until only moonlight remains, dancing across the waves, like the stars themselves have chosen to rest on the surface of the ocean.

Kai looks at me like I'm the only thing that exists, like the sea could dry, the stars could fall, the sky could shatter, and he'd still only see me.

He steps closer, the space between us dissolving like it was never there. One hand finds the small of my back, warm, certain, while the other rises to cradle my face, his thumb grazing my cheek with a reverence that makes my heart ache. Saltwater drips from his dark, wavy hair, landing on my skin, trailing down my neck like the ocean is still trying to reach me through him.

"You're not just my greatest treasure, Mira," he murmurs, voice husky and low. "You're my compass. My reason. You're extraordinary." Then his lips find mine.

My body folds into his without hesitation, without fear. I feel everything, the heat of his touch, the storm building in his chest, the sacred promise buried between every beat of our hearts. The ocean didn't just bless me. It blessed *us*. He's the only thing I'd burn the world for and the only one I'd let the flames take me, if it meant keeping him.

His hands roam, tracing the outline of my waist, my spine, my shoulders, as if he's memorizing every piece of me. He kisses me again, deeper this time, like he's been waiting his whole life for this. For me. And when his lips trail down my neck, my breath catches and sparks ignite beneath my skin.

With effortless strength, he lifts me into his arms like I weigh nothing. And in that moment, wrapped in his arms, with the sea below and the stars above, I know this is where I belong.

I'm straddling his body, my legs barely able to wrap around his torso, feeling the heat of him beneath me. He carries me to our quarters, his hands never once leaving my skin. When he lays me down, it's like I'm something sacred and holy. His gaze roams over me with a hunger that sends shivers down my spine.

He starts at my ear, his lips brushing against it with maddening slowness. Each kiss trails down my neck, across my collarbone, down the length of my spine, igniting sparks along every nerve. He takes his time, worshipping every inch of me.

His lips find my breasts, soft, aching, and my breath hitches. I want more. I *need* more. But he's deliberate, torturously slow, letting his mouth explore me like he's tasting something rare. His hand glides lower, fingers barely brushing the edge of my underwear, and the teasing touch makes my hips rise toward him, instinctive and desperate.

"What are you waiting for?" I whisper, the words breathless, tangled in the haze between us. He looks up, eyes dark and wicked, lit with a storm I recognize all too well. There's something devastating about the way he's worshiping my body, holding back only because he knows it drives me mad.

"For you to beg," he murmurs, voice like smoke and sin, a smirk ghosting across his lips. Gods, he's insufferable. And I want him so badly it hurts. I twist my fingers into his hair, tugging just enough to make him growl low in his throat. "Kiss me," I breathe. "Please... just do it."

His smirk lingers, but his eyes are reverent. And when his lips finally move lower, everything else disappears. The world dissolves, time stops, and all that's left is us. Right here. Right now. In this moment, I am everything. He is everything.

His tongue moves in circles, slow and knowing, hitting every spot like he's been mapping my body in dreams long before this night. One hand slides up, cupping my breast with just enough pressure to make me gasp, while the other finds its way between my thighs, confident, relentless.

Then his finger slides inside me. I arch, a sharp cry ripping from my throat. My hands fist the sheets, legs trembling as he moves with more purpose, his strokes deep and maddening, tongue working in tandem, building a rhythm that sends sparks spiraling through me. Between his tongue and his fingers, I am completely helpless.

He doesn't stop. He devours me. Faster, deeper, like the ocean itself has taken over, waves crashing through me with every motion. My toes curl. My vision blurs. My body pulses so hard I feel like I might come undone. Then, I do.

Pleasure rips through me like lightning, white-hot and unrelenting. I shatter beneath his mouth, my whole body clenching, unraveling, set ablaze. I gasp for air, floating, weightless in the aftermath.

Kai pulls back, his breath heavy, lips glistening. He stares up at me, gaze smoldering. "Pure and utter perfection," he whispers, taking in all of me with a knowing glance.

I can't speak. I just stare, memorizing every inch of him. The way his soaked hair clings to his face. The golden sheen of his skin in the lantern light. The rise and fall of his chest, like I've knocked the breath from his lungs. Like he felt it too. He is breathtaking.

I've always wondered what it would be like. What he would be like. I'd heard the whispers. Seen the way women looked at him, hungry, enchanted, falling over themselves for a glimpse, a glance, a moment. I never truly understood the pull until now. I know why they all craved him. And more importantly, now I know he's mine.

Kai moves up toward me, arms wrapping around my waist, drawing me into him until there's not a breath between us. He presses his forehead to mine, his chest rising and falling against mine as he breathes me in like I'm the only thing keeping him alive.

"You ruin me," he says, the words breaking against his breath. "You tear through my life and leave nothing standing. Nothing makes sense unless it's you. If you're the fire, then chain me to the stake, let the flames eat me alive. I'd burn, screaming your name, if it meant you'd keep looking at me like this, like you've already decided whether to save me or destroy me."

My heart stops, because there it is. A confession, everything out in the open. This is real.

He pulls the covers over us, sealing us in warmth, the outside world fading away. He kisses the top of my head, his arms locking around me like he's afraid I'll vanish. I never want to leave this moment.

Not ever. No more words are spoken. We fall asleep wrapped in each other, our bodies tangled, our souls finally, blessedly, at peace.

CHAPTER EIGHTEEN

MIRA

DROWNED TRUTHS

We're headed to Wonder Lagoon, Anya's home. I stare out at the sea, endless, full of secrets. Anya, my aunt. Today, I forced myself to keep reading. My mother's journals and truths. She once wrote that if she died in her human form, she'd return to her original form in the ocean.

Her death is imprinted in my mind. My father cradling her lifeless body, holding her like it was the last piece of him that still made sense. And then, placing her into the sea with this reverence. He stood there for years. *Years.* Staring out like he was waiting for a ghost to rise from the waves.

I can't be a siren. I refuse to be. There's no way. If I were, why would the ocean choose me? Why would she bless something so vile, so feared, to become her soul? Sirens are cruel. Cold. Heartless. Their souls are twisted, dark things wrapped in terrifying beauty and wicked lies. Mine can't be. Can it? Even though they've protected me my entire life, this is not what I want.

The thought makes my skin crawl. My chest tightens like it's caving in around my heart. Would Kai still want me if he found out? If he really knew what I am, what I might be? Or does he already know?

The questions slice like knives through my sanity one by one. My mind is spinning, thoughts crashing like a storm against a rocky shore. But through the chaos, one fear rises louder than the rest, sharp and unrelenting: What if I lose him?

He's my anchor. My constant. The one I'm tied to, in more ways than I can explain. But I don't want to be bound to someone who might come to hate me. Who might look at me and see only the blood he despises most. Desperate for answers, I reach for one of my father's journals, the oldest one I can find, dated years before I was born. The black leather is soft and fraying at the corners, pages brittle from salt and time. I didn't expect much. Honestly, I didn't think he'd written anything at all.

He was a pirate, after all. Most of them can't read. And almost none of them write. But my father was never like most men.

A thin leather cord holds it shut, wound tight like a secret. I untie it carefully, but the strap disintegrates in my fingers.

Inside, the pages are yellowed and soft, edges curling like they'd once been damp. Some were stained, the ink blurred and bleeding, and for a moment I wondered if the sea had gotten to them... or if something else had. But it wasn't tears.

My father didn't cry. He was a storm. A myth. A man made of salt and steel. Most of the pages were blank, like he'd meant to say something but couldn't find the words or never dared to write them down.

Until I found it. One single page. Half-filled in his unmistakable, rough handwriting, like each letter had been carved instead of written. As if even his thoughts had weight.

Sirena.

Queen of the bloody sirens.

She came to my ship like a ghost, quiet, glowing.

Stars in her hair. Death in her voice.

I didn't fight it.

Didn't want to.

She looked me in the eye. Said,

"Captain Bleu, I've waited a long time. Let me show you a world you'll love."

I stepped off my ship. Willing to go.

Into the black.

Her hand in mine, pulling me under.

Could breathe. Somehow.

Felt like she gave me her soul just so I wouldn't drown.

Couldn't see at first. Water like tar, black and thick.

Then it cleared.

She was floating. Watching me.

Eyes glowing like moonfire.

Skin pale. Shining.

She touched my face.

"I want you to live with me here. You would be happy here. Let me take you with me when you are ready."

Then she took my hand again, pulled me up to the surface...

...and vanished like mist.

I waited.

Gods, I waited every damn day. Starin' at the sea, hopin' to see her again.

I knew then—she was mine. Whatever the cost.

My mother is the queen of sirens? The thought settles in like an anchor in my chest, dragging down everything I thought I knew. It would explain everything, the reason why sirens never came for me. They tore through crews without mercy, left nothing but bones and blood in their wake. But me? They never laid a hand on me.

Even as a child, I remember one of them, her face just above the waterline, watching me with something close to concern. She wasn't trying to harm me. She was making sure I was okay.

They weren't attacking. They were protecting. Watching over their queen and her heir. But my father. I saw him die dragged under by a siren.

Or...

Was that her? Was it my mother? Had she come back to take him home? Had the sirens revived their queen from the dead? Was it a final reunion, or a punishment?

And Taika. Gods, Taika. What kind of dark, ancient magic did she twist to make it happen?

"What's wrong, treasure?" Kai's voice cuts through my thoughts, low and full of concern. He's watching me closely, too closely. He always feels it when my heart starts to race. I quickly slip my father's journal back into my bag, trying to steady my breath.

"It's nothing," I lie. "Just reading some of my father's entries."

His eyes narrow, jaw tightening. "You don't have to lie to me, Mira." His voice softens, but there's something sharp beneath it. Worry. Maybe fear. "I can feel your heart beating out of your chest." My chest tightens even more. I look away, staring anywhere but at him. "You wouldn't understand," I murmured. "I can't tell you."

He steps closer. "Why not?"

"Because," I swallow hard, "if I do, you might never look at me the same again." Silence falls between us. Then, barely above a whisper I add, "You'd kill me."

My heart pounds faster with the realization, Kai has spent his entire life hunting sirens. They've taken his crew, his family... everything. "Kill you?" His voice is quiet, but it hits me like thunder. "Are you mad?" I feel a sudden bolt of pure anger rush through me, his emotions running wild through my veins. I finally look up, startled.

"I would never be the one to put a dagger through your heart." His eyes search mine, steady and unwavering. "If you're scared I'll find something out, Mira, I already know. I've just been waiting for you to say it." He kneels in front of me, soothing me with his presence. I try to hold his gaze but end up looking down, picking at my nails. I feel like a helpless child again. Kai gently takes my hand. "I'm here for you. When you're ready." He starts to stand, but I grip his hand tighter, the words flying from my mouth before I can stop them.

"Am I a siren?" Silence. I brace myself for disgust. For rage. But instead, Kai exhales, and for the first time, I see relief flash across his face.

"Yes," he says softly. "The blood that runs through your veins is part siren." I blink, stunned. "And that's not a curse, Mira. It's a gift. It's a good thing that you know."

I let out a shaky breath at his words. My voice cracks as I glance back at him. "But this doesn't bother you?" I ask. "I have the blood of the creatures you hate coursing through my veins."

Kai kneels again, his hand rising to caress my cheek. His touch is gentle. Steady. "If it bothered me," he says softly, "I would've left you the second you boarded my ship." His thumb brushes across my skin. "I knew, Mira. I knew when Veyra bound our souls together."

His eyes lock with mine, unwavering. "I'll be by your side. Always. No matter who you are. No matter what you are. Nothing you say, nothing that runs through your veins, could ever scare me away." Gods, he always knows exactly what to say. A smile slips across my lips, small but real. He kisses me, sealing the promise between us.

"Thank you," I whisper, the words catching on a breath I didn't know I was holding. My chest feels lighter, like an anchor has finally been lifted. Kai studies me, then reaches up to tuck a loose strand of hair behind my ear.

"One more thing," I murmur.

He tilts his head. "Yes?"

"My mother." I pause. "She's the queen of them. The sirens." Kai doesn't flinch, but the air shifts between us, taut and heavy. "I think she's still alive," I breathe. "And maybe... maybe my father is too." The words feel foreign as they leave my mouth. Even now, I'm struggling to believe them myself.

His brow lifts with a flicker of surprise. "You're sure?"

I shake my head. "No, I'm not sure. But I feel it. Deep in my gut." I clutch the edge of the table, trying to keep myself grounded. "I know she's the queen. That much, I'm certain of." He stays silent, listening.

I hand Kai my father's journal. "Be gentle," I say quietly, my thumb brushing over the worn spine before letting go. He takes it like it's something sacred, his fingers careful, reverent even. I point to the first sentence my father ever wrote.

Kai's eyes widen as he reads, the sun setting his hazels ablaze. His jaw tightens, a slow exhale slipping through his lips as if the words are sinking in too deep to ignore. "I see," he says finally, his voice low. He's processing.

"And my mother's journal says that if she dies in her human form, she returns to her original one." I meet his gaze. "When my father placed her body in the ocean, her blood turned black." Kai's eyes narrow slightly, piecing things together. "And we both know," I continue, my voice firm despite the quake in my heart, "Sirens bleed black, just like the water they swim in."

"And what happened after?" Kai asks quietly, his voice dipping low. "Where did her body go?"

I look down again, my voice small. "I was so young. I just remember her body slipping into the ocean. It was peaceful. Like the sea was welcoming her home. And my father, he never stopped staring out at sea, always looking for her."

Kai's eyes darken with thought. He glances away for a second, jaw tightening. "Hmm," he murmurs, more to himself than to me.

"I know it sounds insane," I say quickly, trying to fill the silence. "But I think they're alive. Both of them. I don't know where, or how, but"—I press my hand against my chest, right over my heart—"I feel it. Like a tide pulling me somewhere."

I hesitate, then say quietly, "There's something else. Anya, she's my mother's sister." Kai's head snaps toward me. I catch the flicker in his eyes, the realization setting in. The pieces aligning. "That makes her my aunt," I add, barely above a whisper. "I'm only just starting to make sense of it, but it changes everything."

"I believe you," Kai says without hesitation. "We'll find your parents. Or they'll find us first. With the ocean blessing you like she did, creatures will talk. If your mother really is the queen..." His gaze locks with mine. "She'll feel it. She'll come."

I nod slowly, the weight in my chest beginning to lift, just a little. Then he smirks softly. "Also, Mira, nothing you say will ever sound insane to me." I feel my face grow warm, and a small smile tugs at my lips.

I glance at him. "With your father killing my mother the way he did," I say carefully, "you and he might've been targets this whole time. From both sides. The sirens and the mermaids."

The words hang between us, heavy with implication.

Confusion swirls beneath the surface of my thoughts. How could my mother and Anya be sisters, one a siren, the other a mermaid? It doesn't make sense. But maybe it's not supposed to. Not yet. It seems that hybrids run in the family.

Kai doesn't flinch. He just steps closer. "Then let them come for me. I'll handle whatever comes at us. Sirens don't scare me, treasure," he adds.

I'm not sure he fully understands what he's saying, not really. Sirens aren't just deadly, they're nightmares. A glance at his arm reminds me that he should know this better than I do.

But Kai's fear isn't of them. "What scares me," he says, standing now, "is knowing how unsafe you are. You're a massive target, Mira. Every creature, every pirate, anyone worth their salt, is looking for you. One mermaid whispering in the wrong ear is all it takes. And there are too many cursed ears to whisper into."

He moves to the door. "We should see how close we are to Wonder Lagoon. And Mira, never, ever trust a mermaid. Their beauty blinds, their words deceive, and their loyalty is paper-thin. That includes Anya.

Family ties or not, they are untrustworthy. Veyra sent us to her for a reason. We find it and then we leave."

I rise, following him toward the door. "We're not just looking for answers about me," I say, voice calm but certain. "We need help finding the fountain." I pause, glancing out at the waves. "And something tells me Anya won't give it up so easily."

CHAPTER NINETEEN

KAI

HOLY & HAUNTED

"How close are we, Jay?" The sun is just beginning to stretch its golden limbs across the horizon, my favorite time of day. The world bathes in amber, shadows long and soft, and the ocean shimmers like molten gold beneath us. There's something sacred about this light, like the sea is holding its breath, waiting for the day to start.

"I'd say we'll be there shortly." Jay takes a drag from his pipe. "Mermaids, Cap? That's what you're after now?"

I cut him a look, sharp and quick. "We're not after them to hurt them. We're after answers."

"Aye, and what of the one that always used to pay you late-night visits?" he says.

I hold his stare. "We are not to speak of her. Not with Mira on board this vessel." My voice doesn't falter.

Then, after a beat: "Mira is something special, isn't she?" His glance is sly, half-curious, half-knowing. He shouldn't ask, but if anyone could, it's Jay.

"Yes," I say, my gaze turning forward again. "She is. And if you ever see her in danger, especially if I'm not there, I want you to protect her with your life."

Jay doesn't hesitate. "Understood, Cap."

I leave him at the helm and head down to the main deck. Morning silence wraps around me, broken only by the rhythmic crash of waves and the occasional whistle of wind through the rigging. I lean over the edge to watch the dolphins trailing us, sleek, silver shapes leaping in and out of the surf like they're escorting us home.

The scent of salt and damp wood fills my lungs. The deck slick beneath my boots, still holding the night's chill. There's nothing like the sea at dawn, silent and waiting. And then, just ahead, I see it—Wonder Lagoon, rising from the ocean like a secret whispered by the tides. A crescent-shaped sliver of land cradles a lagoon of impossibly clear water that shimmers in shades of turquoise, jade, violet, and gold, revealing coral reefs below like a painter's palette spilled across the ocean floor. Schools of fish flicker between them like living jewels, while the lagoon curves in a perfect U-shape, hugged by lush trees, wildflowers blooming in every color, and crystals that glint like scattered stars under the sun.

The reefs form a natural barrier. No ship could dock near their sacred home. Only those they allow in ever reach the shore. And they always know when someone's coming. It's up to them what happens next.

I move to find Mira, to warn her, tell her to prepare herself. But when I turn, she's already there, standing beside Jay like she's been part of this crew her entire life.

Her long, dark curls dance in the sea breeze, catching streaks of gold from the rising sun. She's wearing a crisp white shirt, sleeves rolled to reveal her forearms, tucked into a snug black corset that hugs every curve with wicked precision. Her dark pants lace at the sides, and her boots, scuffed and worn, look like they've seen battles and begged for more. And atop her head, her father's captain's hat tilts low over her brow.

She looks like the fiercest damn pirate I've ever laid eyes on. And she's *mine*. She must feel me staring, because her gaze flicks down for a second, that soft, knowing smile playing on her lips. That smile is the most dangerous thing.

Mira descends from the helm toward me, every step confident, calculated. "Morning, Kai. Looks like we've made it to Wonder Lagoon." Her voice is thick with sleep, rough around the edges.

"We have," I say, eyes lingering on her. "You ready?"

She cocks her head, that half smile curving higher. "I always am. The question is, are you?"

I grin. "Bold words for someone who still has yet to outsail me."

She raises a brow. "I wasn't aware this was a competition."

"Oh, with you, it always is."

She chuckles, brushing past me, her scent of vanilla and sea salt following her as her shoulder intentionally grazes mine, a silent challenge. I turn to follow, grinning like a fool. Whatever waits for us in that lagoon... I already know the most dangerous thing is walking just ahead of me.

As we near the lagoon, Mira stands beside me, calm. There's something about her stillness that unsettles me, like she already knows what's waiting for us and has quietly made peace with it. I haven't. Whatever fate lies ahead, I will never accept one where she's hurt, or worse, lost to me. Feelings I'm having to get used to now. There's no more fighting the pull I feel towards her.

Adella's warning echoes in the back of my mind. She said Anya couldn't be trusted. Called her venomous and manipulative. Veyra said the same, and she's not the type to toss around judgment lightly. However, she's the one who sent us here.

Sure, Adella's words that night were laced with jealousy, that much was obvious. But even in her madness, she cares in her own twisted way. She wouldn't say something just to get under my skin. Not about her. She's not reckless enough to cross someone like Mira, not the daughter of the Siren Queen, not the new Soul of the Ocean. I'm still trying to make sense of how I ended up tied to a woman like that. A woman no man deserves.

If Adella had anything to do with sabotaging Mira, she'd be as good as dead. No one would protect her. Not even me. So if she's warning me about Anya? I'm listening. Because Mira's walking into that lagoon like she's ready to face a storm. And I'll be damned if I let her face it alone. So I'll go in with my guard up and I won't leave Mira's side. Not for a second.

The lagoon is breathtaking, unlike anything I've ever seen. It feels like a dream, like if I blink too long, it'll vanish.

At the center of the lagoon, a massive rock formation juts from the water like a throne carved by the tides. It has to be Anya's.

We lower the small boat to head toward shore. In the distance, I catch the movement of mermaids and mermen. Their laughter echoes faintly over the water. Younglings dart between them, fearless, playful. This is their sanctuary, a hidden world for creatures too mesmerizing to exist anywhere else.

One by one we descend the ladder on the side of the ship to board the boat. First me, then Jay, Smith, and Nate, another crewmate Mira insisted on bringing. When it's Mira's turn, I place my hands on her hips and lift her with ease, steadying her as she steps aboard. Her fingers linger on my shoulders before she settles beside me. I'll take any excuse now to touch, especially after knowing exactly what she tastes like.

A splash to my right draws my attention. I glance into the water.

"You two must come alone. No one else."

The voice is sweet, too sweet. A mermaid rises from the lagoon, wavy green hair cascading down her back like her hair was made from seaweed, eyes the color of blooming red roses, and a shimmering green tail that flicks lazily behind her. Her beauty is sharp, stunning, like it was crafted to disarm.

"Keep the ship safe," I tell the others. "We'll return shortly." Jay looks like he wants to argue, but one glance at Mira tells him now's not the time.

"I wonder why she wants us to come alone," Mira murmurs, head on a swivel.

I grip the oars and begin to paddle us forward. "Privacy," I say gently. "This place is their sanctuary. They'll only allow in who they trust." I do my best to sound sincere, even though a knot of unease coils tight in my chest. I hate that I haven't told her about my encounter with Adella yet, or about Adella at all.

We glide through the glittering water, the boat silent except for the soft dip and pull of the oars. The lagoon holds its breath with us.

I glance forward and I see them. Eyes. Dozens at first, then more mermaids and merman. Even younglings. Slipping up from the water's edge, watching with unreadable expressions, their gazes fixed. There must be over a hundred. They're waiting, expectant.

Mira and I share a wordless glance. We came here for answers. For guidance. For a path to the fountain. But right now, we're more lost than ever.

A few mermen begin to push the boat forward, their sleek tails slicing effortlessly through the water. They guide us toward the stone formation that rises like a throne, anchored in the very heart of the lagoon. With a soft thud, the boat touches the edge of the rock, and silence falls like a curtain.

We step out, our boots crunching against the sand that sticks to the slick stone. The quiet isn't just still, it's weighted and thick with tension. Thoughts buzz around me like screams with no mouths to voice them. No one speaks, but the magic here does. It pulses in the water and thrums in the stone, humming through my bones like a warning.

I hate this kind of uncertainty. I wish I could use my magic to read mermaids and sirens the way I can with humans. But it doesn't work on them, at least, not yet. Maybe I haven't unlocked that part of myself, or maybe it's locked for a reason.

Beside me, Mira's heart pounds like a war drum. I reach for her hand without thinking, lacing my fingers through hers, brushing my thumb across her skin. Her breath hitches, then steadies. We don't speak, both bracing for whatever comes next.

All eyes shift at once. I follow their gaze just in time to catch a dark shape slicing through the water with alarming speed. Her tail skims the surface like a shark's fin, sending sharp ripples across the lagoon. Instinct takes over. I step in front of Mira, arm out, bracing for whatever is about to happen.

Then she emerged. A dark mermaid, unmistakenly Siren blooded. Her hair was jet black, sleek and straight, cascading like ink. Her skin pale as moonlight. Lips blood red. Eyes a deep, unsettling brown that seemed to see too much. Her obsidian tail shimmered beneath the surface, catching slivers of morning light and turning them into blades. She was the darkest mermaid I'd ever seen, elegant, dangerous, and primordial.

Maybe Adella was right. Maybe this was a mistake. Here we are, stranded at the center of their sanctuary.

"Mira, darling. My, how you've grown," the siren rasps, her voice gravelly and raw, like it had been dragged across the very sand that sat atop this throne.

Mira steps beside me, squaring her shoulders, revealing herself. "Anya?" she asked, voice steady, barely, but threaded with steel.

Anya purrs, drifting closer to the edge of the throne. She lifts a hand with slow, deliberate grace, every movement meant to draw attention, to seduce, to unsettle. "Of course, who else? Were you expecting someone else to greet you?" Mira didn't answer. And oddly, her heartbeat stayed steady. Maybe she already knew more than she was letting on.

"No need to be afraid, darling," Anya croons, her voice wrapping around us like smoke. "I would never hurt you. The others, however..." She sweeps her hands to either side, gesturing toward the mermaids circling the lagoon like predators waiting for the word to strike. "I can't speak for them."

Mira stands tall, unwavering. "I'm not afraid of you." The words drip from her mouth like honey set on fire.

Anya smiles, slowly, eerily, like she's seen the inside of more souls than we could count. I lock eyes with her. All I have is instinct, and hers screams danger.

"You must be Kai," she says finally, her gaze sliding to me like a blade. "The infamous Pirate Lord I've heard so much about. You slayed my dear Kraken. What a shame." Her smile was sweet, but her eyes were ice. Of course the Kraken was her pet. "Unfortunately, love, you can't always be her savior."

"I'm not trying to be," I say evenly. "She doesn't need one. But make no mistake, she's not for you. Or them. We came to talk. Nothing more." Anya's expression doesn't shift. Then, in one seamless ripple, she glides forward, nearing the edge of the rock where we stand.

"Mira," she says, her voice a lullaby laced with rot. "You've finally found who you are. But that siren blood of yours... it makes things a little tricky, doesn't it?" Her smile curls like a blade, sharp and knowing. "Have you ever thought about taking a swim? A deep one?" There's a look in her eyes now, something ageless and hungry, but also something else. A flicker of sorrow? Guilt? It is gone before I can name it.

Before I can even turn to look at Mira, to see how she'd taken those words, a splash cracks through the air. A mermaid bursts from the water like a shot from a cannon and yanks her under. I throw my hand out, hoping to latch on to any bit of her. "Mira!" I shout.

I lunge for the edge of the rock, heart in my throat, but Anya moves first. She slams into me, hissing like a serpent. Her black tail slices through the air, and her claws, long, thin, and wickedly curved, rake across my legs, tearing flesh and lighting my nerves on fire.

"Stay put, boy," she sneers, circling me like prey. That smile never leaves her lips, cruel and gleaming, like she wants to rip that title from me letter by letter. Two mermen surface behind me, their hands locking onto my arms like iron shackles. I thrash, but it's useless. Panic surges through me. Mira still hasn't breached the surface. There aren't even bubbles coming up for air. They're drowning her.

"If you care about her at all," Anya says, "you'll stop fighting me." Her tone was calm, detached, maddening. "I have no desire to see her die. I only want to see what she's capable of." She tilts her head, studying me like I'm some fragile, fleeting thing. "She must be tested. She must be prepared. You understand that, don't you?"

I stare at her, really stare, and felt something venomous rise in me. Pure, blinding hatred. This wasn't just a hunger for power. This was personal and twisted. And I will kill her for it. I will gut this monstrous aunt of hers and drag Mira up from the depths with my own hands.

"If you dive after her, you'll only die," Anya says sharply, her voice coiling like a whip. "You can't breathe down there, you sad mortal man. Mira can. She just doesn't know it yet." The surface of the lagoon is still. Too still. No bubbles. No movement. Just silence.

The only thing keeping me from losing my mind is the beat of her heart, steady and strong. I can feel it. She is alive, still holding on. But for how long?

Anya might be right; Mira should be able to breathe underwater. But forcing her down there like this? That, I can't accept. "Let. Her. Go." My voice is low, but it carries, laced with fury. My eyes darken and my jaw ticks.

Anya cocks her head, lips curling in amusement. "Stupid, stupid boy," she mutters, shaking her head like I am some child who doesn't understand the rules of her world. Then she flicks her wrist, dark and razor-sharp scales shimmering along her arms, claws gleaming like obsidian. "Your wish is granted." Before I can move, the mermen shove me off the rock and into the deep.

The surface vanishes above me, just a ripple of distorted light. Silence swallows everything. I open my eyes to a world cloaked in blue, shadows shifting all around. My lungs are already screaming, but I shove the panic down. Saltwater stings my eyes. I spin slowly, searching. No sign of Mira. Just flashes of tails darting between shafts of light like specters. Dozens of them, maybe more, circling and watching.

Where the fuck did they take her? Then, a radiant pulse of light tears through the deep like a heartbeat. I turn, drawn to it. There she is. Mira.

She's *glowing*.

Her entire body is lit from within, a soft, luminous shimmer, like sunlight trapped underwater. She hovers in the center of a wide circle of mermaids, each with their heads bowed in reverence, worshiping her. Mira floats like she belonged to this world, like it answers to her.

I don't have time to admire her. A searing pain rips through my arm. I spin, blood swirling in red spirals through the water. A dark blur glides past.

Anya.

Her eyes lock with mine, wide, merciless, and hungry. She grins. Another slash. This one across my side. She's too fast. Down here, she's not a woman, but a shadow with teeth.

I grit against the pain, my lungs already aching for air, and yank my knife from its sheath. The same blade I once buried in a siren's side when I was just a boy. I survived that siren attack. I'll survive her.

She comes again, lightning quick. But this time, I'm ready. I twist mid-strike, driving the blade into her side. Black blood erupts around us, thick and inky. She shrieks, a sound like a banshee's scream muffled the water. But she doesn't stop. She never backs off.

My vision blurs. The burn in my chest becomes an inferno. I stretch out my hand, grasping for anything. I pour every ounce of magic I have into the water, and the sea listens. A violent current bursts from my palm, a force so strong it knocks her backward, slamming her against the rock of her own throne like a ragdoll. The lagoon shudders. I feel it in every bone.

I may not belong to the ocean. But I can still make it obey me. I am its lord after all.

The black blood spills from her, swirling like tar through the saltwater. Her scream shatters the water, a shriek so raw and violent it rattles my bones. It stabs through my ears, sharp enough to draw blood, even down here. My lungs burn. Every second drags razor-thin. I kick toward the surface, desperate for air, but then she's there again. Her claws clamp around my ankle and yank me down into the dark. I thrash, twist, kick at her face with everything I have left.

And then, Mira is there, glowing and radiant, moving like she was born in the ocean, slicing through the water with terrifying grace.

Then she slams into Anya, full force. The impact sends her flying off me like a cannon blast.

I don't wait. I surge upward, breaking through the surface, and latch onto the nearest rock, the throne. Hauling myself onto it, I cough up seawater from my lungs, every breath scraping my throat like broken glass. Salt stings the gashes that carve into my skin, blood seeping from more places than I can count. But none of it matters.

Because Mira surfaces beside me, radiant, alive, and whole. Water streams down her face and arms as she climbs up next to me.

"Are you okay?" she asks, her voice trembling, eyes scanning every inch of me as she pulls herself up onto the throne to sit beside me.

I can't answer, not at first. I'm too busy staring at her. Breathing. Glowing like the sea has chosen her all over again. "I am now," I say finally, my voice raw. "Where is she?"

Mira turns, scanning the water. Then her gaze comes back to mine, steady but dark. "She swam off when I hit her," she says quietly. "But..." Her jaw tightens. "I don't think we've seen the last of her."

"You can breathe underwater?" I ask, still gasping for air.

Mira nods slowly, a crease forming between her brows. "I can," she says, her voice low. "I didn't know until just now." She glances out at the lagoon, eyes distant. "I think this place is sacred. I feel connected to everything inside it. Like it's part of me. Like I'm home."

I stare at her, trying to wrap my head around what I'd just seen. "And you can swim that fast? As fast as a mermaid? A siren?" She looks back at me, her expression unreadable at first. Then she gives a small, hesitant nod. "I can now. I didn't even try. My body just knew what to do."

Gods. She's extraordinary. Her emerald eyes shimmer in the light, golden flecks dancing like sunlit waves. Wet sand clings to her lashes, and her soaked hair drips onto her shoulders, onto mine.

"You must have unlocked something when the ocean blessed you," I murmur, staring at her like she is a myth come to life.

"I didn't have any of these abilities before," she whispers. I can feel the anxiety rolling off her in waves, so much confusion, so much power she never asked for. I can hear her heart pounding in my ears. She starts to pick at the sides of her nails.

I reach out, brushing my fingertips beneath her chin, gently tilting her face toward mine. "We'll figure it out," I say. "You're not alone.

Whatever this is, we'll face it together." The ocean is beautiful, but dangerous too. Mira is both.

What will it do to her, being the Soul of the Ocean, carrying siren blood? The thought surges like a tide and just as quickly, slips away.

"Hello, Kai." A voice drifts from the water like silk, familiar, mocking. I turn, instantly on guard. Adella.

She glides closer with effortless grace, that smug smile already pulling at her lips. "You don't take advice very well, do you?" she purrs. Her eyes slide to Mira. "Is this your pet? She's very pretty. I can see why you didn't listen." The words are sweet, but the snicker behind them has malicious intent.

I look at Mira and feel it, the fury radiating off her like heat from black sand, her anger barely leashed. Her face is flushed, fists clenching at her sides. Water drips from her skin, trailing down her arms and hissing where it hits the warm stone beneath us.

"Who the hell do you think you are?" Mira snaps. Adella laughs. A cruel, melodic sound as she circles us lazily like a shark that's already won its catch.

"Oh, he didn't tell you?" Adella's gaze flicks from Mira to me and back again, savoring every second. Mira turns toward me, eyes blazing.

She's more than livid, she's gutted. Betrayed. I know her well enough to understand what that means. Mira doesn't just hate secrets. She hates being blindsided. She hates me knowing mermaids at all. This secret might cut too deep.

Adella, of course, doesn't miss a beat. "I'm sorry," she coos, all mock innocence. "Looks like he left out a few details. I mean, how did you think he knew where to find Anya? You believed that clever little Pirate Lord brain of his figured it out all on its own?" She clucks her tongue. "Seems like while you're sleeping—"

"Adella," I cut in. "Enough." She giggles. A light, cruel sound that once used to drag me under now coils like a hook in my chest. That sound doesn't lure me anymore. It repulses me.

Mira turns to me fully, her voice shaking. "You talked to her?" Her face is unreadable, but betrayal and disbelief reveal themselves in her voice. "And you didn't tell me?" she demands. "What the fuck, Kai?"

"It's nothing serious," I begin, but Mira cuts me off before the words even fully leave my mouth.

"Nothing serious?" she snaps, stepping closer. "You didn't think to tell me that some washed-up mermaid floated onto *our* ship and gave you information? While I was what? Upstairs? In our quarters? Fifteen feet away? If *this* is going to work, you have to tell me things, you have to be honest."

She has every right to be seething. But all I can think about is what she said. *Our* ship. Gods help me, I'm obsessed with how those words sound coming from her lips. "You have nothing to worry about," I say, keeping my voice as steady as I can. "I should've told you. I know that's where I fucked up. But that night, it moved fast. Too fast to stop and explain."

Her eyes narrow, still unrelenting. "Which night, Kai?"

I look at her, and even now, even in the thick of this, my expression softens. "The night you found your soul."

Her shoulders drop just slightly. There it is, a flicker of realization in her eyes. That night changed everything. And whatever Adella said, whatever games she tried to play, she was just a shadow at the edge of something far greater. A spark trying to snuff out a blaze.

But of course, Adella won't let it go. "Aww," she shrugs mockingly, circling just beneath the surface. "You two must have such precious memories." Her eyes flash. "Anyway, Kai," she purrs, snapping her attention back to me, "Anya will return. She always does. She's quite the dark mermaid, isn't she?"

Dark mermaids. The old legends say they were once Sirens who chose blood over beauty, sacrifice over seduction. They dwell in the hadal depths, where sunlight dies, where even sea serpents fear to swim. Their fins are obsidian blades. Their voices echo with the screams of drowned men.

Anya isn't just an ordinary dark mermaid. She might be the last true one, the kind whispered about in sea shanties and sailor prayers. The fact that she's surfacing in broad daylight is unnatural. A sign the balance of the sea is shifting.

I rise to my feet, steel returning to my spine. "Watch your tongue, Adella," I growl, "or I'll cut it out and feed it to the Kraken's soul."

She stills. Just for a beat. Then that familiar flicker of amusement returns to her blue sea-glass eyes. "There's the Pirate Lord I know," she says with an all-knowing smirk. One that I know will make Mira even more pissed.

She turns to Mira, taunting with a venomous voice wrapped in silk, but I barely hear her anymore. My own emotions fade, pulled under by the weight of Mira's anger and betrayal. Her heartbreak. It crashes into me harder than any wave, and I can't breathe, not from the fight, not from the sea, but from her.

"Adella," I say, voice flat but firm, "you should go. You've done enough." She tilts her head, amused. "Thank you for telling me where to find her," I add, "but she didn't do anything for us."

Adella swims a little closer, sunlight catching the shimmer of her tail like sparkling amethyst. "Didn't she?" she purrs. She gestures lazily toward Mira. "She found out she can breathe underwater. Swim like a siren. That's something, isn't it?" Then she lets the silence stretch. Lets it sting. Lets the truth settle in like salt on a wound.

"Anyway," she adds with a shrug, "you didn't give her enough time to help. But it's your trip to the locker, not mine." Her gaze drops to the wounds on my side. "Get those gashes to clot soon or you'll wither away, mortal man. Too bad my tears are now dried up for you."

Then, just before vanishing, Adella cuts Mira a sharp look, her sapphire eyes gleaming cruelly. "Careful, Mira," she calls out, silky words laced in spite. "Some souls weren't meant to be saved." With a final giggle and a whisper of a splash, she slips beneath the waves, gone, like she was never there at all.

Mira's dark emerald eyes are still locked on the place Adella disappeared, burning with rage, hurt, and resolve. I reach out and gently tilt her chin, drawing her gaze back to me. There's blood and salt and sand between us now, caked on our skin like battle paint.

She shrugs me off. "Tears, Kai. Mermaid tears." Her voice drips with betrayal. "Do you not understand how sacred that ritual is?"

My eyes widen. "I do. I was young and reckless—I almost died, and she saved my life."

"And now you're bound to her." Her eyes narrow, pure fury slicing through me. "One lucky Pirate Lord, huh? Bound to a stunning mermaid *and* the new Soul?"

"It's not like that, Mira. You have to know that."

Her gaze doesn't falter. "You have her inked on your skin. Skin that I will be looking at every single day for the rest of my life."

Fair point. I draw in a breath, steadying myself. "You, of all people, know what it means to make the impossible decisions, as a captain, as a pirate. I made one of mine when I was young, naive. I wouldn't make that choice again."

I stop before I say something I can't take back because somehow, I'm already fucking this up more.

"You deserve honesty, and here it is. Yes, I loved her. She was the only woman I could say I actually felt even a shred of emotion for. But then some angry pirate came up to me in a pub and smacked me across the face." The corner of her lips fights a smile. "Ever since that night, Mira, you've been the center of my life. You have no competition with anyone."

Her gaze softens, back to her usual self. "Okay."

I narrow my eyes. "Okay? That's all?"

"Yes," she says. "Okay. I'm not giving you any more than that, because you don't deserve it right now."

I let out a dry laugh. She's going to be the end of me. "Fair enough. We should head back to the ship," I say quietly. "I'm sorry she spoke to you. She won't come near us again." I rise, muscles aching, saltwater dripping from every inch of me. The gashes from Anya still bleed freely, but I offer Mira my hand anyway.

She doesn't look at me right away. When she finally does, her voice is flat. "Is that a promise, or just another pretty line from the Pirate Lord?" Her fingers slip into mine. A warning. A test. I don't flinch.

"Promise."

CHAPTER TWENTY

MIRA

SIRENS COVE

I really am turning into my mother. I don't hate it, but it terrifies me, her power and her presence. And now, all these sirens and mermaids seem to know who I am, what I'm meant to become, before I've even had the chance to grasp it myself.

It's overwhelming, your own reflection being a mystery. Looking back, I've always felt the pull of the ocean, like I was born with saltwater flowing through my veins instead of blood. Not just because I'm a pirate who was raised at sea. It's like the ocean's been waiting for me to remember who I am all my life.

Anya was the most unsettling creature I've ever encountered. There was something about her that didn't belong, neither in the water, nor in the world. Anya favors the shadows. Her aura bled darkness. Her voice was raspy, like it had been dragged from the bottom of the ocean's trenches.

"So," I say, just to stir the pot, "you had a mermaid girlfriend?"

He groans, eyes narrowing. "Mira, I've told you—"

"Relax." I cut him off with a smirk. "I'm just playing. You seem to have a thing for women with fins."

He shakes his head with a quiet huff, and I laugh, glancing down at our feet swinging over the edge of the crow's nest. I guess this is our spot. I came up here to read more of my parents' journals, to hear the waves crash against the ship, to feel the sun on my face and the sea breeze twist through my hair. But Kai was already here, perched at the edge, staring out at the horizon.

He doesn't seem upset or stressed. He seems calm. Gods, he's so unbelievably attractive it's unfair. The sunlight clings to his skin, making it glow golden. His tattoos twist over his chest and arms like sea creatures in motion, each one tied to the ocean, and strangely familiar. His wavy dark brown hair hits his shoulders just right, tousled from the wind.

He's perfect. I'm staring at him when I notice it, his arm. The skin around the gashes is puffy and angry looking, veins darkening beneath the surface. My breath catches. "Kai," I say sharply, all the warmth draining from my voice. "Your arm, it's gotten worse."

"It's gotten awfully sinister hasn't it?" he asks, acting like this isn't a big deal.

I reach out to touch his arm, but he pulls back. "Don't," he says, distant and hurt. It's unlike him. I freeze.

"Where is this from?" I asked, my voice dipping. "It looks very infected."

Now that I'm really looking, the veins spread like black spiderwebs beneath his skin, crawling up his arm and reaching toward his chest.

They pulse faintly, alive, like something dark is still moving inside him. The color isn't red—it's the color of deep water, of ink. This isn't just a scar. It's a mark left by the siren that nearly claimed his life as a child.

"I was told something might happen to it," Kai said, eyes fixed on the horizon. "I've been feeling sharp pain lately and the veins are spreading faster than before."

I squint, trying to make sense of it. "What do you mean? Told by who? Can I see it?" He moves his arm farther away from me, putting up a silent wall. "Please," I say softly, flashing him my eyes, steady and unrelenting. Finally, he shifts, offering me his arm. I take it gently.

The scar has split wide open, the skin angry and bleeding. The flesh around it shimmers faintly, something sharp glinting just beneath the surface, like bone, or—

"I was told," Kai says, voice low and rough, "that because I escaped a siren once, because I nearly killed her, she marked me. That I carry a piece of her. And now that she's gone, that piece is waking up. It's just a lot worse than I thought it was going to be. It seems like the siren is trying to kill me from the inside out." I look up at him, my breath shallow. "Her claws, her teeth, they surface through my skin. As if I'm meant to carry her remnants. To protect them." His voice cracks slightly, the pain too obvious to hide.

"In order to make a wish at the fountain, you need a piece of a siren, so this may be true?" I say slowly, the thought crystallizing as it leaves my lips. One of the rarest, most dangerous parts of the map to obtain, pieces of a siren. "It looks like the scar is killing you more than anything."

"Yes, I'm starting to think that as well," Kai says, his gaze still on the horizon. His hazel eyes shimmer gold in the fading light, but something in his expression shifts. He's retreating. Quiet. Guarded.

"What is it?" I ask.

"It's how I found out... that's the problem."

My chest tightens. "I'm not following. How did you find out?"

He finally turns to look at me. Really looks. "You know I'd protect you," he says. "Till the ends of the earth."

The words make my heart drop. Anxiety surges through me, crawling under my skin. What is he about to say? "I do," I whisper, eyes locked on his, my voice coated in fear. "I trust you."

"These creatures, the kappas, they boarded my ship. Right before you found me," Kai says, his voice tight. "They gave me the intel I needed. And I... I made a deal with them." He hesitates. "I didn't know how much you meant to me then."

My stomach drops. "You better not have sold me to the kappas," I say, my voice cold.

"I didn't—" he started, but I cut him off.

"I know the kappas, Kai. They're vile. Wretched. Manipulative. They make you feel needed and then they drown you in the dark. If you made a deal you can't keep," I shake my head, "you're as good as dead. I'm as good as dead."

He looks at me, eyes rimmed with sorrow. "The deal was to grant their captain a wish. To free him, to let him rest." His gaze flicks to the water, then back to me. "But there was another part. They wanted you kept safe. Said when the time came, and they needed you, they'd take you. But I never agreed to that part."

My eyes widened. He reaches for me, grabs my leg, but I pull away from him, like he put fire to my skin and burned me. "That will *never* happen, Mira," he says, voice fierce. "You have to know that. I will gut every last one of them before they even *look* at you."

"What do they want me for?" I ask, my tone flat, emotionless.

He hesitates. "They said you're a key. A piece of the map." His voice slows, like he's picking every word out of a minefield. "They told me to keep you safe until they need you."

My chest tightens and all I can see is red. Has he been pretending this entire time? Acting like my protector just to deliver me to them? Are you fucking kidding me?

I stand, balancing on the beam like it's solid ground beneath the storm in me. I'm shaking, no, vibrating with rage. Smoke could rise from my skin, and I wouldn't be surprised.

"*Mira*, listen to me. Please," he says sharply, his tone bordering on desperate.

"No, I'm done listening to you," I snap. "What the hell is wrong with you?" My voice trembles, not with fear, but fury.

"You've been playing this whole protector role because of some deal? Because you owe them? Every time you said you were keeping me safe... you meant for them." His face tightens, but I don't stop. "You don't care about me. Not really. Everything you do is for you. For the fountain. You are no better than your father." I turn my back on him, the heat of my rage boiling in my blood. But I know my words probably cut him deeper than how I'm feeling.

Even though deep down, I know he wouldn't do that to me. That he would protect me, because of our bond.

I climb down the narrow ladder from the crow's nest, the wind tugging at my hair, Kai close behind. The sun has long since vanished, and now the sky is drowning in pitch black. The moon, my usual guide, is completely swallowed by thick, unnatural fog that clings to the sails and to my skin like it's alive.

Something feels wrong. I pause, tuning into the sea. The air crackles with energy, heavy and tense. Mother Nature is angry tonight. Her waves swell, slamming against the hull with increasing rage. Then, the sky opens up. Rain pours down in sheets, blinding and cold. I grip the ladder tighter, each step downward heavier than the last.

Why are there no lanterns lit? Where is the crew?

"Mira! Stop! You can't go down there!" Kai shouts. His voice cuts through the storm, laced with panic. I freeze, instincts screaming. The air shifts, colder now. I start climbing back up, but then I look down.

A silhouette is emerging from the fog, scaling the ladder at an unnatural speed. Half-man, half-sea monster, tentacles twisting from the sides of his head, suctioning to the wood like leeches. His slick skin shimmers in the slivers of faint moonlight that manages to pierce the gloom. His human eyes lock onto mine, empty and soulless. I knew what he is. A kappa.

I scramble upward, heart pounding, but he's faster. His tentacles lash out, wrapping around my ankle. The suction burns against my skin, bursting blood vessels beneath the surface. His grip tightens, trying to drag me down. I scream. And then, out of nowhere, Kai.

He swings in from the side, gripping a sail rope, crashing into the creature with brutal force. His boot connects with the kappa's face, breaking its hold on me. The impact knocks them both from the ladder and into the abyss below, swallowed by darkness and storm.

Uncertain of what to do, I know the one thing I could do would be to jump into the ocean. But the fog is so dense I can barely see the mast from the mainsail. The rain slams down in sheets, blurring the world into shadows and chaos. Still, I know I'll be stronger underwater. Down there, I wasn't useless. I had senses, power, a connection that made me something more.

But worry claws at me. What are they doing to Kai? To my crew? I can't leave them. A captain never abandons their ship.

I climb down the ladder again, boots hitting the flooded main deck with a splash. The rain has turned the dock into a shallow sea, waves crashing up and over the sides, water rising past my ankles. "Show yourselves!" I shout into the storm, my voice cutting through the thunder.

And they do. About twenty of them emerge from the dark, towering silhouettes rising from the depths, their faces flickering in the eerie glow of a single lantern lit by bioluminescence, casting faint blue-green light on each of them. Half-men, half-sea monsters. Kappas. Tentacles slick with seawater curl from their bodies, their eyes gleaming like sunken treasure. They surround me in a slow, tightening circle. Each one is at least a foot or two taller than me.

I glance down. Scattered across the deck are bodies, some still twitching, some still bleeding, but others... headless. Beheaded kappas. Their heads roll along the planks like grotesque marbles. My heart slams against my ribs.

Kai has already been down here. He moves like a shadow in the dark, silent, brutal, brilliant, and deadly. I know his work when I see it. I stand tall, teeth bared. "Where is my crew?" I shout again as the waves surge around us.

What looks like their captain steps between them, forcing the others to part like a tide breaking around a rock. He's vile, part sea urchin, part nightmare, stitched together from the souls of unfortunate sea creatures. His aura oozes rot. His only eye gleams with malice. "A deal was broken," he says, voice like oil sliding over broken shells. "I'm here to collect."

Before I can move, Kai is suddenly there. He steps out of the shadows like he's been summoned by the storm itself, planting himself between us. His body towers in front of mine, one hand braced against my thigh to nudge me back, shielding me. I can feel the heat of him, grounding me even in the freezing rain. His presence alone is a weapon.

"Varn," Kai says, voice low and sharp.

"Pirate Lord, you spoke of our deal. Now you must pay," the creature's voice calls out, his voice like gravel. Kai moves closer to him, maintaining strong eye contact with the creature.

"I never agreed to that part," Kai continues, stepping even closer. "I only agreed to help you get your damn wish, in exchange for information. That's it. No more. And if you think I'll stand by while you slaughter my crew"—his voice drops into a lethal growl—"you're mistaken. Get the fuck off my ship, or I'll cut every last one of you down. One by one."

The captain freezes. For a moment, he just stares at Kai. "Interesting," he rasps, his voice curling with disdain. "You think you have more strength, more power, than me, Pirate Lord?" He spits the title like a curse and begins to pace, his heavy boots dragging through the water flooding the deck.

Kai doesn't flinch. "I am a lord for a reason," he says coolly, with a small smirk.

The captain halts, head snapping toward Kai. "You think your title means anything when you're standing in front of me?"

Kai steps forward, closing the space between them with purpose. "I think it does," he replies, "when I slaughtered something far bigger than *you* to earn it." The confidence rolling off him is unshakable. His words hit like cannon fire, echoing in the charged silence that follows. The captain says nothing. Then Kai adds, sharp as a blade, "Now what the fuck do you want?"

"I want what you want, boy," the captain says, his voice slick with menace. "I want to find the fountain. But I can't be making alliances with untrustworthy pirates, now can I?"

I glance at Kai. I can feel the slow, steady rhythm of his heartbeat, calm, controlled. None of this rattles him. He thrives in the shadows of conflict. He already knows his next move. "And when," Kai says smoothly, "did I ever give you the impression I was untrustworthy? We're still hunting for pieces of the map, are we not?" The captain groans, half in agreement, half in irritation. "The one part of our deal that's lacking is yours," Kai continues. "I haven't gotten a single scrap of information from you since I boarded your ship."

Varn doesn't flinch. "I've brought more instructions," he replies coolly. "They come at a cost." The captain's eye gleams.

But Kai steps closer, lifting a hand. "No, Varn. My price was your wish. That's all you get. If you want more"—he steps back, placing himself between me and the creature again—"then you'll have to find the fountain on your own." Varn makes a bloodcurdling groan, throwing his clawed arm against the wood of *The Leviathan*.

"You drive a hard bargain, Pirate Lord," Varn drawls, voice thick with mockery. "But I know where the fountain is. Reaching it, however, is your own cursed endeavor. One I can't help with." He pauses, his head tilting ever so slightly toward me. "But she might."

Kai turns instantly, his eyes sweeping over me, confirming I'm still breathing. Still standing. Still his. I meet his gaze and give a small nod, stepping forward. "You won't dare hurt me or this crew," I say, voice steady. "You know what we're worth to the ocean. The deal stays the same."

Varn turns, his dead-black eye, the one that wasn't formed from a human, locking on mine. "I never made a deal with you, girl," he spits, his saliva landing at my feet like poison.

Before I can react, Kai steps between us. "If you made a deal with me," he growls, "you made one with her."

Varn begins to pace again, boots dragging through rainwater pooling across the deck. The storm begins to settle, rain easing to a mist, the sea's tantrum quieting like it, too, is listening. My blood simmers.

"If you have any new information you would like to share, I suggest you do it now," Kai says.

Varn's pacing slows, his shadow rippling against the faint lantern glow as he turns to face Kai. "That scar of yours," he says, voice low. "She's quite nasty, isn't it?" His gaze drifts to Kai's arm. "There's a reason so few survive a siren's attack. They don't just wound—they *claim*. What's inside you now isn't healing, it's *remembering*. Spreading slowly, patiently, until she takes back what's hers."

I'm lost for words. Kai's scar is killing him. Kai doesn't speak, he just stands there, shoulders held high.

"Seems like you have a reason to get to that fountain now, don't ya?" Varn laughs, a wretched sound. "The only way you're going to live is to wish for your health back. There is no cure for a siren's touch, boy. You're as good as dead."

I glance at Kai's hand gripping his sword. The black veins have reached his fingers, crawling across his skin like living ink. This journey just became a hell of a lot more important.

Kai's voice cuts through the stillness. "We don't have time for this, Varn. Make up your mind. If you came to remind me we struck a deal, save your breath. I never forgot. I'll get you your wish. You have my word." Kai steps closer now, voice low, lethal. "But if you lay a hand on Mira, I'll gut you and pray you grow back more twisted than you already are."

The captain turns to Kai, fury radiating off him like steam from boiling water. In the dim glow of the lantern, his grotesque features come into full view, gleaming, monstrous, unmistakably inhuman. "The deal holds, for as long as your heart does. And if it stops..." His grin widens. "She'll pay what's owed in your place," he says, motioning his clawed hand toward me. "But just remember, you can't breathe underwater. That's where you fall short, Pirate Lord." He raises his hand, signaling his crew. One by one, the kappas begin to slink toward the ship's edge, their movements slow and deliberate, preparing to vanish into the churning black sea.

"Varn," Kai calls. "Tell me where it is." The captain pauses. Turns. Their eyes lock, and a chill knifes down my spine. The look Varn gives Kai is void of anything human. No warmth, no malice. Just an empty, unholy calm. Like death dressed in seaweed and salt.

"Siren's Cove," he says.

The name hangs there, suspended in the storm's silence. Then Varn adds, almost softly, "I wish you luck, boy. No one goes in and comes out alive, and that's if they find it." He laughs cruelly as he steps backward onto the rail, a black eye still fixed on Kai. "For both our sakes," he says, "I hope you do." And with that, he drops into the sea and disappears. Then I think, *How many souls have lost their lives due to debts with him, and how many others have gone on this same godsforsaken mission?*

My heart drops. Sirens Cove? Home of the sirens my mother is the queen of? What the hell did she and my father know? What else were they hiding from me? Or was she hiding it from him too? The thoughts hit like a tidal wave, dragging me deeper. What kind of life did they lead? What kind of legacy am I about to inherit?

The storm begins to clear, the fog pulling back like breath. One by one, the creatures vanish over the side of the ship, sinking into the night. The waves still. The sea returns to silence. And the only thing left is the moonlight, soft and pale, washing the ship in silver.

The crew begins to emerge from their quarters, white as ghosts and wide-eyed. I push through them, scanning faces until I find him. "Smith," I say, breathless. "You alright?"

As much as they piss me off, they're mine. My crew. My family. I can't lose them. Smith grabs both of my arms, his grip strong. His eyes roam over me, searching for wounds. "Aye," he breathes. "Only if you are, Mira." He squeezes my arms tighter, his voice quiet, reverent. "You're the only one who can save us."

What the hell happened down there? Smith barks orders, telling the crew to light the lanterns and return to their stations. The night crew moves quickly, stepping into their usual rhythm, while the day crew disappears back into their quarters, shaken, silent, pale as bone. Most of them look like they've seen the Kraken and lived to tell the tale.

"What the fuck happened to them?" Kai asks, coming up behind me.

"I don't know," I said quietly. "Smith didn't say. Just that I'm the only one who can save them all." His words sit heavy on my chest, powerful, but pressing. I want to unlock whatever I am, not just for me... but for Kai. For them. For the ocean.

"You have the power to save the entire sea," Kai murmurs. "You are her soul. It's just about getting you there, so you can become all that you are." I glance down at my fingers, picking at the skin around my nails. My thoughts began to spiral, faster than I can catch them. Kai must feel the shift in me. He reaches out, kisses my forehead. His lips are warm, grounding.

"You're safe," he whispers. "Nothing will happen to you, treasure." The warmth of his words spreads through my chest, soft and bright. I know he feels it too. And suddenly, it clicks—the deal with the kappas. He didn't offer me to them, they're manipulative. I've been too angry to see it, and now guilt crawls up my spine.

"I promise we'll get you there," I say.

"Mira, don't. This isn't my journey anymore—it's yours."

I look up at him, anger flashing in my eyes. "All of this," I say, motioning to the crew, the ship, to me, "wouldn't be here without you. I need you here. More than I care to admit, because you know you can be an ass. But I can't watch you die."

Tears burn at the corners of my eyes. I open my mouth to speak, but nothing comes out.

Kai pulls me in tight, his heartbeat steady against mine. "I'll be okay," he says softly. "We'll make it. You'll get there—that's what matters." He pauses, a faint smirk ghosting his lips. "The sea's not taking me yet."

For someone staring down death he sounds almost at peace, and that's what terrifies me.

I trust him with everything. My body. My heart. My soul. I kiss him, melting into the comfort of his arms. His warmth feels so good against my skin after the freezing droplets of rain. His tattooed hands pulled me close, his touch steadying the storm inside me.

I look up at him, heart pounding with purpose. "Now," I say, my voice steady, "we search for the belly of the beast." I turn toward the horizon, the moonlight casting a silver path across the waves.

"To Sirens Cove."

CHAPTER TWENTY-ONE

KAI

THE PRICE OF MAGIC

My arm throbbed all night, heat radiating from the old wound like it was trying to warn me. By morning, I'd dug out two claws, long, jagged, and serrated along the edges. The same claws that tore into my flesh when I was a boy, now breaking through my skin all over again. It hurt like hell. But it was worth it.

I placed them in a small glass container and stashed them inside the captain's quarters, above our bed, in the drawer only I open. These claws are more than just remnants of a scar. They're one of the biggest, most important pieces to everything. I don't know if more will emerge, but for now, we have two. That's two wishes. One for Mira. One for me. I'd like to give her both, but now, with death breathing down my neck, my wish has to be to save myself, to rip out whatever curse that siren left in me. Whatever this black poison is that's crawling through my veins, it's eating me alive, making me weaker by the day. The pain lingers longer each time, like it's learning how to stay. Saving myself means saving Mira too. Like Veyra said, there's no one without the other.

Siren's Cove has never been discovered by a mortal man. Only one warlock ever made it there, and he never returned to the sea. He lives in self-exile now, tucked deep in the Badlands, where even the tide won't touch him. The entire island is his. Cursed, some say. Anyone who steps foot on that land dies screaming. Whatever he saw in those waters scared him so badly he refused to go near the ocean again. Won't even dip a toe in.

I can't imagine what their home looks like. Sirens slithering like sea snakes through coral caverns, guarding eggs and secrets older than time. The idea of it makes my skin crawl. A place that evil, that primeval, it's not just dangerous. It's unnatural, unholy.

Mira mentioned she wanted to visit Taika, an old witch friend of hers who gave her the map that led her straight to me. Though Taika isn't just any witch. She's the most powerful in the world. If anyone can point us in the right direction or help me understand what the hell is happening to my magic, it's her. Speaking to a witch as old as she is, one who's lived through countless tides and curses... that kind of knowledge is priceless. Rare. Dangerous, too.

But before we leave, there's something I've been avoiding. It's time I check on my father.

I've had members of the crew taking shifts watching over him, though I doubt he even notices anymore. Most days, he doesn't know who's speaking to him. Sometimes he doesn't even remember his own name. Watching him like this, weak, slumped, muttering nonsense under his breath, is like staring into a ghost of the man I once feared.

Once, he ruled these seas, feared and respected. He was a pirate legend, my blood, my example, and my warning. Now he's nothing but a broken shell of a man. His illness wasn't a matter of chance. It was a curse, one he brought upon himself. He made a pact with the devil, and the devil collected. Maybe that's why I've kept my distance. Not out of fear. But because deep down, I wonder if I'm next.

He only gets a few minutes of clarity each month. He's locked away in a tiny room, guarded at all times. The door locks from the outside, but I placed a fake lock on the inside so he thinks he still has a shred of power left. During those rare, lucid moments, Mira can't be anywhere near him. He still wants her dead. Wants to wipe out her bloodline entirely. If he knew she was on board, if he knew what I've been doing with her, with our ship, he'd have my head.

But I'm not him. I have someone to live for. I'll fight for her. Breathe for her. Kill for her. My father let my mother slip through his fingers, ruined whatever they had for the sake of power. He never even told me who she was. Just another secret buried under his madness. Selfish prick.

I take a breath and step inside. "Father," I say quietly as I enter his quarters. The room is small, but not suffocating. There's a narrow bed pushed up against the wall, and a desk cluttered with half-finished maps, old ink bottles, and scribbled nonsense. The only thing that feels alive in here is the window, his view of the sea. The one thing he still loves.

He's seated on the bed, eyes fixed on the waves beyond the glass. Then, slowly, he turns to me. "Son," he says. "You've finally come to pay your old man a visit." Of course. He's lucid. Lucky me.

His eyes are dark brown, shadowed by heavy wrinkles. His long white hair is tied back with a faded blue bandana, the same kind he used to wear when he was feared across every corner of the ocean. He stands when he sees me. Still around my height, though age has curled his spine. His presence feels too big for this room, like it might collapse the walls.

"You alright?" I ask, voice low, as I lean against the stairway just above his quarters. I keep my distance. He's like a rogue bomb... You never know when it'll blow up. The more space between us, the better.

He scoffs, not even looking at me. "What does it look like? I'm fucking sick in the head." His tone is wild, somewhere between manic and bitter. Then his eyes snap toward mine, seething. "And you know what has my blood boiling more than anything?"

I steel myself. "What's that?"

"You brought that bitch of a daughter onto *my* ship. *Bleu's* daughter." I'm on him in two steps. My fist knots in his collar and I slam him back against the wall, hard enough to rattle the desk behind him. My grip tightens, choking him slightly.

"Never call her that," I snarl. "The only bitch on this ship is you." He spits in my face. I don't flinch, but the heat coming off my skin is near volcanic. Magic pulses at my fingertips, itching to lash out, to burn something. I drop him. "Who told you?" I stare down at him.

"Why would I give away any of my secrets to you?" he coughs out. He crumples to his knees, coughing, hands trembling with rage or weakness. "If you don't get her off this ship," he wheezes, "I'll—"

"You'll what?" I cut in, stepping closer. "You'll kill her? Threaten her again and I'll drop your sorry ass at the next port. Let's see how long a sick old man lasts out there." His eyes shift, landing on the sea outside the window. It's the only thing that calms him. But this time, even that doesn't work.

"You'd choose her over your own blood?" he growls.

I crouch down, meeting his gaze, my voice low and dangerous. "I will *always* choose her," I say. "I will kill for her. *Especially* my own blood."

He recoils in disgust—not at my words, but at me. Because the woman he hates more than anything, the daughter of his greatest enemy, is the one whose soul is now tied to mine. And he'll never understand how vital she is. Not just to the ocean, but to me.

"This isn't your ship anymore," I growl. "It's mine. You lost her the moment you made a deal with the devil. And when I slayed the Kraken." He stays on his knees, staring at his hands like they're strangers. Good. Let him sit in that silence. I feel nothing for the man in front of me. Years and years of abuse have boiled down to the abuser on his knees, broken and small.

Everything he did in life was for himself. Gold. Power. Pleasure. He was a slave to temptation, bedding every whore who crossed his path, drowning in rum, leaving wreckage behind like it was his calling card. A disease wearing a pirate's skin.

But I won't lie, he was damn good. Ruthless, heartless, one of the best to ever haunt the seas.

As a father? He was the worst. He beat me as a child—not even a few years old. He wanted me to be so many things from the moment I was born. Strong, but never stronger than him. Powerful, but always beneath his shadow. He saw it early on, that I'd outshine him one day. And his jealousy cost him a son.

"Remember who made you, boy," he croaks, his voice cracked from the strain of my grip. He hauls himself up, leaning on the chair for balance. The fire still burns behind his eyes, but his body is crumbling beneath it. I meet his stare, calm and cold.

"You didn't make anything," I spit. "You were too busy chasing your next fix." I take a step forward. He doesn't move. "The crew shaped me. I made me. Every scar, every battle, every brutal lesson, I survived it. Not because of you. But in spite of you." I lean in, my voice dropping. "My mother gave me more than you ever did. And she wasn't even there." He flinches. "Her magic made me powerful before I could even walk. And you've spent your whole life running from what I was born to become."

He shoots me a sharp look of disgust. "Don't speak of your mother to me."

"Why?" I snap. "Because you don't even know who she is? I was just dropped off on this ship, and you decided you needed an heir. You realized I had magic, so you kept me. And threw her away."

His expression shifts. For a moment, there's a flicker of pain in his eyes. Real pain. I've never seen it before. "I do know who she is, Kai," he says quietly. "I loved that woman. But she chose power over you. Over us."

His voice cracks. "I was a shit father, I know that. But at least you were cared for. She left you. She left me." He pauses, staring past me like he's chasing ghosts. "I never loved another after her. She was my one and only."

I'm stunned. My father has never spoken to me about her, not once. Whenever I tried to find a lead on who she was, all tracks were covered. Even the crew doesn't know anything about her, like some hidden mind control. "What kind of power did she possess?" I ask quietly.

"She's a witch, son. A powerful one," he said, voice low. "That's where your magic comes from. All magic comes with a price. Why do you think I'm sick? Who do you think I made a deal with?"

Horror twists in my gut. Bile rises in my throat. "She did this to you?"

He shakes his head and steps toward me. "I did this to myself. I made a deal with the devil. All magic comes with a price." Then, just like that, his clarity snaps.

His eyes shift. The awareness drains from them, replaced by anger. Wild. Unhinged. His short-lived lucid moment is over.

I wanted to ask him more. What deal did he make? What bargain could turn a man into this? Trapped between death and life, a fate worse than either.

"We have to sail north! Get him out of my way, move him! That bastard's always causing problems. North!" Pacing back and forth, arms flailing, his voice rises into gibberish. He's completely forgotten I'm there.

I exhale slowly and reached for my magic, slipping into his mind just enough to soothe him, redirecting his wild thoughts to stillness. It takes effort, but eventually, he calms. I guide him back to his bed. He collapses into it, fast asleep and breathing steady.

I stand over him, watching the rise and fall of his chest. The man who once ruled the sea, now a prisoner of his own madness. So many things have gone wrong in his life. He deserved most of it, but maybe not all.

I step out, locking the door behind me. *The mighty have fallen,* I think grimly. And now, we have a snake on this ship. Because whoever told my father that Mira was on board will live to regret it.

CHAPTER TWENTY-TWO

KAI

LAGOON HEART

We dock at an island called Lagoon Heart, a quiet, remote spot known for its still waters and steep prices. We're running low on everything after weeks at sea: food, fresh water, rum. Especially the rum. Which is the number one necessity on a pirate ship. A happy crew with rum running through their veins is a well-oiled crew.

As soon as we anchor, Mira and I make our way to the docks to track down whoever's in charge of supply dealings. Prices are high. Not many merchants make it this far out, which means anyone who does can charge whatever they like. And when they see pirates? Prices double.

There's this myth that pirates always have gold to burn, that every ship hides treasure below deck. It's bullshit. Most of us are scraping by like everyone else.

He recognizes me the moment he sees *The Leviathan*. He knows exactly who I am and takes full advantage. I give him extra, not because I'm fooled but because I respect confidence, even in a man stupid enough to try and scam me.

The crew scatters across the small island town once we secure supplies. It's the kind of place where everyone looks like a pirate or a local, and no one cares who you're running from. Safe from the royals. Safe from watchful eyes. Even though this island is just east of Coral Haven, maybe a two-day trip, there's no real threat from them here.

Most of my men flock to the nearest pub, probably sniffing around for booze, brawls, or a warm bed. If there are any working girls on this rock, they'll be there. Spending months at sea does a number on a man. So when we dock, I let the crew do whatever the hell they want, so long as someone's watching the ship.

Mira and I have a few crewmembers help load the ship before I catch her hand, giving it a tug.

"Come on," I say, motioning for her to follow. I've visited this island before. Lagoon Heart, a quiet place with stunning views and one of the most breathtaking waterfalls I'd ever seen. I figure she could use a moment away. We both could.

"Where are we going?" she asks, her green eyes catching the sun like sea-glass.

I give her a small side smile. "I thought we could use a break from everything. Do you not trust me, treasure?"

Her cheeks flush a soft pink. "I do. Always," she says, voice warm, almost shy.

She doesn't ask again, just slips her hand into mine and follows. We walk the shoreline, then enter the jungle. Tall palms shade us from the sun, and bursts of hibiscus bloom in rich pinks and fiery oranges. Exotic birds call out in sharp whistles, a song of their own.

"It's beautiful here," Mira murmurs, eyes wide with wonder.

"Yes," I say simply, guiding her up a moss-covered trail. "Wait until you see this." We turn the corner and there it is. The hidden lagoon.

The water is crystal clear, emerald-green foliage clinging to the rock ledges like it's been painted there. Sunlight filters through the canopy above, catching just the center of the pool, where vibrant coral glows beneath the surface. Soft white sand hugs the edge of the water. The waterfall crashes down the rocks, silver and endless.

The air is thick with the scent of salt and jungle flowers. She lets go of my hand and takes a step closer, speechless. She doesn't just fit into the landscape, she completes it. Two ethereal things in one place, both too beautiful to belong to this world.

I turn my attention to the scenery for just a moment, then I look back at Mira. She is already undressing. "Well? You were planning on getting in, right?" she laughs, stripping without hesitation. Completely bare. My gods.

Her body in the sunlight, she looks like a goddess. Glowing. A dream I don't deserve to have brought to life.

I fumble with my clothes, suddenly desperate to be closer to her. I unsheathe the twin swords from the X on my back and drop them into the sand, the sound dull against the rush in my ears.

Mira dives into the warm water with a splash, her head popping up moments later, hair soaked and clinging to her skin. She moves joyfully, weightless in the lagoon. Droplets shimmer on her as the sun kisses her freckled shoulders. Her wet hair falls across her chest, covering what I want to see, hiding them so perfectly it's just enough to drive me mad.

I dive in after her, letting the saltwater wash over me, cleansing something deeper than skin. The water here feels alive and fresh. I swim toward her and drag her playfully beneath the waterfall. She shrieks and splashes at me, and I laugh before lifting her into my arms and holding her close, the water crashing down around us.

Her skin is warm. Soft. Every time I touch her, I feel like I've come home. Like there's nowhere else in the world but this.

I toss her gently back into the water, grinning. She surfaces laughing, breathless and bright. Gods, that laugh, that smile. It's the most intoxicating sound I've ever heard. Her joy hits me like sunlight, piercing, blinding, and real. And for a moment, I'm nothing but happy.

She swims over to me, slow and hypnotic, eyes locked on mine like she already knows what's about to happen. When she reaches me, I cup her face in both hands and kiss her, soft at first, then deeper, her body pressing into mine, bare and weightless in the water.

My arms wrap around her waist, drawing her closer until there's no space left between us. Her skin is slick and warm, and I can feel every breath she gives me, every inch of her against me. My fingers trace the curve of her back, teasing her chest until I feel her gasp into my mouth.

She reaches down, and when her hand wraps around me, I nearly lose control right then. But not yet. Not like that. I shift us beneath the waterfall, guiding her gently as I step onto a smooth ledge of stone just beyond the water's edge. The world narrows to her, just her, and the way she looks at me, half-wild and glowing in the mist.

She straddles me, her legs wrapping around my waist, and I press her gently against the mossy wall behind us. Water rushes around us, but all I can hear is her breath, ragged and wanting, and her heart beating out of her chest.

I let my fingers find her, slowly, learning the rhythm of her body. She's already aching for me. "Do it," she whispers, voice trembling against my ear. Her words send a shiver down my spine.

"Do what, treasure?" I murmur, brushing my lips against her jaw, her neck, teasing her with everything but what she wants. She arches back, fighting the urge to beg. My hand slides behind her head, cradling it so she doesn't hit the rock. My other hand keeps her pinned just where I want her—desperate and beautiful and mine.

I lay her down on the flattest stone I can find, water glistening across her bare skin. She doesn't care about the rough edges. Neither do I.

"What do you want, Mira?" I ask, kissing her chest, my mouth finding her nipple.

She squirms beneath me, soft moans falling from her lips. "Please..." she breathes, barely able to speak as she reaches for me again.

Her touch is electric, every stroke driving me closer to the edge of insanity. My body aches for her. Every part of me burns, and this time I won't stop.

Her curves glow under the golden light, slick with water, like she's been carved by the sea itself. I want to be selfish, to keep her here with me forever. In this place. In this moment.

I lift her easily, and she wraps her legs around my waist without hesitation. Her skin on mine. Her heart races like mine. I kiss every inch I can reach, slow and reverent, worshiping her like the goddess she is.

"Are you sure?" I ask, voice low, pressed against her ear. She looks up at me, those sea-glass eyes wide, shimmering with something deeper than want.

"Yes," she whispers, breathless. "I've never been more sure of anything."

That's all I need. I kiss her again, deeper this time, anchoring her to me as I ease into her. She gasps, sharp, beautiful, a sound I want to hear again and again. Her nails dig into my back. Her hips roll against mine in perfect rhythm, meeting me with every breath, every pulse of heat between us. I grab a fistful of her hair and gently pull her head back, exposing the length of her neck.

I kiss her there. Bite gently. Mark her as mine. I move faster, deeper, chasing the sound of her moans, the shiver in her breath, the way she clings to me like I'm the only thing keeping her grounded.

She comes first, head tilted back, body trembling. I follow, losing myself completely, coming undone in her arms. And for the first time in my life... I don't feel cursed—I feel whole.

I sit down with her still straddling me, her arms looped around my neck. Her hair clings to her skin, half wet, half wild from my hands, and I can't stop looking at her. "You're exquisite, Mira Bleu," I say, voice low and sincere. My eyes can't stop taking in every single inch of her. Pure. Holy. Beautiful. Her smile lights up every dark place inside me.

"You're my always, Kai Eldoris," she whispers. Her words warm me, a feeling I'm not used to. She isn't just a part of my life now. She is my life—the only treasure I'll ever need in this godsforsaken pirate world. I cup her face with one hand, the other resting gently on her back. She leans into me, and we kiss again, slow, unhurried, until the sun melts into the sea.

CHAPTER TWENTY-THREE

MIRA

FLESH & BLOOD

We make our way back through the jungle under the glow of a full moon. Fireflies light our path, flickering softly around us like they can feel the energy still humming beneath our skin. Kai leads the way, never once letting go of my hand. His grip is tight, protective, like he expects something to come from the shadows and take me.

Then I smell smoke. "What is that?" I ask, looking up at him. "Stay close to me," Kai says sharply. I do without question. He has a sixth sense for danger. I've seen it too many times to doubt it. He always knows before anyone else does.

As we near the opening of the jungle, the glow ahead brightens. Flames. The small village has been overtaken, engulfed in fire. Screams echo. Steel clashes. Pirate flags wave in the smoke-choked air.

It is chaos. The town is under siege. I scan the harbor desperately, trying to find *The Leviathan*, but the smoke is too thick. Shapes move in the firelight, fighting, falling, fleeing. I can't make out anything clearly.

"What the fuck is happening," Kai growls, rage seeping through every word. He reaches for his weapons, twin blades strapped in an X across his back. The moonlight and flames carves shadows across the muscles and dark veins spread on his arms as he moves, all sharp angles and deadly focus.

I unsheathe my cutlass, the familiar weight grounding me as we move toward the burning town, smoke stinging my throat. Taking the black bandana from my hair, I wrap it around my nose and mouth. Kai suddenly turns and grabs both of my arms, his grip firm, his eyes locking on mine.

"If anyone comes for you, you run. You don't look back. You swim straight to the ship and don't stop. The ocean answers to you. That's where you're safest." There was desperation in his voice. Fear he wasn't even trying to hide.

"I know how to handle myself, Kai. Don't forget, there was me before there was us. Not just anyone. A captain," I say sharply. Something flickers in his eyes, hurt, maybe. Or guilt.

"I know that," he says, softer now. "You don't have to remind me." He says this like he was repulsed that there was a life I led without him in it. He turns away and leads us toward the chaos.

"I'm going to the coastline. I might be able to spot the ship," I say, scanning the horizon.

"No. Stay close to me," he orders. But before I can argue, something shifts behind me.

There's a rustle in the bushes. I turn just in time to see a massive figure emerge from the fog and the smoke from the fire. Seven feet tall, shoulders broad as a ship's mast. His skin looks like weathered driftwood, his face torn with old scars and his eyes hollow.

He lunges. I barely have time to move. Kai is already there. Steel flashes and in one brutal motion, Kai slices across the man's gut. His blade carves clean through flesh and muscle, and the man drops to his knees, entrails spilling to the ground. He collapses. Dead. Blood soaks the earth at our feet.

Kai turns to me, eyes dark and wild with fear. "This is an ambush. These pirates are here for you. We have to leave. Now." There's no room for debate in his voice.

"How the hell do you know?" I snap.

"Because, Mira, people know who you are now. You're not safe. We have to leave."

I stop in my tracks. "I'm not leaving my crew."

He turns, jaw clenched. "You will if they aren't smart enough to be on that ship by the time we return." I cross my arms and look him up and down, with a man's guts spilled at our feet from one quick stride from Kai. I still stand my ground.

"And what makes you so sure the ones after me aren't already on the ship?"

His eyes go dark. "Because no pirate is stupid enough to step foot on my ship, not when they know who's on it." I search my mind for who could already be there. Then it hits me like a wave crashing over the bow. His father. Kai warned me about him being locked away before I boarded *The Leviathan,* I haven't seen him yet. He must be tucked away pretty well.

"Let's go. Now." He grabs my hand, and I let him lead me, my body pulled forward by instinct and dread. As we walk the coastline, flames flicker across the water. I can't stop thinking about the people who lived here, the ones who didn't make it out. Who lost everything because someone's looking for me.

Fire is the cruelest death I can imagine. If I have to go, I'd rather be taken by the sea. Dragged down by a siren. At least that would feel like something earned.

Through the thick smoke and rising heat, we see them, island folk clashing with invaders, fighting to protect homes. Pirates looting and laughing like devils. "Who do you think it is?" I ask, my voice barely a whisper.

"I don't care to know," Kai mutters. "I just want you on the ship."

The moon paints a silver path across the sea as we slip along the shoreline like shadows. We're invisible out here.

Until he sees us. The largest pirate of them all. He must be the captain. "Kai," I whisper, "He's coming." I brace myself for the impact of whoever this pirate is. Kai moves without a word, stepping in front of me. His body blocks the moonlight, his shadow falling over mine.

A massive figure steps through the haze, shoulders squared and arms thick as iron chains. His coat, singed at the edges and layered in gold and red, clings to him like battle-worn armor. Straps of old rope crisscross his chest, and his beard braided with coins and carved charms, tokens of every ship he's conquered. One eye is cloudy, the other pure gold, gleaming like a cursed jewel. When he smiles, his jagged teeth catch the light, and for a heartbeat, he looks like a man who's eaten gods for sport, a legend bled into myth, and proud of it.

"Like father like son, aye, Kai?" the man calls out. Kai says nothing. He stands his ground, too calm, too quiet. The captain may be larger than life, but Kai is bigger where it counts. He is the Lord of Pirates, and no man outranks him.

"If you give me the girl," the captain says, voice like gravel soaked in blood, "you can leave with your life. Sounds fair, aye?" Kai steps closer, shrinking the man with nothing but his presence.

"Touch her," he growls, "and I'll slit your throat in front of your entire crew. Just enough to let you choke on your own blood." The flames flicker in his eyes, matching the wildfire behind him and the one inside him.

They aren't strangers. That much is clear. "Don't tell me," the captain sneers, his eyes dragging toward me, "You've fallen for the *creature*." His gaze is cold. Inhuman. "She's nothing but a bargaining chip. An expensive one. Now hand her over."

The words slap me like a crashing wave. A fucking creature? Not a woman or a soul? My blood boils. "Fuck you!" I blurt out. Kai moves his arm, holding his sword out in front of me. The captain lets out a low chuckle of a laugh.

"That arm of yours has the sea's curse, aye?" His eyes measure up Kai's body, pinpointing any weakness. "You don't have too much time left, do you?" he mocks.

I can see Kai's jaw ticking. He dismisses the comment the captain made. "Step back, Archer," he warns, voice cold as steel. *Archer.* I know that name. My father beat him in battles many times. However, he did give him a run for his coin.

The name unlocks something deep in my memory. I'd heard whispers of him long ago, back when my father ruled the sea. Archer was a name pirates didn't speak lightly. He was a master of the duel, one of the few who gave my father a run for his treasure. He was the closest to the title Pirate Lord, that was until Kai slayed the Kraken. I hadn't thought of him in years, not until tonight. And now I've seen him with my own eyes. Felt the weight of his threat.

"I'll kill you. No one touches her."

Archer raises his sword. Kai mirrors him. The sound of their blades colliding rings through the air like thunder. Sparks fly. Two more pirates surge forward to defend their captain.

Kai doesn't flinch. He strikes first, one clean, devastating slice across the chest, and the man collapses at his feet. Dead before he hit the ground. It looked effortless.

I turn just in time to catch movement from the corner of my eye. A man charges at me, gun in hand and eyes locked on mine. I move quickly.

Then, a gunshot rings through my ears. The gunshot cracks through the air, louder than anything I've ever heard. My body hits the sand hard. The force of it knocks the breath from me. I look down. My arm is bleeding, just a graze. But I'm not the one who falls. The attacker crumples at my feet, his face half gone, blood pooling into the sand.

Standing behind him, gun still raised, is Smith. "Mira, up. We need to go," he says, voice flat. There's a look in his eyes, one I can't quite place, but it feels wrong.

A heavy, twisting feeling settles in my gut. A warning. *Don't go with him.* "Mira," he says again, stepping closer. "Let's go. I'll get you back to the ship." His voice is too calm, so unlike the man I know. There's something twisted lurking just beneath the surface.

I look over to see Kai still locked in battle with Archer, holding his own. Blades flash in the firelight. I take a step back from Smith. The look in his eyes gives him away. It isn't him anymore. He's never looked at me like I'm something to win or bargain with. Unease ripples through me, followed by heartbreak so deep it nearly splits me open. He's always had my back. Always.

But he's made a deal. He's made a deal with the devil. My eyes narrow. "What are they promising you?"

His stare darkens, like something ancient has rooted itself behind his gaze. "*Power*," he says, smiling. But it isn't his smile. It's something else. Something so dark and twisted, possessed.

Then he lunges. I roll in the sand, barely dodging him, scrambling to my feet. And I run. I run like hell, toward where I know the ship has to be. Please let it still be ours. Please don't let them take any more of my crew.

Thoughts race through my head, knowing I'm going to have to end him. I remember one night on *The Siren*, years ago, just the two of us sitting beside a small lantern while the sea rocked beneath us. I couldn't have been more than fifteen years old. He looked at me with tired eyes and said, "You've always been like a daughter to me. And one day, I won't be there. So you fight. You run. You kill if you have to. Even if it's me."

Like he always knew this day would come. He knows every move I make before I make it. That's the worst part. He trained me, and now he'll use that training against me.

He has to be possessed. He has to be. Because the man I love, the man who raised me, would never betray me. So I keep running. My legs burn and my lungs claw against the smoke, but I don't stop.

I finally see the ship. And the water surrounding it has gone black. *The sirens.* They're here. I don't know whether to feel relieved they've joined the battle or terrified of why.

Their song begins to rise, soft at first, then louder, carrying through the burning sky like a curse wrapped in silk. It slithers under my skin, curls around my ribs. Men start to stagger toward the shoreline. The water darkens further, inky and unnatural, reaching for the land like it's hungry.

I step into the shallows, heart pounding. Please let Kai still be alive. Their song grows louder with every step I take toward the shore. I know they can't walk on land, but the closer they come, the more lethal their voices become. A single verse can shatter a man's mind. And now, they're singing for me.

A massive hand yanks me from the water and slams me into the sand. The wind tears out of my lungs. Before I can move, his blade is at my throat.

"Stupid brat," Smith hisses, breath ragged. "You carry all this power while everyone else rots." The steel presses into my skin, sharp enough to split it. Warm blood slides down my throat, trailing along the edge of his blade.

"I spend my life protecting you," he spits. "Every broken bone, every scar, I take those for you. And what do I get? To watch you play captain? Spoiled. Soft. Blind to everything we gave up." His hand trembles, just slightly, like he's battling himself. "You becoming captain is the worst thing that's ever happened to this crew," he growls. "To me."

He sneers down at me. "You're a witch," he says, voice dripping with venom. "And you deserve to burn." He spits into the sand, but I keep my eyes locked on his, those eyes that once watched over me like a guardian. Now they are obsidian black. Empty. Possessed. Or worse... willing.

My fingers inch toward my cutlass, slow and quiet. Then in one fluid motion, I twist out from under him and slice into his leg. He roars and spins around. I quickly scramble to my feet. Steel meets steel.

"You think you can take me?" he snarls, breath ragged. "I taught you everything you know." My blade doesn't waver.

"Then you're facing a weapon of your own making," I say, voice cold as the sea. I drive him back, step by step, toward the black water and toward what waits beneath.

He's slower now, older and heavier. My strength isn't in my size, or even my anger. It is in my clarity. In knowing exactly who I am, and who he no longer is.

I slam the hilt of my cutlass into his face. His nose crunches. Blood sprays. Still, he smiles through it, teeth stained red, wild and ruined.

"I have to say, Smith," I breathe, never lowering my blade. "I didn't think it'd be you." He sneers, blood still dripping from his nose. "But I guess"—I step back, arms crossing over my chest—"one more life gets claimed because of mine tonight."

His eyes widen. "You stupid, foolish man." I spit at him; he opens his mouth, no doubt ready to spit more poison. But he never gets the chance. A webbed hand shoots from the black water. Claws—long, jagged, and hungry—sink into his ankle like a trap snapping shut.

Smith screams out in pain. The siren yanks. His body slams against the sand, dragged so fast the mist tears up in sheets. He claws at the earth, kicks, and howls. One final scream, then silence.

He's gone. Swallowed by the black water. Gone beneath the surface with no trace left behind. His soul now belongs to the sirens.

I walk to where his body was claimed and let my toes touch the dark water. Relief floods me. The black, salty tide seizes me like I belong to it. Maybe I do. I step deeper into the ink. Gold light blooms around me beneath the surface, flaring like fire beneath the waves. Behind me, the town is in flames. Smoke claws at my throat, the taste of ruin thick in the air.

I look up and see them. Sirens, dozens of them, swimming toward me through the darkness. One surfaces in front of me. Her voice slices through the chaos, sharp as broken glass yet hauntingly angelic. "Mira," she says, "you will always be protected. We are your home."

Her eyes shimmer like stars scattered across the night sky. The sirens are not beautiful, not by any human standards. Their bodies are covered in jagged black scales, each one edged like a blade. Their hands are webbed, fingers ending in long, hooked claws designed for shredding.

But still, I don't flinch. "We will help take you back to your ship," she says. And despite everything, the war, the fire, the betrayal, I feel calm. How can something so eerily terrifying make me feel this safe?

I swim underwater toward the ship, fifteen sirens at my sides. They move like shadows through the black water, silent and lethal. When I reach the ship, I grab the rope ladder and climb, saltwater dripping from my skin.

At the top, I turn back. The siren who spoke to me hovers just beneath the surface, only her eyes above the water. "Thank you," I say softly. "Please help me get Kai back. Don't harm him. He's part of me."

She blinks slowly, then smiles, revealing a row of gleaming, razor-sharp teeth. "We know who he is," she says. "He will make it back safely. You have my word." Then she slips beneath the surface, her body gliding through the water like silk, leaving only a small ripple behind as the moonlight dances across the black water.

CHAPTER TWENTY-FOUR

MIRA

STILL WATERS

My bare feet touch the deck of the ship. My crew and Kai's were all here. Kai was right. They were smart enough to make it back. "Cap'n," Nate calls, stepping forward. "You okay?"

I don't answer right away. My eyes cut across the deck, my hand instinctively brushing the hilt of my cutlass. Staying close to the ship's edge, where the sea waits, comforting, deadly, *mine*. It's a strange thing, realizing you trust the ocean more than the wood beneath your feet.

"I'm fine," I say, voice steady. "What the fuck happened?"

Nate hesitates, taking a cautious step forward.

"That's far enough," I warn, sharp and sure. He freezes, hands slightly raised.

"They hit the island hard. We couldn't find you or Cap'n Kai. We thought the safest move was to regroup here. The town's gone, torched.

They were looking for you." His voice falters as he glances around the crew. "Smith... he was paying someone off. Last time we made port. They've been tracking us since."

A cold, slow fury rises inside me. "You knew Smith paid someone off and didn't tell me?" I growl. "Did you think we wouldn't find out?"

"I didn't know until tonight," Nate replies quickly, eyes wide. "If I had, I swear I would've said something. Most of us thought he was paying off a prostitute, as usual." I narrow my eyes at him, searching for a crack, a tell, anything. But there is nothing. His eyes, clear and sea-blue, give nothing away.

Still, something in me stays on edge. My trust, once given freely, now has thorns. And I don't plan on bleeding for anyone ever again.

I look up at the rest of the crew. Every one of them wears the same haunted expression, concern etched deep into their features. Before I can speak, Kai vaults back onto the ship. The second I see him, the tension in my chest loosens. Relief crashes over me, stealing the breath from my lungs. Just knowing he's been out there, onshore with too many ill-intentioned pirates to count, has my stomach churning, bile rising in my throat. After what we just shared, the thought of losing him now makes something inside me claw to the surface.

But a part of me also knows that Kai rarely loses. He is the first and only Pirate Lord for a reason. He carves that title out of blood and grit. Pirates worship him for it.

Kai steps toward me, slipping an arm around my waist to turn me. Then both of his hands come to rest on my arms, steadying me in place. He searches me, eyes burning gold beneath the moonlight. His gaze drags over every inch of me, inspecting.

When he sees the dried blood at my chin, he brushes it away with his thumb, gentle, yet fierce with intent. His touch lingers for a second, as if trying to take the pain from me.

He has a long gash down the left side of his face, slicing from his brow to the edge of his jaw. My breath catches. I reach up and touch the cut, fingertips brushing away flecks of sand, the gesture tender but filled with worry.

He has blood all over him. I can only pray it isn't his. "I'm okay," I say softly, offering the words before he can even ask. He gives a slight shrug, eyes already scanning the crew.

Then his voice cuts through the silence. "If any of you is a traitor," he says, low and deadly, "I'll kill you in front of everyone. I'll make sure they all watch you die a pitiful death. If that's you, I suggest you walk the damn plank now. And *pray* to whatever god you believe in that I don't catch you."

He starts pacing the deck, each step deliberate. His hair is soaked, dripping seawater onto the wood. His jaw ticks as the rage in him boils. I wonder briefly how his swim with the sirens went, what they said and what they showed him. Did he even swim with them at all?

Under the moonlight, he looks carved from vengeance itself. His fury stretches him taller, makes the air around him hum with menace. Every muscle is tight with restraint, but only barely. He's livid, at Smith, at the betrayal, at how close danger had crept to me without him seeing it first.

I look around the deck. His crew looks terrified, as if they've seen what he can do before and have no desire to see it again. My crew, while tense, is calmer. They haven't yet witnessed the full extent of Kai Eldoris's wrath. But they will understand it soon enough.

"Jay, come with me. I want a full report. Everyone else, back to work," Kai orders, his voice like steel against the crashing waves. He turns without waiting for acknowledgment, walking with the confidence of someone who's already made up his mind. Jay follows close behind, both of them disappearing into a part of the ship I haven't explored yet. A war room, I assume. Which then leads me to the thought, where does Kai keep Captain Eldoris stored away?

For a moment, I consider going after them. But something tells me to give Kai space, to let him cool off and strategize. He needs that, and frankly, so do I.

What I want is simple: to strip out of my salt-stiffened clothes, crawl into bed, and watch the waves slap against the hull while I bite into something sweet. Chocolate. I always have a secret stash.

But the ache in my chest doesn't fade. Smith's betrayal leaves me feeling hollow. His words sting like a box jellyfish, sharp and venomous. I can understand his grief, maybe even his bitterness. Watching crewmates die protecting me isn't easy. But he knows what he signed up for. He knows what this life demands.

Smith was the closest thing I had to a father. He helped raise me. Protected me. Watched over me when no one else would. He taught me how to tie my boots when my fingers were too small to get the knots right. He was there when I cracked my ribs in a training match and said I took it better than most grown men do. He trained me for battle, taught me how to fight smart, taught me how to survive.

If he truly had been my father's first mate, then he knew everything about my mother, about the choices my father made. About the risks of protecting someone like me. He was supposed to be my ally. Now I'm starting to see why Neressa slaughtered all of her mentors. So no one alive knows her next move.

When my father was off chasing some cursed treasure, it was Smith who trained me and who watched over me. Smith who told me to never let anyone take me, not even him. But that man is gone. And now, so is the lie he wrapped around me.

His betrayal will weigh heavy in my heart. But his death will float, light as a feather, now that I know who he truly was.

I'm left uneasy, haunted by Smith's final words. Power, he said, like it was worth more than life itself. Worth more than the crew, than me. Does no one realize that killing me would shatter the ocean's balance? That my death wouldn't just end a life, it would unravel everything?

I'm still trying to understand the weight of what's been placed on me. To make peace with it. But I know I *have* to live. Not for myself, but for the sea and for Kai.

The poisoned Soul of the Ocean has grown sick, twisted by greed, betrayal, and ancient rot. I am the only thread left holding it all together. The only hope to restore what's been lost. Every step I take from here on out is for the creatures who swim beneath the waves. For peace, for this war that is being built from the deep trenches to be stopped. For Kai. And for the sirens, creatures I once feared, now deeply tied to me. Misunderstood, mythologized, and feared for all the wrong reasons, but they are not monsters. They are fiercely loyal and they're my home now. I want to know them for what they truly are.

I can only pray Kai finds it in his heart to open up to them too. To see that they were there the moment I needed them most. It was as if they could feel my fear, my rage, the betrayal in my heart. Read my intent. They knew exactly what I was doing when I lured Smith closer to the water's edge. I wasn't scared, not then. Because when the sea turned that haunting, beautiful shade of obsidian black, I knew I wasn't alone.

Kai made it back to the ship safely, through black waters that would've swallowed any other man whole. The sirens must have escorted him. I want to know what happened out there. What was said and what wasn't. I want to be a fly on the wall during his conversation with Jay.

I haven't made it back to our quarters. I wander instead, my thoughts swirling like the tide. Staring out at the ocean, the moonlight glittering across the surface, I feel the ache of everything. My mind unspools at sea. I wonder if the sirens are silently gliding through the night water beneath the ship. The water always does that to me, wraps around my soul and pulls at all the knots I've tucked away.

Very like me, I suppose, to be lost in the sea's beauty. I am a Pisces, after all. And Kai is a Scorpio. Of course he is. Born in the season of storms, tethered to secrets, shadows, and the pull of deep waters. He once told me his favorite part of our quarters is the windows, not just for the view, but because he likes to watch the sunrise break over the sea. He said it reminds him that no matter how dark things get, the ocean always finds its light again.

We're both water signs. It makes sense now, why I feel everything so deeply, and why he hides everything he feels like it's a weapon. He is the storm, and I am the tide, pulled to him no matter how far I try to drift. Dangerous, beautiful, and impossible not to love.

"Cap'n?" Nate's voice breaks through the hum of my thoughts. I turn to face him. He stands a respectful distance away, hands loose at his sides. He's maybe ten years older than me, but his presence carries a calm authority that makes men listen. Salt-and-pepper strands streak through his dark blond hair tied back at the nape of his neck. A deep scar curves along his jaw, a faded reminder of battles long past. He joined my crew a few years after I was born.

"I want you to know, Smith never told any of us what he planned. Not about leaving. Not about hurting you," Nate says, his voice low but firm. "I've watched you grow from a wild little girl into a captain men will follow into the storm. The crew on this ship, your crew, they're here because they believe in you. We'll protect you with our lives. That's what your father would want."

He pauses for a breath, the flicker of something unspoken passing through his expression. "I can't speak for Captain Kai's men," he adds, "but we're with him too. Anyone who has your back the way he does earns our respect and loyalty."

His words settle in my chest like warmth after a long, cold swim. I hadn't realized how much I needed to hear them. "Thank you, Nate," I say. "Your loyalty is all I could ask for." He gives a short nod, the kind shared between people who've been through hell and still keep going. Then I turn and make my way to my quarters.

I undress, peeling off the soaking wet clothes and letting the sting of the cold night air bite at my skin. The lantern flares to life, its soft glow casting shadows across the room as I sink into our bed. A long-sleeved shirt lies draped over the chair—lightweight, worn, and saturated with the scent of tobacco and sea salt.

I curl beneath the satin blankets, facing the long window. The sea shimmers in the dark, and I let the sound of waves lull me. I must fall asleep waiting for him, because I wake to sunlight kissing my face, warming my skin like a promise.

I roll over, sensing him before I see him. "Morning, treasure." Kai's voice is low and raspy, gravel laced with heat, the kind of sound that sends goosebumps down my spine. I turn and see him standing at the door in nothing but his underwear, a cup of coffee in one hand. The steam curls around his face in delicate swirls, catching the morning light.

His hair is damp, tousled from sleep or sea, I can't tell. I don't care. He looks like sin and salvation all at once.

"Morning," I say, my voice soft but with worry. "Are you okay?"

He sits beside me, the mattress dipping beneath his weight. "Yeah. Just... figuring out a plan."

I narrow my eyes. "A plan? For what?"

He reaches for my hand, wrapping his fingers around mine. "To protect you. Mira, you're not safe. You need to go somewhere, somewhere no one can find you. To train, to strengthen. Not that you need it, but it could help you protect yourself in battle."

I pull my hand back, holding his gaze. "First off, I can protect myself. Never bring that up again. Second, I'm not leaving you. I'm not leaving my crew. And I will never abandon this mission. We are going to find that fountain together. We're going to make our wishes together. We are going to save you." I glance at the black veins spreading down his arm and his hand. "Do you understand?" My voice doesn't waver. I need him to know there's no version of this story where I run.

He exhales slowly, nodding. "Understood. But we need better ways of keeping you safe." He hesitates, just long enough to make my heart skip.

I meet his gaze, steady and unflinching. "We're pirates, love. Nowhere's safe." A slow smile tugs at his lips.

"Luckily, I had a conversation with the sirens last night."

My eyes widen. "And?" I ask, my pulse already racing. Unlike Kai, I've never been good at keeping calm when it matters most.

"They're going to help us," Kai says. "They'll show us where Sirens Cove is." He pauses. "But like everything else... it comes with a price."

A chill slides down my spine. "What do they want?"

He walks to the desk, grabbing the black long sleeve slung over the chair. As he pulls it on, my heart pounds louder in my ears. "They want the all-powerful witch," he says, buckling his belt, attaching each weapon with careful precision. "And they want you to help them get her."

My blood runs cold. "Taika?" He doesn't answer right away. He just crosses the room slowly until he stands at the edge of the bed. The morning sunlight pours in through the window behind him, casting a golden glow across his face. It catches the flecks of green and gold in his eyes, turning them into wildfire.

"Yes," he says. "It's time the witch burns."

CHAPTER TWENTY-FIVE

KAI

DEALS & BLOOD

Anger burns through me at Smith's betrayal, simmering in my blood. Knowing how much it's tearing Mira apart makes me sick with disgust. I want to be the one to drag him to the plank myself. But death by a siren feels more fitting. More painful. More poetic.

The rage fuels me as I finish off Archer, slitting his throat. I search him as he lies gasping, blood pooling in the sand beneath us. I find a seashell in his pocket, one that looks exactly like Mira's. Even in his final moments, his eyes widen in fear when I take it from him.

I lean close, my knee pressing into the blood-soaked sand, my voice a low growl. "The moon controls the tides. And they're never in your favor, mate. Not even the stars will weep for you. Your bones will rot beneath black water where the sirens wait to drag you under. Tell the

Kraken his killer sends another soul to choke on." I stand, the sand clinging to my hands, to my bloodied clothes. Another infamous pirate dead by my blade. I slip the seashell into my pocket, turn my back on him, and walk to the shoreline.

Mira wears a small vial of liquid around her neck and always carries a seashell in her pocket. I've never asked what they mean, figured maybe they were something from her parents, or another life she never talks about. But seeing something so similar on Archer makes me wonder.

A pirate like Archer never bothered with sentiment. His heart, if he ever had one, was as cold as the ice caps in the far north. He was infamous, scandalous, a name whispered like a curse across the sea. Gave me a slight run for my coin, but I took the title. Something he could never live up to. His death won't go unnoticed.

He struck deals with creatures from the depths. And when those deals soured, he bargained with even darker forces to save his own skin. Whispers always followed him, rumors that he'd made a pact with a witch whose magic was as vile as it was potent. Dark magic. The kind that could pull even the strongest souls into the abyss and devour them whole. I'd never touch that sort of power. Being strong on your own, without selling your soul to monsters in the dark, that's real power. That's the kind of power Mira and I were born for.

I press the shell to my ear, and a chorus of eerie whispers spills out. I can't make out the words, but I know this is no ordinary sound. It's dark magic, something I don't want anywhere near Mira.

I slip the seashell back into my pocket and step into the black water, heading for the ship. Halfway there, a siren surfaces in front of me, watching with unblinking eyes. I don't slow my pace. I look past her, searching the deck. When I see Mira climbing up the ladder, a wave of relief washes through me. A sigh I didn't realize I was holding slips out. She's *safe*. That's all that matters.

"You love her," a voice whispers from the water, curling into my ear, cold as the grave. I glance around but see nothing in the black water. The darkness stirs up an old memory. The depths nearly claimed me once, and part of me still hears them calling. Except now, I don't flinch. I keep walking deeper, the cold wrapping around me like an old friend. Maybe I'm just hearing things.

Then I hear it again. "Don't you?" A dark fin cuts through the moonlit water before disappearing beneath the surface. I'm not alone.

"Show yourself," I demand, my voice steady. A head rises from the water, skin pale and slick, abyssal eyes wide and reflective, catching the moonlight like twin mirrors. She blinks, the motion strange, her gaze flicking in a direction no human eyes could turn. Her eyes hold starlight, vast, cold, and unreadable.

"It's good that you do," she whispers, her voice like breaking glass. "It's what keeps you alive, after all." She smiles, revealing razor-sharp teeth. The sight of them sends a chill down my spine. Not much scares me, but the sirens do.

She lets out a laugh, a high, shrieking sound that burns in my ears, then dives beneath the surface, gone as quickly as she appears.

I begin to swim, pushing through the black water, the moonlight glinting on the waves, guiding me back to the ship. Then she surfaces beside me again, gliding through the water with unnatural ease.

"I can help you," she hisses, voice thin and sharp. "And her." I follow her gaze, seeing where she looks, up at the ship, where Mira stands silhouetted against the light.

"And I'm supposed to blindly trust you?" I ask, keeping my strokes steady.

She ignores my words, slipping in front of me, moving like a serpent through the sea. "I can show you the way to our cove. But you must do one thing for us," she whispers.

"If you tell me where Sirens Cove is," I growl, "I'll give you anything."

She smiles, her mouth filled with jagged blades. "You love her enough to give up anything?" she coos, as if it was even a question.

"Anything?" I spit. She leans in closer. "Everything," I say, steady, deadly calm.

"We want the witch, the all-powerful one. Then the fountain will be yours, if you can find it once you're inside the cove." She snickers, the sound hissing through her sharp teeth. Her sisters join in, their laughter curling around me. She acts like I give a damn about the witch. Mira is the one who cares, not me.

"I'll get you the witch," I say sternly. "Be ready to take her." I reach the ship, grabbing the ladder and pulling myself up. I look back down at the water, locking eyes with the lead siren.

"I love her," I say, my voice low, steady. "To the ends of the earth, to the very depths of the sea, I will love her. I'll give you what you want, but only if you give me what I need in return. Know this: every single breath I take is for *her*. You need her alive, just the same."

I hang there, one arm hooked on the ladder, swaying with the water beneath me. She hovers close, silent, watching me with those unblinking eyes. Strange, how a siren, a creature made of hunger and death, could almost seem comforting.

"Hmmm. Good boy. Smart boy," she says, then slips beneath the waves, gone. Anger burns through me again as I climb the rest of the way up to the deck. Smith's betrayal twists in my gut like a knife. If there was anyone else on this ship thinking of harming her, they'd find out exactly what kind of monster I could be. Their death would be cruel. Slow.

Magic prickles at my fingertips, pulsing just beneath my skin, begging to be released. It has been reacting stronger lately, like it's tied to my rage. Or maybe it's been fighting against the infection of the scar. Trying to keep me alive. I still haven't figured out how to control the magic, how to let it out without losing myself. But I will. And when I do, gods help whoever tries to hurt her.

I climb up the ladder, soaking wet and seething, and there she is. Mira. Standing as close as she can to the railing, her arms wrapped tight around herself. Even if she'll never admit it, she's terrified. And she should never be terrified on my ship, *our* ship. I can hear her heart pounding in my ears, wild, unsteady. Mine, in moments like this, only grow calmer. Cold. Calculating.

I want to kill every single one of the crew, loyal or not, for standing there useless, just watching her. Not one of them offered a blanket. Not one of them moves to help. Rage pulses through me, hot and thick, begging to spill out like lava.

I look her up and down, every inch, making sure she's whole. That speck of blood on her chin makes my vision blur with fury. Her blood. *My blood.* Even the smallest drop, it was mine. And it was spilled.

There are specks of sand stuck to her eyelashes, tangled in her hair. She looks battered by the night, and all I want is to scoop her into my arms and burn the world down for daring to touch her.

When I call for Jay, I want answers. I want loyalty. "What the fuck happened?" I growl as he lit the lantern in the study. I watch him carefully, scanning him head to toe for any sign of guilt or deception. "I couldn't tell you, Cap'n," Jay says, steady but tired. "He was just gone. Disappeared at sunset."

My brow twitches, eyes narrowing. "What do you mean he was just gone?"

Jay shakes his head. "I mean he was with us at the pub, then he wasn't. And then the town went up in flames. No one knew where he was. We all knew how important he was to Mira, so we kept searchin'. Couldn't find him. Couldn't find you either, so we headed back to protect the ship."

His voice is genuine. Jay has never lied to me. But neither did Smith, until he did. That betrayal creeps under my skin, making me question everything. I never thought twice about Smith. Never thought he'd turn. Not after how fiercely loyal he's been to the Bleu family name.

"I don't think any of you realize how important she is to me," I say, voice low as I stare down at the map sprawled across the large oak table.

"I understand, Cap," Jay says.

I look up, meeting his icy blue eyes dead-on. "I don't think you ever will." The words come out colder than intended.

I start pacing. "But I need your loyalty now more than ever. She needs it. If I fall, you follow her. You protect her. Until the end. Understood?"

Jay leans against the doorway, arms crossed, his face hard. "You have it," he says with a nod, steady as stone.

I believe him, for now. I give him a nod, gesturing for him to come closer and take a seat. Then we turn our attention to the map, plotting where the hell Sirens Cove might be and how we are going to take down the most powerful witch in the world.

"You want to just hand her over? You think she's that easy to catch? She's the most powerful, lethal witch for a reason," Mira snaps, standing her ground. She lets out a sharp sigh. "I can't let you take her, Kai. She and I have a deal. She has ties to my family. You're underestimating her. You don't just pick her up. She will kill you."

I watch her as she paces across our room, hands moving wildly as she talks. The morning sun catches the curve of her hips, the softness of her thighs. Her hair is a mess and her face flushes with anger. Gods, she is beautiful.

"I made a deal too, Mira," I say, voice low. "One that will help you. One that will save us. What better way to find the cursed cove than by the ones who reside in it? I thought you trusted the sirens?"

"I absolutely trust them," she fires back. "But I will never risk your life for anything. There will be another way into the cove." Her words strike me straight through the chest. She is a dream come to life, fierce and soft and impossible to let go.

I stand up from the bed and walk over to her, cupping the side of her face, gently forcing her to look up at me. My other hand slides around her lower back, pulling her closer. Her big, beautiful green eyes gaze up at me, shimmering like the sirens' sea, deep and endless.

I kiss her softly. "I won't risk you either. You're the most important thing in this entire sea. We've both made our deals, but we need to prioritize. What did you promise Taika?" My voice is firm.

"A wish," she says quietly. "I promised her a wish." I search her face, trying to read her. She gives nothing away.

"What does she want to wish for?"

Mira looks down, then back up at me. "I don't know. She was vague. She said it wasn't for my ears to hear yet, just that her wish was dark."

A chill sweeps through me. "Dark? You promised her a dark wish? Mira, she'll wish for something twisted, something with black magic. You can't give her that. The fountain is pure, so no dark magic can be near it."

She pulls away from me. "You don't know that. Remember, she gave me the map that led me to you. Why it turned red, I don't know, but it brought me to you."

I stroke the stubble on my jaw, watching her, studying her every move. "We need to find her," I say, leaving no room for argument.

She doesn't say anything at first, just pulls away from me slowly. I let her go with ease. She starts getting dressed, her movements quick and focused. "Mira," I say, watching her, "you need to lead the way. I don't know how to find her. My best guess is Alek, but once we're inside those haunting seas... I don't know where to start." I have a feeling my magic could lead me. But someone like Taika is only found when she wants to be. And honestly, I've avoided Alek my entire life.

She glances up at me while lacing her boots. "I know. I just..." Her voice catches in her throat. "I don't want us to make the wrong move. What do you plan on doing when we find her?" Worry clouds her eyes, heavy and real.

"I'll figure that out when we get there," I say. "We'll hear what she has to say. Then we'll decide, together."

Mira shakes her head and stands, heading for the door. She pauses, hand on the handle, turning back to me. "I will follow you to the ends of this world," she says quietly, "but I won't stand by and watch you lead yourself to your own death. That path, I cannot follow."

She straps on her belt, securing her weapons, then takes her father's hat and sets it on her head. In that moment, she looks every bit the captain she was born to be, even the air shifting around her as she steps out of the room.

CHAPTER TWENTY-SIX

MIRA

SEVERED BLOODLINES

I left our captain's quarters with my blood boiling. I knew he could hear my heart beating out of my chest, could feel the rage pouring off me in waves. I don't know why he thinks this is a good idea. He's going to put everyone in danger, mostly himself. He's always throwing himself into the fire like he thinks he's invincible. Maybe he is.

Trying to take down the most powerful witch alive is a death wish. Even if we somehow make a deal with Taika, it would just be another debt hanging over our heads. A deadly debt, owed to an even deadlier witch.

I had to leave the room before I pushed him further, before I told him exactly why we shouldn't go after her. If the sirens are asking for Taika, they need her for something. Maybe they have a debt to settle too. Part

of me wishes they would have come to me instead of Kai. After all...
I'm one of them.

We spend the day sailing. I avoid Kai as much as possible, which isn't
hard. He and Jay are locked away in the study plotting gods know what.
I'm tired, and all I want is the open sea and the quiet, endless horizon.

The sun has long since set. I climb the ladder to my favorite spot high
up on the ship's tallest sail, where the ocean breeze kisses my face and
the night feels endless. Up here, with the world quiet and still, it always
feels like if I just reach out far enough, I could pluck a star from the sky
and tuck it into my pocket, saving a wish for another night.

Below, the deck is mostly dark aside from a few glowing lanterns.
Some of the crew linger near the railings, smoking, sipping rum, and
swapping old sea tales. I love this time of night when nothing is
happening. When the world feels hushed and the moonlight turns the
ocean into a silver mirror.

I listen to the waves splashing against the ship's hull and feel the
gentle sway of the deck beneath me. I lick my lips and taste salt, the
ocean's breath on my skin. The sea was my first love. It was supposed
to be my only love until he came along

Making my way down the ladder from the sail, I decide to explore
the parts of the ship I've never dared to before. Taking advantage of the
quiet night, I slip past a few crewmates, nodding to them as I pass. I
keep my steps light, careful not to startle anyone. Before I boarded *The
Leviathan*, Kai told me his father was still here, very sick but still alive.
I haven't heard a word about him since. Part of me wants to ask—the
other part doesn't care to dig. For all I know, the bastard could be dead.

But an uneasy feeling settles over me, prickling the back of my neck.
For the first time on this ship, I felt unsafe. I quicken my pace, glancing
over my shoulder, seeing nothing.

Then a strong hand grabs me, yanking me into a side door so fast I can't fight back. Whoever this is knows exactly what he's doing. The tall figure shoves me down a few steps, picks me up again, and slams me into the wall. Pain explodes in my skull, my vision going hazy. I try to focus, but the room is nearly pitch black, only the moonlight spilling in through a small window.

"So you're the one who's brainwashed my son," a voice rasps from the dark, cold and venomous. "Such a pity." My heart stutters in my chest. Captain Eldoris. The man who slaughtered my mother in front of me when I was just a child. The man whose life mission is to wipe out my entire bloodline. Now he has me.

If he's as insane as they say, he's a loose cannon. He could kill me right here and no one would know. Kai has no idea where I went. I haven't seen him since morning. If he were following me, I would have noticed.

I am alone.

"A pity?" I spit at him, trying to steady my breath.

"Mhmm," he groans, locking the door behind him with a click that makes my blood run cold. Now it really is just him and me.

Rage burns through me. I want to gut the bastard who destroyed my family, the monster who haunted my nightmares.

"Pity I'll have to kill you like your mother," he sneered, stepping closer. "My son will be heartbroken, but he'll get over it. You're just another dumb wench."

Red bleeds across my vision. My voice trembles with fury. "I'm not just another one," I hiss. "I am *the* one. And you've already made your last mistake." If he kills me, Kai will fall too. "If you don't want to watch your son die, then put that blade down. Because killing me is killing him."

He moves like smoke, quick and twisted. "He's tied to you?" he spits, venom thick on his tongue. "What a disgrace." He steps closer, and the cold in his eyes slices deeper than any steel. "Maybe I'll kill you both. Tear out his heart by ending you. Let him drown in the bond he never asked for."

He lunges at me, his long, bony fingers wrapping around my neck. He lifts me off the ground effortlessly. I gasp, clawing at his hands as he squeezes, cutting off my air. He reeks of tobacco and rum, his eyes wild. "I make no mistakes, child," he growls. "You are a disease. I could end it all now. Wipe your bloodline from the sea forever."

His grip tightens and my legs kick uselessly as I try to fight back. He's too strong. I feel helpless—exactly how he wants me. I've never let my guard down this much before, and now it might get me killed.

He has me pinned to the wall, no room to move, no room to breathe. Everything starts going fuzzy, my ears ringing like a war drum. Then I hear the faint noise of a lock unclicking. "What the fuck did I tell you about touching *my treasure*, old man?" Kai's voice is low, lethal. "You wish to die where you stand?"

Eldoris drops me, and I crumple to the ground, gasping for air. My throat burns, bruises already blooming beneath my skin from where his fingers crushed me. I can't catch a breath. My body aches from the fall, from the lack of oxygen. Bile rises in my throat, but I swallow it down, focusing on the scene in front of me.

Eldoris steps toward Kai, rage twisting his face. "I could have rid the world of her cursed bloodline," he snarls. "You always find a way to fuck things up. You've been in the way since you were a child. Now you tied your soul to this filthy disease? Maybe I should kill one of you, so I can watch the other die."

I can't see Kai's face, but I can feel his anger radiating through the room, thick and suffocating. His shadow grows larger as he steps forward, his magic crackling just beneath the surface. "If this is what you've become in your lucid moments," Kai says, voice cold as steel, "then there's no point keeping you alive."

Eldoris moves closer, sneering. Kai drew his sword, the moonlight glinting off the blade. "You'd kill me for her?" Eldoris roars. "Your own blood? Your father!?"

"I would kill anyone for her. *Especially* my sick twisted father." The next sound is wet and final, Kai's blade sliding through Eldoris's stomach. The old man chokes on his own blood as his worthless body slides off the blade and hits the floor. The scent of iron fills the room, stinging my nose, thick and metallic.

Kai stands over him, staring down. Eldoris gurgles, blood bubbling up his throat as he choked out his final words. "Taika... my love... free me..." His voice drains away with his last breath.

"What the fuck? What did he just say?" Kai growls, his shadow falling over the lifeless body.

I can feel the crack in his heart, the weight of what he's done pressing into him like a crushing wave. All I can think is that Captain Eldoris, the man who haunted my nightmares, has just been brought down by the one person no one ever saw coming.

The room reeks of blood, old smoke, rum, and death. My mind reels to make sense of what I've just seen.

Why would Eldoris's final word be Taika? Why would he beg her to free him? Was there something between them Kai hadn't told me? But even as my thoughts spiral, one truth anchors itself in my chest. Kai killed him. Not out of spite from Eldoris being a terrible father, but for me. He severed the past to protect our future. And I don't know if I'll ever find the words for what that means, for what he means.

Kai rushes over, scoops me up like I weigh nothing, and carries me out of the godsforsaken room I didn't even know existed, leaving his father's body behind to rot. No one has ever fought for me like that. No one has ever chosen me like that.

Back in our quarters, he lays me gently on the bed and lights the lantern. Then he sits beside me in silence, his hazel eyes swirling with gold and green and firelight, like molten honey dripping down a moss-covered branch.

His hand brushes the side of my face, then slides down to my neck. His eyes go wide with fury, his heartbeat slowing to that eerie crawl that means he's on the edge of something dangerous. He doesn't have to say a word. I know the bruises must look bad. He looks breathtaking like this, all sharp lines and soft shadows, the moonlight spilling in through the window and highlighting every perfect angle.

"Can you breathe okay?" he asks, his voice tight with worry and his eyes softening as they meet mine.

I try to speak, but it feels like swallowing glass. "Enough," I croak out, raspy and broken.

"Good. Drink," he murmurs, holding out a glass of water. "It'll help open your airway a little."

I take a sip of the water, wincing as it slides down my raw, burning throat. Kai doesn't say a word. He just watches me, his gaze tracking every tiny movement like he's afraid I might disappear if he blinks.

A few moments pass before I find enough strength to speak. "Are you okay?" I rasp out. I don't care about myself right now. All I can think about is him, what he's just done. He's lost the only parent he has left in this world. And he's the one who ended it.

I know he's ruthless. The tales of him cutting down men twice his age, taking ships by force, earning the title of Pirate Lord at such a young age, they aren't just stories. But seeing it with my own eyes... seeing how far he'll go to protect me still stuns me.

Now he has ended two pirate legends in the matter of days. No one will come for him again. "I'm fine, Mira," he murmurs, eyes flicking back to my throat, his fingers brushing gently over the bruises forming there. "I need you to be okay."

I can feel the rage simmering in him, hot and crackling just beneath the surface, like lava about to explode from a volcano. The magic under his skin pulses with it, wild and electric. "I can feel you," I whispers, laying my hand gently over his. "Everything inside you."

He looks at me, broken and unyielding all at once. "He wouldn't have stopped," he says, voice low and raw. "Not until you were gone. I didn't want to do it, but there was no other way." He swallows hard. "If I'd let him live, I would've lost you."

I reach up, brushing my fingers along the side of his face. He closes his eyes, leaning into my touch like it's the only thing keeping him from slipping under. When he opens them again, something burns there, grief and love. "I know," I say softly. "I know what it cost you."

He looks at me like I am the last light in a world he barely believes in anymore. "I love you, Mira," he whispers. "I would burn the world for you."

Then he kisses me, slow and sure. Every part of me feels warm, safe, whole. Gods, he is everything. Hearing those three words from his lips makes me feel complete.

"I love you too, Kai," I breathe. "My quiet. My chaos. My home." His expression shifts, like the stars themselves have lit up just for him. He moves closer, resting his forehead against mine, his breath steady as he inhales me in, like he's memorizing the moment. Then he presses a kiss to my cheek, soft and sure.

If I hadn't just been nearly choked to death, we'd already be tangled in each other. But for now, just lying here wrapped in each other and the warm glow of the lantern is enough. In this moment, it feels like our souls have tied themselves together all over again. And I never want it to end.

CHAPTER TWENTY-SEVEN

KAI

MOTHERLESS

My father's body slides off my sword, silver and crimson glistening in the moonlight as he collapses to the floor. Blood sprays across my boots. I don't feel anything.

I'm too late.

My gaze finds Mira where she fell. Her neck is ringed in bruises, his handprints seared into her perfect skin. Her lips are parted like she tried to call for me, like she thought I'd come. I was *supposed* to come. I was always supposed to be right there for her. He took her breath from her, drained every bit of her.

I fall to my knees beside her, my sword slipping from my hand with a dull clang. "No," I whisper, voice raw. "No, no, no." I touch her cheek, her skin still barely warm. "*I'm so sorry.*"

Rage tears through me, blinding and feral. I don't stop until there's nothing left but silence and the sea howling outside.

I was too fucking late. Too slow. Too human. And Mira is gone.

I wake gasping for air, the sheets clinging to me, damp with cold sweat. For a moment, I don't know where I am. The room sways, shadows crawling across the walls like they're still alive. My pulse hammers in my throat as I turn—

Mira.

Alive. Perfectly alive in bed beside me. The bruises around her neck are there, but faint in the low light, fading shades of purple and blue. Her chest rises and falls, slow and steady. She's safe.

I reach out, afraid she'll vanish if I blink. My hand trembles as I brush her cheek, her freckles scattered like tiny stars across her skin. Relief floods in so sharp it aches. The thought of losing her is unbearable, even in a nightmare.

I pull the covers higher around her shoulders, tucking her into the warmth, as if I can protect her from the ghosts still clawing at my mind. Then I stand, dress, and buckle my sword to my belt. My legs feel unsteady, like reality could give way and toss me back into the nightmare at any second.

Outside, the night air is cold, salt biting at my lips. I head for the helm, breathing in the crisp morning air, trying to believe. The dream still clings to me, heavy and wet, like blood that won't wash away.

Some of it was real. I did kill my father last night.

"Taika, my love. Free me." The echo from his words haunts me.

Dawn creeps over the horizon in a slow bleed of gray. I'm at the helm, guiding us toward Alek, the place Mira said we'd find her. They say Alek is where witches are born from bone and salt, where the fog is so thick it weeps. Where the sea bows out of fear. You can only enter if you're expected. If not, the fog will find you, and it will suffocate you.

My father's words churn in my gut. "The woman chose power over you. Over us," he rasped, eyes already dimming.

I don't want to believe it. Gods, I don't. But the truth is pressing down on me like a rising tide. I thought I was the only one in my family alive who had magic. But now, the pieces are clicking into place.

"She is a witch, son. A powerful one." *Taika.* The name crashes through me, sharp and final. The most powerful witch the world has ever known. The oldest. Untouched by time or death. Nothing has ever been able to take her, not war, not sickness, not even death itself. If death dared to knock, she'd answer the door and walk away untouched. She'd bargain with it and win.

She is my mother. Taika is my *mother.*

I grip the helm until my knuckles whiten, the wood biting into my palms. Between the sting of sleepless nights, the poison burning slowly beneath my skin, and the storm of thoughts clawing at my head, I feel like I'm going mad, coming apart one breath at a time.

The siren I spoke to that night knew. She knew that once I found out, I'd hesitate. That I wouldn't have the heart to hand over my own mother. That blood might win.

But what she could never understand is that my blood isn't what defines me. Taika may have given me life, but she also left me with a father who was barely human. A man who wore his legend like armor and raised me with fists and fear. She knew I had magic. She knew I could die from it if I used it wrong, or worse, I could kill someone else. She knew he wouldn't help me. That the crew would be the ones to raise me.

Still, she left. For what? Power? What kind of mother chooses power over her son, her family?

Now I'm faced with the same choice, but it's already been made. I would do anything for Mira.

I would drown the world if it meant getting Mira to that fountain. What I once thought I'd wish for has long since faded, swept away like dust in the wind. Everything has changed since her. With my life now being tied to hers, I have to make sure this sinister scar doesn't take me down. I have to wish for my health, to save us both.

But the sea is still watching. Waiting.

Until the ocean and everything in it sees her for who she truly is, she'll always be hunted. They either see her as a threat or a prize. Some might have already made deals with witches, or with sirens who've long since turned wicked, just to get close. They'll come for her. And when they do, I'll be ready.

I lean against the helm, watching the world wake. The crew shifts with the light, those who manned the night slipping into rest, while others take up the ropes and scrub the decks. The scent of breakfast curls through the wind, tangled with salt spray. It smells like home, bread, pork, potatoes, and yesterday's fish frying in a blackened pan. Grease and smoke cling to the air, thick enough to taste. It's the smell of survival.

Above us, the sky blooms with soft pinks and molten gold, the clouds glowing like they've been lit from within. Light dances on the ocean's surface, painting it in pastel fire. And still, through it all, I can't stop thinking of Mira.

I'm too deep in my thoughts to notice the shift at first. My mind is spinning, unraveling the knot of truths I wasn't ready to face, until I hear it. Singing.

An alluring siren song thrums through my skull, pain and sweetness tangled in every note. Images of drowning in black water rise up, dark, merciless, and somehow disturbingly euphoric.

I look to check but there's no black water, no dark magic creeping along the tide, just a clear morning, the sea glowing a brilliant crystal blue.

I can't make out the words, but I feel them. Feel them down to the marrow of my bones. Like something or someone is trying to speak to me through my blood.

"Cap'n, I can take over from here. We're headin' west?" Jay's voice cuts through the haze. I don't answer right away. "Cap'n? You alright?"

"Fine," I mutter, trying to ground myself. "Yeah. West. We're looking for a city called Alek." Jay gives a grunt and takes the wheel, pipe hanging from his mouth. He smells like he just ate pork and potatoes from the kitchen. Smoke coils upward, twisting into the morning light like it's listening too.

I watch him for a beat, heart hammering. How is he not hearing this? "You don't hear that?" I ask, voice lower now.

Jay raises his brow. "Hear what?"

The chill hits me instantly. "The singing," I say. "You don't hear the singing?"

His stare doesn't waver. "Ain't no music but the sea today." I turn back toward the horizon, the voice still floating just at the edge of my mind, distant but insistent. A sharp pain shoots down my arm, the scar pulsing like it's alive. There has to be more to it—more than flesh and bone. The siren isn't just in my blood anymore. She's in my head.

"Hmmm," I mutter, rubbing the back of my neck. "Maybe you're right. I'll go check on Mira." Jay gives a nod. Before I walk away, I turn my back to him. "Did you take care of him?" I ask, not meeting his stare.

"Yes, he's with the sea now."

That was all I needed to hear. I nod slightly. His voice had a flicker of grief in it. I could tell he wanted to pry more, but I can't talk about what happened. I step away from the helm, heading toward my quarters. But the moment I leave the deck, the singing grows louder.

It chases me down the corridor. I'm losing my fucking mind.

I'm so distracted by the voice, I don't see the small figure until I nearly plow into her. "Shit, treasure, I'm sorry." I grab Mira's arms to steady her.

Her hands settle on my chest. "What's going on, Kai?" she asks, eyes narrowing with concern. "You look exhausted."

"Nothing," I lie. "Did you sleep okay?" I try to shut out the noise still whispering in my head. I try to focus on her, on the way her dark hair spills down her shoulders, on the emerald fire in her eyes. But even as she looks at me, grounding me, I can still hear it.

She takes a step back, her spine pressing against the door to our quarters. "Don't bullshit me, Kai," she says, low but firm. "Something's going on. Tell me."

I hesitate. Her eyes are searching mine, sharp with worry. "I... I keep hearing this singing. It's getting louder." I run a hand through my hair. "It's nothing. Don't worry about it."

I walk past her into the room. She follows, closing the door behind her. "Kai," she says, gentler. "You can't pretend what happened with your father didn't happen. You killed him. I can't lose you to madness like he lost himself. And we still need to talk about Taika."

Her words land hard, but I don't respond. I sit down on the edge of the bed, elbows on my knees, head in my hands. My temples throb like something's clawing from the inside. I barely slept. My mind's been spinning since it happened. The nightmare of losing Mira and reliving slicing a blade through my father is on repeat.

My father's blood still stains my sword. The darkness he brought on this ship is only clinging tighter in his absences, like it's looking for the next place to root. Word will spread, and when it does, his enemies won't care that he's dead. They'll come for the next in line.

"She is my mother." The words leave my mouth like a curse. My head stays bowed, hands still pressed against my face. Trying to avoid the conversation of my father.

I hear Mira's soft footsteps. Then her head appears between my knees, eyes peering up into mine. "I know," she whispers. "I thought so." Her presence soothes something sharp in me, something I didn't even know I was holding. But I can't let it soften me. Not now.

"It doesn't change anything," I mutter, voice tight. "We still need to hand her over to the sirens."

"You don't have to make up your mind right now." Her voice is gentle now. "She's alive. She could help you with your magic. Don't you want that?"

"I don't." I sit up, jaw clenched. "She means nothing to me. She left when I needed her most. She's no one. Just another bloody witch." I shake my head. "If giving her to the sirens keeps you safe and gets us to the fountain, then that's what I'll do. I'll figure out my magic some other way."

Mira straightens, arms crossed. "Don't you think I get a say in this?" she asks, her eyes narrowing with that fire I know too well.

"You do, treasure," I say, rising to meet her gaze. "But I don't think you realize, we're not on some grand journey to reunite me with the mother who abandoned me. We're doing this to get to the fountain.

You're the Soul, Mira. The only one that matters. Everything in this ocean breathes because of you. I breathe because of you. I won't risk that. Not for her. Not for anyone."

She starts to walk away, then pauses, her voice calm but firm. "I think I'm more than capable of protecting myself. And your happiness?" Her gaze flicks to mine. "It matters to me. In case you've forgotten, our souls are tied. I felt your heart shatter the moment your blade went through him. Every piece of that pain, yours became mine."

Her words hit hard. "I want happiness for you, Kai. You are all I have. All I want. Your heart matters. More than you'll ever know." She lowers her voice. "And what you don't know is that I would kill for you. Drop dead for you. Walk the plank for you. I'd jump into an abyss, so long as you're holding my hand on the way down. My heart beats for you. So your happiness, your soul? Yeah, it matters to me."

She steps in closer, standing between my legs. Her eyes lock onto mine, her voice sharper, fiercer. "So tell me what you really want. Don't fucking lie to me."

Through hell and high water, I love this woman. My hands find her hips, her skin warm beneath my palms. Her hair spills in soft curls just above her lower back, brushing my hands like silk.

Talking to Taika might be the only way to get answers. Not because she's my mother, but because of her magic. She's feared for a reason. If anyone can wake whatever power's buried in me, it's her.

"I want to find her," I breathe. "I have a few questions to ask."

She gives me a warm smile. "Then we'll do just that." She kisses me, slowly. When she pulls back, her eyes hold mine. "I see now why the map turned blood red when you touched it."

My brows furrow, but the truth sinks like a stone in my gut. "Because I'm her blood," I murmur. "The map wasn't just for you. It was for her. It was a test."

Mira nods slowly, her confidence unwavering. "Then let's pass it," she says, that sweet, devious smile of hers as steady as the tide. It's all I need.

She turns toward the door, moving with that quiet grace that's always undone me. The singing that had been swelling in my head, maddening, fades at last. Maybe I'm losing my mind, but the one thing that calmed the storm was her.

Now it's time I get answers. Seeing Taika will be a challenge, but one I'm up for. One that could turn the tides in the best way or destroy everything if I'm not ready for what she has to say.

CHAPTER TWENTY-EIGHT

KAI

SERPENT'S WAKE

We're two days out from Taika's domain, maybe less if the wind holds.

My arm starts to throb again. I wrap it tight with fresh cloth, binding it just in time. Whatever part of the siren is pushing through this time, I want to catch it clean. Last time, two claws tore through my skin. This time, I'm hoping for at least two more. Mira and I both have debts to pay, one to the most powerful witch to ever live and the other to the most vile sea creature to ever live. The black veins have slowed their spread, but the pain inside them is consistent.

Each piece that surfaces is a promise. One wish, if we make it to the fountain. With the way things are going, we'll need every single one. My health is getting worse. I refuse to die. I won't let Mira pay for my curse.

Powerful creatures are beginning to notice us, the kappas trailing our every move. I can feel them just at arm's reach, lurking beneath the ship. The deals Mira and I have both made to two very powerful beings are not easily escapable. We're running out of time. *I'm running out of time.*

It's midday. The sun burns high above, the deck alive with motion, ropes hauled, sails trimmed, boots pounding on planks.

I see Mira perched high atop the mast, a queen on her throne, surveying her kingdom of endless blue. The salty wind teases her curls, and the sea breathes in rhythm below her.

The noise in my head hushes at the sight of her. She looks down, sensing my gaze.

Her posture shifts and she points toward the horizon with certainty. I turn. A dark storm is churning.

Clouds roll in like a thick unnatural fog, swallowing the sky in a single breath. The hush that follows is eerie.

I turn to signal Mira down, but she's already moving, sliding down the ropes with graceful ease. My mind flashes back to when she swung over from her ship to mine with such grace, such fluidity. So much has changed since then. We've been on a journey one would write books about. "Ready the ship!" I call out. "We're heading into a storm!"

The crew jumps into action. Sails are lowered, ropes tightened, cargo lashed down. Every man aboard moves like clockwork. A violent sea will show us no mercy, we have to be ready.

Then I hear her voice behind me. "Into the eye of the storm, aye, Captain Kai?"

I turn. There she is. Soaked in sea spray, wind threading through her hair, eyes gleaming like she belongs to the storm. She smiles, her eyes lighting up, not like she is walking into a tempest, but like she's the tempest. For a split second, I don't fear the storm at all. There's a hint of mischief in her voice, the kind that always gets to me.

"It seems so," I reply, smirking, but deep down, this storm feels wrong. I glance past her and catch a shadow slicing through the water between us and the storm.

"What is it?" Mira asks, turning just as it vanishes.

"I saw something," I say, stepping toward the rail. "There's something in the water. This isn't a natural storm, treasure." Her eyes snap to mine, wide. "We need to turn the ship around. Now." I leave no room for argument. "Turn the ship around!" I shout up to Jay as I sprint for the helm. He stumbles aside, pipe in hand, as I grip the wheel and wrench it hard.

The crew scrambles, shouting orders, dropping sails, tying down anything not already secured. The ship groans beneath us, the wheel fighting me like it doesn't want to turn. But I force it away from the storm. Away from whatever's out there.

I've never run from a sea monster in my life, but I'll never gamble Mira's life for another tale in the dark, especially if I saw what I think I saw.

Whatever the fuck is out there, it's guarding something. Maybe a breeding ground. Maybe a graveyard. Either way, it doesn't want us near. We've been lucky so far, avoiding sea monsters, but there are plenty. And what I saw, could be one of the worst of them all. A tarlock.

A massive sea serpent with amethyst and charcoal-black scales, each edged like a blade. They're nearly impossible to kill. Their teeth alone stretch four feet long, gleaming like polished daggers. These creatures are born in the deepest trenches, surfacing only to breed. The dragons of the sea. Even the Kraken had been known to steer clear.

"What did you see?" Mira's voice cuts through the storm. Steady, but laced with fear. "I feel cold," she says after a beat. Her voice shakes. "If it's what I think it is, we're not going to make it."

I feel the cold, too, seeping into my bones. It's the look in Mira's eyes that truly guts me. Her fire has been snuffed. Her light dimmed. As if whatever's out there already took something from her.

"We're going to be fine, treasure," I say, trying to keep my voice steady. "We've changed course."

She looks up at me, her eyes narrowing into that cool, steel gaze. "What. Did. You. See. Kai."

I soften my voice, my face, anything to ease the edge in hers. "I think... I saw a tarlock. I could be wrong. But I'd rather not find out." My hands are still on the helm, steering us clear of the storm, of the beast.

Her expression shifts like a tide turning, fear blooming like frostbite. "A tarlock?" she echoes, stepping back, eyes locked on the churning storm in the distance. "You think you saw a tarlock?"

"Mira," I say gently, "it's okay. We turned in time. We're clear of it." Even I don't believe what I'm selling.

She shakes her head, slow and certain. "No. You don't understand." Her voice is laced with dread. "They follow." She tightens her jaw. Her eyes scan the horizon. "I'm connected to everything that lives in this ocean. Especially powerful creatures. Whatever that thing was"—she swallows hard—"felt me. It knows what I am." Her voice dips to a whisper. "We disturbed its peace, and now it will disturb ours."

Mira bolts down the main deck. "Get away from the sides!" she yells. "Everyone, middle of the ship! Climb if you can! Now! If you stay down here, you'll die!" Her panic is contagious, rolling through the crew like a wave. I push through the chaos.

"Jay, take the helm. Keep us heading east. The farther we get, the better."

Jay nods and grips the wheel, his pipe forgotten. "It was a tarlock, wasn't it, Cap?" I meet his eyes and give a single nod. "I saw it too," he adds. His face goes pale. He grips the helm tighter, knuckles turning white. I've never seen Jay rattled before, not in storms, not in battle, but this has him shaken. And that says everything. It is one of the deadliest creatures to ever come across in the sea. If not the deadliest.

I spot Mira and grab her arm, spinning her toward me. Her chest heaves. I can feel her heart hammering through her rain-soaked shirt. Her eyes shine with fear. "Calm down," I tell her, keeping my voice steady. "Panicking the crew will only make things worse."

Tears threaten her lower lashes. "They need to know," she says, voice breaking. "They deserve a chance. I'd want to know. I'd want every chance to survive." A tear slips down her cheek. Thunder cracks overhead, and then rain comes down harder.

"Climb," I say, brushing the wet hair from her face. "Get up the mainsail. I'll be right behind you, but I need to grab something." She hesitates. "I *promise*, Mira. Go."

I press a kiss to her forehead, and she runs for the ladder. As soon as I see her climbing, I turn and sprint toward the lower deck. There's only one weapon that might actually give us a shot.

It's complete chaos on deck, shouts, crashing waves, the creaks and groans of wood strained to its limit. I spin toward the starboard side, and there it is, rising from the depths like a nightmare come to life.

The sea serpent, massive, and furious, surges upward, water cascading off its coiled, scaled body. Waves batter the ship, and it's not even close yet. Its eyes, gods, its eyes. A molten, blood-orange glare that pins us like prey.

It's staring straight at us. Straight at me. The tarlock is larger than any beast I've ever seen. Its full body hasn't even cleared the surface, and it's already three ships long. Maybe bigger. Every word I've ever known for "monstrous" feels too small.

Somehow it knows I'm the captain. It knows I'm the one who trespassed. Its gaze locks on me with a rage that feels ancient, personal. My stomach turns. The taste of bile creeps up my throat. This is death, dressed in scales and fury, and it's coming for everything I love.

If we survive this, it will be nothing short of a miracle.

I sprint below deck to retrieve the black spears. Forged from a metal rarer than gold, enchanted by witches, they're strong enough to punch through even a tarlock's scales. We've only used them once before, on a lesser beast. Now we have three left. Three shots. Three chances to survive.

I shove barrels aside, dragging them off the locked chest at the back of the gun deck. Inside, the arrows gleam. I sling two across my back and grip the third tightly. Every ship should have these. Most don't.

"Man the cannons!" I bark to the crew as the ship lurches violently. The tarlock struck its first blow. I hit the floor hard, pain blooming in my shoulder as cannons careen across the deck. Wood cracks. Men shout. "Get the cannons back to position! Wait for my command!" The crew scrambles, boots thundering over wood as I sprint back up the stairs.

Mira. Where is she? The thought barrels through everything else in my head. I need eyes on her, need to know she's safe. But a darker thought slips in as I run. *Can she tame it?*

She's bound to the sea. The most powerful beings can feel her, and maybe this one does too. Maybe she could stop it, or maybe trying would get her killed. It's a risk I'm not willing to take.

I reach the ladder, the mainsail thrashing above me. Rain lashes against my face like needles, the wind roaring in my ears, trying to shove me back with every step. The rigging is slick, my fingers numb. It's the only place I can get a clear shot, either straight down the beast's throat or at its underbelly, the only two places it can be killed. Or so the old man's tale claims.

The ship groans beneath us, wood shrieking as it twists, waves slamming against the hull like fists. The tarlock coils around us in a relentless circle, churning the sea into a whirlpool, dragging us off course like a toy in a tide pool.

Mira's already there. Clinging to the ropes, soaked and shaking, her eyes locked on the storm-black sky. She turns just as I reach her level, her face pale, her body braced against the fury, like she's been waiting.

"Are you hurt?" I shout, breath ragged. She turns, tears streaming down her face, the wind whipping strands of her hair across her cheeks.

"Not yet," she says quietly. Her voice is final, like death already knows her name.

"No." My grip tightens on the rope as the sail pitches wildly. "No, Mira. I need you to hold on. You hear me? Hold strong."

Her eyes find mine. There's a softness there that cracks something deep in my chest. "I love you," she says, barely louder than the storm. "You know that, right?"

"I do," I whisper. "Gods, I do. But what are you—" My voice catches. I already know. That smile, the one she gives when she's decided something I can't change. "Mira," I choke out. "Whatever you're thinking, don't."

She reaches for my hand, cold fingers trembling as she presses a kiss to my knuckles. "I have to, Kai. For you. For the crew. For the ship."

The wood groans beneath us, a sickening crack splitting the air. "It's tearing us apart. I can tame it. I have to try."

She leans in, forehead brushing mine. "I'm sorry," she breathes. "We'll all die if I don't."

My heart splits clean in two as I lunge for her, desperate, wild, a man undone. But she slips through my grasp like mist. She lets go. Not just of my hand, but of everything, safety, fear... me.

"I love you, Kai Eldoris," she says, the storm in her hair, the fire still alive in her eyes. "To the end." Then she's gone.

She soars with arms open, body arched like a queen diving into her throne, a siren called home by the sea. She looks like both things she was born to be, a captain and a myth. Her curls fan behind her like smoke, her body cutting through the air with impossible grace.

There is no splash, only a silence that screams louder than thunder. And then, stillness. The ship stops rocking. The wind dies. The clouds pull back. The ocean waits. And so do I.

She's going to try to tame the most ruthless beast.

CHAPTER TWENTY-NINE

MIRA

OF SCALE & SOUL

The moment my blood ran cold, I knew what I had to do. Knew Kai would never be okay with it. But if anyone could get through to the tarlock, it was me.

I felt his heart shatter the second I let go, piece by piece, the breaking echoed through my own chest like glass cracking in slow motion. Tears spilled down my cheeks into the air between us, silent goodbyes carried on the wind. Because this could be it. If I fail to tame the beast, if it doesn't listen, this will be the end for both of us.

It's all on me now.

I saw the weapons strapped to Kai's back, the one he carried in his hand, ready to pierce through scale and bone, but something inside me rebelled at the thought. The tarlock isn't just a monster, it's part of the sea my home and heart. I can't allow him to pierce through the beast.

And if it's protecting something precious, we have no right to strike first. If there's a chance for common ground, I have to find it. We can't afford to make enemies of the ocean's most powerful, lethal creature.

So I jumped. The salt wind rushed through my hair. My tears streaked sideways, torn from me by the force of the fall. The sea rose up to meet me, and I was home.

The moment the water closed around me, I felt it in my bones. My skin drank it in like it had been starved. I could finally breathe again.

I dive beneath the ship, swimming hard toward the beast. I need to stop her, pull her attention away before she drags *The Leviathan* under completely. Ironic that the ship was named after a creature just as deadly. The tarlock is circling fast, creating a massive whirlpool, trying to drown the ship so no one can fire back. It is a smart tactic, terrifyingly strategic. But I won't let her finish it. Not while I still have breath.

I can feel it in my blood that whatever comes next, the sea is with me.

Then I see her. Blood-orange eyes glow brighter beneath the surface, brighter than anything I've seen in the ocean's depths. The moment she senses me, she stops, her colossal form cutting through the water like a living shadow. Scales sharp as razors shimmer along her body. Her talons are the size of our mast, and her teeth can cleave a man in half with ease.

She is the most terrifyingly beautiful creature I have ever laid eyes on. Serpent and dragon, nightmare and goddess. Her face is sleek and deadly, otherworldly in its design. And she stares right at me. Holds my gaze. The world slows to a crawl. The ocean quiets as she watches and waits.

I meet her stare, unblinking. I feel her grief and rage deep in my bones. She isn't a killer; she is protecting, hurting, searching for peace.

"*Mira,*" a voice echoes inside my head, soft like a hymn sung from the edge of heaven. I look around, startled, breaking eye contact with the creature. "*Mira. The Soul.*" It is her. The beast.

She is speaking directly into my mind. Magic? No, this is something else.

"*Not magic, dear Mira,*" her voice comes again, gentle as a wave. "*We are connected. I know you feel it.*" And I do. I just haven't understood it until now.

I swim closer, slowly, the water parting around me like it knows where I need to go. She is still some distance away, but I need to see her up close, to look into her eyes and truly understand.

"*Name?*" I ask with my thoughts, reaching out through the bond, something new for me. "*Keta,*" she answers. Fierce and beautiful.

I reach her at last. She doesn't move to strike or bare her teeth. She simply watches me, massive eyes tracking my every movement, glowing like twin suns in the dark. "*I didn't know it was you,*" she says, and there's something almost regretful in her tone. "*If I did, I would never attack.*"

"*I'm sorry for my ship,*" I tell her quietly, swimming up toward her face. "*But they didn't know. They don't understand.*" She dips her massive head slightly, acknowledging the apology. I hover there, close enough now to feel the slow pull of her current, the sheer force of her presence.

"*Can you spare them?*" I ask. My voice is steady in my mind, though my heart pounds inside my chest. I know the one thing Kai is holding on to above water is the beat of my heart.

She stares, and I wait, hoping the bond between us is strong enough to shift the tide.

"*Spare them? I'm not going to kill. I just want them gone. These are ancient waters for my kind. No man shall cross. Most Tarlocks would attack, but I sensed you the moment your body touched the sea.*" She is breathtaking, radiant in the way she glides through the open water. Ancient and terrifying in the sheer mass of her being, every single inch of her is razor-sharp.

"*Thank you,*" I dip my head slowly, in a small bow. "*We'll be on our way.*"

She lowers her massive head until her glowing eyes are in direct contact with mine. "*You are a beautiful soul. Stay safe. The ocean needs you, Mira—female ruler of the sea. If ever you need me, call my name. You know it now.*"

I blink slowly, then swim the last few feet between us, placing my hand gently against her snout. She closes her eyes, leaning into the touch. Her scales, to my surprise, are warm.

"*I'll see you soon, Keta,*" I say down the bond. "*May your waters stay guarded, and your days be peaceful.*" I lift my hand off of her snout.

Before I can swim away, I hear her voice again. "*There is great unrest churning in the sea,*" Keta says, her tone calm but endless, like the tide just before a storm. "*You must guard yourself well. The Pirate Lord is bound to you. Trust in him.*"

Her ancient eyes met mine, unblinking and unreadable. Then her voice sinks lower. "*An army rises beneath the waves, one far greater than me. Greater than you. It is being forged by the Soul, and she does not wish to sleep. But she has turned dark. Cruel. She must be stopped. That burden now falls to you.*"

Anger surges through me. I knew the Soul had gone bad, but that goes against all that it is there for. The Soul was meant to preserve balance, not poison it or raise monsters to destroy what little light we had left in this sick world. "*Let her build her army,*" I say, my voice like flint, my eyes narrowing. "*Let her rise from the deepest trench she can find. I was born of this sea, and its fury runs through me. And I don't bow to anyone that's forgotten what it means to belong to it.*"

Keta gives a slight nod, the glow in her eyes deepening. "*You, child, are the light. The Soul is dark,*" she says, her voice echoing like a distant tide. "*You know my name. Call it when the sea turns against you, and I will come. I will save you.*" Her words settle, anchoring my soul.

Before I can move, Keta shifts, graceful and deliberate. She rises beneath me, scooping me up with a gentleness that doesn't match her size. She carries me through the waves, back to the ship. Then, with an eerie ease, she lifts me from the water. The water parts between her sharp talons and she sets me down on the main deck, right next to Kai where I belong.

She holds his gaze, unflinching. He doesn't look away. "*If he is the one your soul is tied to,*" she says, "*then he, too, is under my protection. May your journey to the fountain go smoothly. Don't waste your wish.*"

She looks at me once more, eyes softer. "*Remember, you know my name.*" Then she turns, slipping silently beneath the waves and vanishing into the depths from which she came.

Kai's hands are on me in an instant, gripping my arms and scanning every inch of me, wild with worry. "What the hell happened?" His voice is controlled, but his gaze is a storm. Panic, fear, disbelief.

Water drips from my hair as I lift my chin, the entire crew frozen around us, waiting. "I bonded with a tarlock," I say, steady and sure. "Her name is Keta." Shock ripples through him like a wave.

"You did what?" he breathed. "How is that even possible?"

I try to rise, but my legs give way beneath me. Kai catches me before I can fall, hand firm against my back. I meet his eyes. "She wasn't trying to kill us, she was just protecting her home. But there's something worse coming. Something darker. We need to go."

His jaw tightens, but he nods. "We'll take the long route," he says. "We'll find Taika. But not through cursed waters." Kai's grip tightens on my arm as he helps me to my feet. "Mira, what do you mean you bonded with her?" He steadies me until I can stand on my own, but my legs feel like they'll only work underwater.

"It means if I ever need her, she'll come," I say simply. "The crew is safe. The ship is safe. We can move on now, shall we?"

Kai lets out a slow breath, his eyes shining with something softer than awe. "Every time I think I've seen all there is to you, you surprise me. You're unparalleled, Mira."

I lean in slightly, voice low, just for him. "And if you ever need her"—I tap his chest—"call her name, Keta. She's bound to you now, too." His smile fades, jaw tightening, eyes softening with something close to pride, like he's trying not to show just how much it moves him. Because now, we have the most powerful being in these seas on our side.

CHAPTER THIRTY

MIRA

REFLECTIONS

The ocean feels wrong. Too still. Like it's bracing for something. We're still headed to Alek, to Taika. The thought of facing her under these circumstances knots my gut. I'm not afraid of what she might do, but I'm afraid of what it'll do to him.

Kai masks it well, but I can feel the storm brewing inside him. A son aching for answers, a wound left open for far too long. Every time her name is spoken, I feel his heart twist. I feel the weight of what he's never said. And it terrifies me, because I don't know if meeting her will heal him or break him.

I can't help but wonder, why did the map she gave me lead to him? Was it drawn from her own desires, a mother's quiet hope that her son still lived? Or was it truly shaped by mine? Or both?

We haven't touched the map since we found Veyra. I haven't touched anything Taika gave me, not the shell she said to use if I ever needed her, not the vial of mermaid tears that could heal even the deepest wound. They're relics from someone I no longer trust. The vial of mermaid tears never leaves my neck. The one who gave them to me may be far from pure, but the tears, at least, are not.

I'm scared that everything she gave me is cursed. That every gift was a chain in disguise and I was too blind to see it.

Kai informed me we're running low on supplies, weapons, food, even rum again, and insisted we stop at Seal's Island. He always tries to dock there during his voyages. Says the merchants give him the best deals, especially on the things he values most: steel, salt, and spirits. Especially the rum. Gods forbid we run low on the rum.

I didn't want to stop. I wanted to power through as much sea as possible. Something's shifting in the ocean that I can feel, and my gut is rarely wrong. But Kai's right. We need what we need.

Seal's Island was only half a day away from where we encountered the tarlock. Since then, Kai's been locked in the study room with Jay, poring over every map and scrap of parchment, hunting for anything that could lead us closer to Sirens Cove. He's been in there for hours.

I've been at the helm scanning the horizon for any more unwelcome visitors. The ocean is both beautiful and brutal. One wrong turn, one moment of hesitation, and she can swallow you whole, delivering you to a place no soul has ever seen. That's what makes her so dangerous. She's unpredictable, always shifting like a living thing.

As I stare out at the horizon, my mind drifts to the Soul of the Ocean. The one who came before me. The one who now clutches the title like a blade held to the throat of the sea. Who was she, truly? Was she once human, like me? Or born a creature, siren, mermaid, witch, something older?

How long did she live before the ocean chose her? Was her transformation slow, or instant? Did it hurt? Did she love someone the way I love Kai? And if she did, did she have to give him up to become what the tides demanded of her? Questions I can't answer. Not until it's my turn to become her.

She must be endlessly exhausted, carrying the weight of every soul in the sea. Feeling their pain, their joy, their rage. Every creature's death echoes inside her—every scream swallowed, every war ever waged bleeding through her veins.

Maybe it broke her and that's why she turned cruel. Built an army out of fear. Twisted her power into something dark. Maybe she simply couldn't carry it anymore and decided the ocean should suffer with her. After I fight this war, fighting for every creature that swims beneath the waves and sails above them, I refuse to become the darkness that already bleeds in these waters.

The sun dips low on the horizon, casting golden light across the sea, and there, just ahead, I spot Seal's Island with my naked eye. It is far larger than the scattered isles I've grown used to. Bursting with color and sound, its painted buildings climb the hillside like stained-glass steps. It looks like Magda, feels like home, but it isn't. It only reminds me of what I left behind: *The Siren,* my people, the pieces of myself I would trade for this journey. Neressa. The ache comes fast, blooming in my chest like a bruise.

I feel him before he could even touch me. Kai's warm hand slid to my waist. I turn around to look up, locking eyes with him. "Hi, *treasure,*" he says, his smile crooked and voice rough like weathered rope. I smile, unable to help myself. "What's going on in that mysterious head of yours?" he asks, eyes searching mine.

Where would I even begin? A thousand thoughts swirl behind my eyes, none of them easy to name. "We don't have enough time for that," I say, teasing. "Let's just focus on making port, and maybe grabbing some rum?" He grins. My back presses against the helm, his arm brushing mine as he steers, his other hand still resting lightly at my side, like he couldn't bear to let go.

"I *always* have time," he says softly, "to listen to every single one of your thoughts, Mira."

My name on his tongue still sends a chill down my spine.

The crew begins scrambling with anticipation, their boots clattering across the deck as they prepare to make port. Kai was right. They need this break for more than just supplies. This is what they look forward to: the brief thrill of land under their feet, rum in their hands, and the touch of a woman.

I don't answer Kai's inquiry of what's on my mind. Instead, I kiss him. It's easier that way. A kiss to make him drop it, at least for now. But Kai isn't the type to let go, especially when it comes to my thoughts and my heart. I love him for that.

The crew makes their way down the gangplank, their laughter echoing into the growing night, leaving just a few of us behind to keep watch. It's always done in shifts, and tonight, it leaves me and Kai alone on the quiet deck.

I start to walk away when he reaches out, gently catching my hand. "I can feel you hurting," he says. "Talk to me. What can I do?" His words stir something warm in my chest.

I look up at him. "It's nothing you can fix. The ocean feels wrong. Unbalanced. Something is coming. I don't know what or when, I just feel it."

Kai pulls me closer, one arm wrapping around my waist. "Then we'd better find that fountain," he says with a crooked grin. The flame from the lanterns flickers in his hazel eyes, dancing across the tattoos on his skin. The moon paints him in silver. In the soft hush of night, with the ocean at our backs, he looks more alive than ever. I always see him differently after dark. Night Kai is my *favorite*. I gently shake myself from the thought and meet his gaze again.

"Shall we go grab a drink?" I nudge his arm, barely moving him, though I know he lets it shift, just enough to please me. Kai chuckles low in his chest, that rare sound that hums through the air and settles under my skin. He nods once, offering me his hand.

"But first," he says, his voice dipping, eyes glinting beneath the moonlight. "A quiet deck and a full moon? Maybe we stay here a little longer." He pulls me in by the waist, his touch rough and warm against my skin, and kisses me slowly, deeply, until I'm already unraveling at the taste of salt, smoke, and him. The ocean sways beneath us, matching the rhythm of my pulse. I break away, breathless, meeting those wild hazel eyes that always undo me.

"Show me the way, Captain Kai," I whisper, teasing, watching the fire catch in his gaze.

He lifts me effortlessly, pressing me back against the helm as his lips find the curve of my neck. My captain's hat slips from my head, landing somewhere on the deck. The night air hums around us as he lowers me to the boards, his touch reverent, deliberate. Fingers trace the ties of my corset, loosening each one with aching patience. Every breath feels heavier, every inch of exposed skin touched by the chill of the sea breeze—and by him. I have nothing on aside from the large black long-sleeved shirt, and my undergarments. Kai moves under my shirt, kissing my stomach, then my ribs, then my breasts. My breath catches. He knows exactly how to make me tick.

I throw my head back with a light moan. He looks up at me from inside my shirt, and I smile down at him, "That smile, treasure—it could undo kingdoms. And right now, it's *completely* undone me."

He stands, pulling off his shirt, then his pants, the sight of him stealing the air from my lungs. He spreads the fabric across the deck and eases me onto it, shielding my skin from the cold, splintered wood. I remove my shirt. As he sits next to me, I move to straddle him. "What do you want?" I tease, knowing exactly what he wants.

He sits up, keeping me straddling him. "You know what I want, my love," he murmurs, voice low and rough.

I trail my fingers along the hard lines of his stomach, tracing the edges of his muscles. "I wish you'd tell me," I whisper, teasing, challenging him.

His eyes darken, turning hungry, wild. "*You,*" he breathes. "I want all of *you.*"

He pulls me into a kiss that feels like it might set the whole world on fire. Our bodies press together, every inch of him warm, solid, mine. His tongue brushes against mine, deepening the kiss, making my entire body ache with need. There is something about him under pure, raw moonlight that makes me want him even more.

One of his hands cups my cheek while the other slips lower, tracing the curve of my waist. He moves slowly, savoring every touch, memorizing me with his hands.

"No," I whisper, stopping him gently as he starts to move down. He looks up at me, confused, hungry. "It's my turn," I breathe, my voice soft but certain. "To please you."

The look on his face, gods, he looks like he might lose control just from hearing those words. I move to grab my shirt that was loosely thrown off to the side and smile as I cover his eyes with the sleeves.

"Oh?" he growls, low and eager, ready for whatever I was about to give him, he lays his back onto the cool deck. I kiss my way down his chest, taking my time, worshipping every inch of golden inked skin and taut muscle. He lets out a quiet moan, his body tensing beneath me. By the time I reach his hips, he's already straining for me, breath ragged, every part of him begging for more.

I wet my thumb and brush it lightly over his tip, drawing a deep moan from his chest. Gods, the sight of him, blindfolded, breathless, completely at my mercy, makes me want to give him everything, to let him ruin me in every way he wants.

I lower my mouth to him, taking him in slowly, using my hand to cover what I can't with my lips. His hands tangle in my hair, tugging gently, urging me deeper, but I pull back, breathless, my own need overwhelming me.

I slide off my undergarments, guiding him into me, savoring the way he fills me, the way my whole body seems to come alive around him. "Fuck," he moans, voice rough and desperate. His hands grip my hips, but I move slowly, teasing, wanting him to feel every inch, every second.

I lean forward, kissing his neck softly, whispering his name into his skin, wanting him to know there will never be anything better than this, than us, in this single, perfect moment.

"My treasure," he rasps, his voice thick with need. "You feel so good." His hands slide up from my hips, tracing the curve of my waist, moving higher to my breasts. His fingers tease my nipples, light and slow, making me shiver and gasp. Then his mouth is there, warm, hungry, his tongue circling, his teeth grazing just enough to make me whimper.

I shatter around him, moving helplessly, clutching at his shoulders as waves of pleasure rush through me. He holds me steady, then flips me slowly onto the deck, pressing me down as he moves inside me, fast and relentless, until I can't see and can't breathe, only feel.

He finishes with a low groan, collapsing over me, his breath hot against my neck. Pulling off the shirt, he looks into my eyes, voice soft and reverent. "You're ethereal." His words melt me, turning my heart to lava.

"So are you," I whisper with a small smile, tracing the dark lines of his tattoos along his neck, the moon bathing us both in silver ribbons.

He turns, grabbing my captain's hat from beside us and setting it lazily on my head. I'm wearing nothing but the hat when he kisses me, slow and warm. "Look at you," he murmurs against my lips. "Wrecking me without even trying." I can't help but smile, my cheeks flushing red under his gaze.

"So... about that drink?" I say, suddenly craving something amber and burning. He smiles, reaching for my shirt and handing it to me with that lazy confidence that always makes my stomach twist. "Let's go."

We get dressed—my corset laced half-heartedly, his shirt hanging loose—and head down together, stepping off the ship and into the glowing pulse of the island town.

CHAPTER THIRTY-ONE

KAI

SINISTER SHORES

Seal's Island. It feels good to be back. Too many moons and sunrises have passed since I last stepped onto these docks. There are only a few places that ever feel like home beyond the sea, but this island, this crooked, smoke-sweet stretch of coastline, holds a piece of my heart. Just like Mira has Magda as her home, this is mine. Seal's Island holds many of my memories on land as a kid. Running through its smoke-filled streets, stealing pastries from market carts, playing ball with the younger kids until the sun went down. It's the only place I ever really felt like a child.

Mira and I make our way toward one of the main pubs, walking down the gangplank with our fingers intertwined.

The night air wraps around us, thick with salt and smoke, fires burning along the shoreline, pipes curling sweetness into the breeze. It smells like old stories and safe harbors. I feel content here. Settled, almost. Especially with Mira by my side.

"After the war," I start, and a drunk staggers past us, barrels clattering as he goes. Mira laughs.

"Yes?" she asks, tilting her head.

"What do you see for us?"

Her emerald eyes catch the lights and glitter like diamonds. "I haven't thought that far," she says, "but whatever happens, so long as we live through this, that's what was meant to be." She scans the lively town as we move deeper into it.

"Have you thought about life after all this?" she asks. I watch her every small movement, reading the way she shifts, the way her smile steadies.

"Yes."

"And?" she presses.

"I see us ruling the seas together—taking down even the royals, if we get that far." I grin. She bursts into a clear, delighted laugh.

"The royals? Kai, come on." She nudges me, incredulous and amused.

"You don't think we can take them down?" I say.

"No, I didn't say that. But our battle is in the ocean, not on land. When we win the war at sea, we have won it all. Don't you think so?"

"I think we can have it *all*."

She smiles and nods her head.

My attention drifts from our conversation the closer we get to the town. Something feels off. The shadows shift too quickly when I'm not looking. Mira says I have a sixth sense, that I can feel things before they happen, and maybe she's right. Even in this moment, with her laughter in my ear and the warm glow of tavern lights ahead, I feel myself bracing.

I don't know what for, but I've learned to trust the quiet before the storm.

We step into the pub, and my mind flashes back to the first time we were in one together. The way she glared at me, calling me a bastard like she meant it. It's hard to believe how far we've come. From enemies chasing the same map to sailing the seas side by side, facing the kind of danger most wouldn't survive.

Even back then, when I claimed I couldn't stand her and swore I didn't care, I always hoped she was just a step behind me. Even if I didn't understand why. I think some part of me wanted her close.

I order two rums from the bartender. Around us, our crew makes their rounds, some catching up with old friends. Most of my side of the crew were born here. Others are already slipping off with women they clearly came here to find. I used to be one of them, searching for the same escape right here in this pub. But since Mira boarded my ship, not a single thought like that has crossed my mind, especially after what I just did with her, to her, on *The Leviathan*.

"We're close, you know?" Mira says softly. I glance at her, squinting. "To her," she adds. She means Taika.

"Yes," I say, colder than I mean to. There's not much else to say. I know what needs to be done, and Mira won't like it. But this isn't about Taika. It's about Mira. If the sirens want the witch, they can have her. Mira always comes first. Always. Getting her to the fountain is all that matters. Not saving some selfish, power-hungry witch, even if we share the same blood.

I take a long swig of rum and set the cup down. "Don't worry," I say, sensing the unease rolling off her. My hand finds her thigh, grounding us both.

"It's hard not to, Kai," she says, voice low. "You haven't said much. I just... I don't want to lead us somewhere I might lose you." Her words land like an anchor in my chest.

"You won't ever lose me, treasure." She smiles, placing her hand over mine, her thumb brushing softly across my skin. "It would take a lot more than some old witch to take me away from you."

Before she can answer, the doors to the pub crash open. A group of pirates storms in, knocking over tables, sending drinks flying, throwing fists without reason. A brawl erupts in the corner, and my hand instinctively goes to my sword.

"There she is," one of them snarls, locking eyes with Mira.

I'm on my feet in an instant, stepping in front of her and drawing my blade. "What the fuck do you want?" I growl, ready to strike.

The leader steps forward, tall, and broad with slicked-back silver hair, sporting a glass eye and a pegleg. He smiles, and silver teeth catch the lantern light. "Isn't it obvious?" he says, voice deep and scratchy. "We came for the Soul. The one they say will rule the sea. We've got business with her."

I shift slightly, keeping Mira behind me and feeling the steady rhythm of her breath. "You must be mistaken." He laughs, an ugly, grating sound that churns my stomach. "Make it easy on yourself and hand her over. If she ain't who I say she is, why get your blade out over some dumb broad, aye?"

That's it. My blood surges hot beneath my skin. Every foul inch of him is a challenge. I can feel the magic simmering at my fingertips, waiting to be unleashed. One more word, and I'll make sure those silver teeth of his hit the fucking floor.

I raise my sword to cut off his head, but he's already there, like he knew my move before I did. Steel crashes against steel, his blade catching mine with precision that feels inhuman. The two men flanking him leap into the fight, blades drawn, but my crew is right behind me. Swords meet swords. Fists fly. The pub turns into a storm. I keep my focus on the silver-toothed bastard. His grin doesn't falter. He's fast, too fast. And then, just like that, he vanishes. Gone. As if the shadows have swallowed him whole.

I spin, scanning the pub, blade still raised. Only my men stand beside me now. Mira is behind me, weapons drawn, ready for anything. "They possess some sort of magic, Cap'n." Jay appears at my side, already stepping in front of Mira like he vowed to do.

We wait. But nothing comes. Just the stench of smoke and blood and something unnatural. If they're ghosts, there'll be no flesh to pierce and no blood to spill. And yet, I've heard the stories of spirits taking over the living, puppeteering them from within. Nyx.

Whoever sent them now knows exactly where we are. Which means this island, the place I've always called home away from the sea, is no longer safe. Not for Mira. They weren't just passing through, they were waiting for her. They knew I'd come home.

"We should go, Kai," Mira says quietly behind me. "We got what we came for." I can feel her rapid heartbeat. Whatever those things are, she felt them in her bones, just as I did. But Mira always keeps a cool, confident exterior.

"Let's go." I grab her hand without hesitation and pull her through the crowd, Jay right on our heels. "Get the crew," I order. "We need to leave. Now."

Jay nods, scanning the pub. "Understood, Cap'n. This island... It doesn't feel like it used to." I shoot him a knowing look, and he disappears into the crowd to gather the others.

He's right. Everything about this place feels off. Twisted. Almost sinister. I can't place it exactly, but I know one thing with absolute certainty. Whatever just touched down here, whatever's watching us now, I won't let it anywhere near her.

"Kai," Mira says, unease lacing her voice. Her green eyes flick toward the horizon, glowing with worry beneath the moonlight. I follow her gaze. The ocean is unnaturally still. The moon casts its silver glow over the water, and that's when I see them, their heads breaking the surface, watching us.

"The sirens," she whispers. "They're calling to me."

I don't know if this is a trap or something worse. "I'll go with you." She shakes her head, calm but firm.

"You will not. They could drown you. Not all of them know about us. Let me go alone. You need to stay here."

I reach out, gripping her chin just enough to turn her face to mine. "That wasn't me asking," I say, leaving no room for argument. She blinks, caught off guard, but she doesn't fight me. Doesn't say a word.

Then she turns away, stepping into the freezing water. I follow, close behind. The moment her boots touch the sea, something shifts. Her body relaxes. Her heartbeat slows. It's as if the ocean itself reached out to calm her heart.

Only the light of the moon and the distant flames flickering along the beach illuminate the shore. I can barely make out the shapes in the water, but I can feel them. The sea is as black as night.

"They aren't singing," Mira says. "I don't think they're here to kill. I think they want to speak with me. If you follow, don't go too far. If things turn, I might not be able to find you in the black waters." She's right, there's no song. They came in peace, rare for sirens.

"They'll come to you if they want to speak," I tell her, hoping she'll listen. We step deeper into the water. Fog creeping in, curling across the surface, making it harder to see.

The water around us begins to glow, a soft blue pulsing from beneath the surface. Then they appear, sirens, silent as ghosts, moving through the black like shadows. One swims forward. I recognize her as the same one from the night Smith betrayed us.

"Mira and the Pirate Lord," she says, her voice cold and lifeless. "You are not safe here." She came to warn us. "This island is infected. Possessed. Mira cannot stay." She moves closer, her webbed hand reaching for Mira. "Take her and go, boy."

"His name is Kai," Mira says firmly. The siren's expression shifts, her head tilts, eyes narrowing.

"My apologies. Kai." She apologized? Mira has that kind of power now? To make even the most stubborn of species bend at her word?

"What happened to the island?" Mira asks.

"That is not for you to know," the siren replies, dark eyes glinting under the moonlight. "It is not safe. You must go. Now." Mira steps forward. The siren blocks her path, voice sharper now. "Go no farther. The waters aren't safe either..."

"It's dark magic," I tell the siren.

She grins, slow and sharp. "Hmm. Smart boy. Smart Kai. But you are not strong enough to be near it, not yet. You must have found out who you've come from."

I say nothing. She swims closer, dipping beneath the surface, then rises again, eyes narrowing, amused. "Do you still wish to complete the task I gave you?"

I open my mouth, but Mira steps in. "He won't be making any promises."

The siren snaps her gaze to Mira, the water stilling around her. "Do you know what will happen once we are rid of her?" she hisses. "Do you understand what will be unlocked for him? He will possess all of her power and more. He is the heir to magic. The holder of it. You hold him back, girl, and it is you who will suffer. He could die. *You* could die." Heir of magic? The only thing I'd ever inherited was my ship and crew. Not this.

"I'll get you the witch," I say, the words like stone in my mouth. I feel Mira's fury before I see it. She turns, livid, trudging through the black water, walking away without a word. "Mira," I call after her.

The siren speaks. "It's what's best. If you want to reach the fountain, this is what she commanded. Bring us the witch, and she will take you to it." Mira stops and turns around.

"She?" Mira's voice cracks like a whip.

"Your mother," the siren replies with a gleam of cruel delight. "She's alive. And she will take you to the fountain. Personally."

The siren turns with a single motion and vanishes into the depths.

CHAPTER THIRTY-TWO

MIRA

EVERY BREATH

The siren's words pulse through me like thunder. Disbelief drowns out everything else, and Kai grabs my hand as we make our way back to the ship.

"She's alive," I whisper, as if saying it aloud might shatter the illusion. I had a feeling after reading the journals, but hearing it, knowing it as a fact, feels like my heart shattering all over again. I don't remember the walk back. I black out everything around me, my thoughts hijacked by memories of her. Her lullabies and her warmth. The way she used to brush the salt from my hair. For a moment, I feel like a little girl again, standing on the deck of *The Siren*, safe under her shadow.

But the joy is short-lived. Uncertainty creeps in like a rising tide. What if she's not the same woman I remember? What if the years or her grief have changed her? What if she never knew what became of my father? Or worse, what if he didn't die that night?

We leave the island and set course for Alek. It's about a day away now. "Are you okay?" Kai asks as he sits beside me on our bed. I'm wearing nothing but his long-sleeved green shirt, which drapes over me like a dress.

"Shocked," is all I manage to say.

"We'll find her," he says gently, reassuring me.

"If she's been alive all this time, why hasn't she come for me?" My voice cracks a little.

He shakes his head. "I could ask the same question," he replies, a half-smile tugging at his lips. "You're not alone," he says with the gentlest tone, and for some reason, as twisted as it is, it's the most comforting thing he could have said to me.

I smile, leaning into the comfort of him. My back rests against the headboard, and he shifts, laying his head across my lap. I run my fingers through his curls. He smells of sea salt and tobacco, like home. His hand strokes my thigh slowly, grounding me.

"She might not remember me," I whisper. "Or maybe she's been watching. Every time there was a siren attack, they never came near me. Never touched me." I pause. "Not even once."

Kai looks up at me with those piercing eyes and a soft smile. "You're unforgettable, treasure. She remembers you." His words wash over me like warmth sinking into frozen skin. "She probably couldn't come near you. It would've put you in danger," he says softly. "Look how many are after you already. If she revealed herself too soon, you'd be dead. Watching from afar, that might've been the only way she could keep you safe. And if you'd never stepped foot on my ship..." He trails off, his jaw tight. "I don't even want to think about it."

His emotions shift like he's been pulled under ice. His jaw tightens and ticks. The thought of losing me makes him feel sick. But he's right, without Kai and the crew, I wouldn't have survived. I'd be a ghost drifting through the sea.

"What happens if I die?" I ask softly, the question trembling out of me. "What happens to the ocean? Its soul?"

Kai's expression changes to a look I haven't seen yet, heartbroken and confused at the same time. "I ask myself this question every day. I don't want to find out." He sits up, to look in my eyes. "It looks like we have a clear path to the fountain, but we have to turn the witch in..." He stops to take a breath and gather his thoughts. "Have you thought about what you're going to wish for?"

The thought hasn't left my mind since we set out to find the fountain. "I'm still trying to figure it out. I know that's bad, but a lot has changed in my life. My original wish was to bring my parents back but that's changed. Now you're sick, that's the number one reason why we *have* to get to the fountain."

He smiles at me, caressing my face with his hand "I can wish for my own health. Don't waste your wish on me," Kai says.

"It's not a waste of a wish if it saves your life." I smile down at him. "Which, as you know, saves mine too." He lets out a soft laugh.

"You can pick your own wish at your own pace, treasure, there's no pressure for you. I pulled out two more siren claws from my arm, so we have four wishes now." He moves to reach for his neck and pulls out a necklace with four siren claws on it. "Whatever your heart desires, you'll get."

"What's your wish?" I ask quietly. "Your scar?"

He nods. "To be cured of this siren curse," he says, sighing. "Originally it was for your safety, but now I think saving me is what is going to keep you alive longer."

My heart sinks. I hate that this scar has poisoned him. My eyes find the black veins trailing down his arm, slowly starting to take over his chest.

He watches me look at the curse, a smile playing on his lips. "Don't worry," he says with reassurance.

"How could I not be worried? It's spreading."

He brushes a strand of hair behind my ear. "Because we will get there. It will be okay, even if I'm sick for a little while." He's just so sure and confident all the time that it bothers me. If I had a dark curse running through my veins, I would be worried sick every second of every day.

"Okay, do you promise we'll make it there?" I ask, knowing that he can't promise me that fully, but it helps take away some of the unsettling feelings arising.

"I promise, Mira. I won't let us die." His words linger, suspended between us. "There is no world without you in it," he finishes, his gaze locked with mine. "We will make it through this."

"I love you." It's all I can get out.

He smiles, then sits up, and kisses me. "I love you, my treasure." And then he takes me, again and again, until sleep finally claims us, tangled in each other's arms. Naked beneath the moonlight, the soft flicker of the lantern painting golden fire across our skin.

Just us against the world and everything that stands in our way. But together, we'll take it all on.

Because together, we are everything. In a world so vast, we've become the center of it, our bond eternal, beyond any end we could ever fathom.

Chapter Thirty-Three

Mira

Shell of Secrets

When I wake, my thoughts are razor sharp. We're inching closer to facing the most powerful witch the sea has ever known.

The memory of my mother still clings to me, her body drifting lifeless in the tide, the ocean wrapping around her like a grave. I remember the exact moment my father's soul shattered. The blade touched her skin, and something in him fractured, never to return. He carried that grief like an anchor with every wave he sailed. But even in all that sorrow, he was unbreakable, his love for her so fierce, so consuming, it cracked the world open.

I think I knew then that's what I wanted. That rare kind of love. The kind that ruins you and rebuilds you. The kind that scars and saves in the same breath. Now that I know what they both sacrificed for one another, I know what they had was pure, unrelenting love.

And now, I have it. In the quiet moments, when the storm stills, he calls me treasure, like I'm the rarest thing that's ever drifted through his world. He's the rhythm in my tide. The fire in my blood. The calm in my chaos. He's the map I never knew I was following.

My mother evidently knows I'm alive and thriving. The commands she's sent through others are evidence enough. Telling me to bring her the witch means she's either confident in my ability to make it happen or reliant on Kai to do the heavy lifting. She must know who he is to me and who he is to the witch.

My father's journal said she's the Queen of the Sirens. That means she and Veyra must know each other, two forces born from the same source: Mother Nature herself. But Mother Nature isn't all rainbows and blossoms. She's also storms and fire. Veyra is the gentle beauty in all things. My mother is the tsunami you pray never finds your shore. But who is the corrupted Soul? What physical form does she hide in? And what has she done to take the skins she's been living in?

Kai is already gone when I stir, but he leaves behind a hot coffee, a glass of water, and extra blankets in case I miss the warmth of his body beside me. A small smile creeps across my lips at that.

I get dressed slowly, adding more weapons than usual to my belt. I need to be ready to see Taika today. I take a sip of the coffee, letting it wake me from the inside out. It's just past sunrise, and neither of us has gotten much sleep. Still, I feel as prepared as I can be for what is coming.

I wonder now if Taika knew Smith was a traitor. She barely looked at me that day. Her eyes kept snapping to him, tracking him like a threat. She felt it. But she did warn me. Her voice echoes in my head even now. "*You wish to protect those with bad blood in their veins?*" She knew the person I was standing next to would sell me out.

While searching the room for smaller weapons to strap to my thigh and calf, my fingers brush against something cold and familiar. A seashell, nearly identical to the one Taika gave me. My blood runs cold. How does Kai have this? *Why?*

It was just sitting there out in the open, that somehow makes it worse. I trust him. I do. I know he'd never lie to me about seeing her, but my thoughts begin to spiral anyway. Seashells like this are rare and personal. My father had one too, given to him long ago. Maybe this one came from Kai's father? Maybe it's nothing, or maybe it's everything. I grab the shell and leave to find him.

I spot Kai on the deck, leaning against the railing with his coffee in hand. The sun kisses his skin, illuminating the ink on his body. His hair is damp, dripping onto his shirt. He must've just bathed. He has to be the cleanest pirate I've ever known.

He turns around like he can feel me coming, that sixth sense of his always one step ahead.

"Good morning, my treasure," he says with an alluring smile and a raspy voice. Then his gaze drops to my hand. He stills. He steps toward me slowly, carefully, like the space between us is charged. "What's this?" he asks, gently curling his fingers around my hand.

"I could ask you the same thing," I reply, not backing down.

His eyes narrow, studying me like I'm a riddle. "I took it off Archer," he finally says. "After I killed him. I searched his body and found this. I wasn't hiding it from you, if that's what you're thinking." He nods toward the shell. "You carry one just like it every day."

I open my mouth to respond, but he cuts me off. "Mira, this is dark magic." His voice is tight. "You shouldn't be carrying something like this."

"What do you mean? It's not dark magic." I say, but even as the words leave my mouth, doubt crept in. Who am I to argue with someone who has magic in their veins about what's dark magic or not?

I open my mouth to speak again, but he cuts in, testing me. "Where did you get yours?" I break his gaze, turning to stare out at the sea. "Mira," he presses, "if someone as vile as Archer had this, it can't be good." I look back to him, then slowly pull the shell from my pocket. "It's from Taika. She said it was a direct line to her, if I ever needed help."

I hold the shell in my palm. Then the pain hits. A searing heat licks across my hand like fire. I drop it with a cry, the shell clattering to the deck. Kai catches my wrist instantly.

"She can hear everything," he mutters grimly.

He snatches the shell from where it's fallen. Without another word, he hurls both shells into the sea. I see the wince flash across his face. She burned him too, but he says nothing. He turns his full attention to my hand, cradling it with so much care that my throat tightens. His eyes lock with mine. "She knows we're coming."

My body goes rigid. "How could she have heard everything... through a shell?" I ask, my voice shaking. Kai doesn't answer at first. He is already heading toward the quarterdeck. "Kai! Tell me what's going on! Don't walk away from me," I demand, stomping after him.

He stops, turning to face me. "We can't go to her. The only advantage we had was the element of surprise, and it's gone. We have to turn back." He's right. We are sailing straight into a trap.

Then he adds, "When you were little, did anyone ever tell you that if you held a seashell to your ear, you could hear the ocean?" The realization hits me like a knife to the gut. My stomach twists, bile rising in my throat. She's one clever witch. It's too late for us.

That thick, dark fog begins to roll in, just as it did the first time I saw her. It swallows the ship inch by inch, curling through the rigging and over the deck. I grab Kai's arm and hold him close. "We're here," I say.

He looks down at me and presses a kiss to my forehead. "I know. May the tides be with us." He covers my mouth and nose with a cloth, then does the same for himself. The crew around us coughs and gasps for air, same as before. But this time, we aren't here seeking help. This time, we've come to collect.

CHAPTER THIRTY-FOUR

KAI

THE SOUL'S CURSE

The ship jolts, pitching beneath our feet. Mira nearly goes down, but I catch her before her knees can hit the deck. The fog thickens, dragging across the wood like a curse, suffocating everything in its path. My lungs fight it off, but it clings to the air like poison.

I glance to the side and see a dock rising from the sea like it's been waiting for us, like we're late for a meeting. My ship is already tethered to it by magic of her doing. Lanterns hang on winding vines, the flames dimmed unnaturally low. She doesn't want us to see clearly. One sense dulled by fog and shadows. She's setting the rules before we even get to the table.

Mira and I make our way to the ladder. Before we descend, Jay finds me. He looks like he's been ready for this moment longer than I have.

"If we're gone too long," I tell him, "take the strongest of the crew and come find us. Don't leave this ship for any other reason, even for a breath."

He nods and presses a newly sharpened sword into my hand. "Understood, Cap'n. We'll be waiting." I grip his shoulder. A silent thanks. The blade won't help me in what's to come, I know that much. Magic prickles at my fingertips. This isn't a battle that can be fought with steel.

I climb down first, keeping my eyes locked on Mira as she follows. I watch every step she takes. One wrong move and this place will eat her whole. But she has been here before, so she knows that more than I do.

The bridge greets me with a groan, wood lashed together by magic, creaking under my boots. I reach up and lift Mira by the waist, setting her down beside me with care. Even her weight, as small as she is, makes the thing shudder. It feels like we'll fall right through it.

The water is black enough to swallow starlight. They say the waters around Alek were cursed by the first witch to ever bleed salt. Her magic sank into the tide like poison, and it's been festering ever since. Her sinister soul, cursed to the witch waters.

The surface lies still, yet beneath, the water stirs and remembers, watching like a living graveyard. Every wave knows the names of the damned who dared to trespass. There are souls trapped below, faces illuminated by the flicker of the glowing lanterns, stuck in the same expressions they had when their soul was claimed.

Mira and I wrap our cloths tight around our mouths and noses, a thin barrier between us and the thick, toxic fog clinging to everything. It burns the lungs if you're not careful. "Are you ready?" she asks, her voice muffled but steady as we approach the vine-draped hut ahead, small, crooked, half-swallowed by moss.

"As ready as I'll ever be," I answer. "But if anything goes wrong, anything, you run. You get back to the ship. Don't look back."

"I won't leave you," she says firmly. "You know better than to ask that of me."

I stop walking. Turn to her, stepping in front of her. Her eyes shine even in this dim, sickly light, those impossible emerald eyes that always see more than I want them to. "You will," I say, sharper now. "You'll go back. I won't watch you die at the hands of my mother." She doesn't argue, just turns her head and keeps walking. Her silence says everything.

The stench hits me first: rot, damp earth, the sour tang of blood. It clings to the back of my throat, thick and unrelenting. Her hut smells like death.

As we draw closer, the fog thins just enough to see the outline of the crooked doorway. Mira and I pull the cloths from our faces, eyes watering from the fumes. I pause with my hand on the doorframe, forcing myself to breathe through the dread knotting in my chest. Then I open it.

There she is, sitting in a chair as if she's been waiting for me, like I was late coming home and she was ready to scold me, like she is a real mother. As if she'd ever earned the right to call herself that. The room is worse than I imagined.

Withered animals hang in rusted cages, twitching and groaning, trapped in something that wasn't life but wasn't death either. Glass jars line the far wall, filled with floating limbs and body parts of creatures I can't name. A parrot perched overhead keeps muttering the same three words, "Death, ruin, and run." A warning.

Black magic soaks this place, thick and pulsing. I can feel it in my bones. Taika sits upon a throne of bone and moss, likely the remains of those she's claimed. Her lips and teeth are stained black. Her skin, though pale, is smeared with blood and dirt. She smells like the earth after a storm, but hungrier and rotten.

She's not beautiful, but she's powerful. For all she could've done, all the good she might've wielded, she chose this. She turned purity into violence. Innocence into ruin. And I'm the blood she left behind.

"*Son*, how nice of you to finally pay me a visit. Here to kill me, are you?" *Son*. How fucking dare she. She says it so casually, like she hadn't abandoned me to rot in a world without her. Her voice is gravel, like she's spent centuries screaming into the void or smoking her lungs to ash.

I don't speak, refusing to give her the satisfaction. But Mira steps forward, her voice steady and clear. "Taika, what do you want to wish for?"

That catches her off guard. The change in her body language is instant. Her posture softens and her gaze shifts, trying to become someone gentler. A mask. "Girl," she says with faux sweetness, "I told you, this wish is for your ears only."

Mira doesn't budge or blink. "Whatever you say to me goes straight to him, and you know that. Now answer the question, what is it you want to wish for?" Her stance is unshakable. Eyes narrowing, her chin lifts. She stands there like she belongs in this cursed room more than Taika does.

Taika steps forward, her movements deliberate. I move without thinking, placing my body between her and Mira. My arm is instinctively outstretched, ready to block, to burn, to kill if I have to. But Mira gently nudges me aside out of defiance. She doesn't fear Taika, not anymore.

"I wish to be freed," Taika says at last. Freed? She wants death? I can grant that gladly, just as I did with my father.

"You wish to be freed?" Mira echoes. "Then why have you fought for so long to survive?" Taika doesn't answer at first. She turns, her fingers tracing along the clutter of chaos of one of her tables, bones, feathers, rusted blades, glass jars filled with trinkets of torment.

"You think this is living, girl? This hut? This prison?" She gestures around her, the vines curling in like claws. "I was locked in here years ago. Let out only when she decides it's convenient." *She?*

She moves toward the wall, her hand trailing across its damp, rotting wood. "I haven't seen the ocean," she mutters, "haven't felt the sea breeze on my face since..." Her beady dark eyes find mine. And her voice, raw and almost human, lowers. "Since you were born." She says it like a confession. Her bony, dirt-caked finger lifts, pointing directly at me.

"Why did you leave?" I ask, my voice low. If she's been trapped in here, then whatever caged her must have been more powerful than her. The thought makes my blood run cold. Taika nods slowly, her gaze falling to the floor, where mold creeps between rotting wood and earth. "I made a deal," she whispers.

Her posture changes, shoulders hunching inward. Her eyes dull, the memory draining her. "With who?" I ask. She doesn't answer. She begins to pace, lips moving with words I can't catch, murmurs slipping from her mouth. I reach out, grabbing her arm. It is like touching a corpse, cold and stiff. Taika's eyes widen, startled by my touch, like a ghost's hand has found her in the flesh.

"Tell me who," I growl.

Her head snaps up. Her eyes, once pale and murky, are now pitch black, a void where a soul should be. "There are things we don't name, boy," she hisses, her voice not entirely her own. "Things more deadly than I. More twisted than the kappas. Old things... things that don't need to touch you to kill you, but poison your mind instead." She leans in closer, her whisper brushing against my skin.

My heart feels like it stopped beating. My father had a similar curse put upon him. Mira must sense the shift in me. Her fingers brush the back of my arm, soft and steady. I swallow hard. "So you didn't poison my father?"

Her eyes snap to mine, wounded. "I would never hurt him," she says, her voice cracking. "He was the only thing I ever truly loved. I'd trade every ounce of magic, every drop of power I have, just to hear his heart beating in my ears again." Their souls were tied. That's the only way she could have heard her other half's heartbeat.

She looks away, but I can see how her gaze softens, lost in a memory. For the briefest moment, she doesn't look like the monster I've built her up to be in my mind. She looks like someone mourning the one thing that made her human. "It was mercy," she adds quietly, voice raw. "What you saw, that wasn't the worst of it. It was only the beginning. You saved him from what was coming."

My eyes narrow. "You knew?" I ask.

She meets my stare with a gaze that pierces straight through me. "I knew the moment I felt cold. The human in me, or whatever was left, died when his heart stopped beating. I'm what remains, because of my curse," she whispers. "And I knew you'd be the one to take his life. I saw it in a vision."

Guilt twists through me, but I hold my ground. "I did what I had to do," I say, "to protect Mira."

She turns to face me fully then, emotion flickering behind her eyes. "You are your father's son," she says. "Whether you like it or not." Taika stops pacing. "I know it was the right thing to do, son," she says softly. For the first time, she sounds like a mother, reassuring her son. I hate how it splits my heart in half.

I've spent my whole life hating her, believing she abandoned us, that she poisoned my father. But this is something so much bigger than her or any of us. And we walked straight into it. She's standing in the heart of it with me.

The room falls into an eerie silence, broken only by the rattling of cages and the quiet shuffling of whatever else lurks within her hut. "Why do the sirens want you?" I ask. "What did you do to them?" Taika's grin twists into something unsettling.

"If you want to be freed," Mira says, stepping forward, "then we need to know the truth." Taika begins to hum an old siren song, warped and off-key, as she drifts around the hut, moving objects, muttering, her mind clearly splintered, poisoned like my father's.

"I used to do bad things to them," she finally says, hauntingly casual.

"Such as?" Mira asks.

"I had pirates capture them. Bring them to me," she continues, turning over a cracked bottle on the table. "Then I'd use their scales, their tears. For spells and potions. Afterwards... I'd let them go." She lets out a snicker, blackened teeth glinting through cracked lips. There's no remorse in her voice, not even a flicker of shame.

Fury flashes through Mira, sharp and barely restrained. "You did this because you wanted to?" Mira asks. "Or because you were ordered to?"

Taika turns slowly, the grin crawling across her face like a shadow. "Both," she whispers.

Mira's heart is pounding. Rage surges through her, I can feel it as though it's my own. "Do you even know who I am?" she demands, raising her voice.

Taika doesn't flinch. "I know exactly what you are, girl. I've known since the day you were born."

The color drains from Mira's face. I want to end this woman where she stands, but Mira beats me to it. "And you thought it was a good fucking idea to ask me for a favor?" she snarls. "After what you did to my bloodline?"

Taika stops fiddling with the mess on her table. Her expression shifts to something almost proud. "I thought it was my most clever idea yet," she says, voice low. "I knew the sirens would come for me eventually. And they'd use you to do it. You were my way out. I hoped they'd drag me down, drown me, so I wouldn't have to rot in this hell any longer. But I also knew"—she pauses, cruelty slipping into her tone—"you owed me a wish. And you'd use it to free me. Not out of kindness, but out of duty. Then my soul could finally escape. Because the only thing stronger than what binds me here is that fountain." Clever witch.

Mira goes still. All the fire in her eyes fades, and suddenly they grow cold.

"If it's death you crave, then death you shall have," I say grimly. "The sirens will see to it that it's slow and cruel." Taika's smile widens as she turns a handful of tiny bones over in her palm, bones too small to belong to anything kind.

"Good," she rasps, her voice cracking like dry earth. "Let it come. That is exactly what I wish. And you dear boy, you're living a very slow and cruel death already. Aren't you?" Her gaze finds the black veins on my arm.

"A siren's curse isn't reversible. You're lucky you've been able to live this long with that wretched thing in your veins," Taika says.

"I know what I have. I don't need you to tell me," I say with my hand raised.

"Hopefully you both have enough pieces of a siren for all the debts you owe and enough to save your souls." She lets out an evil laugh, and the critters coil in their cages.

Mira steps forward. "I'll free you," she says. "But only if you tell me what has a hold on you. What's keeping you here." Taika's fingers begin to tremble, the bones snapping under the pressure, brittle splinters falling to her feet. The sound cracks through the silence.

Her eyes lift, wide, glassy, and rimmed with terror. Then, barely above a whisper: "*You.*"

"What did you say?" I growl, stepping forward. Her hand rises slowly, stained with soil and time, a single long finger pointing directly at Mira. "You," she repeats, louder now. Certain.

I move in front of Mira on instinct, blocking the witch from reaching her. But Mira steps out from behind me, undeterred. "Me?" she asks, her voice low.

Taika's gaze never wavers. "Yes," she breathes. "The Soul. The song. The ocean. You." Taika's voice coils through the air like smoke. "You are the new Soul, are you not?" My heart drops.

"I am," Mira answers, claiming her title with conviction.

Taika's eyes gleam, dark with something ancient and bitter. "Then you are what controls me." The truth hits like a wave crashing over rock. Mira, my Mira, isn't just tied to the ocean. She is the ocean. She will become all that is good... and all that is ruin.

"The Soul did this to you?" Mira asks, voice tight, uncertainty curling at the edges. Taika nods, gaze locking with hers, unblinking and intense. Mira doesn't flinch. "Then what did you do to deserve it?" she demands. "What did you do for the Soul to bind you here?"

Taika doesn't answer. Instead, she turns away, her attention drifting toward her endless clutter. Her hands move quickly, grabbing vials of dark liquid, mixing them with stained fingers like none of this matters to her. "If you won't answer, we're done," Mira says coldly. "Rot here for all I care."

She turns heading for the door. But Taika's voice comes again, quieter. "It gave me a choice," she says. Her hands were slick, the color of blood dripping down her wrists. "I chose wrong."

She wipes the red across the tattered edge of her dress, smearing it like penance. Then she turns, her eyes on mine. "I chose power over love," she says. "I chose power... over you." Her voice cracks, barely more than breath. "I'm sorry, my son," she says. "I chose wrong."

There are a thousand things I could say. Accusations. Demands. But one question rises above them all. "What were the choices she offered you?"

Taika starts pacing again, back and forth like a caged thing. Her voice drops into a hollow murmur. "That I cannot say. It is a test. One most don't pass." Her eyes flash at me. "Not even your father." My chest tightens.

"It was angry with me," she continues, her voice slipping into memory. "But I didn't know then what I know now. That your soul was already tied to hers, even before she drew her first breath." She turns to Mira, pointing once more with that long, skeletal finger. "Fated mates," she says, like it was a sacred curse. "A rare, violent bond. Stronger than even the Soul itself, because it is the Soul."

My breath catches. Taika looks between us, at me, at Mira. Her voice turns reverent. "The Soul is not just the ocean. It governs all life. It chooses vessels to carry it forward, and it has chosen her."

Mira doesn't move. Taika steps closer. "But know this, Kai, your soul is tied to it too. You are its other half. Its flame. Its peace." Her next words land like a dagger.

"Mira will never be able to rest. But you will." Silence. "She will live a lonely life after you're gone. And there is nothing you can do to stop it." My heart slams against my ribs. Mine might already be drawing its final breath. She's been cursed with my soul, bound to someone who will wither before she ever learns how wide forever stretches.

"That is when the Soul grows cold," Taika says softly. "When it loses its other half. That is when it forgets how to feel. When it becomes cruel... and unstoppable."

Mira looks at me. "Then I know what I will wish for," she says softly, her eyes full of calm.

"But the Soul eventually finds a new one to take its place," she continues. "That's what's happening with me, isn't it?"

Taika lets out a laugh, the sound scraping against the walls. "After more than a thousand years, yes. It's finally ready to sleep. To rest."

She tilts her head, her blackened teeth visible in the low light. "It's not all darkness, girl. It's light, too. It's both. The ocean has its crystal-clear waters where the pure hearted live. And its darkest depths where the most vile creatures are born and live. It depends on who you are... before it chooses you. Depends on the life you live. It chose you because of how pure you are."

Mira glances around the hut, taking in the bones, the jars, the rot clinging to the rafters. Then she asks, "So it chooses when it wants to rest?"

Taika shrugs. "I am not it. I can't speak for it. But I can tell you this, whoever held the Soul before you was cruel. Is cruel." She steps toward us, slowly. "That's why the ocean is unbalanced. That's why nothing feels right. It hasn't for a very long time."

Then she says it. "There is an army coming. One built from dead souls. They cannot be killed." The words hang in the air.

"Is there anything else we should know before we hand you over to the sirens?" I ask. Taika freezes, then slowly turns to face me, staring so deeply it feels like she's peeling back every layer of who I am. I stand tall, and something in my posture makes her step back.

"My greatest regret," she says, voice trembling, "in all my long, cursed life... was not choosing you, my son." Her breath catches. "When I'm gone, when my soul is finally put to rest, you will inherit my power. All of it. You'll need to learn how to control it, how to wield it without destroying yourself. Find Fog. He will teach you."

Her words settle as I watch the fragile, filthy creature before me. This is my mother. This is what remains of her. I step closer. "Then I think it's time you join my father." Her eyes widen, not with fear, but with something unholy. Glee.

"It won't be a peaceful death," I add. "The sirens have no mercy left for you." Taika's lips curl into a wicked smile, black and gleaming.

"I welcome a painful death."

CHAPTER THIRTY-FIVE

MIRA

UNTIL THE STARS BURN OUT

After we secure Taika in the brig, I retreat to our quarters and start rifling through more of my father's journals. I've gone through every single one, but there's nothing—no clues, no maps, no hidden notes.

"What's wrong?" Kai asks as I sit on the floor, surrounded by weathered pages.

"I just feel like I'm missing something," I say, brows furrowing as I flip through another entry.

"Such as?" he asks, his tone soft but curious.

"I need to go back to Magda." I meet his eyes. "I know that's a big ask, but I feel like the answers I need are there—at home. On *The Siren*."

He moves to sit beside me, the last of the sunlight spilling through the windows and pooling across the floorboards. "It's not a big ask," he says quietly. "If you ever want to go home, I'll never get in your way."

I feel myself blushing at his words, embarrassed that even the simplest thing he says can pull that reaction from me. "To Magda then," I say, a smile spreading across my face. Something feels whole in my heart. After being out at sea for so long, the thought of home warms me.

He returns it, a hint of warmth in his eyes. "What are you looking for?" he asks, brow furrowing.

"I'm looking for a clue, something big that I missed. When I left *The Siren*, it was in such a hurry. I don't think I went through all of my father's things thoroughly enough. Maybe whatever he was hiding holds the answers we need."

"I'll tell Jay to change course. We'll be in Magda in a couple of days."

The Leviathan is the fastest ship on the sea. What took *The Siren* three days to sail from Magda to Alek will only take us two. Which is what we need, since time is running short with Kai getting worse, even if he won't admit the pain he's in.

He kisses my forehead, gentle and fleeting, then rises and slips out to change our course.

I stand at the side of the ship, leaning against the railing as Magda finally appears on the horizon, the colorful buildings alive with the pirates that reside there. Relief floods through me, carried on the salt-heavy wind as I take a long, steadying breath. Kai stands at the helm, and I can feel his gaze even before I look. When I turn and smile, it's to let him know that *I know he's watching*. He lets out a quiet laugh, his lips curving into that rare smile, eyes never leaving me.

We steer toward the far side of the island, the place where we left *The Siren.* The moment I see her, I swear I hear her groan in recognition. My chest tightens. Seeing her again makes my throat ache; the wave of emotion is almost too much to hold back.

We dock *The Leviathan* beside her. I don't wait for Kai. My feet move on their own, carrying me toward *The Siren.* Then I spot movement on the deck. Neressa steps out, just barely into my view.

I stop walking and stare up at her. Neressa looks like she belongs on the ship, though she's as tied to the land as I am to the sea. Since *The Siren* is docked on land, she's able to be on board. She lifts a hand and waves at me to come closer, so I do.

Kai comes up behind me. "Do you want to go alone?" he asks, his voice gentle. I look up at him, my boots sinking into the wet sand.

"Yes. Come up in a little bit. I have a feeling Neressa wants to speak to me privately."

He nods, respecting my wishes, though something in his eyes tells me he's wary of her. And honestly, who wouldn't be? She's terrifying.

I climb the ladder, the enchanted teak groaning under my weight. "Hello, love. I've missed you." My hand lingers on the railing, long enough to let *The Siren* know I'm here. When I finally step onto the deck, tears sting my eyes. I didn't realize how much I missed her until now.

I glance toward the helm. Neressa sits in an old wooden chair, feet propped on the wheel like *she's* the captain now. I make my way toward her, each creak of wood and memory beneath my boots.

"I see you've made yourself at home," I say as I walk up the last step.

"You did say I could move in." She smiles. Her fog-colored eyes catch the dying light from the sun.

"Did you?" I glance around. Everything looks exactly the same.

"No," she says, lips curving with amusement. "I saw you coming and decided to grace you with my presence."

I let out a low laugh. When I reach her, she stands and wraps her arms around me. It's longer than her usual quick embrace, tighter too.

"I've missed you, Mira." She releases me and studies my face as though she's trying to read me like a book to find out everything I've gone through. "I heard about Smith." Her tone sharpens. The anger returns at the thought of him. What he did to me, to the crew. The words he spoke to me.

"What a fucking traitor. If I had known..." Her jaw tightens, eyes darkening to storm gray, the shade that comes right before she kills.

"He did have a painful death, trust me," I say.

Her eyes snap up to mine. "Oh?"

"Sirens." That's all I have to say. She nods once and walks away from me, leaning on the railing beside the helm. "Why are you back? How's Kai?" Her voice carries a rare hint of genuine concern.

I move to stand next to her, resting my hands on the same railing. "I need to do some more digging through my father's things. I feel like I missed something last time."

I pause, letting the silence settle, feeling *The Siren* hum beneath my palms, the ship's old magic pulsing through the wood like a heartbeat.

"As for Kai," I continue, "he's... well, so much more than I ever thought he could be."

She turns to look at me, and her expression softens. "You love him?"

"More than anything."

She smiles faintly, looking down at her nails. "Good. He's kept you alive this long, I'm sure he'll take care of you." I look away, trying to break her gaze. "What is it?" she asks. She never misses anything.

"He's dying." The words scrape out of me, barely more than a whisper. My throat tightens. I've been so strong in front of him that finally saying it out loud, especially to Neressa, shatters something inside me.

"He's dying? From what?" I can't answer right away. The knot in my throat only tightens, stealing my voice away from me. "Take your time," she says quietly. She's gentle with me, so gentle it almost hurts. I fear I'm the only one she's ever saved that emotion for, that I know of.

"His scar," I say quietly. "He got it when he was a boy. It was cursed. It's called—"

"The siren's curse." Neressa finishes for me. "That's one of the few curses that can't be undone," she says, her voice lingering with empathy. I nod, fighting back tears. "How bad is it?" she asks.

"It's spreading. The black veins are down his arm and across his chest now. He's had a hallucination of a siren song. I think it stemmed from the scar."

Her expression hardens. "When you make it to the fountain—"

"Yes, I'll save him," I say before she can finish.

She tilts her head. "You must really love him, to give him your wish."

I let out a low laugh, shaking my head and choosing not to reveal how many wishes we really have. "Love makes you do crazy things, aye?"

"It will be okay, love," she says softly. "You're strong. You'll get there." Then her eyes sharpen, that familiar glint returning. "Now, what are we looking for?" Changing the subject before I become a complete mess.

I lead her to my father's quarters. When I open the door, it creaks louder than I remember. "Look for anything with a lock on it," I say, stepping inside. "Or something that looks like it wasn't meant to be found."

We start rifling through everything, drawers, shelves, the desk, under his mattress. Nothing. Not a single thing. The room feels as bare as the bottom of a ship's hull.

Then my eyes catch on the closet. His clothes still hang unorganized, untouched by time. I push them aside, and there it is, a small lock hidden in the back, built into the wood of the closet, a number dial glinting faintly in the low light.

"Interesting," Neressa murmurs from behind me, the sweet scent of cinnamon curling in the air around her. "What do you think it could be?"

Four digits. What four digits could he have possibly been attached to? I start guessing. His birthday—*zero, four, twelve.* No.

His favorite number, twice—*five, five, five, five.* Nothing. Then I try my birthday. *Zero, three, twelve.* It clicks open.

"Your birthday," Neressa says quietly.

"My birthday," I echo, my voice barely a whisper. My eyes sting, tears gathering at the edges. I unlatch the rusted lock, the metal groaning in protest. As it snaps free, a piece of paper slips out, the final entry of his journal, aged, weather-worn, and stained with what looks like blood.

Coordinates and a letter. The moment my eyes meet them, something shifts. A calm washes over me, foreign and familiar all at once. I feel them, deep in my bones, like they're calling me home.

Neressa places a hand on my shoulder. "I'm going to leave you now, love. This is for your eyes only. I'm here when you need me." I meet her gaze and nod. There's nothing more to say.

When she's gone, I make my way to his old, dust-covered bed, the sheets still wrinkled from the last time he laid there. I sit down slowly, the air heavy with the ghost of him.

The coordinates point directly to the heart of Sapphire's Ocean, the most beautiful and mysterious sea in existence. Known for its deep blue trenches and waters so clear at dawn, they shimmer like glass. As soon as the moon is out, the surface reflects the stars so perfectly, it feels like you could dive straight into the heavens and come back drenched in starlight. But beneath that beauty lies silence, depth, and ancient magic. It's the least explored ocean for a reason.

I open the letter, his handwriting messy but readable. My father's final message, one meant for the sea, but never sent. A message in a bottle.

Sirena,

I promise you, I'll find you. My love, my wife, the mother of our extraordinary daughter. I had no choice but to put Mira above all else. She had to be kept hidden, protected. No one could know who or what she truly was. If they did, they'd try to take her from us. Neressa is the only one who knows. I've made mistakes, too many to count. I've failed her as a father, and I know that. But one day, I pray she'll understand the weight I've carried, and why I did what I had to do.

I know you're still out there. When your body returned to the sea, you likely lost your memory, but I didn't. Not for a second. I remember everything. The sound of your laugh, the storm in your eyes, the calm in your touch. You were the fiercest soul to ever cross my path, and the sea has been colder without you.

I swear on the Soul herself, I'll find you. And when I do, I'll bring you back to me. I'll make you remember. I've searched the entire ocean for you, and now I know where you are. These coordinates are a promise. I'm coming.

Mira will have her mother again, even if we're separated by water and sky. She's more like you than you know. I know she can breathe beneath the surface, she just doesn't know it yet. She belongs to the tides, like her mother. Teach her, when the time comes. Even if you can't be beside her, you live in her. She carries you, always.

I'll never stop searching. Till the sea swallows me and the stars burn out.

Yours Always, Bleu

Tears burn hot trails down my cheeks as I read, my vision blurring with every word. I glance at the date. He wrote this the day he was taken by the sea, dragged into the depths by a siren. My father must have hidden the letter and coordinates when we entered the battle that took his life.

He never got to send it. He never was able to hunt for the cove. Their love was a graveyard of what-ifs. If he had found the cove, would he have been welcomed in? A message meant for my mother, lost to the tide of their love story. It's like he knew he was going under that day. His handwriting, how clean the letter was, he made it special for *her.*

My father loved her and me with everything he had. He wasn't perfect, but he gave up a life with her to protect me. And that's all a daughter of a notorious pirate could ever ask for.

His words carve something permanent into my soul. He raised me to be strong, to face whatever storm came my way. He was selfish, always searching for a way to numb the pain of my mother's death—a pain he often took out on me. But his love was never fickle, buried beneath the anger and the rum. I just wish he'd said it to me—at least once more.

I watch the tears fall onto my pants, tiny drops of grief soaking into the fabric. I let them dry. Then I wipe my face, stand tall, and tuck his final words into my pocket.

I take in the room one last time, my fingers brushing over the pillow where he once laid his head. Then I move back to the closet, shut the secret vault, and scramble the numbers.

When I step out onto the deck, Kai is there, waiting. He's standing at the edge, eyes on the horizon. The sun is setting, casting a golden hue across his skin. He turns as soon as he senses me. The moment his gaze meets mine, he smiles.

"Hi, Kai," I say softly, a small smile finding its way to my lips as I walk closer to him.

"Why are you crying?" His brows pull together. I hand him the coordinates I found. His expression shifts to pure shock. "Is this—"

"The coordinates to Sirens Cove," I finish for him.

A slow smile spreads across his face. He steps closer, cups my cheeks, and kisses me. "You were right, treasure. They were here." The sun hits just right, turning his hazel eyes to pure gold.

"When have I ever been wrong?" I tease. He laughs, wrapping his arms around me.

"But you're upset—why?" he asks softly. He never lets a single one of my emotions slip past him.

"There was a message attached to the coordinates," I say quietly. "A message in a bottle that was never sent. My father wrote it for my mother, hoping she would somehow find it." I take a slow breath. "I found it hidden in a vault inside his closet. The code was my birthday."

Kai's lips curve into a smile. "Which is?" he asks, genuinely curious.

"My birthday?" I tease, letting out a soft laugh. "You claim to love me but don't even know when I was born?"

He laughs, shaking his head. "Between keeping us alive and marching straight into the biggest war this sea's ever seen, it just hasn't come up." He shrugs his shoulders. He has a fair point.

I laugh again, the sound breaking through the heaviness. "It's March twelfth."

His eyes narrow with mock suspicion. "Do you know mine?"

Shit. I only know his sign—from whispers in taverns. "I know you're a Scorpio."

Kai smiles. "Yes." He pauses, narrowing his eyes. "November twelfth," he says.

"Also born on the twelfth," I reply, a small smile tugging at my lips.

His eyes light up. "It's like we were fated mates or something," he jokes. It's one of my favorite sides of him, the one no one but me ever gets to see.

I laugh, the sound soft and real. When I look up at him, he's still holding me, smiling down. "Let's find the cove," I say. He nods, that familiar determination flickering behind his eyes. Then he steps toward the edge of *The Siren*, where the ladder waits.

I pause, taking her in one last time. Every plank, every rope, every whisper of magic in the wood, a deck that used to be so full of chaos and warmth, now empty. This feels like a goodbye I'm not ready for.

"I'll be waiting for you on the shore," Kai says softly, before disappearing down the side of the ship.

I stand there for a moment, the echo of his words lingering in the air. Then I turn and walk to my quarters, letting myself breathe it all in, the scent of my sheets, the desk where maps once sprawled, everything frozen exactly as I left it.

A hot tear slips down my cheek. I close the door behind me.

I climb the stairs to the helm, each step slow and heavy. When I reach the wheel, I rest my hand against it, the wood warm beneath my palm. "I'll be back for you, okay? I promise." *The Siren* groans in response, like she understands.

"I'm sorry," I whisper. "You know I love you. Let Neressa captain you if it comes to it. Even if she isn't full blood, you can trust her. And keep her safe." Another groan rolls through her hull, softer this time like a sigh.

My fingers trail along the helm as I turn to leave, the magic humming faintly under my skin, like she's saying goodbye too.

"I'll see you soon, girl," I whisper as I climb down the ladder, the sea air thick with salt and promise.

Kai waits for me on the shore. We walk back to *The Leviathan* hand in hand, our steps quiet against the sand. The sun paints the sky in shades of pink, purple, and gold. The perfect sunset.

Up ahead, Neressa leans against a palm tree, watching us. When our eyes meet, she gives a single nod. I return it, a silent promise passing between us. Something tells me this is the last time I will see her for a very long while. The thought plucks a heartstring in my chest. Kai's hand slides to my back, steadying me as if he can feel the ache in my heart.

It's time to save his life. To Sirens Cove.

CHAPTER THIRTY-SIX

KAI

LOVE & LOSS

I wake before Mira, as usual. She always sleeps a little longer than me, tucked into the warmth of the sheets. I leave her there and make my way to the kitchen, boil water for a bath, and soak in the quiet that only early mornings can bring. Just the night crew works above, moving like shadows across the deck.

The fog this morning is thick, haunting, like the world has been swallowed whole. I keep a careful eye on the ocean, scanning for any sign of blackened waters. I don't want the sirens arriving sooner than expected. There's still one more conversation I need to have before they come for the witch.

Having Mira by my side, selfishly, has been the greatest adventure of my life. One I never want to see end.

I make my way up the stairs to the quarterdeck, taking over for the crewmate who had been steering overnight. Gripping the helm, I turn us toward the coordinates Mira gave. She found them on *The Siren* but wanted to keep her father's writing, so she wrote them on a separate piece of parchment. Her handwriting is elegant and fluid, each curve of the cursive like she's woven beauty into every number. Even something as simple as her writing is stunning.

The ocean stretches out before me, calm yet eerily still, like a predator waiting to strike. There's something unsettling in the air, an unnatural quiet that claws at my senses. It's the calm before the storm, that haunting silence where every second feels stretched and heavy, a warning whispered just beneath the surface. But even in that unease, I find solace in one truth: Mira is in our bed, asleep, wrapped in warmth and safety, untouched by whatever darkness looms on the horizon.

I watch as the sun begins to rise, burning away the thick fog that clings to the water, casting the ocean in a brilliant, glossy sheen. The deep blues bleed into rich indigos, shimmering with turquoise as the sun kisses the surface. It feels like the sea is showing off, flaunting her mythical beauty, taunting me with her allure. And as the salty spray mists my face, I'm reminded of my true first love. She never lets me forget her, the sea.

I listen to Mira's heartbeat echoing softly in my ears, slow and steady. The one thing in my life that I find full comfort in. I sense she's awake the moment it quickens. Still, I stay at the helm, wanting her to find me on her own, to gather her thoughts in peace.

Whatever waits inside that cove is close. Too close. We arrive ahead of schedule, moving faster than we usually do. We haven't had to stop once. Part of me suspects Taika is behind it, down in the brig, quietly controlling the sea.

Once Jay wakes and comes to relieve me at the helm, I know it's time. I need to visit Taika one last time. He approaches with a tired grin, rubbing the sleep from his eyes. "Morning, Cap'n."

"Jay," I nod, stepping aside. "I wanted to thank you."

He gives me a confused look. "For what?" he asks, brow furrowed. "For protecting her. The crew. Me."

Jay blinks, caught off guard. "Since when did you get all sentimental on me?"

I smirk but don't look away. He sobers, the corners of his mouth lifting into something quieter, more loyal. "I've always had your back, Cap'n. Since the day I met you. I'm not going anywhere now."

His words sink deep. I clap him on the shoulder and leave him at the helm, knowing I can trust him with everything I care about.

With that, I step back from the helm, the chill of the morning clinging to my skin as I turn to go below deck. I've spent enough quiet moments preparing my words for Taika in my head, but still, there is a heaviness in my chest as I make my way down. I haven't seen her once since we dragged her from that cursed little hut in the sea. Part of me expects the force that kept her confined there to rise up and try to stop her from leaving. But there's been no sign of it. Maybe it's because of Mira. Maybe it trusts her.

Our brig is small. I never saw the point in keeping prisoners. If someone is dangerous enough to lock up, they're dangerous enough to kill. No use wasting food and supplies on someone marked for death. But Taika, she's different. She's the last part of the map.

I make my way below deck, the instant chill nipping at my skin. A flicker of remorse creeps in, knowing she's been down here freezing. I placed her in the farthest cell on purpose, away from any wandering ears she might try to manipulate into setting her free.

Taika sits on the wet floor, clothes soaking and clinging to her skin. Mira, ever compassionate, had insisted we give her something fresh to wear, since the rags she arrived in were nearly rotted through. I found a dress deep in the hold, and when I handed it to her, her eyes widened. It was hers from a life long gone, back when she was with my father. The fabric is the color of deep red wine.

She sits cross-legged now, meditating, still and silent. But the moment I step close enough, her eyes open. Black as the void at first, unsettling, bottomless. Then, slowly, they shift into something almost human once her gaze settles on me.

"Finally here to visit me?" Taika asks with an uneasy smile.

I step closer to her cell. "I am."

The only reason I'm keeping her locked up is for the crew's sake. I can't risk her making deals or killing someone in their sleep. If she escapes, whatever magic binds her to her word will kill her, or worse, send her back to that rotting little hut in the sea. If the sirens want her, they'll surely get their hands on her. Mira and I need her now more than ever.

"So, boy," she says, rising from where she was meditating, water dripping from her soaking dress, "you must have something to say to me?"

I shrug and walk over to the cabinets along the far wall. I can't stand by while someone sits freezing and soaked, not even her. I grab a few blankets.

"Those won't do any good, dear boy," she calls softly behind me. "I can't feel the cold." I turn and hang them on the bars anyway.

"I didn't know you were down here soaking wet," I say quietly. "If I had, I would've done something."

She steps closer to the bars of the cell, stopping just in front of me. "It's good to get used to the water," she says, her voice flat. "I'll be drowning in it soon enough." There is no doubt she knows that is how she will die.

"My magic," I say, the words sharp. "I need you to tell me more about it." The least she can do, after everything, is give me the truth. The real path to the power that's been buried inside me since birth.

Taika wraps her long, bony fingers around the bars. "It's strong," she whispers. "I told you. Find Fog. He will help you."

My eyes harden. "I want to hear it from you, not some stranger I've never even met. How do I unlock what's dormant?"

Her eyes narrow, almost gleaming in the dim light, and she tilts her head slightly. "I'm a stranger to you too, am I not?" she says, the words cold enough to freeze bone. Then she hisses bitterly. "I told you... I have to die for you to unlock it all."

I tune into Mira's heartbeat. It's steady, but climbing. She is looking for me. I look back at Taika, pacing again, like always. She never seemed able to sit still when we talked, like the truth might burn her alive if she stopped moving.

"I don't blame you." The words leave me quietly. Controlled. She stops in her tracks. Her eyes grow wide. Tears pooling instantly, clinging to her lashes.

"How?" she breathes, her voice cracking. She's been waiting a lifetime to hear those words from me.

"You made one bad deal that cost you everything," I say quietly. "You fucked up, and you paid the price with a lifetime of pain and suffering. You lost your family, but knew they were still breathing. Still out there." I pause, my voice lowering. "Mourning people who are still alive is harder than if they were dead."

She moves her hands to her face, her shoulders trembling. She looks like a ghost of herself, an innocent woman who has finally let the last of her walls fall. Her cries are silent at first, choking and trembling.

"Every day," she starts, her voice breaking. She swallows. I give a slow nod, letting her know I am listening. "Every day, I wished I could see you. Both of you." She removes her hands from her face, placing them on the bars.

"I tried everything. The potions, the spells... I was always trying to find a way to reach you. But all I could make out were fragments. Tiny images of your faces. That's how I watched you grow. Through flickers. On your birthday each year, I'd see you, just for a moment. I always looked forward to November."

My heart feels heavy in my chest, like it had swallowed a stone. And then I feel her. Mira. She is near the stairs, lingering in the shadows, letting me have this moment alone with my mother.

Taika begins pacing again, water dripping from the hem of her dress. I wait. "Take your time," I say. She stops and steps back to the bars, her black eyes locking on mine.

"Never make a deal with the devil," she whispers. "I'm sorry I lost you. I'm sorry I lost him. I loved you both. I should've figured it out. I just... I couldn't find the right spell."

Her long, bony fingers wrap around the bars. I reach out, placing my hand on top of hers. Her skin is ice cold. "Our family is fucked up," I say. "But you tried. That's what matters. He loved you. I think he made a deal with the devil for you, too. His last words were, 'Taika, my love. Free me.'

Her expression shatters. She grows paler, if that's even possible. "He said that?" Her voice is thin, a cold wind behind it.

"Yes." I let go of her hand. She steps back, releasing the bars. "Hmm," is all she says at first.

Then, after a long silence: "His soul isn't resting," she murmurs. "He's in pain. I'll find him. I'll bring him with me."

I blink, confused. "What do you mean?"

"Don't worry, dear boy," she says. "I'll take care of it. The afterlife is hell if you're not at rest. Only immortals know that pain." I nod slowly, unsure what to say.

If his soul wasn't resting when I killed him, does that mean he was immortal? I watched him die. I heard his last breath. Just like Mira's mother. If she came back, could he? Or worse, did he already have an original form? And if both of my parents were, or are, immortal, what does that make me?

"Thank you. You will heal this world, my beautiful boy." Her voice trembles, but the smile that follows is warm. "You and her, you will heal it together. Please, don't use your power for evil, vile things. Use it to mend what's been broken."

She smiles again, soft and motherly, like I'd come home with a scraped knee and needed to be told I'm okay. It disarms me completely. "We will free you," I promise. "You have my word." Her eyes close slowly, then reopen, tears balancing on the lower lashes. I never thought I'd see emotion like this from her.

"I love you, dear boy," she whispers. "Never forget how much I love you." She looks around the brig one final time, her gaze lingering on the stairwell. She can sense Mira's presence.

"That girl is your compass," she says softly. "Let her lead you wherever she wishes. She will always be your heart. Never choose anything or anyone over her. You were written in prophecy, Kai. You are meant to change this world for the better."

She crosses her legs on the wet floor, slipping back into a deep meditative state just as I say, "I love you too." I turn to walk away but glance back one last time. She is smiling. Tears run freely down her cheeks. This is the happiest she's been in decades. I feel a smile sneak across my face. I'm glad to be the one to give her that.

I look away from Taika to find Mira, sitting quietly on the steps, waiting for me. She gives me a smile so soft and so full of understanding that it settles the storm in my chest.

She's heard everything. I reach out my hand, and she takes it, her touch gentle and grounding. I pull her up, and she presses a kiss to my lips, light and full of quiet reassurance.

Together, we turn and climb the stairs, leaving behind my mother, my past, and the weight of a bloodline that never loved me back.

All of it, locked in the cold.

CHAPTER THIRTY-SEVEN

MIRA

THE COVE AWAKENS

Kai has four siren claws strung around his neck, a silent declaration that he's ready to make the wishes he's been holding close to his heart. "You should probably hide those from the sirens," I warn. "Wearing pieces of one of them might not sit well." His intense gaze locks on mine and he wordlessly tucks the claws beneath his shirt.

"Thank you, treasure," he murmurs. "Are you ready?" We can both feel it, an invisible pull tightening with each passing second.

The sun vanishes behind a wall of fog, a heavy veil swallowing the ship whole. It clings to the sails, curls around the rigging, and slips over the deck like ghostly fingers. The sea is eerily still, pressing against my chest.

We stand near the starboard side, just below the quarterdeck, where the railing curves outward toward the sea. The wood beneath our boots is damp with mist, the ropes around us slick. From here, the water looks endless, a sheet of silvery blue disappearing into the fog, like we're sailing straight into the unknown.

"I am," I say softly, then add with a smirk, "Are you? We can still make a run for it."

He glances down at me, a tired smile ghosting across his lips. "You know I'd take you," he says. "Don't tempt me."

He pauses, then leans in, his voice low, like a vow wrapped in salt and storm. "But once we finish what we've started, I want to marry you."

My heart swells so fast it nearly hurts. He wants to marry me? A pirate? Pirates don't get married. That's for royals, for dreamers, for those who still believe in fairytales. For the common folk with simple lives and safe homes. This isn't something I ever imagined I'd be worthy of.

Tears burn the backs of my eyes. One slips free, carving a silent trail down my cheek. Before I can even breathe a reply, he drops to one knee. My hand is already in his, steady and sure. In his other, he holds a small teak box, the same wood my ship is built from.

"Mira," he says softly, "*my treasure.*"

His thumb traces slow, reverent circles across the back of my hand, anchoring me in the moment. His hazel eyes lock onto mine, rich with emotion, glinting with unshed tears. In that look is everything, love, devotion, *home.* He is wholly and completely mine.

Then he speaks. "Though our souls are bound, and that's the rarest magic in all the seas... I need you to know something." His voice trembles slightly, but his gaze is steady, full of quiet certainty. "I want you, not because of fate, not because the gods tied us together, but because you are everything. I choose you. Every day, I will choose you."

My hand covers my mouth, trying to not let myself completely fall apart. He takes a breath, then continues, voice growing stronger, more certain with each word.

"I've lived a life of killing, of chasing treasures, of sailing through the fiercest storms, always hungry for the next thrill. But then... you." The world stills. "You stole my heart the second I saw you in that pub. Within seconds, you became everything. You changed me, down to my very core. You're the very blood that runs in my veins. You beat my heart. You, Mira, are a treasure. One I can't live without." His grip tightens, fierce but so gentle.

His voice cracks as tears and tears well. I never thought I'd see the infamous Pirate Lord down on one knee, tears spilling from those stormy hazel eyes, looking up at me like I am the only thing that has ever mattered. He lets go of my hand and slowly opens the box, revealing the ring nestled inside.

It steals my breath. The center stone is a rare blue diamond, cut in the shape of an emerald, glowing like ocean light caught beneath the surface. Smaller diamonds trail along the gold band, delicate as stars scattered across a midnight sky. My breath catches in my throat.

"My father gave me this ring years ago," he says quietly, reverently. "I never knew why, until now. I love you, my treasure. Will you marry me?"

The tears come in waves, unstoppable, spilling silently down my cheeks as emotion swells in my chest.

I can't stand above him for another second. I drop to my knees beside him, the weight of it all pressing into my bones. My hands find his face, cupping it gently, like I need to hold the shape of his love in my palms, to remind myself this is real. That *he* is real.

"I will marry you, Kai Eldoris," I whisper, my voice trembling with the weight of everything we are and everything we've survived. "You already have me, my heart, my soul, my blood, my fire. You've had it from the beginning, even when I didn't want you to. Even when I tried to fight it. You are my home in every lifetime. I choose you in this life and the next. In every version of the world, I'll find you. I'll love you through storms, through silence, through death. You have all of me. Forever."

I reach up and gently brush the tear from his cheek with my thumb, treating it like something sacred, because it is. He exhales shakily, then pulls me into his arms, lifting me from the deck like I weigh nothing, but am everything.

He kisses me like a vow, like it is both the first and the last kiss we will ever share. The world disappears. There is no past, no prophecy, no war waiting beneath the waves. Only us and the vow we make beneath a haunting sky.

"Aye, Kai got himself a bride!" Jay calls out as he leans on the railing. The crew stops what they're doing and erupts into cheers, their voices echoing across the deck like waves crashing against the hull. Kai slides the ring onto my finger, and it fits like it knew my hand before I was ever born. Laughter, whoops, and shouts of celebration surround us, and for a fleeting, perfect moment, it feels like we've won. Like maybe pirates can have happy endings after all.

Who would've thought? Two people born of chaos and cursed bloodlines. The Pirate Lord and a siren-born girl, both drowning in each other. Our souls were made for this, fated from the moment we were born. I am so in love with him, it hurts. A beautiful ache that stretches through every rib, every bone, every breath. And then...

Silence. The cheers fade like a dream slipping through my fingers.

Kai gently sets me down, his arms still lingering as if reluctant to let me go. I don't need to ask. I feel the shift in the air, too. A chill crawls up my spine at the weight of something watching. A ship looms through the fog, all too familiar.

"The kappas," Kai mutters. Their ship hovers just beyond, cloaked in silence and deathly still. This kind of quiet only means one thing.

They are already in the water.

Kai steps in front of me, shielding me with his body. His eyes are sharp, but I see the worry laced beneath. "I'll protect you with everything I have," he promises. "But this isn't just our fight anymore. It's the battle of everything born from darkness. The kappas. The sirens. The pirates. It ends here."

He turns to face me fully, his hands gripping mine. "If I'm not at your side, you have to protect yourself. Do you promise me that, Mira?"

I look up at him, heart pounding like war drums beneath my ribs. "Promise," I whisper, sealing it with a kiss that speaks all the things I am too afraid to say out loud.

"It is so nice to see love," croaks a voice, hoarse and splintered, like barnacles scraping the hull. "I don't see that much anymore." I turn slowly, every inch of me tensing as my eyes land on him.

Varn.

He stands like a nightmare risen from the ocean's depths, water still clinging to his skin. His presence reeks of death and power, the scent of brine and decay clinging to him like a second skin. Before I can breathe, Kai slides me behind him with a motion so fluid my body follows without hesitation.

I find the hilt of my cutlass at my side. I draw it with a steely whisper. My grip tightens. My jaw locks. I'm ready.

"Varn," Kai says. He squares his shoulders, rising to his full height, even though Varn towers over him, half-sea creature, half-man, his skin slick and glistening with everything he's dredged up from the deep. But it doesn't matter.

Kai's presence expands, larger than fear, bolder than death. Confidence rolls off him like thunder on the tide. He is the sea, and he is ready to fight for everything that matters.

"Kai Eldoris, you have a debt to be paid." Varn's voice slithers through the air, sending a chill straight down my spine.

Kai takes a slow, deliberate step forward, his entire frame radiating strength as he looks up at the towering creature. "I can't pay it until I find the fountain, now can I?" His voice is steady, but the defiance in his eyes burns.

Varn's eyes flick to the crew, who stand at attention like they too sense something is about to break. With a harsh tap of his sword against the deck, he summons his own crew from the shadows, figures slithering up from the sea, silent and soaking in menace.

His gaze never leaves Kai. "I wish to change what I wanted," he rasps, thick with a dark, knowing resolve. "I want the bloody witch. The one you come from. She is of value." Varn knows—somehow, he knows that to reach the fountain, he can trade her for entrance.

The air between us goes cold. I can feel the heat of Kai's anger radiating off him like the sun beating down on the ship's deck. His jaw clenches, broad chest rising and falling with the storm brewing behind his eyes.

"You made your deal, Varn," Kai growls, his voice low and rumbling like thunder. "Stick with it." Varn's face twists. He isn't used to being challenged, especially not by a human. But even now, as rage flickers through Varn's monstrous features, it is clear that Kai's power is more dangerous than any weapon the kappas could wield.

"If you don't give me what I want," Varn hisses, "then I will be forced to rain blood all over your ship. Till I leave with what I came to get."

Kai doesn't flinch. "You don't get to keep changing your mind," he says. "One moment you want a debt settled. Next, a witch. Pick a path, Varn. And don't change it." Kai's eyes darken. "I don't take threats very well," he says. "Especially not on my ship." His grip tightens around the hilt of his sword, his knuckles turning white. As Varn raises his massive weapon, Kai moves with a perfect calm, lifting his blade like it's an extension of himself. Steel to steel, man to monster.

"Keep your original deal," Kai says, each word a blade of its own. "And I'll give you your wish."

Varn's expression turns darker. "I've decided I'd like to stay alive a little longer," he says, voice slick with venom. "So I'll be handling some unfinished business." He grins, feral, vile. "Besides, playing with little mortal pirates is fun in my free time." His eyes drag across the crew. Then Kai.

Then they land on me with an unsettling hunger that turns my blood to ice.

Kai moves in front of me with a speed that leaves no room for hesitation. His back becomes a wall of stone between me and the nightmare before us.

"Don't." Just one word, sharper than the blade in his hand. The force of his protection, his raw, unwavering resolve to keep me safe, is more terrifying than anything Varn can conjure.

Varn's eyes drop to the ring Kai slipped onto my finger only moments ago. A slow smirk spreads across his face. "Oh... she's the key to your heart," he taunts. "She means more now than she ever did before.

Her blood, boy, it'll be on your hands." He keeps his vile look and adds, "Your wife's blood." *Wife*. My heart warms at the word. Something that I never thought I could be.

His stance remains rooted, his grip solid, his gaze locked. He isn't just shielding me. He is declaring war. A pirate's life may be soaked in violence, but at this moment, Kai is no longer just a pirate.

He is a storm, relentless in his need to protect what is his. He became the lord of the seas within seconds.

"There will be no deal," I snap, my voice cutting clean through the rising storm. I step from behind Kai, planting myself between him and the monster who thinks he can make us choose. "Your deal was made. You take it, or you leave. Funny, I feel like I'm repeating myself. Am I not?"

Varn's gaze sharpens, seething with insult. Before he can act, the ship lurches violently beneath us. Wood groans, sails whip, and the sea roars its fury. We all stumble. My breath catches as I find Kai's grip on my arm, tight, grounding. He's already in motion. "Look," I whisper, pointing toward the horizon. But we both already know. The air has shifted.

Then, with eerie calm, Varn taps his sword twice on the deck. Tap. Tap. The sound is final. A death sentence.

We've arrived. Sirens Cove.

No land in sight. Only the sea, churning like it knows what's coming. We are surrounded. Trapped. And whatever waits below, whatever ancient wrath has been stirred, will not be stopped. I take Kai's hand, steady my breath, and lift my chin toward the storm. If this is how it ends, then let it be the kind of ending they'll sing about for centuries. The kappas will not win this.

Let them remember that I didn't run. Let them know I chose the fight. Let them know Kai and I were with each other till the very end. A siren and pirates' tale as old as time.

"I was born from the tide," I whisper, voice unshaking. "It's time to let it rise with me."

CHAPTER THIRTY-EIGHT

KAI

HEARTBEAT

A fucking whirlpool erupts beside our ship, massive, snarling, violent. A vortex of black water spirals faster and wider, like the sea has unhinged its jaw. The fog thickens, turning to smoke.

And then I feel the sirens. Their presence darkens the horizon, and for the first time in my life, the sight of inky black waves brings something close to relief. They've come for blood. For once, they're on our side. Or so I hope.

I don't take my eyes off Mira for a single goddamn breath. Even as my blade slices through kappas like paper, their bodies falling at my feet, their heads rolling across the deck like cursed dice, she's right there beside me. Her blade is slick and dripping with the dark blue blood of the kappas, the same as mine. She slices them down like they aren't two feet taller than her. Her hands are sure, her stance unshakable. This war is ours to win.

The sirens' discordant lullabies thread through the air and tangle the kappas' minds, drawing them off balance. It's a lullaby I haven't heard before. This is a song for the kappas and the kappas alone. None of my men are even fazed by it. It isn't enough to end the battle, but it's enough to make the monsters falter. Their eyes glaze, their movements stutter, giving us seconds. But that's all we need to cut them down.

Except Varn is still coming. He moves through the carnage, slicing through my crew without hesitation, eyes locked on Mira with unholy hunger. His shape is more beast than man now, taller, thicker, covered in seaweed and slick with saltwater, but all I see is red. The kind of red that only comes when the one thing you love most is threatened. And I *will* end him.

The rage races through my blood like lightning. He doesn't get to touch *her*. He doesn't even get to look at her. He wants war?

I am war.

I swing my blade, cutting down another kappa with a clean, brutal strike. Bone cracks and blood sprays across the deck like blue ink spilled from the sea. But then he appears. The one who always follows Varn's lead is a towering shadow nearly as monstrous, a hybrid of man and shark. His skin is rough and gray, like stone worn smooth by the tide, the menace in him oozing with every step.

"I've been waiting for this," he rumbles, voice low and cold as the deep.

"Then you know your life ends here," I snap through gritted teeth.

He lunges, fast and wild, wielding jagged weapons crafted from saw-fish and swordfish. His strikes are fast, but I move quicker, sidestepping with trained precision. Steel clashes against bone, sparks flying, and I drive my blade forward, slicing across his stomach.

The cut split him wide, his insides spilling like rotten cargo torn from a wreck. The sight churns my gut, but I don't hesitate. Still, he grins.

A hideous, unholy grin, filled with rows teeth. "It doesn't hurt, you know?" he rasps. "I'm already dead." The way he says it, so calm and sure, sends a chill slicing down my spine.

The sirens' song grows louder, their melodies warping the air around me, twisting through my mind. It's not just noise, it's a message. They're speaking to me, trying to send me a warning me.

Then my blood runs cold.

Mira.

Her heartbeat spikes, frantic, and terrified. She's moving fast, but not toward me. No. She's been cornered, I can tell. My chest tightens as the pieces slam into place. She was just beside me. How the hell did she get over there?

He took her.

While I was distracted by his monster of a second-in-command, Varn used the moment to pull her away, drawing her toward the quarterdeck, toward the sirens. But now she's trapped. I curse under my breath, rage and panic flaring like wildfire in my veins. I have to get to her *now*.

Mira's locked in battle with Varn, fighting with every ounce of fury in her. She's holding her own, blades flashing, but she's alone. I can't look away, but I can't move yet either. I still have a monster in front of me. If I don't finish him, I'll never reach her.

The sirens' song crescendos to a scream, a warning. Something is coming. Something is wrong. I can't lose her. Not now. Not when we're this close. She has to make it to the fountain. We have to make it there, *alive.*

My head splits open like a lightning strike, pain radiating down my arm, causing my hand to seize up. The sirens' voices drill into my skull, a thousand serrated knives behind my eyes. But I don't look away. I keep my gaze locked on the bastard pinning me down. I struggle to lift myself up.

He slams me against the deck with all his monstrous weight, bone-crushing and brutal. His face hovers inches from mine, shark-like teeth jagged and dripping with spit, a beast ready to rip me apart.

Deep in my chest, my magic stirs. It pulses through my veins, an ancient thrum, igniting my fingertips with fire. My wrists are pinned, but the energy crackles beneath my skin, building, swelling, demanding to be unleashed. I don't need a spell. I don't need a sacrifice. I just need anger.

I summon every ounce of fury inside me, every betrayal, every scream I never let out, and pour it into him. The shift in the air is instant. He freezes, eyes wide. He feels it, feels me.

The temperature spikes violently. My rage becomes heat and *power*. He grunts, confused and panicked, as the force under his hands begins to burn him alive. His grip falters and his skin blisters. Steam hisses between us. I push harder.

I make him feel every ache I've ever carried, every time I was left behind, every drop of blood spilled in my name. I flood him with the fire of my grief, my anger, my truth, of me needing to get to *her*. He twitches, muscles spasming under the weight of something he can't fight.

His guttural scream tears through the air. My power erupts from my chest like a tidal wave of heat and light.

"You're a fucking warlock," he spits in disbelief and pain. Then comes the crack, a violent, sickening snap that splits the air like lightning. He convulses, his limbs jerking uncontrollably as the power I've unleashed tears through him. His body can't hold it. With one final shudder, he collapses in a smoking heap on the bloody deck.

The air is thick with the stench of scorched flesh and iron. The storm howls around us, the clouds recoiling from what I've become. I stand over him, chest heaving, breath ragged. I behead him for good measure. My hands still glow faintly with the aftershock of the magic that had scorched him from the inside out. I tasted what was buried deep inside me, and it was terrifying. Addictive. My fury burned him alive. If this is just a fraction of what I'm to become, I'm ready to take it all now.

I grab my sword from the deck. My focus narrows to Mira. Her heartbeat pounds in my ears like war drums, my compass in the chaos. She's holding her own, two cutlasses flashing, steel clashing in an X to block a strike. But then, Varn kicks her legs out from under her. She hits the deck hard, and before I can take another step, Varn's hand connects with her face. The crack echoes. She crumples. My heart stops.

He leans over her, muttering something I can't hear. She doesn't respond. Her heartbeat slows like she's slipping under, leaving me.

I run. Jay appears out of nowhere, moving fast. His blade sinks into Varn's back, a clean, brutal strike, but it does nothing. I knew it wouldn't. Varn is too strong. Only a beheading could temporarily take him down, but Jay knew that too. He knew, and still he went for it.

It's the distraction I need to get to her. Varn turns slowly, almost mockingly, and drives his sword straight through Jay's stomach, swift and fast. Lifts him. Holds him there, high, like a trophy. My body stops moving, but everything inside me breaks. My lungs seize, the air ripped from me before I can even scream. My oldest friend, my right hand. His blood runs down Varn's sword, coating his arm like a badge of pride.

Jay's eyes find mine, just for a second. Then they don't. His body goes limp. And I can't breathe.

I watch his body crumple, then fall, rolling down the steps like he was nothing, like he's just another casualty of war. He lands at my feet with a sickening thud. The blood still pouring from him now stains every step I've ever climbed to meet him. Steps we used to walk together, leading to the helm, his sanctuary on this ship.

I look down at him. His eyes are empty, his soul is gone, and his blood paints the path I have to take to get to her. I step over him, my heart a battlefield of agony and vengeance. Varn just made the biggest mistake of his life.

I lift my gaze to Varn. He turns and sees me.

The ship lurches violently beneath me, but I don't stop. I move faster, eyes locked on the quarterdeck. The sky is a blackened void, the wind screaming. The ship tilts further into the whirlpool's pull, dragging us into a mouth that wants to swallow us whole. The world is spinning. Everything is unraveling, but I don't care. The sirens fall silent. In the space they leave behind, the world goes still.

I climb, my heart thundering lungs burning. One more step. One more second. But when I reach the top, my world ends. I freeze. The breath is ripped from my lungs. The sound of the world, gone.

His blade is already through her chest. I freeze.

I can't feel her heartbeat. The rhythm that's lived inside me since the day we were tied, gone. Our bond snaps. The thread that always tethered us together tears clean through, leaving behind only darkness. Veyra's voice echoes through my mind, cruel now in hindsight: "*You protect her heart.*" She knew. Gods, she knew.

Mira's warmth, her fire, is vanishing before my eyes. Something inside me shatters, like glass cracking under a pressure too great to bear.

Every ounce of hope I have left drowns in this moment. Her light... my light... is fading. And all that remains is rage. Unforgiving, unrelenting, unstoppable rage.

I fall to my knees. It feels like I'm the one who's been stabbed. Jay's blood soaks into the wood beneath me, staining everything it touches. My hands shake. My lungs can't fill. Still, I rise.

I walk toward her, each step heavier than the last. I need to see what he's done to her with my own eyes. I *need* to hold her.

She slides off his blade. Her body hits the floor with a sickening thud, limp, lifeless, in a pool of her own blood. It soaks into the boards beneath her, spreading in violent red streaks, then darkening. Her blood is changing, turning from crimson to a deep, unnatural black. Siren blood.

I don't have time to fall apart. I can't, not yet. My grip tightens around the hilt of my sword, the weight of it suddenly immense, fueled not by duty, but by devastation. I turn, blade raised, and meet Varn's with a brutal clash. Steel rings out like a violent scream that splits the air. The ship groans beneath us, tilting and crying out like it, too, is mourning her.

Varn has the gall to smile. He has Mira's blood on his hands. Jay's still drips from his sword. "You should've made me a deal, boy," he spits, words thick with venom. "You could've saved them." I strike again. His blade meets mine, but I don't stop.

"You're the reason she lies dead at your feet," he hisses, stepping into me, his voice low and cruel. "Her blood is on your hands." And then he laughs, so twisted, so inhuman that it makes my vision blur. My pulse thunders in my ears as I look down, just for a second.

Mira is still and silent at my feet. The light in my life, extinguished like a candle in the wind. Anger starts to bubble up inside me, rising.

And what rises is a wrath born of grief and blood and ancient magic. Something not entirely human.

The sky above darkens. The clouds churn, writhing and twisting, more violent than the waves below. They swallow the last remnants of the sun, casting the world in a sickly twilight. Rain comes down in sheets, thick and punishing, turning the air into a silver veil.

The storm is alive. In its chaos, something shifts. Then I hear it. Her *heartbeat*. It's faint and distant, but it's there, like a drum calling me home. Our bond, severed just moments ago, sparks back to life. She is reaching for me. Flickering in the dark. Not gone. Not yet.

I look down. Water spills across the deck, rushing over her lifeless body. As it kisses her skin, she stirs. The sea itself is breathing her back to life. Her fingers twitch first. Then her chest rises. A gasp, soft and shuddering, pulls into her lungs like it is her first breath all over again.

She's not just alive, she's becoming. The storm welcomes her. Crowns her. Saves her. Even the skies cry for her. Mira isn't a girl anymore. Not a pirate. Not even just a siren. She is reborn in the eye of the storm, forged in salt and thunder, chosen by the sea to rise again.

I focus my full attention back on Varn, raising my sword higher.

He makes a fatal mistake, stepping left instead of right. I strike. "I will *never* free you," I growl. With one ruthless swing, I behead him.

His monstrous body crashes to the rain and blood slicked deck. His headless form thuds down the steps until it lands beside Jay's body, two ghosts of war, fallen side by side. Blue and red blood soaks the deck.

But even as the silence closes in, I can feel the unnatural stir of his immortal curse still coiling deep beneath the surface. He'll return. I feel it in my bones. But that doesn't matter now.

Because she is breathing. The wind howls like a chorus of vengeful spirits, and the storm rages harder. Through the chaos, my magic hums, alive, awake, and waiting for my command. I know, with a certainty as deep and wide as the ocean itself, when Varn rises again, he'll face me. And when time comes, I'll make sure he never crawls back from the hell he came from.

I drop to my knees beside her, gathering her into my arms with a care that borders on desperation.

"Mira?" Her name escapes me like a prayer, ragged, trembling, sacred. I brush the blood and rain soaked strands of hair from her face, my forehead resting against hers for a fleeting second. She's warm. "Treasure... please," I whisper. "Say something."

Her eyelids flutter, barely cracking open. For a heartbeat, she just looks at me, unmoving. Then a tremor passes through her, barely there, but enough. "Wa... water," she rasps. Her voice is so soft I almost don't catch it, but when I do it cuts me open. Water. She needs water, to breathe, to heal, to live.

I watch as her hand weakly moves toward her chest, fingers twitching, searching for something just out of reach. I catch her hand in mine, holding it gently, following the silent plea she can't voice. "What is it?" I ask, my voice cracking. "What are you trying to show me?"

My pulse pounds in my ears as I slowly uncurl her fingers, one at a time, until I see it. The vial. The one she wears around her neck. Tears burn my eyes as I hold it in my palm, the liquid glittering like starlight. I stare at it, pulse hammering in my throat. "Is this it?" I breathe, barely trusting my voice.

Her head gives the slightest nod, and then, softer than a sigh, her lips part. "Mermaid tears." Of course. Her secret all this time. The most sacred magic of the sea, the essence of life itself. Hidden not to be used in battle or bargaining, but for this. A gift meant to heal any wound, except the one that ripped through me the moment I saw her fall.

I crack the vial open, and the scent of fresh morning rain escapes. Carefully, I slide one of her arms behind my shoulder, lifting her just enough to pour the tears over her chest, the place where her heart nearly went still.

The moment the liquid touches her skin, the change is immediate. Her pulse strengthens. Like a distant drum echoing from the depths, it grows louder with each beat. Her chest begins to glow, soft at first, like the horizon at dawn, then bright, fierce, golden. Her heart is reigniting.

The shadows clinging to her begin to lift. And though she still looks fragile, like a soul caught between life and death, I feel her strength returning, pulsing with every heartbeat. Her magic is awakening, re-membering.

The ocean is her sanctuary, her lifeblood, always calling, always waiting. When the saltwater touches her skin, it sinks deeper than the surface, soaking into her bones. She needs it to live, more than the mermaid tears. More than anything I can give her on this ship. She needs the sea.

Somehow, I know I have to let her go for her to be able to live. I gather her in my arms, her body so light it breaks me. Each step toward the edge of the ship feels like walking through a storm made of time, like every second I hold her back from the ocean is one too long.

"I'm so sorry," I whisper, my voice breaking as I look down at her face, her light flickering like the last breath of a flame.

I'm so sorry.

I failed you.

I was too late.

I move down the stairs, my boots echoing over wood drowned in crimson. Rain pours in sheets, soaking us to the bone. Around me, chaos still reigns. Swords clash. Men scream. The final notes of war ring out. But none of it matters.

Not when she needs the sea. Her breath is shallow and her body limp. I can still feel it, that faint thread between us. She once told me that the ocean is the only place that's ever truly felt like hers. When the saltwater kisses her skin, it welcomes her like a long-lost daughter.

I hold her tighter as the ship spins closer to the heart of the whirlpool, dragging us like a leaf down a drain. My heart thunders in my chest. I can't lose her. Not here. Not now. We're so close.

I hear a voice, angelic yet eerie. "Drop her, Kai." My eyes scan the black water. Sirens cling to the sides of the ship, their haunting faces breaking through the black churn of the sea. I don't know which one spoke.

"No," I choke out, my voice already fraying at the edges. "I won't drop her here. She won't make it." My arms tighten around Mira's body, her warmth fading fast. The rain keeps falling, and I pray it's enough to buy us time.

"You're killing her," the voice insists. "Let her go."

Then a figure rises from the waves, her presence unlike any other, but familiar. "You know who I am," she says, her voice like silver threaded with moonlight. "I know you can feel it."

And I do. My heart recognizes her before my mind does. Sirena. The Queen of Sirens. Mira's mother. The storm swallows nearly everything around her, but she shines through the dark like the moon itself reborn in the water. Her long wavy hair floats around her, caught in the sea's embrace. Her piercing blue eyes slice through the downpour and chaos, locked not on me, but on her daughter. She looks more inviting, more beautiful even, than any other siren I have ever seen. Her skin glows faintly with bioluminescence, freckles scattered like stars across her collarbones, mirroring Mira's. Of course it's her. Of course the sea would call its daughter home through the woman who first belonged to it.

For the first time in all this madness, my legs give out. Because this is fate. It's her bloodline and her legacy, and I can't change that. Mira's heartbeat, faint as it is, begins to echo louder in my soul.

"Sirena?" I choke out, my gaze fixes on the churning waters below. The storm rages around us, but it is nothing compared to the one tearing through me. I hold Mira tighter, as if my arms alone can keep the world from pulling her away.

But it's too late. Gods, I know it's too late.

Rage burns through my veins, at myself, for not getting to her in time. At him, for taking her from me. At the world, for letting this happen.

"Yes," Sirena says softly. "Please. Let me heal her. Let me have her." Her words echo in my skull, painful and sacred. "You will see her again," she promises. "You've done your part. Let me do mine. She needs me now." I don't want to hear it.

I don't want to believe it. "I need her," I rasp, my voice shattering under the weight of everything I feel. I look down at Mira again. *My Mira.* Her skin is pale, her lips losing their color. The light in her eyes is gone. She's slipping away again.

Sirena's voice trembles now, thick with grief and something else only a mother can feel. "Please," she says. "Let me help her... or you'll lose her forever. You know this." I clench my jaw, the fight draining from me. I want to scream. I want to demand that I be the one to save her. That I'm enough.

But I know Mira doesn't just belong to me. She belongs to the sea, and she needs it more than she needs me. She needs her mother. She needs home. Even if I can't bear to let go.

I look down at Mira. Her emerald green eyes are wide, unblinking, staring into me with a haunting intensity, like she is trying to memorize every part of my face. Black blood slips from the corners of her lips and eyes, streaking her skin like a goodbye she can't voice. Even with the mermaid tears coursing through her, it isn't enough. She is dying.

"Drop me, Kai. It's okay," she whispers, and my heart shatters. "Neressa... find her." The words barely leave her lips. Neressa. Gods, she's going to kill me. I promised to protect Mira and I failed.

"I will," I say, and my voice doesn't feel like mine. She gives the faintest nod, and I pull her closer, pressing my forehead to hers. "You will find me, okay? And I will find you. This is not the end." My voice cracks, and I hate how broken I sound. "You'll make it to the fountain. And when you do, don't waste your wish on me. You hear me? You have to live. You *have* to be okay."

I kiss her forehead, my hands trembling as her warmth slips away. Her hand, slick with blood, rises weakly, brushing my cheek. "I love you, Kai Eldoris," she whispers. "I will find you."

Her gaze never wavers. I cling to it like it is the last anchor I have. "Is that a promise?" I ask, my voice breaking. And she smiles, faint and full of love.

"Promise. Remember... till the very end."

I kiss her. One last time. Tasting her blood. Salt. Her goodbye.

"Don't let them hurt you," I say. "You are stronger than they'll ever know." I kiss her again, fiercer this time. One final prayer. "In every lifetime. Till the very end, treasure." I whisper.

I look down at Sirena, her arms outstretched, waiting to catch Mira. Rain pours around her like silver, but she remains still, luminous in the dark.

For a brief, breathless moment, a rush of unshakable trust floods my chest. *She will protect her. She will bring her home.* With that, I let go.

My chest tears open as I watch Mira's body slip from my arms. She falls slowly, weightless, a dream unraveling. Every second stretches into forever. Until Sirena catches her with grace. The Queen of the Deep cradles her daughter.

A dark figure catches my attention beside them. *Anya.* She rises with the storm and the black waters. Instant regret pools in my stomach. The worst possible creature to rise from the waves, and now she has my Mira.

Then they're swallowed by the black abyss. The sea closes over them. And a hollow stillness spreads through me. She is gone.

But I feel it, her heart. That once-fragile rhythm is back stronger and steadier. Each beat blooms like a second chance. It is her. *Alive.* Somewhere in that endless, sacred sea, she is still with me.

The ocean begins to close, swallowing the remnants of the chaos as Mira disappears into the depths of the black water. The whirlpool, once a monstrous, devouring force, begins to lose its grip. Its violent pull softens. The storm quiets. Beneath the fading roar, the sea begins to reveal its true form, crystal blue, clear and serene. But there is nothing peaceful about it.

Mira is gone. Taken. The sirens and Anya dragged her beneath the surface, into the dark, into the unknown, toward the fountain. The very creatures I'd sworn to destroy, every last one, now hold the one person I couldn't lose. My entire life, I'd vowed to wipe them out.

Then it hits me, sharp and sudden. The fountain isn't hidden somewhere far away. It has been beneath us this whole time, under the very whirlpool that had threatened to tear us apart. Their cove. Their sanctuary, it lies at the bottom of the ocean, the deepest, most unreachable place in the world.

I didn't see it before, but now I understand. The whirlpool isn't a chance, but a summons. The sirens called the storm and tore open the sea to take her.

In that moment, they control everything, the sea, the storm, my fate. The ocean obeys them. The tides bend to their will. And with a single thought, they close the whirlpool. Just like that, the tempest vanishes, swallowed by silence so thick it presses against my ears like a vice. I stand at the edge of the ship, staring down at the glassy water. Still, calm, and mocking me.

The sirens used me. Used all of us. They took the one thing I love more than life itself. The sea has claimed her, and I am left with nothing but the wreckage of what used to be hope.

When the whirlpool vanished, silence fell, gut-wrenching, unnatural silence. The stillness claws at me, making my thoughts louder, crueler, impossible to escape. It feels like a dam inside me is about to burst.

I walk across the center of my ship, my boots heavy against the deck. The battle that had raged moments ago has frozen. The kappas stand motionless, stunned into stillness, as if even they could feel the shift in power. Maybe they sense what I am about to become.

"Get. The. Fuck. Off. My. Ship." The words rip from my throat like a war cry, each syllable soaked in fury.

The kappas freeze. Without their leader they're just desperate animals clinging to someone else's power. I watch as they scatter like vermin, retreating to the ocean they crawled out of.

My magic pulses beneath my skin, trembling with rage, begging to be unleashed. It roars, craving destruction and ruin. It wants to make the sea bleed for what it has taken from me.

I stalk across the deck to where Varn's severed head lay, his eyes frozen in that final, pathetic expression of shock. Without hesitation, I grab it and hurl it into the ocean. "Rot," I snarl. "Let the sirens take what's left of you." I don't care if the sea devours him or spits him out. I just want him to suffer. I want his vile soul trapped in an eternal abyss, cursed to scream where no one can hear him.

"Throw the rest overboard," I bark at my crew, my voice sharp as steel. They obey in silence, dragging his mutilated body to the edge and casting it into the depths.

Whatever is left of me, the part of me that loved, that hoped, that believed, sank with *her*. I'm not the same man anymore. I don't want peace or survival. I want revenge.

A wail rips from my chest, primal and inhuman, tearing across the ocean.

The ship groans beneath me, trembling under the weight of the storm that rages in my veins. My magic surges out of me, wild and unstoppable, pouring from my mouth, my ears, my fingertips. I can feel it splitting the air apart. The deck shakes like it is caught in the grip of an earthquake, boards creaking, sails whipping. The sea around us heaves, waves colliding with a force that mirrors the chaos inside me.

The ocean is a battlefield. It's me. And the sky, hell, even the sky answers. Thunder cracks, lightning tears through clouds, and the wind screams with me, howling my pain back to the gods. But nothing will ever be enough to unleash my fury.

I stand at the center of it all, magic crackling off my skin like lightning, and I make a vow. I'll find them, every last siren, and I'll burn them from this world. No mercy. No surrender. No soul spared. They thought they could take her from me. Thought they could use me. Break me. But they didn't realize, they created something worse than any siren alive.

I step forward, hands braced on the rail, eyes locked on the horizon. Let them run. Let them hide. I'm coming.

"You've unlocked your powers, son." I turn toward Taika. She's still alive. She hasn't been there when I've needed her, not once. Just a ghost in the corners of my life, a shadow I could never outrun. But now, after everything, after Mira, after Jay, she is the one left standing.

It makes me sick. I spent every ounce of myself trying to save Mira, trying to outrun fate, trying to make sense of the storm inside me. But I'm done chasing what's already lost. Because now I see it clearly, with a clarity that only comes after destruction.

This is more than a war. It's a game, and I've just been handed the winning card. My power, bloodline, and title. This is what the sirens wanted all along. And now I'll use it to take everything back. They had to have made some sick twisted deal with Varn. To get me distracted, to get her away from my side and slaughter her. What kind of mother puts a blade through her own daughter's heart? The thought makes me slightly thankful for the woman standing in front of me. The tell all of the betrayal? Anya, grinning up at me like she'd just won a chest of gold.

I stare at Taika, drunk on secrets and confidence. But whatever hope she has of playing mother now is gone, burned away in the fire that has taken Mira from me. There is no bond here. No warmth, nor family. Just power.

"And?" The word cuts through the air between us like I meant it to draw blood. She doesn't flinch.

"Let's get her back," she says. "I'll help you." My eyes stay locked on the black water ahead. The waves slam against each other like fists in a fight, rising higher with every breath. But the ship doesn't move, not even a shudder. The sea finally knows fear. It knows who I am now.

"Who let you out?" My voice is colder than the water below.

"No one did. The cell broke open." Of course it did. I nod once, slow and silent, salt stinging my skin, rain burning through the grime and blood on my face. The ocean sprays me like it's trying to remind me I'm still alive. It doesn't matter. She's gone. And now the world is colder.

But I have something else now. A weapon. And I'm going to use it.

Taika steps beside me, calm, like she hasn't just watched the world burn. "You see, son? You command the tides, just as she does. You can wield water. You are far from human. You're immortal. So is Mira." Her voice is smooth, almost proud, but it makes my skin crawl.

I turn my head slowly, my gaze drifting from her face back to the ocean, *our* ocean. The sea that has chosen us, blessed us, and bound us. She is right. The ocean touched me the same way it touched Mira that night. That night everything changed. When salt met skin and the stars carved fate into our bones. We weren't just chosen. We were born to be this. Two souls made from the same storm, split into two bodies. Bound by something deeper than blood, deeper than magic.

My soulmate, flame, light, treasure, she is gone.

Rage surges through me like lightning in a storm, each heartbeat a thunderclap in my chest. I'm not supposed to be standing here with Taika. Not after everything we lost. We traded the wrong person. *We traded the wrong fucking person.* My jaw clenches, my fists curl tight.

"It should've been you," I spit, my voice raw, deadly. "Not her. Never her." The fury inside me cracks open. The sky splits and the sea answers.

A tidal wave roars on the horizon, a towering wall of black water rising like a beast summoned from the deep. The crew screams with panicked voices, boots slamming against soaked wood, as they rush to take cover below deck. But I don't move. I am the storm now, and I want the world to drown with me.

"You've caught sirens before?" I ask, my gaze fixed on the tidal wave surging toward us.

"Yes. Many." Taika's voice carries a quiet, unsettling pride.

"I need you to do it again." From the corner of my eye, I see her nod once.

I try to breathe, but it's like the ocean has wrapped itself around my chest, crushing and relentless. Her memory clings to me, salt, blood, the phantom weight of her slipping through my arms. I close my eyes and I see her face, the storm behind her gaze, the promise she made with her final breath. The sirens took her to save her... or so they claimed.

I turn to Taika, my voice carved from the wreckage of everything I've lost. "I don't know where they've taken her, or what they truly want with her, but I will find her. I will turn this ocean to *blood* till I do."

A Note on Dyslexia and ADHD

I wanted to take a moment to shine a light on two things that shaped who I am, ADHD and dyslexia.

ADHD (Attention-Deficit/Hyperactivity Disorder) is a neurodevelopmental condition that affects focus, impulse control, organization, amongst many other things. For many, it feels like having a hundred thoughts running at once, but within that chaos, there's passion, creativity, and deep curiosity. ADHD minds see the world in color when others see it in black and white.

People often view ADHD as someone who just can't sit still, but in reality, it's so much more than that. To me, ADHD is a brain full of ideas, seeing life in full color, holding multiple conversations at once, and knowing our boundaries. It's a superpower most wish they could have.

A quote I live by that has always helped me embrace my ADHD: *"You're mad, bonkers, completely off your head... but I'll tell you a secret... all the best people are."* - Lewis Carroll

Dyslexia is a learning difference that affects how the brain processes written and spoken language. It can make reading, spelling, and writing more difficult, but it has nothing to do with intelligence. People with dyslexia often think in pictures, patterns, and stories, they just translate the world differently.

Growing up, both of these made me believe I couldn't be a writer. I struggled through school, staring at letters that never seemed to stay in the right order, and felt like the world wasn't built for how my mind worked. But now I see that the way my brain works is what allowed me to build this world, one filled with magic, ocean tides, and the beauty of imperfection. In my own way, this is my personal superpower.

If you've ever been told that you're "different," I hope this reminds you that different doesn't mean less. Your imagination, your ideas, and your voice are worthy, no matter how you process words on a page.

You are not broken, and you are not less than. You just see the world a little more wildly.

ACKNOWLEDGEMENTS

Sirens Cove comes from many inspirations in my life, movies, books, my hometown, and the people I've known along the way. Writing this story has fulfilled me in ways I can't even explain.

Growing up, I struggled deeply with dyslexia and ADHD (as you read on the previous page), but I always had these wild worlds in my head that I couldn't get onto paper, unless through illustration. If I could tell little me, "Look, we wrote a whole book and published it," it would've completely changed how I saw myself.

With that being said, none of this would have happened without the following people who helped me with nothing but love and belief.

To my parents, Bill and Jennifer, you've shown me a love that every daughter deserves. You never gave up on me, no matter how hard I fought you. You sat beside me for hours helping me write, even when it was frustrating watching letters jumble into something only I could read. I used to say, "I'm not going anywhere in life," and yet here we are. I wouldn't be who I am, where I am, or have written what I have without you. Thank you for being my biggest supporters. I love you both endlessly.

To my other half, my rock, my love, my husband, Maxwell. You've been incredible throughout the making of *Sirens Cove*. Thank you for your patience, your love, and your quiet acts of care, hyping me up when I'm down, bringing me warm food when I'm glued to my laptop, refreshing my glass of water mid-edit. Thank you for loving me the way I always imagined love should feel.

To my little brother, Billy, thank you for always being my first best friend. Thank you for supporting every wild idea I ever had, whether it was building a fort that took over the entire living room or listening to the crazy stories I would come up with. You've always believed in me in the purest, simplest ways, and I'm grateful for you every day.

To my editors, Alyse and Alexandra, thank you for helping shape *Sirens Cove* into the story it was always meant to be. You guided me in ways I didn't even know I needed and this book wouldn't be where it is without your hard work, dedication, and the love you poured into every word. I can't thank you enough.

To my cover artist, Mary, who brought this world to life through her incredible artwork, not just on the cover, but through the character art and map as well. You turned imagination into masterpieces, and I'll forever be grateful.

To my best friend, my sister in all but blood, Cara. You've been endlessly supportive from the very beginning. From the moment *Sirens Cove* was just an idea to seeing it become real, you've stood by every version of it with love. Thank you for being here, for every word of encouragement, for being such a huge part of this journey.

To my close friends, Michelle, Elise, Brittney, Maddie, Elaine and Caroline, you've been through every up and down with me. From the first words on paper to turning an idea into a series, you've been there every step of the way. I'm endlessly grateful for each of you.

To Mr. Schmidt, my high school English teacher, thank you for never giving up on me. For accommodating my learning struggles, for making my assignments in fonts and colors I could actually read, for helping me discover my favorite genres. You made me fall in love with stories. I'll forever be grateful for that and for every time you made the entire class laugh.

To the incredible online community I've found, you've helped me grow in ways I never imagined. Your support has been astronomical, and I wouldn't be here without you.

And last but not least, to my hometown. From the little bookstore café *BookWorks*, where I wrote eighty percent of this book, to the ocean, to the people who make up this beautiful place, you've been my inspiration. I couldn't ask for a more supportive community. I love you all.

If you're still reading this, you've made it to the end and I can't thank you enough. Thank you for being a reader. For bringing books back to life. For taking a chance on mine.

I hope I made you laugh. I hope I made you cry (oops). But most of all, I'm just so happy you're here.

See you all soon,

Allie Belle

ABOUT THE AUTHOR

Allie Belle is a fantasy romance author from Monterey, California, where she spends most days writing beside the ocean, her greatest muse, tucked away in a cozy café with a cappuccino in hand.

Growing up with severe dyslexia and ADHD, she learned early what it meant to fight for the stories inside her. What once felt like her biggest weakness became the very thing that sharpened her imagination and her determination. She built worlds to escape into, then slowly realized she was building a future for herself, too.

She writes romantic, poetic, atmospheric fantasy filled with magic, danger, and deeply emotional characters, stories where sirens sing, pirates rule the tides, and love is as treacherous as the sea. Sirens Cove is her debut novel and the first installment in The Sirenborne Chronicles.

When she isn't writing, Allie can be found sipping coffee in her favorite cafés, wandering bookstores in search of new worlds to fall in love with, curled up with her cats, or laughing with family and friends who have supported every chapter of her journey.

You can connect with her on Instagram @alliebelleslibrary and on Threads @allieebellee, where she shares bookish content, writing up-dates, and behind-the-scenes glimpses into the magic she's creating.